Glorifying Terrorism:

an anthology of original science fiction.

edited by Farah Mendlesohn

Rackstraw Press

Published by Rackstraw Press

23 Ranelagh Road, London N17 6XY

ISBN: 978-0-9554688-0-3

Cover by Curio-CityCatKilla: Haylee Fields and Mike Harwood

http://www.citycatkilla.com/

Typeset in Jenson, Frutiger and Courier by Feòrag NicBhrìde.

Printed in the United Kingdom.

To all the terrorists who are now revered elder statesmen.

Contents

Introduction
Andrew McKie

The purpose of the stories and the poems in this book is to glorify terrorism. More specifically, they attempt to break the law proposed by the British Government designed to outlaw anything which might be read or interpreted as that.

Of course, this current Government knows you could ride a coach and horses through this legislation, and that it isn't supposed to apply to the contents of this book, not really. But that's what this current Government says, now.

My purpose is not to introduce or analyse the work which follows, except to commend it to the attention of anyone interested in what is perhaps the earliest clear ideological crisis of the 21st Century, and to hope that it will be a spur to debate. It is likely that you, like me, will violently dislike or disagree with the implications of some of the entries in this anthology; indeed, I will go further; I suspect that I disagree more with the political views of the authors of the majority of these pieces than most of its readers will. But I am happy to stand beside them because of the one thing on which we do agree: freedom of speech.

It is as well to be clear at once that, in liberal Western democracies, liberty is not licence, and that no freedom is unfettered. Full-blown Libertarians may wish it otherwise, yet even their ingenuity may be hard pressed to find an accommodation with Jihadists who advocate as a moral duty the extermination of them and all they stand for. Trotskyites and others on the Left may claim a moral equivalence between the force exerted by the State and its enemies, but it is a notoriously partial ground, and depends on your sympathies – the Israelis or the Palestinians? the Irish Republicans or (in the six counties) the democratic majority Unionists? the Cedar Revolution in Lebanon or Hiz'bollah? the Russian Federation or Chechen separatists?

A bid for neutrality in these No Man's Lands does little good. Even on the football terraces of Glasgow or Liverpool there is a race memory of difference which goes back three centuries or more before the founding of the clubs. History, even – perhaps especially – invented history, encompasses all our narratives, as great glorifiers of terrorism such as Sir Walter Scott knew. As Orwell pointed out, even the declaration that art is not political is in itself a political statement.

And so, while it is almost laughable to hear the BBC describe the beheading of a Western captive in Baghdad by some terrorist group as the work of Iraqi "insurgents" or "militants" (the more so since most such outfits are imported murderers), the fashion in which it is ridiculous depends upon what has fashioned your own political views.

History may resolve some of your doubts. What could be wrong with Stirling's memorial to William Wallace, Scots inventor of guerrilla warfare, or even Mel Gibson's wildly inaccurate film about him? Or the plaque unveiled earlier this year to Irgun's bombing of the King David Hotel? Or the comments by the British Prime Minister's wife that we should try to understand what drives young Palestinians to become suicide bombers? Or Nelson Mandela's autobiography, which doesn't disguise his connections with an armed resistance to apartheid? Michael Collins or de Valera? Che or Fidel? Leon or Vladimir? The decadent Europhile neo-Papist (but Royal) Stewarts or the voice of non-Conformist, Parliamentarian small-landowner England (but Puritanical and Regicide) Cromwell? Custer or Crazy Horse?

The fact is that our views of all those contests are coloured not only by our own political standpoint but by results. Though a horrible thing, I would strongly disagree with the view that the bombing of Dresden was a war crime, but it is routinely regarded as that in Germany, and by people without the slightest sympathy for the Third Reich (I don't know Günther Grass's opinion).

Whose governments were Left or Right wing: Pinochet's; Franco's; Hitler's; Stalin's; Castro's; Deng Zao-Ping's? Whose were open and whose restrictive in terms of freedom of speech: Nero's; the Venetian Doges'; Charlemagne's; Louis XIV's; Thatcher's; Ortega's; Haughey's; Gorbachev's; Kohl's; Mitterand's; Berlusconi's?

Since you are an intelligent reader, I suspect that I disagree with you on at least three of your answers to the questions above. Since you are an intelligent reader, I suspect you disagree with at least three of your own answers, and find at least three more which contradict others.

Which brings us at last to the contradictory and thought-provoking work which follows. A literature of the fantastic has, paradoxically, less opportunity to trim, conceal and spin than has everyday journalese (itself a tautological phrase).

The success of all science fiction and fantasy is rooted in three things. First: it must make, or build. We demand from it worlds that we have not imagined, but which, when they are constructed, we can imagine visiting. Second: it must remain consistent unto itself; in other words, if it falls apart, it can only do so in its own terms (you can't have vampires in space opera, or spaceships in Faerie, unless you've set it up that way).

Third, and hardest to explain, but easiest to spot for anyone who reads any kind of fantastic literature: it must be true in some way. Which is just a way of saying that good sf and fantasy are always talking about how the world is, and how it might be. Sometimes (John Brunner, John Wyndham, Philip K Dick) as prophecy or awful warning. Sometimes (Ursula K Le Guin, Arthur C Clarke, JRR Tolkien) with an almost optimistic yearning. But whichever it is (and all the writers suggested as examples of one tendency have moments of demonstrating the opposite), it is about elucidating the present, rather than predicting the future.

Indeed, it is the freedom of sf and fantasy that makes it the most flexible literary form for this purpose: the excursions into the fantastic by Borges, García Márquez, Havel, Lem, Bulgakov, Kafka and others in the last century were often born of restrictions on what could plainly be said. British publishers may have refused *Animal Farm* on the ground that no one wanted to read anthropomorphic fables; in the countries where it mattered, everyone got the point. When *The Master and Margerita* came out in serial form, the magazines flew off the shelves: no one could quite believe the authorities had not realized what it was about.

But of course they hadn't, as they never do. The most vocal opponents of Tony Blair and his ever-more authoritarian declension of Home Secretaries (at the last count David Blunkett, Charles Clarke, John Reid: though who knows by the time of printing?) do not claim him as a Kruschev. I am sure all of them believe that they are doing their utmost to combat the terrorist threat.

Which allows us to return to the restrictions which liberal Western democracy has always placed upon freedom of speech, and against which voices have been raised since before Milton's *Areopagitica*. But whether the logic of the arguments advanced (implicitly or explicitly) in the pieces which follow create a case for greater freedom of speech, one thing is evident about the new curtailment of expression. It will achieve nothing, cannot, indeed, achieve anything productive in the "war against terror".

The purpose of terrorism is to make ordinary life unsustainable by creating random assaults on the population. The hope is that resisting the ambitions of the terrorists becomes less important than the horrors which may be consequent upon resistance. The game is not worth the candle, they hope we will say. And the result is that families are displaced from Catholic or Protestant areas of Belfast, from Jewish or Palestinian sections of Jerusalem; Bosnians, Serbs, Croats, Hutus and Tutsis, and who knows what group next, shuffle from refugee camp to refugee camp.

It is perfectly respectable for legislative bulwarks to be raised against such bullying. And so we have in Britain a law against the incitement to riot; we have numerous public order acts; we have laws against incitement to racial hatred, and laws, or proposed laws, against discrimination on the grounds of sexuality, ethnicity or religious conviction.

But, as I have said, this collection is not primarily about the logic of that existing legislation, but asks only why, when it is already in place, any new law should be required. If some Imam urges the slaughter of all Jews, he may be prosecuted as the law stands. If some Roman Catholic thinks all Protestants damned, or vice versa, he may say so; but if he does so in a particularly incendiary situation, he may be charged with offences under the Public Order Act.

Some believers in International Socialism (Trots) have been arguing since I was in nappies for violent perpetual revolution; though the adherents of that doctrine may feel they have been victimised by the state, the state has in fact provided me with the opportunity to read the maxims of their founding fathers at the taxpayers' expense at every public library, and paid for their adherents to attend places of further education, where they can try to sell me more copies of their tiresome newspapers. Neo-Nazis, when they can avoid calling for measures which offend against the law against incitement to racial hatred, have no difficulty publishing their arguments. I personally have no trouble in ignoring those arguments as both wrong-headed and repugnant. I can, however, see no way in which either group should not be allowed to advance its case which does not at the same time compromise the ability of, say, the Liberal Democrats or the Scottish Nationalists to do the same.

The question, for liberals, for conservatives (who are, in the British tradition, liberal) for socialists (who are, in the British tradition, liberal) is one of proportionality. Whether or not we want unfettered freedom of speech, there is at least a case for the law prohibiting open calls for the assassination of individuals (this is not theoretical, as the Rushdie case demonstrates) or groups (as both the conflict in the Balkans and Islamist and Nazi assaults on Jews demonstrate).

I am writing this in the country from which liberal Western democracy, inherited from Greece, spread throughout Europe. It is also the centre of Western Christendom; not, perhaps, a doctrine which many of the writers in this book wish to advance against the threat which proudly opposes it, but a tradition which allowed the evolution of the civilization we are now engaged in defending.

Getting here, thanks to a terrorist scare the day before I left Britain, involved a prohibition on carrying laptops, mobile phones and – most difficult for a family with three children, one of them an infant – a ban on liquids, including close examination of baby milk, on planes.

I don't like those curtailments on my freedom of movement, but I understand them as a reaction (even if over-zealous) to a perceived threat. I have myself been fairly close to terrorist bombs several times – South Quay (one failed bomb, one successful); and in Soho and Covent Garden (the Admiral Duncan, the White Swan, the bomb near Centre Point). I was on a train stopped on its way to King's Cross on 7/7.

So I don't mind these tiresome, temporary, impediments to liberty, because they are temporary and proportionate. Having everything X-rayed and taking off your shoes at an airport may do some good; so may making it illegal to call for the extermination of an entire people on the basis of their religion or ethnicity by birth.

What is absurd is to call for a law which prohibits anything which might be characterised or interpreted as "glorifying terrorism". And, in the peculiarly post-modernist interpretation in statute, by anyone. You, like me, may not think it enough for Tony Blair to assure you that he's "a pretty straight kind of guy". You may start thinking quis custodiet ipsos custodes or, if you're of a slightly different political cast, who, whom?

You'd be right. There's an important battle going on here, and one which probably only became clear to the West after September 2001. It's a battle for what we believe in, but whether we're reactionary Presbyterians or Catholics, liberal middle-of the-roaders, radical Trotsykists or Libertarians or, probably most acutely, devout Muslims who want to hold to traditionalism without being labelled wicked, when it comes to legislation we would do well to ask what we were taught to ask of any remark: Is it necessary? Is it true? Is it kind?

The trouble is that it's a maxim which relies on the good faith of our masters. I have, as you would expect from someone who has made a living writing editorials for The Daily Telegraph, a certain scepticism about this Labour Government. But I have also understood, and indeed supported, certain aspects of its stance on the invasion of Afghanistan and Iraq, its support for America, its anxiety to tackle what I think is a genuine assault on the values of Western society. That, I'd guess, won't be shared by many of the writers who follow.

What we do share is a demand that we inhabit any area of thought we choose; an assumption that the imagination not only should not but cannot be policed, and a refusal to take the word of "moderate" governments that their illiberal, shoddy and badly-drafted legislation does not intend us to be its target.

Under this legislation I can think of plenty illegal sf classics, from *Dune*'s suicide commandos to short stories by Bob Shaw, John Varley and Bruce Sterling. So can you. All we are asking is that we continue to be allowed to think of them; that the people writing for you in this book continue to be allowed to think of them, and others. If we are not going to be allowed to think as we choose, we choose to be targets – not for terrorists, but for our own legislators.

Andrew McKie
Montepulciano, August 2006

The Comrades Decide To Continue Their Struggle

Jo Walton

Aravan returned to the hiding place beneath the rocks ashen faced. "We are too late," he said, his voice full of sorrow.

"How, too late?" Prince Pers asked, the brave spirit which had withstood exile and a thousand risks undaunted by the dread in his counsellor's face.

"Too late, my prince. The usurper Gorgion has used the holy balm and taken the crown."

A shocked murmur ran through the comrades, but none spoke aloud. Pers bowed his head. Then, seeing this, the warrior-woman Aleta set her hand on her sword Boldheart and spoke. "You will always be my true prince. You are the son of King Farahan."

Pers smiled on the beautiful face of the impetuous heroine, and her heart leapt, even as your heart, reader, would have leapt in her place. "Yet though I am the true-born son of my father, raised in distant exile, Aravan taught me that legitimacy in rule here in Hatheria passes by annointing with the holy balm. Because he was not annointed I have taken up arms against Gorgion, and led the struggle, striking from the shadows and our gathering strength. Now that Gorgion has annointed himself, he is the legitimate king, and his name must be entered in the lists of kings that lies on the High Table in the Sanctuary of Hatheria. And our actions, my comrades, could be given an ugly name."

"If Gorgion's name be entered into those lists, let it also be said that his reign was short!" Aleta cried, and the comrades cried with her and banged their spears on the ground.

At this, old Aravan took heart and spoke again. "My other news is that none support Gorgion save the Yushions."

"The Yushions have an unsavory reputation, and I believe I have met none of them since my return," Pers mused. "Tell me, wise counsellor, why they alone support Gorgion?"

"Gorgion has promised Crookback Yushion that he will mend the face of his wall-eyed daughter, that Crookback might marry her as is the ancient detestable custom of Yushions. Crookback's lame-legged son brings flyblown meat for Gorgion's monsters, and is made knight."

"A plague on Crookback, and on his wall-eyed daughter and lame-legged son! No true Hatherians support Gorgion. Pers forever!" Aleta declared, standing straight and tall. Again the comrades cried out in agreement, shouting their prince's name. The sun, lowering now over the unhappy kingdom of Hatheria, lingered on the figures below the rocks, gilding them with golden rays.

Pers looked on the faces of his companions. "Whatever they say of us in time to come, whether they think us terrorists or saviours, I will continue to fight for Hatheria!"

The comrades cried out again in joy, swearing to obey their prince and free the country. And so, dear reader, would you and I have cried, had we the good fortune to have been there, and such great deeds as the comrades did would we emulate, if ever it fell to us to live in such a day.

Hijack Holiday
Ian Watson

Author's Note: This story was written 9 months before, and first published 6 months prior to, the events of September 11th 2001.

Our flight out of London Heathrow has been in the air for two hours, chasing the sunset across the Atlantic bound for Bermuda. Passengers are still occupied with their dinners of venison medallions in Madeira sauce which was preceded by lobster salad. Lowered shelves and food trays impede movement even in first class seats – actually, there are only first class seats in this luxury jet, a hundred and forty or so seats, and almost each one occupied. Quite a gathering of multi-millionaires from Europe, the Americas, and Japan, mostly under-forties although some older people are present too. All special people. Actually, although you don't bump into a multi-millionaire every day, there are oodles in the world, but amongst those oodles these ones are particularly special.

Jill and I are sitting towards the front of the plane. A smartly-suited fellow hurries past, followed closely by a young woman in trendy combat clothing shouldering a big bright ethnic woven bag embroidered with tiny mirrors, and then another man in casual designer gear.

A moment later guns emerge from the bag — mini-sub-machine guns of tough black plastic. They're sneaky weapons which an X-ray machine would show as faint and harmless objects, yet slickly they snap into a new and deadly shape.

"Nobody move!" that young woman calls out. Her companions disappear through the galley towards the cockpit, forcing a stewardess ahead of them at gun point.

Naturally, people do move a bit. I certainly look round. A few armed men and another woman are at the rear of the plane, menacing passengers and the other flight attendants.

"We are taking over this flight in the name of Zenji Had! Any passenger leaving a seat without permission will be executed. Otherwise no one will be harmed."

Zenji Had! The apocalyptic cult leader, currently in prison in Israel...

Jill squeezes my hand.

The hijack has started.

"You'll be well treated. Your safety's guaranteed. Special Forces will rescue you – it's good training for them."

"Will weapons all be loaded with blanks?" Jill had asked the man from Unusual Holidays, a smartly dressed dark-haired chap in his early twenties named on his business card as Peter Chough, pronounced chuff. Following our phone call of enquiry, he had come to our mansion in the Warwickshire countryside for a personal, private presentation.

"Hardly! If that was so, the hijack would be a charade. You do want your money's worth. Which is why the android pilots and flight crew know nothing of what will happen."

"Not even an inkling? A suspicion?"

"They're programmed not to suspect, even if you shout out loud, 'Hey, this flight is going to be hijacked – seven of the passengers are armed.' The crew will simply smile and reassure you and carry on."

Androids are pretty essential these days as commercial pilots and air-crew because they can put up with all the stresses and strains of the job better than people. The screaming baby, the air-rage smoker, and especially all the time zones and jet lag. In the case of air traffic control, what with the skies being so crowded, an android is much more reliable at the computer screen.

"Our money's worth," I echoed. "It's quite expensive."

"Well, a hijacking *is*. The plane might end up in need of a complete refit. That," and he grinned with boyish charm, "is why only adventurous millionaires need apply. People who have done everything else."

This pleased Jill. She glowed.

I asked, "Are the hijackers androids too?"

"No, no, they're genuine human beings. Nor are they actors. They believe in their cause. They will all be under the temporary sway of Persuasion. For them, this will be an unusual experience too."

Persuasion was a, what's the name, nano-drug, nano-virus? It could reprogramme a person's beliefs. The American government denies that Persuasion was developed in its own military laboratories. Whatever the truth of this, the substance was now in use by some unscrupulous regimes in Africa and Asia to defuse opposition and rally support. Officially, Persuasion was banned in the western world. How had Unusual Holidays got hold of any? If asked, Peter Chough would merely tap his nose. I had heard rumours that some cult leaders made use of Persuasion.

"Do you mean to say that the hijackers as well as the passengers are customers of yours?"

The young man tapped his nose. "That would be telling."

"You could package a virtual reality hijack," I pointed out, "and it would seem to be thoroughly believable."

"You'd still know it was a pretence and you could quit any time. And where would the media headlines be? The media are going to think this is for real. Just imagine all your friends tuning in and scanning the news, and well, envying you after the event. Good heavens, it *is* real. It's actually happening. So much nowadays is unactual. Virtual safaris, virtual Moon visits."

"Have Unusual Holidays been responsible for any other hijacks?"

The young man touched a finger to his lips. "Aha, not saying. Would *you* tell any of your friends that your ordeal was staged?"

"Not likely," said Jill.

"You say that Special Forces will rescue us. So *where* we finally land after our mystery tour must be fixed in advance, right?"

Again the young man remained inscrutable.

"Surely the end destination has to be pre-arranged. Your company can't have agreements with scores of nations just on the off-chance. That isn't possible."

"Aha." The young man grinned broadly. "Another reason, perhaps, why your holiday is just a bit on the ultra-expensive side. I don't wish to spoil the surprise of making new acquaintanceships during your travails on the flight, but you may well discover that no other lottery winners are on board with you. A suddenly acquired fortune tends to be splashed on more obvious holidays. It takes a discerning lottery winner to seek such an unusual experience."

"We thought so," agreed Jill. "We wanted to be different."

"And so you shall be. When you approached us, did you have any idea that a hijack holiday might be on offer?"

None at all. Complete surprise. What if we're spoilsports and tip off a journalist? Before Mr Chough would even show us the Unusual Holidays brochure, he had insisted on us signing a legal confidentiality document which he'd brought along.

He eyed us, knowing that Jill was hooked, and therefore that I was also. "It'll be the experience of a lifetime. Unrepeatable. Unique."

Had there never been any other hijack holiday – and never would be again? Perhaps there were only enough multi-millionaires with the necessary pizzazz (or sufficiently jaded) to sustain one such caper.

After Jill's gaze had lit on the hijack listing she had barely glanced at the other unusual holidays on offer in the brochure – such as a week on a space station, big-shark-hunting in the Pacific, volcano-bungee, or tidal-wave surfing (with wings to deploy and flee free above the devastation as the mountainous wave rampaged ashore). No, being hijacked was *her*. It had frisson, and a sort of vast inverted glamour. Jill always had been keen on sexual bondage.

Already our plane is veering, commencing a wide turn. We'll never see Bermuda, although admittedly we did not expect to.

Trendy Combat Woman calls out, "You will obey all our orders!"

"Oh yes," breathes Jill, letting her raven hair fall forward, half hiding her face.

Maybe TCW notices this.

"You will all sit up straight so that we can see you. Place your hands on your heads *right now!*"

Jill clutches my hand almost painfully, then she obeys, as do I.

Jill's mother was (and still is) a strait-laced person. Given present circumstances, I suppose strait-laced is the wrong term to use. Let's simply say frigid. Jill is far from frigid – however, her upbringing implanted certain inhibitions about enjoying her sexuality to the full. She and I had discovered that bondage released her from these inhibitions because when she's unable to refuse or resist she does not feel personally responsible. *Vincilagnia* is the term for arousal due to bondage. Sounds to me like the name of an Ancient Roman town. Let's visit Vincilagnia, Jill. Oh yes, let's! Such are her cries of ecstasy that we sometimes use a silk gag to muffle those.

In our imaginations we often visit imperial bedrooms and harems and tents of Araby, assisted by a few garments and props – in addition to such useful items as curtain sashes, being softer than ropes, and rope for slow prolonged caressing, and shoulder-length zipper mittens which confine Jill's fingers and pad her wrists for handcuffs, or exhibitionist spreader bars to hold her arms and legs apart and flip her over on the bed – as well as latterly a specially made Chinese Chair which clasps her automatically when she sits down and then unfolds into a bed – not to mention a parachute harness to suspend her from a framework in a room in our new mansion with specially reinforced ceiling. I enjoy the sense of power these situations give me.

Since we became multi-millionaires (although hardly mega-millionaires) thanks to the double-rollover win on the lottery, somehow our domestic amusements had palled just a little. All of a sudden compared with previously we controlled so much wealth that being controlled, or rather feeling controlled, was a bit difficult even though we bought more complicated equipment such as the Chinese Chair and the parachute harness with ceiling supports. Hijackers would see to Jill being thoroughly controlled. This would be bondage in a novel style prolonged for an unpredictable number of days. Mind you, Jill had teetered over the Abduction to the Harem holiday, but we would not have been able to share that. And I might have been jealous. We were an item, Jill and I. We had never invited others of like tastes to join in.

Would the hijacking give me any sexual thrill on top of adrenaline rushes? I would be participating in Jill's secret excitement which would build and build over a period of days, and after we were rescued and alone in a hotel somewhere, *well*… I foresaw an explosion which I would detonate.

Are some of our fellow passengers similarly motivated? Some are probably masochists. I glance around at women's and men's faces, unable to decide, though not really needing to decide because our own games are personal.

Private, yet now in a sense being acted out in public.

Meanwhile I am powerless.

"*You*," TCW shouts at me, "face the front!"

How long will we need to sit like this? Even with fingers laced and with the support of the back of the seat, my arms are beginning to ache. Smart Suit rejoins TCW, leaving Casual Designer to supervise the flight deck.

"No talking or whispering!" This is addressed to the Japanese couple across the aisle alongside us. Both become expressionless.

"Aw, shit," from the seat in front of us as a pair of hands vanish from view.

Gun in one hand, SS strides forward and his palm descends forcefully. The slap is very audible.

"Hands on head!"

Hands reappear shakily. I can hear the heavy, shocked breathing of the victim of the blow.

"But we're to be well treated," protests his female companion.

"Shut up, rich bitch!" The palm hovers, about to pounce again.

"Don't," the woman begs.

"I told you to shut up!" SS does not hit her, maybe because he would need to lean across her companion. Instead, he orders, "*You*, stand up and step into the aisle right now."

An easy enough manoeuvre, given first class leg-room.

The woman's blue-dyed hair is gelled into curling ram's horns. She wears an armless, iridescent trouser suit. Quite a few gold bangles adorn tanned bare arms which could benefit by being a bit slimmer. Several jewelled rings are on her fingers. She may have had a face-lift. Just at this moment the android stewardess emerges into the galley — maybe she has been told to supply coffee for the hijackers.

TCW instructs the ram-headed woman, "Remove all your clothes except for your panties if any."

The woman protests. "Why?"

"Because I order it. Do so now! You will still be dressed in your jewellery."

The humiliation. Is this what the woman came on holiday for? Unlikely – Jill and I never described our own kinks to Unusual Holidays to enter on a data base for the use of the hijackers.

When the stewardess attempts to intervene, SS simply turns and shoots her. *Shoots her*. Tiny bullets, maybe carbon-fibre, slam into the stewardess. Blood welling from her blouse, she collapses backwards upon the galley floor, and lies still.

Distinct from the steady throb of the engines I hear gasps and whispering and whimpering.

"Silence!" bellows a man's voice – with a French accent? – from the rear of the plane.

"Now obey me," continues TCW, "or suffer the consequences."

Her victim complies. Soon the woman stands clad only in black lace panties, her tanned thighs somewhat puckered by cellulite, though her breasts have probably been uplifted. When SS uses the discarded black bra to tie the woman's hands in front of her, Jill moans softly.

"Jill," I hiss, *"the stewardess is dead."*

Jill replies faintly, as if gagged, *"She's android, isn't she? She can be restored."*

"Can she be?"

Neither of us know enough about the workings of androids to say one way or the other. Artificial persons certainly have some rights. They definitely aren't robots; they're assistants to humanity. And now such a one lies shot and unmoving. Is this a pretence – a piece of theatrical realism?

"Sit down again," SS tells the near-naked woman.

Which she does gladly, though more awkwardly than when emerging from her seat.

As we fly back into deepening night, for in-flight entertainment TCW treats us all to an interminable lecture about the life and surreal political philosophy of Zenji Had, delivered in a chanting sing-song which makes it difficult to follow, yet woe betide if we do not pay attention and fail to answer questions correctly. During the course of an hour and a half most of the passengers lose some or all of their clothes in this ideological version of strip poker. At least we're allowed to take our hands off our heads although trips to the toilet are not permitted until the end of the lecture, by which time some people are squirming.

In our pre-jackpot life Jill and I managed a print-on-demand coffee bar/bookshop with catalogue terminals at each table. We have comprehensive minds so both of us ought to be able to cope well enough with the contents of the lecture, yet Jill muffs her questions – deliberately? – and loses her jacket and blouse. The plane's interior is beginning to resemble an outing by a nudist club. An android flight attendant collects all the discarded clothing to heap at the front.

Zenji Had is not the notorious fellow's real name, of course.

What of his screwball philosophy that justifies such acts of nihilist sabotage as blowing up a dam in India and triggering avalanches in the Alps? The notion that sweeping human civilization aside will clarify and enlighten and bring survivors closer to Bod-Allah-Gaea, the deity of the Earth, is nuts. *Bodallagaea, Bodallagaea*: a mantra of madness. Our captors chant and compel us likewise to chant for what seems half an hour until our brains, and the plane, are resounding with one nonsense word and we can hardly think clearly any more.

Bodallagaea suggests a painful allergy – a growing hostile reaction of the Earth to the human race, especially I suppose to the rich who consume more resources. Symptoms of the allergy include wild storms and floods and unseasonal blizzards. *Allagaea, Allagaea!* Sounds like a Hallelujah Chorus. *Bod, Bod, Bod, Bod...* sounds like ominous footfalls coming closer, or perhaps a cosmic dripping tap. The fact that our captors are under the influence of Persuasion and are not actually followers of the terror-guru is beginning to elude me.

Once we have partly lost our minds as well as a fair amount of clothing, it's time to start in on our intangible possessions. TCW and SS produce little laptop computers. A couple of the comrades act as bodyguards while SS and TCW make their way along the aisle. Goodness, how much our hijackers know about us! Not merely our names which are on the passenger list, but quite full financial profiles. Share portfolios, accounts, investments, brokers. Some high-level hacking has gone on preceding the hijacking, the entry point presumably being our credit card payments for the trip. Now extra security details are needed, which most people carry in their organisers or in their heads. In defiance of air-line safety regulations those laptops uplink to satellites. Liquidation of assets and electronic transfers of millions takes place – to be stored in a safe holding account and credited back to us in due course along with the interest that accumulates. This is rather exciting, like a zany auction, the exhausted bidders punch-drunk by Bod, if not by Bud – we've had nothing more to drink yet. Passengers divest themselves. Reluctance is met with dire threats. Unusual Holidays has thought of everything – these hijackers are now posing as aerial highwaymen, and we are stripped not just of clothes but, temporarily, of our wealth.

So far I have had little opportunity to acquaint myself with any of our fellow passengers. But at long last wee-wee is permitted. As I'm waiting in the queue for the toilet I murmur to the chap ahead of me (burly and hirsute, stripped to his underpants), "How do you rate the holiday so far?"

Without turning his head, he mouths tightly, in an Italian accent, "Too much, too much!"

Too much what? Money paid beforehand? Funds confiscated on board? Too much in-flight activity? Too much piss in his bladder? Or maybe he is expressing amazed praise.

"Silence!" shouts a hijacker.

Afterwards, two androids tour with the drinks cart. The kidnappers have certainly worked out plenty to occupy us. The fallen stewardess still lies where she fell.

Presently – *"Fasten all seat belts tight!"* – our plane is descending... towards what airport?

"Cover your windows!"

We aren't even going to see. French Accent patrols the aisle, checking that all windows are masked.

We land, we taxi for quite a while. FA continues his patrol. Finally the plane halts and the engines die.

I do sneak a look while FA is furthest away. Black night and stars, vast blankness apart from a few lights of distant buildings. The temperature falls slowly until we're shivering, Jill worse than I. SS and CD drag the body of the stewardess out of sight but nothing else happens.

An hour passes. Gooseflesh abounds. Teeth are chattering. It's impossible to sleep. Jill hugs herself. We may be in North Africa. It's cold at night in the desert. How stiflingly hot will it become by day?

Blessedly, TCW shouts, "Get dressed!" The android flight attendant who collected our clothing earlier now redistributes everything – but at random. Jill receives a bra too big for her, and a cashmere sweater, for which she's certainly grateful. Some men receive women's clothes, and vice versa.

TCW announces, "The Zenji Had Commando will now release three hostages in exchange for refuelling. Do any passengers suffer from serious medical conditions?"

Wise, wise. Some people who signed up may have thought they were fit enough for such a holiday yet now are having second thoughts, prompted by palpitations.

A score of hands go up – whether legitimately or not, who can say? TCW glares at the passengers, and a few hands go down again. Personally I feel tempted, but I would be chickening out of the rest of the holiday, and surely more surprises are in store for us.

Three of the older passengers depart, somewhat shamefaced.

Just before dawn we take off again. Once in the air, we can unshade our windows. We're flying high over brightening desert, southward. Such waves of dunes like a golden ocean. Has to be the Sahara. Apart from the passenger release, whatever exchanges occured between the ZHC and the ground remain a mystery to us.

Niger? Chad? A baking immensity of barren ground, military vehicles in the distance, tiny black faces. The temperature inside the plane is soaring. Jill plucks feebly at her sweater. This time we haven't been obliged to mask our windows, though we are hardly engaging in much sight-seeing.

"Unless our demands are met," declares TCW, "we will crash this plane into the Great Pyramid. Allagaea, Allagaea, Bod Bod Bod!"

Before we can roast aboard our prison, the plane takes off again – indefatigable androids! – and soon we're heading north-westward approximately, presumably towards Egypt – just a stone's throw from Israel, where

Zenji Had languishes, or raves, in jail. We're now not merely a hijack but a flying bomb. The hijackers have managed to rack up tension by another notch.

As regards stones being chucked, how much damage would our fairly large plane impacting at 450 miles an hour do to the Great Pyramid? Enough to persuade the Egyptian authorities to beg the Israelis to do a deal? Why should the Israelis care? Dramatic damage to the Great Pyramid might even boost the flagging Egyptian tourist trade, bedevilled by fundamentalist Moslem militancy!

How can our hijackers compel the pilot or the co-pilot to smash our plane into such a target when the death of all aboard will be the result? Maybe the ZHC have spare ampules of Persuasion with them. Of course this is all a big pretence.

Despite our apparently lethal new status, I drift off to sleep, quite exhausted.

Jill nudges me. A jet fighter is pacing us. I can see the pilot, helmeted and snouted.

Costs money to scramble a plane.

TCW appears, rubbing sleep from her eyes, so she must have bunked down for a while.

"I have an announcement. Our demands have not yet been met. We shall not target the Great Pyramid."

That's a relief.

"Instead, we shall destroy the Dome of the Rock in Jerusalem."

She explains the significance. Third most sacred shrine in the Islamic world. Muhammad travelled to heaven from the outcrop of stone it now shelters. Administered by Moslems courtesy of the Israelis, the Dome also occupies the site of the ancient Jewish temple which many Jewish ultra-orthodox militants aim to rebuild. If Israeli intransigence in the matter of Zenji Had's release causes the dome to be obliterated, riots such as never seen before will erupt in Israel and Palestine and throughout the Islamic world, probably even a war or two. This is much bigger than bashing a bygone Pharaoh's memorial. If Israeli is attacked, Israel may go nuclear. *Bod Bod Bod, Allagaea, Allagaea!*

This is all very exciting, but isn't it becoming rather *major?* Jill and I had been promised headlines – but *Doomsday* headlines?

We have no proof that any of this is actually happening. That the hijackers have actually threatened Egypt or Israel. We may simply be flying across the empty Sahara, no repercussions in the offing.

What about that war plane pacing us? Hired by Unusual Holidays from some African country glad of the revenue? Rented as a prop (ho, with jet engines, and missiles slung under its wings)...

The androids distribute wrapped breakfasts of cinnamon bagels, cream cheese, lox, smoked trout, rye bread, and mini-bottles of chilled Champagne. We would have received these before landing in Bermuda. First class fare, yet. I feel seriously confused. After our ordeals Champagne goes straight to the head. A couple of passengers are sick in the aisle.

"You eat too richly!" screams TCW.

Coffee follows, to keep us on our toes. Or off them.

Did we cross southern Egypt? Was that the Red Sea below us? Are we heading for Sinai? The previous war plane has been replaced by two fighter jets emblazoned with the Star of David. Sublime theatre! Surely the Israelis are too serious about security to scramble two fighter planes unless they mean business?

The toilets have begun to smell.

If our hijackers truly believe they are who they think they are, what control is there upon what they choose to do? In bondage there's always a safeword guarantee. Utter the agreed word and the captor must immediately free the prisoner. The safeword should be one you wouldn't routinely use. Such as Malaria. Or Nebuchadnezzar. Or Afghanistan. Jill always uses the word Hexagon. As soon as she utters this, the spell confining her – handcuffs, whatever – will promptly be whisked away, hex gone away. (Or when she's gagged, she blinks six times in rapid succession.) Will a safeword be broadcast to our plane at some stage to terminate the holiday? Meanwhile, we are a loose cannon zooming around the sky.

Presently TCW announces, "If we proceed any further Israel will shoot us down. Accordingly, with the welfare of passengers in mind, we will refuel in Cyprus and head for France. France dare not shoot down a civilian jet. There would be outrage. We will crash into the Eiffel Tower!"

We're on a tour of the Wonders of the World – without actually seeing any of them. To demolish the symbol of France: such an action would be very much in keeping with the spirit of Zenji Had.

"This time, we shall not warn of our intentions! We will demand to land at Charles de Gaulle airport to release hostages and negotiate. But instead we will fly into the Eiffel Tower. It is possible that there may be some or even many survivors."

Oh cue disaster movies, *The Towering Inferno* and such – movies such as are never shown on any passenger flight, yet now they screen in my mind: our plane impaled, blazing or soon to blaze, in the wreckage of Monsieur Eiffel's tower, passengers trying to scramble out on to twisted girders high above the ground. Brilliant. Here's a new turn of the screw of tension.

Are those genuine Israeli jets outside? We're changing course, and they're peeling away.

Cyprus stop-over, as promised. Three more of the older passengers are released. The Cypriots send airline food on board, fare more Spartan than we enjoyed hitherto. I'm beginning to experience cramps. Jill too, and many of the other passengers, I expect. People are stretching their legs and arms, almost as if a co-ordinated exercise session is in progress. Noting this, TCW leads us all in another round of the Bodallagaea chant.

Bondage may require up to 48 hours to produce its full effect upon the willing victim. The person inflicting the bondage needs stamina and diversity so that the game can proceed in an intense and focused way. In my experience, the binder can become more exhausted than the bound, and despite naps our captors are showing signs of tiredness – a stumble here, a yawn there – yet they remain stalwart, fixed in their purpose.

On release, those who were previously bound are often submissive and grateful. This is why, even quite a while afterwards, hostages often identify with their former captors. Fundamentally it's a sexual thing. Despite aches and the smell from the toilets I feel that this whole plane has become eroticised, and this applies subconsciously even to those who have not previously experienced or inflicted bondage.

Towards evening we take off. I imagine our route westward across the Mediterranean threading its way along the edges of the various national flight control zones so that no one effectively controls us. In our bondage we are strangely free, cut loose from the world and its mundane ties, exalted in our indignity. I am very happy with our very special holiday, and Jill often smiles radiantly to herself.

How many TV sets around the world are tuned to our progress?

Lights are dimmed. Though the scratchy window I can make out the Plough pointing the way northward as we fly up across France, escorted by what must be Mirage jets.

Below, blooms the occasional city or town. Lyon? Vichy? Auxerre?

Two of the hijackers remain in the cockpit. The five others stand at the front, holding their weapons, like a peculiar guard of honour. Soon we will land again – yet will even Paris be our final destination? I feel a sense of limitless destinations.

"We are cleared to land at Orly," announces TCW. Orly is to the south of Paris. The French do not wish us overfly their capital so as to reach Charles de Gaulle. Even so, Orly is only a few minutes flight time from central Paris. If we overfly Orly no one will shoot us down over the city. The casualties on the ground could run into hundreds.

"Cover your windows!"

We're descending, unable to see. Perhaps other passengers, to the rear, ignore her order. Being so far to the front, I cannot disobey.

Descending, descending. Engines boosting then throttling back then boosting again.

I hold Jill's hand tight in mine, imprisoning it.

We're flying level. This must be the final approach.

"I have an announcement," shouts TCW. "You believe you are on an unusual holiday. You are not! You think we are deluded to believe we are the Zenji Had Commando. But we *are* the Zenji Had Commando. We know it is impossible to free Zenji Had from Israel. Our demand is a pretence. Our mission is to destroy a national emblem as dramatically as we can at the cost of our lives – which we give gladly. We can never freely walk away from this airplane, therefore we choose death. The world is too full of people! People poison the Earth! But our other mission was to rob you. You have been milked of billions of Dollars and Euros and Pounds and Yen to buy nuclear weapons from ex-Soviet republics. Unusual Holidays only existed for this purpose – a master stroke of Zenji Had-ish inspiration. By now all the money you transferred is the hands of our comrades. That is why we have delayed until now."

A woman screams, believing what TCW says. Five of those wicked-looking guns are levelled at us captors belted in our seats. We can do nothing but sit.

"Bodallagaea!" cries TCW. "Bodallagaea! Bod, Bod, Bod. Compose your minds by Bodding! Your bodies will soon be destroyed."

There's no proof of this, no proof. Still flying level, the plane picks up speed.

Some fellow at the back must have slid his window-cover up. "It *is* Paris! We're so *low* – !"

The one thing he *won't* be able to see is the otherwise unmistakable Eiffel Tower which will be dead ahead if TCW is telling the truth. Dead ahead is our blind spot.

TCW cannot be telling the truth. This is the latest and finest finesse of our holiday.

Jill begins to chant softly, "Bod Bod Bod." She is blinking rapidly. Some passengers are panicking and clawing their windows shields up, but many join in the chant. The drumming of Bod mounts ever louder, like some sports crowd cheering on a favourite, like some political rally voicing their approval of a Saddam.

I wonder about the other holidays which were on offer. Supposedly on offer. The volcano bungee-jumping and whatnot.

Oh this is the holiday of a —

Civilization

Vylar Kaftan

1. Beginning

You have a civilization! It doesn't matter which one—let's say it's modern Western civilization. It's got fast food and sporting events, which is all you really need. Western technology gives you great military power—you have fantastic unstoppable tanks, and heat-seeking missiles to keep you safe. It's a good place to start.

You could also have chosen a remote aboriginal tribe in the center of Australia—one with nuts and berries, and spears and ropes. Or you could have chosen Communist China, or that group of scientists living in Antarctica. But let's stick to modern Western civilization. Let's give you people, too. We'll call them John and Jane. If you have a civilization, then you probably have at least two people in it.

Now, with your civilization comes a political system. Maybe your system is a democracy, and everyone gets a vote except the felons and child molesters. Maybe your system is a republic, and you market it as a democracy because it looks better on the brochures. Maybe your system is totalitarian, and you force everyone to enjoy the sound of that complicated word. Totalitarian!

But! A major choice awaits you. Are you traditional, bound by the past, certain that the old ways are the best because "we've always done it that way, so there"? Or are you radical, lured by the future, always hoping that the new ways will be better than the old because "we've never done it that way, so there"? Be warned, the future of your civilization depends on your choice. John and Jane's lives are at stake.

If you choose tradition, go to section 2.
If you choose radicalism, go to section 5.

2. Tradition

You're a traditionalist. Or a blind follower. Or just someone who reads everything in order, from start to finish. It doesn't matter; you end up in the same place anyway.

So, you have a civilization. You have TV dinners and expensive cars. You hold elections. This is the way it's always been done, and this is the way it must be. Never mind those fruitcakes in wigs who fought against the colonial powers. They were supporting Freedom and Liberty and other words that make great advertising. The corporations live off the people and the people trust the corporations. John and Jane relax, knowing that everything around them has worked for centuries.

Things stagnate. You hold more elections, or pretend to. The people in power have always been in power. The world is the way it's always been. The police have always arrested people in the streets. The freedom to speak has always been restricted in the name of security. The corporations destroy the people and that's the way it's always been, and why would you question that, citizen?

Congratulations! You've got fascism!

Go to section 3.

3. Fascism

How nice for you, that you look so good in jackboots and a uniform! Your secret police are so dangerous that they're sexy. They kick the enemies of the State in the street, like Rockettes in steel-toed boots. You sleep with national security books on your nightstand and a revolver under your pillow. Or maybe you just have secret meetings of secret societies in secret boardrooms, sealing fates with secret handshakes. The artists fill the gulags, and hey—cheap labor! So what if it's not fair and equal? Equality is for hippies. John and Jane trust you to keep them safe at all times.

When you're fascist, you're always right, because God or Satan or your left boot told you what to do. Divine power is with you! That means that you're right, and you'd better make sure everyone else knows it too. Let's go to war!

Go to section 7.

4. Complacency

You've been in power an awfully long time now. Why pay attention any longer? There's too many good shows on TV (or in the bullring, or in the arenas, or whatever you've got). You talk about the great sporting events on television and visit fast-food drivethroughs. You worry about whether your toothpaste is *really* doing all that a toothpaste should. After a while, you stop paying attention to anything at all. John and Jane are off doing something, but you're not sure what. This is the way it's always been, and this is the way it will always be. Is this progress? You aren't sure.

Go to section 2.

5. Radicalism

You decide to experiment. Artists love your society. Painters color skyscrapers, and sculptors make art of garbage. Directors shoot movies in black light and show them in darkened theatres. Musicians shred the works of previous centuries. Corporations hold festivals to mock their own logos.

People are changing things from the way they've always been, just to make changes. Broken furniture becomes the new fashion. Everyone lives with six uncles and an aunt. John and Jane change their names to Isthmus and Quagmire. No matter what the new idea is, it must be better than the old. You remember that you haven't changed governments in a while. Throw out the old! Bring in the new! It's time for a revolution!

Go to section 6.

6. Revolution

You hand out pamphlets in the street. Citizens march in protest of everything. The Hero of the People takes over in a bloodless coup. The former powers all commit a penitent suicide: on the same day, in the same prison, under your watchful eye. How convenient! You take note of all the former rules—because if that's how they did it, now you must do it differently. You charter a new Constitution in a different font from the old one. Oh good, this regime is much better than the last one!

You suppress the counter-revolutionaries. They want to change everything. Any disagreement in society must be squelched. John and Jane must have their freedom. For the good of the new regime!

Go to section 4.

7. War

Oh boy, it's war! Your regiments march like clockwork toys. Colonel Mustard is your general, with his dashing moustache and monocle. Your hats are quite classy, with a feather for each soldier (for officers, two!) On the streets, your noble supporters weep with pride as their loved ones march past. The people support the Cause (both sides, if it's a civil war). Or if they don't, you silence them, for national security. Jane blows John a kiss as he shoulders his weapon and heads away. He'll come back a hero, and they will marry.

Your soldiers fight bravely. They pose for photos every time they save a small child from Tyranny. There's no blood—at least, not in the photos. The enemy can't oppose the side of Truth and Justice, which you're quite certain is you.

Congratulations! You've won the war! Now for the next step: What kind of society do you want to build? Is your future an ideal Utopia, or a dark Dystopia?

If you build Utopia, go to section 8.
If you build Dystopia, go to section 9.

8. Utopia

Medicine: Disease has been eliminated, and people live to be 120 in perfect health. As a result, your people have more time to contribute to society and to enjoy their lives.

Agriculture: Food is mass-produced by advanced techniques so that there is plenty for everyone. Special additives in the food guarantee nutrition and health for every citizen.

Employment: Everyone is guaranteed a job that pays a living wage, so that all people have the means to support themselves.

Housing: No one is homeless. Citizens are guaranteed safe, affordable housing.

Education: Citizens may study any available information. The government provides the entirety of human history and current events, and encourages people to read.

Law: All issues are decided by fair courts. Mistakes are never made.

Government: The government wants to make sure the citizens are happy.

Wow! What a wonderful world you've built for yourself. Now, all that remains is to help everyone else enjoy Utopia!

Go to section 10.

9. Dystopia

Medicine: Disease has been eliminated, and people live to be 120 in perfect health. As a result, your world is overpopulated and resources are scarce.

Agriculture: Food is mass-produced by advanced techniques so that there is plenty for everyone. Special additives in the food guarantee obedience to the government.

Employment: Everyone is guaranteed a job that pays a living wage, so that people are trapped in nightmarish jobs that they can't leave.

Housing: No one is homeless. People without homes live in institutions, where they are subjected to conditioning and experiments.

Education: Citizens may study any available information. The government provides the information that citizens are authorized to see, and records who is reading it.

Law: All issues are decided by fair courts. Mistakes, of course, are never made. How could they be?

Government: The government wants to make sure the citizens are happy.

Oh dear. What a horrible world you've made for yourself. Hey—those people next door, in that other place? They have Utopia, and you don't. Misery loves company. It's time to change some things.

Go to section 10.

10. Zeal

Rows of smiling identical people sing a patriotic anthem in perfect tune. In Utopia/Dystopïa, you are never alone.

Your society is happy, or it's not. Someone else has it better, or they don't. But you're sure about one thing: other people are different from you. And that's dangerous.

Everyone else must share in your happiness or unhappiness. Everyone else must be just like you. Like Jane. Like John.

Oh boy, it's war again!

Go to section 11.

11. War, Again

I hope you're not surprised. It always comes back to war. The details change, but the patterns remain the same.

The last war was just for fun, but this one is serious. You're blowing the left arms off babies and burning 10,000-year-old monasteries. You perfect the technique of keeping a soldier alive despite mortal injury; the technique is quite helpful for spies on suicide missions. Your soldiers pray to God in the field, but you don't have time to answer. You're busy making military decisions. This war is serious, and hard choices must be made. John marches off again, and someday will return to Jane. Or he won't. That's war.

The question is, did you win? Will you dominate these not-like-you people and rule them with an iron hand? Or did you lose, and now face the destruction of your society?

If you won, go to section 12.
If you lost, go to section 14.

12. Tyranny

You're mad at these people, these pathetic creatures you conquered. They started that horrible war! Now you must teach them a lesson.

You make them build bigger stadiums and better fast food restaurants. Perhaps it's tyranny, but it's oppression with a smile—because you love them. That's why you want them to be like you. *Just* like you. And once they learn your lesson, they *will* be like you. You want them to enjoy their world as much as you enjoy yours. Or hate it, the way you hate your own. It's all for the good of John and Jane, who really should appreciate you more.

Unfortunately, your smiles aren't enough to convince them of your love. There's always room for assassination.

Go to section 13.

13. Assassination

Oops! Someone got crabby and killed your leader, in the shower. It's terribly messy, with brains splattered on the bathroom wall.

Who do you blame? Why, it's obvious. It's the vice-president secret police Communists students Boy Scouts Mothers Against Drunk Driving anyone who isn't you. People not you are responsible! People not you must pay!

Retaliation is swift and effective. You kill their leader. And the other leaders. And some people who aren't leaders. And they kill more of your leaders. And non-leaders. The streets flow with blood.

Is this war again, again? No, it's just collapse. Government structures tumble. Schools are boarded up. Garbage piles up because no one removes it. People burn textbooks for warmth. John and Jane live on scraps from their neighbors. Maybe someone finds an atomic weapon, and maybe they use it. Maybe they don't need to.

Whichever way it happens, you've reached the apocalypse.

Go to section 14.

14. Apocalypse

Oh no! Your civilization is destroyed. No more fast food. No more sporting events. No more two-for-one buffalo wing specials.

It's a mushroom cloud, billowing away in the breeze. Or a plague where everyone's skin explodes with toxic pustules. Or intense radiation that boils the brains of 98% of the population.

All of the nice families with 2.5 children (maybe happy, maybe not) are vaporized like rain in a volcano. Or the corpses pile up like ants that ate poisoned bait. The survivors walk among the living dead—stealing granola bars from their purses but leaving the wallets, because who needs money anymore?

Nuclear winter sets in. Or a biological disaster. Or just sheer depression.

But there are a few survivors. There always are. And they can start over.

Go to section 15.

15. Survival

Groups of ragged survivors struggle across the wasteland, or rubble, or abandoned cities. John and Jane take things one day at a time. Their challenge is to live until the night—then to live through the night, and to live another day.

Food and shelter are scarce. Many people don't make it. With time, the population balances so that it can support itself on the meager resources. This takes months, or it takes years. But when enough time passes, a small tribe sits in a cave, or at an oasis, or by a river. John (or Jane) says, "Remember how much better things used to be?" The others throw rocks at him or her, and demand not to be reminded. They want to forget the dead times that can't be revived.

But Jane (or John) watches, and waits, and remembers.

Once the others have truly forgotten—and the past has become myth—s/he has an idea. S/he says to the others, "I will lead you to happiness and freedom! Everyone follow me!" John (or Jane) unifies the tribes. Jane (or John) thinks that s/he has a new idea, better than anyone's ever had, something that will work. As always, certain choices must be made. But Jane and John are no different from you, in the end. They aren't smarter or wiser. They're just someone else.

Go to section 16.

16. Beginning, Again

Did you think the choices were terrible? They were.

Are you disappointed in where your choices have led you? Don't be. Other leaders have tried, and failed. The future is full of the same choices as the past. Nobody likes the choices, but civilization keeps moving.

Do you feel that you're at the beginning, again? You are. It's a circle. But there's always hope for change—hope that the circle becomes a spiral staircase.

Look, here, see this. A room, with a table. It's evening, or night. Look closely at the three people sitting around the table: John, Jane, their child. John smiles. He needs a shave, or perhaps he is bearded. Jane serves lasagna, or chicken casserole, as she tells her family about her day. The child is a girl, or a boy. The child sits in a highchair and gazes adoringly at John and Jane. After they eat, the parents take the child upstairs, singing a lullaby. It's been a good day.

Their world is radical, or traditional. They vote like responsible citizens, but they're more excited by the child learning to walk. The child grows up in revolution, or not, and marries a man, or a woman, or no one at all. S/he raises a family in Utopia/Dystopia or a world that is neither. When the apocalypse comes, s/he stays with the kids, who are grown up themselves and having a child. Despite the destruction, a baby is born.

You have a civilization.

The Lion Waiting

Kira Franz

They came to the sculptor's country after they had sucked the oil from all the other sands and jungles in the world. They discarded those other nations, dropped them like a farmer's boy leaves the husks of tangerines behind him.

They had remembered this land where the people's skin was the color of the treasure they sought. And mouthing the usual list of virtuous excuses, the whites invited their soldiers in with them.

The sculptor first tried to praise the white men in his country. He had sold much work to white people and remembered some fondly. "They are not so bad," he told his neighbor. "They are kind and innocent, if you talk to them one at a time." But after a friend of the neighbor disappeared into the white soldiers' prison, the sculptor's tongue stuck to his teeth.

The sculptor continued to go about his business, carving slabs of wet clay with curving knives and tiny wooden paddles. Sometimes he would make masks because the white people liked to buy them – solemn tattooed faces that became stone in the fire. Once he would have cast each figure in bronze, but now metal was too expensive. Now they remained clay.

The sculptor didn't mind. When he set his sculptures on the ground, he imagined them surfacing out of the mud, like fish from the sea. The masks he laid on the soil seemed like surprised visitors blinking their empty eyes at the sun. One day when his grandson stole a mask, the sculptor assumed it had melted back into the earth – at least until he heard the boy giggling in the mango tree.

A few days later, the sculptor's grandson danced too near a land mine. He survived the explosion, but the hospital had no antibiotics and no IV's and no power to run its magical machines.

The boy's death changed the sculptor's face, made it a mask more set and sad than any he had carved. The sculptor began to go to meetings late at night. He began to ignore the people who shrugged and murmured, "When will the goat grow strong enough to kill the leopard?" He began to memorize the poetry of sulfur and sodium – "Lithium, calcium, aluminum, phosphorus, potassium..." he recited to the masks, whose open mouths would close before they would betray him. And he began to take his wares every day to the market just outside the white encampment, where the white soldiers came to buy orange and blue striped cloth and carved calabash bowls.

Whenever there was an opportunity, the sculptor would tie a small bag to a market stall or a friend's cart. "A token," he would say. "For good luck." Once a white soldier stopped him and inspected the packet.

"Copper?" the soldier asked, letting the powdered metal seep through his fingers like red-gold water. The smell of the metal, the same as blood, rose in the air. "What's this for?" The soldier's voice took on a tone the sculptor knew, and his friends nearby feared for him.

But the sculptor smiled at the soldier. "A merchant's superstition, sir," he explained. "For prosperity. Copper calls to copper, you see." And the soldier, unable to find a reason to arrest the sculptor, let him go on his way.

One day, before the sculptor rolled his wagon of masks and sculptures to the market, he strapped on a heavy vest – all the pockets full of one secret or another. He poked at the pockets, whispering to each as though to comfort a small creature within. Over the vest, he draped his loosest robe.

As he started on the road, he felt he was wearing the leather and chain armor of his ancestors. Then, as step followed slow, overloaded step, he began to wonder if he had become one of his own sculptures in the sun. "I will harden," he said to himself. "I will be beautiful."

At the market, the sculptor smiled at the fruit seller on one side of him and nodded to the calabash carver on the other. He bought some puff-puff for the two boys begging near his stall, then shooed them away when their lips were snowy with sugar. The younger boy was always laughing and so reminded the sculptor of his grandson.

When a large group of soldiers arrived at the market, the sculptor stood and held a funeral mask over his head. "Who will buy this lovely mask?" he called. "Look, see how the eyes of this ancestor gaze upon us all." No one answered, though the fruit seller rose and gestured to a few friends. Together, they strolled to the far end of the market while the sculptor remained, twisting his wrist this way and that so the sun could turn the mask's hollow cheeks into shadows and its glittered teeth into dancing light. The group of soldiers began to pass the sculptor's stall.

Then the sculptor yanked a cord from his vest like a thread that needed pulling. He heard a soft hissing, a small pop, and then a great sound and flame consumed him and made him stone. The explosion of flame swallowed up the market stalls nearby, and the soldiers as well.

But the sculptor had stroked copper and potassium, borax and magnesium, peering at them, sniffing them, tasting them, feeding each to his kiln to see what the fire would make of them.

When the fire burst from the sculptor's vest, it snatched the secrets from each pocket, then, emboldened, it sought out the hidden sachets he had tucked throughout the market. As the flame gobbled those alchemical charms, it turned golden or green or blue or pink. The market became a rainbow of fire, like the dusty sky when the sun rises behind the eastern plateau.

The whites who watched saw only a riot of colors devouring their soldiers. But the sculptor's people could see the great golden lion in the midst of the flames, roaring and calling to them in all its power.

Only a very few could see both the lion and the burning. One was the older of the two beggar boys. After the fire died down, he went to his little brother, even though the embers raised blisters on his scarred feet. The laughing boy had been joking with a soldier in the back of the group and watching the ground for the coins the soldiers always dropped for the children. Now the older brother knelt beside the younger, but found he could not touch the boy for a long time.

But in the months and years after, many people would tell their children a story, beginning with "There once was a sculptor...." And a few of those children would love the story, and remember only the glory of the lion.

Engaging the Idrl

Davin Ireland

I

The desert here is pink and rocky and shrouded in darkness for much of the day. The excavation site is slashed with grey spills of rubble that could be collapsed towers or random seams of granite. To the east, great clouds of mortar dust boil across the plains, scouring the arid landscape, depriving it of fresh growth. Only the Idrl remain. Oblivious to the wind, seemingly blind to the desolation, they drift through the emptying topography like azure phantoms, the robes that stain their hides a deep, lustrous blue snapping petulantly in the breeze. They refuse to talk to us or communicate in any way, for they consider our troops to be an occupying army.

Our generals are therefore left to draw their own conclusions about what went on before mankind arrived on Serpia Dornem.

Gruel says he knows. After listening to his story, I am inclined to agree with him. The Idrl did not build these ruined cities. Nor did they occupy them. They are instead a separate nomad species, periodically emerging from hibernation to roam the land and take whatever sustenance their dying world has to offer. The mysterious Architects, however, strove for greater things.

II

A transport carrier arrived unannounced this morning. Its harried crew whisked us away to a salt flat fifteen hundred clicks east of base camp, and dumped us there to await further instruction. None came, and when the adverse weather conditions disrupted our communications equipment, some of the younger men grew visibly anxious. Then Gruel himself appeared towards the end of afternoon, tiny reconnaissance craft bobbing and groaning against increasingly heavy turbulence. The perpetual scream of mortar dust had whipped itself into a sandstorm of vicious proportions, yet the latest intelligence took precedence over all.

"We depart at eighteen-hundred hours," the corporal announced, and took shelter on the leeward side of the craft. He would say no more and prohibited further discussion between the men. Forty minutes later we took to the skies.

"Right beneath us," Gruel cried above the shriek of the engines. We had been in the air for maybe a half hour at the time. "Tell me what you make of *that*."

I looked down. The pink and grey shelf of desert that followed us everywhere we went had suddenly vanished, only to be replaced by what turned out to be forty-thousand square kilometres of unfettered parking space – an asphalted lot of such grotesque proportions that it extended all the way to the horizon in three different directions. And not a motor vehicle in sight.

Who were the Architects, I ask myself. What made them do this? Precious little evidence remains beyond the cities themselves, and these have been stripped, razed, and abandoned in a way that suggests the destruction was thorough and wholly intentional. By the look of it, the only exception is a parking facility identical in character and composition to anything one might have found outside a conventional strip mall circa 2010. With the exception of size, of course. This thing dwarfs anything Earth had to offer by several thousand orders of magnitude.

Tomorrow we will learn more. For the remainder of this evening, we'll kick our heels and wait for the survey team to complete its remote sweep from orbit. Naturally, the Idrl sense moves are afoot. They have ceased roaming the sterile plains and watch us cautiously from distance. The calm dignity these beings exude stands in stark contrast to their magnificent trailing robes, which ripple and flutter incessantly on the gritty air currents. A displaced show of emotion, perhaps? We may never know. Meanwhile, certain members of the unit already exhibit the first signs of battle fatigue, though we have fought no war.

III

Tang and Spritzwater, two of my best men, are refusing to go on. They shed their laser carbines shortly after dawn this morning, and now stand with their backs to the spent orb that is this system's sun, shadows trailing before them like tired ghosts. They say there is something wrong with Serpia Dornem. They say the planet is haunted. I am beginning to believe them. When we performed a perimeter sweep at 2300 hours last night, rocks, pinkish sand, and lazily flipping dust devils were about the extent of it. As the false dawn coloured the sky, a monstrous city loomed in the east.

My men blame the natives. Even those of us who retain a degree of objectivity are becoming unnerved by their austere presence, which grows by the hour. During breakfast I counted eleven Idrl gathered about a cluster of the spiny-leaved plants that cling in the cracks between the parched rocks. By first inspection their number had swollen to seventeen. They filter down from the arid hills to the south – gaunt, weary, faces expressionless yet eloquent as pantomime masks. This is not uncommon for a race subjected to prolonged oppression. A spectacle is unfolding here, and the spectacle is us. We have found the one city the Architects overlooked – or perhaps it has found us – and now we must investigate.

Later.

The nearer we get, the greater the extent of the challenge. In the swirling wastelands between base camp and city, we spied a dead tree. It stood naked and branchless in the wind, sand-blasted for what may have been centuries on end, the very last of its kind. Oloman was dispatched to investigate, and returned minutes later in a state of high agitation.

"You have to look at this," he said, tugging at my sleeve, "you have to look at this right away."

We deviated from our game plan just long enough to verify the lieutenant's claims, which were irrational in the extreme but perfectly justified. The tree was not a tree at all, but a roadsign: a rusting iron pole pointing the way to a city with an eerily prophetic name. Venice Falls. The words were still legible despite the corrosive effects of the wind. There could be no mistake. Out here in a region of the galaxy visited by no human, there exists an urban settlement large enough to accommodate the entire population of New York City.

And it has an English name.

The Idrl appear unmoved by our discovery. They form a serene gathering to our wind-choked huddle, steadfastly refusing any attempt at dialogue, even though the surreal possibility exists that we may actually speak the same language. Nye has tried to tempt them with extra clothing and with food, but all is ignored. Even when an older female, badly undernourished and clearly hypothermic, allowed her eye to wander in the direction of the rehydration kit, her fellow tribal members closed ranks about her. We have not seen her since.

IV

Much as I suspected but dare not mention for fear of spooking the men further, this metropolis is a full-scale reproduction of an Earth city circa 2010, faithful in every detail except one. There are no people here. None except us, that is. We wander the empty streets in aimless fascination, weapons drawn but pointed at the ground. Sand dunes clog the intersections, erosion blights the shopfronts; but any wear and tear is incidental, a tawdry gift of the elements. I stare at the red-brick apartment buildings that line the sprawling avenues, at the reproduction brownstones with their salt-stained walls, at the magnificent steel and glass towers that pierce the gloomy sky – and wonder again who the Architects were and why they should have built this place.

Were they intending to populate it with immigrants from our own planet? To forcibly humanise the Idrl for their own ends? To create a holiday resort? Such notions strike me as absurd. The dying sun, the alkaline soil – a bleaker aspect is difficult to imagine. And yet they *must* have had a reason for such folly. Acquiring enough knowledge to make a balanced judgement on the subject would take decades of investigation, and we only have weeks at best. In the meantime, the men are determined to make a start. Without my consent, Oloman used the butt of his carbine to smash a movie theatre window and thus gain access to the sealed lobby. Inside, our torches revealed plush red carpets, a ticket booth, even a hot dog stand advertising various brands of popcorn and ice-cream. None of the food on offer was actually available, but that didn't detract from the authenticity of the moment. It seemed so real that I half expected an usher in a velvet suit to emerge from a side door and escort us to our seats.

But not everyone shared my enthusiasm.

"It doesn't smell right," Oloman complained, "like fresh paint and new carpets shut in for thirty thousand years."

"And no movies," agreed Nye. "Look at the poster frames: they're all empty."

It was a pattern that was to be repeated throughout the city. Bars with no liquor, trash barrels without garbage, corporations bereft of employees. And beneath it all, lurking at the very edges of perception, the unshakeable conviction that we were being watched.

"Of course we are," I declared in exasperation, "the Idrl are everywhere. The fact they choose not to show themselves doesn't mean they're not around."

But my words failed to allay the unit's increasing sense of unease, and in the end we retreated with weapons raised and hearts aflutter. Venice Falls is an unsettling place.

V

Tang and Spritzwater are gone. We arrived back at base camp an hour ago to discover the radio damaged beyond repair and half our stock of rations missing. This is not the work of the Idrl. If the men are to believe that, however, we must locate and capture the deserters before the spiral of suspicion and paranoia becomes too great. Already some of them are starting to question my authority.

The search begins immediately.

Ranging through the powdery foothills beyond the city, we encounter the entrance to one of the stately Idrl burrows. The rock-lined tunnel leading down into the ground is high enough for a man to stand upright during his descent, yet from just a few feet away it appears no more conspicuous than a natural fissure in a seam of granite. We enter, calling out the names of the missing as we navigate these labyrinthine corridors. Occasionally we find signs of occupation but no actual occupants. These people have nothing. The few oxen-like beasts that survive on this desiccated globe are reared and worked to exhaustion underground, never to see the light of the pale sun. The lapis lazuli the Idrl mine for their own personal use – the one commodity this barren place has left to offer – we would gladly take off their hands in exchange for food, water, and crops engineered to survive the inhospitable conditions. But that would be dishonourable, it seems. So instead they survive on a diet of insects and the coarse spiny plants that thrive out here in the desert, taking hope from the knowledge that, quite incredibly, they are almost there. The Architects are gone, we could very well be next. Freedom, at any price, is almost within their grasp.

I wonder what the Idrl will be left with once we return to space?

An answer of sorts has arrived from an unexpected source. The search for the missing men having proved fruitless, we withdrew to the surface in pairs, myself and a soldier called Gosling bringing up the rear. Just prior to breaking the surface, Gosling angled his flashlight at the ceiling. The scalding white torch beam revealed a long niche carved into the rock along the top of the cavern walls, and here, stowed like so much excess firewood, lay the mummified remains of countless generations of deceased Idrl. Intrigued by the discovery, we retraced our steps, following the dusty seam of corpses to its source. The oldest, driest specimens were stored at the heart of the burrow, nearest the fire pit, which is where the Idrl sleep, cook and keep warm. It made sense for their carbon store to begin here, nearest the flames, where the dead could do their bit to sustain the living. No wonder we never found a burial site.

Back at the entrance to the burrow, we made another discovery. Huddled next to the freshest addition to the line of shrivelled corpses crouched a juvenile female – shivering, barely alive, no larger in my estimation than a six-year-old girl. Hunger had collapsed her face, preternaturally enlarging the eyes. But already she had learned her people's way. When I offered my coat, her gaze drifted to the rock wall opposite and she was lost to me. Almost. But then an idea struck me. The chocolate bar was freeze-dried, vacuum packed, and perfectly fresh. When I broke the foil package and waved it beneath her nose, the child's nostrils quivered spasmodically, and a tremor of anguish seemed to travel through that pitifully slight form. For a moment, just a microscopic sliver of a moment, her eyes betrayed all of the misery and the suffering and the longing in her tiny heart. Then all of the fight, all of the emotion, seemed to bleed out of her, and she was lost to me once more.

"Move out," I whispered to Gosling, and we broke the surface together in uncomfortable silence. But at least I had confirmation of that which I had suspected all along: the Idrl are not the empty vessels they pretend to be. They feel, just as we do. They hurt; they hope.

VI

Tang and Spritzwater are now officially missing. I reported their disappearance this morning when a second transport carrier dropped by with news, supplies and a fresh radio. After consulting the high command, it was decided we would make one last sweep and then return to headquarters for the final assessment – the one that will decide the fate of our mission entire. Already Serpia Dornem is being discussed in terms of a washout, and that suits the men just fine. I myself retain mixed feelings on the subject.

I think I understand the nature of the problem now. I honestly believe I am starting to comprehend the size of the dilemma the Idrl face. They are a dying species on a world that will soon be extinct. They have spent the last thirty-thousand years subjugated and occupied by a race who were at best indifferent to their existence, and who at worst may have enslaved them. Perhaps they no longer understand the meaning of compassion. Their lives are brief and cruel and filled with all the bitter harshness of winter, even in the warmest of months. Perhaps they need someone to show them that not all visitors to this place are hostile, and not all outsiders are to be viewed with distrust.

All I need is a chance.

We continue to follow the winding pathways through the foothills to the south, but few believe the deserters – if deserters they truly be – would seek refuge in exposed outlands when the corrupt monolith of Venice Falls squats so predominantly to the east. They are much more likely to be drawn by the prospect of shelter and the comforts of home, no matter how strong their initial reluctance. Still, we must be thorough and we must be sure. And the search has not proved a complete waste of time. Bit by bit, the land is giving up its secrets. We discovered a deep quarry veined with countless fractures and many millions of the tough, spiny plants upon which our hosts depend. We also discovered a broken loom near a deep, natural well. Attached to the loom was a cup filled with powdered lapis lazuli. So now the picture is somewhat complete. The Idrl eat this plant, feed it to their livestock, weave its sinewy fibres into robes that are subsequently stained blue with the crushed lapis. If you add in the not unreasonable amounts of geothermal energy generated beneath the surface, you have an entire ecosystem right there.

Returning the city at noon, the men are somewhat cheered by the knowledge that the approaching storm will not hit until we have completed our projected sweep, and are on the way back to base for our final pickup. As we draw nearer, Oloman's behaviour becomes increasingly erratic. So great is his distraction, in fact, that word of it filters up the column to me, and I am forced to drop back and confront him. The last thing I need right now is another Tang or Spritzwater.

"What the hell is going on," I demand, "your attitude is making the men restless."

In lieu of an answer, Oloman turns on his heel so that he faces back the way we came, finger jabbing in the direction of our dusty tracks. The dry soil here is heavy with iron oxide, and our footprints describe a pinkish-red arc that trails all the way back to base camp. He then flats a hand in the direction of the old signpost that marks the way to Venice Falls. It stands perpendicular to our position, about a mile distant, and I can just make it out through the murk of late morning.

"We've got company," Oloman informs me, and then narrows his eyes.

"But not Idrl."

Another species, perhaps? My field glasses are useless against the membranous skeins of dust that drift lazily across the intervening plain. I therefore make a decision based on instinct. Oloman may have his weaknesses, but foolishness is not one of them. "Collect Gosling and Nye and follow in my wake," I tell him. "Send the rest of the men on into the city."

We reach the signpost just as the last of the forward party melts into a decaying business district on the edge of town. The little girl is no more forthcoming than on the previous occasion we met, though her whole body betrays the incredible risk she has taken in coming here. A pronounced pulse-beat bangs at her throat, and her overly large eyes dart frantically to and fro in their sockets. Not another species, then: just a smaller version of same. Now, at least, I can begin the process of redressing the balance, of showing a little kindness where before cruelty reigned supreme. Dropping my carbine in the dust, I produce the uneaten chocolate bar from my flak jacket and offer it to the girl. There is no hesitation this time: she snatches the confectionary from my hand, consumes it in six diminutive bites – chewing, swallowing, unable to disguise the terrible need that lives inside of her.

"Rations," I mutter, and four packs hit the dirt. There is no longer any point in offering, I merely load the pockets of the girl's robe with food, and pat her gently on the head – all too aware, as are we all, that it is at such moments history is made.

Recalling the notion that the Idrl may actually understand something of English, I call to the girl as we depart. "Tell your family we are their friends," I cry. "Tell you tribe we mean them no harm. We are not here to hurt you, we can help. Tell them soon."

My words are lost in the rising moan of the wind. Perhaps it is for the best. Perhaps the gesture alone should speak for us. As long as we march towards the city, the little one remains in place – watching, waiting, possibly savouring the taste of our friendship and the notion that not all strangers are aggressors. One can only hope.

VII

The storm is almost upon us. Angry thunderheads roll in from the horizon, purple-white lightning veins the clouds. We do not have much time. Sensing that the end is near, we fan out through the streets, the names of the missing echoing back at us from abandoned buildings.

I cannot stop thinking about that little girl. With one simple gesture, one overt act of kindness, the relationship between Human and Idrl may have changed forever. If they come to us for more, we will accommodate them as best we can; if this entire people require refugee status, we will provide it. The hardy crops and other supplies initially offered as trade items will be granted as gifts, part of a larger goodwill package that will grow in size until the Idrl can no longer deny the sincerity of our motives. We will not rest until freedom and democracy are established in this arm of the galaxy.

I am already dreaming of petitioning generals and world statesmen on the Idrl's behalf, when a call goes up from the next block. The cries are eerily faint against the overwhelming groan of the wind, but reverberate hollowly among the glass-fronted towers. I race down the sand-clogged avenue, past homely little Italian restaurants with generic-sounding names, past lofty investment houses with grandly-furnished reception areas, past diners and hardware stores, supermarkets and coffee shops — all of them empty, none of them dead because they were never alive. They are stillborn, unborn, aborted.

Tang and Spritzwater are cowering in a walkdown when we find them. They claim to have fled into endless blank acres of parking lot after we left them yesterday morning, only to awaken hours later in the very heart of the city with no memory of how they got there. They have been trying to find their way out ever since. The story sounds contrived, I admit, but their fear is only too real. No matter. I drag them up to the sidewalk by the hair and shove them in the direction of base camp, my anger at their behaviour tempered only by the knowledge that our time here is coming to an end.

IIX

Trudging back through the gloom and the gathering winds, we find ourselves veering inexorably in the direction of the signpost that marks the way to Venice Falls. Is it curiosity that draws us on, or a deeper need to confirm, one final time, that this is not some vast illusion. The men are excited. Certain of them discuss the snaps they will take of themselves with the city in the background, others express a wish to take the sign home with them as a souvenir. The mood is upbeat and euphoric, and remains so despite the knowledge that we are under scrutiny from the south. For at the summit of each foothill stands a lone Idrl, robes swirling, posture unreadable. The sky has turned the colour of an old bruise, and the resulting light tinges the ground beneath their feet an ominous purple. Lightning flickers at our backs, illuminating those austere figures but revealing nothing of what resides in their hearts.

We encounter the girl one last time. She is still in the same place. The pockets of her robe still bulge with untouched ration packs, a brown smear of chocolate still decorates that delicate mouth. As ever, the blue stain of her garments flutters endlessly on the strengthening breeze. One of the men — I think it Gosling, but it could just as easily be me — allows a horrified moan to escape his throat. It appears the natives have found yet another use for the spiny plant they rely on so much. Its platted fibres creak gently back and forth as the little girl twists in the wind, the weight of the ration packs elongating her already slender neck. Once and for all, the Idrl have answered our gesture of kindness with an unequivocal statement of intent.

Only now am I beginning to comprehend our predecessors' motives for leaving this place after investing so much in it for so very long. Victory is not a question of superior firepower. It is not even a matter of right and wrong. It is simply a matter of conviction, and of belief — and who would dispute that the Idrl's is far, far greater than ours ever could be.

MS Found on a Hard Drive

Ken MacLeod

1. Dark Country Covers

They sang dark country covers in a hundred Highland bars. Their roll-ups were American Spirit; Black Bottle their *usquebaugh*. The 2010s were a tense decade. In the years of the eastern wars the United States was well afraid of an EU *militaire*. Winter and Calder sang dark country covers. They spoke to their wives on mobiles, and in the dark to other lovers. They stepped up to the mike one night in Glencannich Hotel bar and took a request for the Jacobite '*Sè mo laoch, mo ghile mear*'. They knew it well but the words had changed on the hand written page. They sang it well though the lines were strange, and thus they met their fate.

The song told of an exile prince, a man they couldn't kill, a man whose voice could fools convince to die on street and hill. But who was now the hero, the fighter bright and brave? It was no more the bonnie prince but a *bodach* in a cave. It was the man who sent the planes, who brought down the towers, who threw the troops an RPG when they expected flowers. And by this time too many folk had laid too many flowers, on fresh graves of Highlanders who'd died in the eastern wars. They died in the blast of IEDs, they died in burning tanks, and while we hate their killers we hate more the bloody Yanks. Winter and Calder sang dark country covers until the coppers came and the whole crowd was roaring the bearded *bodach*'s name. Now every night we'll sing his fame in a hundred Highland bars for while we're ruled by bloody Yanks – *sè mo laoch, mo ghile mear*!

2. Just Revolution

'What's the Catholic position on the Provisional IRA?'

I had lunchtime cider on my breath and a challenge in my truculent tone. The university's Catholic chaplain, a Jesuit, silently and smilingly forgave me both. He sat me down and poured me a cup of tea. He may have smoked; he looks, in my memory, a little like Sherlock Holmes: lanky limbs, receding hair, sharp eyes and sharp nose.

'The Church, historically, has developed the doctrine of just war,' he said. 'From it, we can derive criteria for the just revolution: justice of the cause, necessity and proportionality of violence, and probability of success. Let us assume the justice of the initial cause. Necessity means that no peaceful means of redressing the injustice can reasonably be said to exist. Proportionality means that the level of violence resorted to is related to the depth of the injustice and the severity of the force applied to deny justice. Probability of success means that there must be a reasonable expectation that the resort to violence will in fact result in victory for the just cause.

'Now. In cases such as, let us say, South Africa or Rhodesia, or certain countries in Latin America, where the injustice is deep, a large majority of the population is denied the means of peaceful organisation, where revolutionary violence can be and indeed is aimed directly and almost exclusively at the agents and instruments of the state, and where for reasons almost implicit in these conditions a popular victory is at least possible, the Church might very well regard the criteria for a just revolution to be met. Some priests in these countries, as you know ... But. With regard to Northern Ireland ... well, for an informed and concerned young man such as yourself I need hardly spell out the grave difficulties of making such a case.'

He looked at me as if he'd said more than enough.

'What about the role of the IRA in weakening British imperialism as a whole?'

If he was surprised by this change of tack he gave no sign.

'Ah!' he said. 'Imperialism! Yes, that's a very interesting point. But you see, even if we accept for the sake of argument the Leninist concept of imperialism, we can analyse it into various structural injustices, political and economic: usury and so forth. On all of these the Church has made its position quite clear, and through various campaigns and charities it does it best to address them. On the structural nature of the injustice I quite see the point, yes ... but none of that, really, can be considered as being in any way seriously affected by the activities of the IRA.'

'So if the IRA's killings aren't justified, why aren't its members excommunicated?'

His expression became a little pained. 'Excommunication is a very grave step, which I don't think you fully understand. The Church distinguishes between an error of judgement made in all sincerity, and sin, committed with a will to do evil. The moral standing of a given action is a matter between the individual and the priest who hears his or her confession. And it's with them, I'm afraid, that I would have to leave that responsibility.'

'I think I understand,' I said. 'Thank you.'

We chatted on lighter subjects – alienation, exploitation, that sort of thing – and I left. I hadn't come seeking clarification on the moral standing of the Provisional IRA. I had just wanted some reassurance that it wasn't a Papist plot.

3. Devil's Advocate

Reasons why terrorism is preferable to just war:

1. Soldiers are mostly young men, who know the value of life and have a lot to look forward to. Among non-combatants there is a broader spectrum of people who have already had a life and people too young

to know what they're missing.

2. Furthermore, killing young men distorts the age and sex structure of the surviving population, whereas indiscriminate slaughter of civilians merely reduces its numbers.

3. Soldiers have demonstrated that they possess the virtues of courage, if they are volunteers, and of civic obedience, if they are conscripts. Non-combatants have not. Killing soldiers reduces the overall moral calibre of the population.

4. Young men and women are a greater genetic and emotional loss to their relatives than young children, the middle-aged, or the elderly.

5. Terrorism is more cost-effective than just war in all terms including human life, and that by at least two and often more orders of magnitude. By means of terrorism the following communities have secured or significantly advanced their political rights: the Jews in Palestine, the Palestinians in Palestine, the Catholics in Ireland, the Protestants in Ireland, the Basques in the Spanish state, the Black majority in South Africa, and many more. Thousands have died in these terrorist campaigns, whereas the costs of political recognition secured in just wars – such as that of Vietnam or France – have run into millions. Populations supporting national liberation movements, such as the Timorese, which eschewed terrorism in favour of more legitimate guerilla tactics, have suffered far more severe repression than populations supporting terrorist movements.

6. The avoidance of war is almost always an almost unalloyed boon, whereas the avoidance of terrorism has enormous costs (including avoidable wars). Consider the consequences of the failure or non-occurrence of terrorist actions against the Stalin and Hitler governments in the late 1930s, for example. Serious and sustained consideration should be given to the possibility and possible costs of absent or insufficient terrorist activity today (on such issues as climate change, mass poverty, electoral fraud in imperialist democracies, persistent and incorrigible media misinformation and manipulation, existing tyrannical regimes, etc).

7. The terrorist has a better chance than the soldier of exercising the virtue of self-preservation, including in organisations that practice suicide terrorism.

8. The purpose of terrorism is to terrify: kill one, intimidate a thousand.

> This applies particularly to state terrorism: recently established and unstable revolutionary governments should weigh the costs of immediate terror against those of counter-revolution, and act accordingly. An example which may be widely accepted is that of the televised execution of Nicola and Elena Caucescu, which demoralised their supporters and thus reduced the duration and intensity of armed opposition. An example of an insufficiently terrorist revolutionary government was that of the Sandinistas in Nicaragua: those they spared became the contras, just as the Tsarist generals spared by the Bolsheviks went off to lead the White armies.

For these and other reasons, the glorification of terrorism is a civic good, particularly in a situation where the thousand-fold more destructive practice of just war is incessantly glorified and terrorism is incessantly, ignorantly and unfairly denigrated.

4. Prediction

In my novel *Newton's Wake* I imagined two folk-singers, Winter and Calder, recalling how they had in a past life been pressured into singing the amended version of the Jacobite song referred to at the beginning of this piece. (The exact wording, implied but not given in the book, is below.) To imagine that Scottish Highlanders might at some time in the future glorify the terrorist Osama Bin Laden might seem a slander on my compatriots, or at best far-fetched. I'm not so sure. It is at least possible to imagine a concatenation of political circumstances - conscription under a closer special relationship and a widening war – in which that could happen. It is not as widely known as it should be that people far removed from the Muslim world welcomed the 9/11 attacks: in Bolivia, in Nicargua, in South Korea and the Congo. As I watched the fireballs of Shock and Awe blossom over Baghdad, I predicted that the next spectacular terrorist attack on America would be welcomed with mass, spontaneous, uncontrollable demonstrations across the underdeveloped world. I will take no satisfaction if that prediction is confirmed, but three years on I see no reason to doubt it.

5. Mo Ghile Mear, trad., version current circa 2020

Sè mo laoch mo Ghile Mear
'Sè mo Chaesar, Ghile Mear,
Suan nà sèan nì bhfuaireas féin
Ò chuaigh i gcèin mo Ghile Mear.

Syne my brave darling disappeared
Naught know I but pain and sorrow
no news we heard, his death we feared

in th' cruel caves of Tora Bora.

Sè mo laoch mo Ghile Mear
'Sè mo Chaesar, Ghile Mear,
Suan nà sèan nì bhfuaireas fèin
Ò chuaigh i gcèin mo Ghile Mear.

Freedom's fierce and gallant knight,
a high-flown laird with gentle eyes.
A blade of fire upon the night,
he'll wreak destruction from the skies.

So drink his health and sing his praise
his far-famed face and sloganned name.
In every house be one who prays
he'll scorch the tyrants with his flame.

Sè mo laoch mo Ghile Mear
'Sè mo Chaesar, Ghile Mear,
Suan nà sèan nì bhfuaireas fèin
Ò chuaigh i gcèin mo Ghile Mear.

The Sundial Brigade

James A. Trimarco

Antonio Buccini saw the street vendor every day, here in the plaza beside the Uffizi gallery. He was a dark-skinned black man, very tall and dressed in robes of sheer purple with a white dashiki. On his table, blue-gray incense fumes snaked around elongated masks of wood, some of them with nails hammered in for hair or a slice of copper pipe glued on for a mouth.

"African masks, statues, incense," he said again, and a crowd of Tyrraneans rushed up to fondle his wares. Antonio shouldered past them, his sweaty arms sliding on their raspy yellow robes.

He turned and watched them for a moment. In a way, they weren't so different from the tourists that Italy had always attracted. People of every size, color, and shape stood among them. Some dressed in bulky yellow sub-space robes that hummed as they cooled the air around them. Others, perhaps more willing to brave the summer heat, dressed like ordinary Italians. Antonio's girlfriend, Elona, said she told them apart by the scars on their hands where the sub-space keychips were implanted. But Antonio didn't need to look for any scars. A certain softness around the eyes and a peculiar slump to the back gave them away every time.

He turned onto a side street and found his favorite butcher shop. The air inside was much cooler and the sweat on his face became a splash of cold. He put his hands on the glass counter and felt his stomach twist at the sight of juicy ham hocks, fat sausages, ground beef. His breath clouded on the glass.

A loud clap made him jump. Giovanni the butcher glared at him from across the counter, hairy forearms crossed over his bloodstained apron.

"Why do you do it?" asked Giovanni. "Why do you drool over my meat when you know you can't pay?"

"Well, I . . . ."

"You haven't found a job, have you?"

Antonio shook his head.

"Ay-ay-ay!" Giovanni moaned. "It's been how many years since you've had work? I'd make you sweep the shop, but you can't even use a broom. Why do you do it?"

"You know why."

Giovanni's face went still. All the force and bluster drained away. He gestured with his head to a corner of the shop. Two men sat at a table, sipping cappuccinos and whispering in their language. The ventilation pumps in their coarse yellow robes purred and thrummed.

Antonio nodded, then raised his eyebrows. "It's . . . just the economy. I've been on the waiting list at the employment agency for years. The secretary says it could happen any day now."

"You lazy bum. I should throw you out on the street."

Antonio shrugged his shoulders. "I'd like two kilos of salted ham, four links of sopressata, very dry if you please, and a kilo of ground beef. Put it on my tab."

Giovanni picked up a ham and heaved it onto the slicer, grumbling softly. The Tyrraneans turned to watch them. Their soft skin, the color of coffee with milk, flushed and reddened. One of them spoke a command phrase and a silvery sub-cam materialized over the center of his right palm. The pieces corkscrewed out of the air and sucked together with a hissing sound like water on a hot pan.

"*Maledizione*," said Giovanni. "We're amusing them. Here come the cameras."

The man gave another command and a sub-gun made from what looked like shiny red plastic appeared in his other hand. He didn't point it at anyone, but Antonio knew what it meant.

"Have you finished wrapping that meat?"

"I'd like a package of condoms, please. Extra thin."

"That's three euro, Antonio."

Umberto glowered down from his kiosk on the Ponte Vecchio. All around him gleamed a constellation of items ranging from the cheap to the tacky: packages of crisps clipped to an old length of extension cord; disposable cameras in brightly colored cardboard boxes; lotto tickets; postcards with pictures of the Uffizi, the Duomo, and the Ponte Vecchio itself. Antonio had heard rumors that Umberto could get other things as well, things much harder to find.

"Could you put it on my tab?"

"I'd like to smack you, *ragazzo*," said Umberto, his mouth twisting below the brush of his white moustache. "Is there anybody in Florence you don't owe your hide to?"

"If I don't have a job, it's not for lack of looking," said Antonio. "It's the damn E.U. that makes it impossible."

"Right," said Umberto, letting a sarcastic growl into his voice, which, like most people of his advanced age, carried an oddly clipped accent from that other language he had spoken all his life. His eyes scanned the street, where throngs of Tyrraneans moved in every direction, pointing and sighing over the shape of a drainage pipe or the texture of a cobblestone. The air rang with the hum of the ventilation units in their suits, punctuated at irregular intervals by the hiss of a cam-globe crossing over from subspace.

"There have always been people like me in this country," said Antonio.

"But it's not right. I have to work, while you do nothing all day."

Antonio laid his arms over his friend's countertop and smiled sweetly. "Do you really think that living with my mother and begging for scraps is my idea of the perfect life? I'm no idiot. I went to engineering school. Did you know they trained me in their language when they first returned here? They wanted me to work for them. That was before they figured out what they really wanted."

"They didn't want us to be able to understand them, that's for sure," said Umberto. He placed a condom wrapped in shiny plastic on the counter. As Antonio took it, he saw the silent rage in his friend's eyes. He'd heard people gripe about the situation a thousand times, but he'd never seen anyone look so close to the edge. Antonio grabbed the condom and stuffed it in his pocket. Before he left, he took Umberto's hand and squeezed.

"It's going to be all right, my friend. Even the greatest museums must close their doors some day."

Antonio rang the bell to the little apartment he shared with his mother and waited for her to let him in. He'd given his key to Elona, his girlfriend, to borrow. Even in the miserable refugee camp where he'd lived in the first years after the flood, a vein-scanner on the door had screened his guests automatically. No one had to carry keys.

His mother opened the door with a cigarette dangling from her lips. Her arms swung with hanging fat as she went back to the table where Elona sat in a wicker chair.

"Oh, *figlio mio*," she said. "Did you bring us some meat?"

"Of course," he said, glancing at the faces of several Tyrranean children in the window. They pointed and laughed at his mother. Then a large hand slapped their faces—a mother herself, perhaps. She said something Antonio couldn't hear and the children watched more somberly.

"Don't look at them," said Elona, making the quick taking-a-picture gesture that she used when talking about the Tyrraneans. "I've been trying all night to forget that they're there." She raised a cup of wine to show him exactly how she'd been doing that.

"How did you get the wine?"

"I don't ask you how you got the meat, do I? Just sit down and have a glass."

"You didn't bring those technology magazines I asked for, did you?" said his mother.

Antonio sipped the wine Elona had poured for him. It felt good going down his throat, especially if he looked away from the window.

"Those magazines are forbidden. They're not true to period."

"I don't care about that," she said. "And don't quote their words to me. What's wrong with our real period, eh? What is wrong with 2310?"

"You want them to assign you every bad habit in the period because you can't follow the rules?" said Antonio, his voice rising to a shout. "You didn't use to smoke, you didn't use to eat too much, you didn't use to drink. What vice will they give you next?"

Elona clucked her tongue. "Go easy on her, Tony. How would you like it if you'd been older when they came? At least we were just coming out of school. But your mother already had a good career. She was telling me about all the programming she wrote for the cars that drove themselves."

Antonio took another draught of wine and leaned back in his chair. He felt like taking off his shirt and slouching in front of the TV with the next glass. Funny how easy it was to slip into the very stereotypes the Tyrraneans were dying to see.

After a dinner of *pasta e fagiole* with broccoli rabe and a cup of gelato for dessert, his mother went to bed. Antonio listened to the splash and clatter of Elona doing the dishes. He would have helped her, but it wouldn't have been true to period. When she finally finished, he pulled her close and kissed her. Her mouth had a slightly acid taste that he noticed when she was tired or frustrated, but he didn't care. He half-led her, half-carried her to the couch, where he kissed her some more and took her shirt off. Elona, who was Albanian, had whiter breasts than he'd ever seen on an Italian girl. She had blue eyes too, but it was those white shoulders and breasts that made him want to devour her, protect her, stay with her. He reached into his back pocket for the condom he'd got from Umberto.

"No," said Elona.

"Wha?"

"You heard me. They're watching."

"They were watching last time."

"Sure they were," she sung, wriggling out from underneath him and slipping back into her shirt. "And you know what my curator told me? She said, 'Albanian women in the twenty-first century didn't have sex before marriage.'"

"What? But the streets were full of whor-, I mean, prostitutes, from Albania. Everybody knows that."

"I guess that's not what it says in their research," said Elona, "*thankfully.*"

A rasping sound came from the window, and Antonio saw it slide open. A Tyrranean man climbed in and nodded at them. He had a smooth round face with features from Europe and Africa and Asia mixed together, and short curly hair. He wore a white cotton shirt and grey slacks.

"*Buona sera,*" he said. "My name is Moddo. Sorry to bother you, but for the past ten minutes you've been talking about nothing but our regulations. That's not what we need to see. You've got plenty in your real lives to talk about. Forget about us and live your lives!"

The Tyrranean smiled. Like most of his people, something about his smile struck Antonio wrong. His face might have seemed attractive in the pages of a magazine, but his skin was as smooth as a stick of butter. When someone like Giovanni or Umberto smiled, it was the accumulated troubles Antonio saw there that made him smile back. He didn't feel that with this man.

"You can't blame us," said Elona, pulling her shirt down to cover her belly. "We can't even remember what our lives were like."

"Then let me remind you," said Moddo, his chest puffing out self-righteously. "Your world was flooded. Hundreds of millions of refugees crowded the few dry cities. The wars over fresh water got uglier each year. It was just what we were afraid of when we left. We returned from Mars to find you living like animals."

"That's not true," said Antonio. "My mother was programming advanced AI navigational systems. Life was getting better."

Moddo's smile disappeared. Water hissed on a hot pan and a shiny red gun materialized in his hand. His face shivered as if he might cry.

"You'll never know what it was like," he said. "A hundred and eighty-five years without a blue sky, without the ocean, without sunlight. We lived surrounded by machines until we forgot everything that made us human. We rescued your world. All we want in return is to know where we came from, to know who we are!"

Antonio stared at the sub-gun. They did not destroy the body like ordinary guns. Instead they whisked it into sub-space, the alternate universe the Tyrraneans had discovered and harnessed while living on Mars. Although no one knew for sure where the people who got shot ended up, most people believed it was a random point in the middle of outer space.

"All right," said Elona. "We'll do what we can."

"*Grazie*," said Moddo. He climbed through the window and into the gentle darkness of the night.

Not long after that, Antonio had an appointment with his curator, Yoshi, at the Department of Human Heritage. Antonio explained his situation in the Tyrranean language.

"So you're unsatisfied with your role as a beggar," Yoshi said when he had finished. "That's hardly surprising. The unemployed of the early twenty-first century were also unhappy. Your emotions are true to period, that's all."

"But it's entirely wrong," Antonio insisted. "I did well in school. I wanted to be an engineer. If this was the real Italy, someone like me wouldn't have to live like this."

Yoshi's mouth curved into the sterile non-smile of a bureaucrat with no time for sympathy.

"What's more," said Antonio, "Elona won't marry me unless I have a job. Her curator has forbidden it."

Yoshi stared down at his desk. He looked as if he was concentrating on a difficult mathematical problem.

"I did not expect to be convinced by you. But it's true that most Italians were married by your age, so I would be disrupting truth to period if kept you from marriage by denying you a job. I'm sure I can find someone else to fill your role."

Antonio said a tiny prayer for that person, whomever he might be.

"I have an opening for a guard in the Uffizi," said Yoshi. "I could get you started there in a few weeks."

"But I studied electrical engineering. Can't you find me something in my field?"

"It'll be fine," said Yoshi. "All the good work is in museums now."

Antonio and Elona walked along the narrow streets of their neighborhood. The tawny brown walls of the houses glowed brightly in the afternoon sun. All of this had been destroyed during the flood years, but Tyrranean construction bots had restored it to period true. Several times Antonio tried to take Elona's hand, but she pulled it away every time.

"What's wrong with you?" he demanded.

"Do you think we're alone now?" she asked. "I've got something to tell you."

Antonio glanced around and noticed the silvery glow of a sub-cam behind the shutters of a nearby house. Its microphone would catch everything said on the block, and who knew how many more there were around?

"I saw my curator today," she said. "He told me a funny joke." She made the picture-taking gesture and nodded her head at the sub-cam. He knew what she meant. She was about to tell him something she wasn't supposed to talk about.

"Three women are in school to be teachers. One is American, one is Italian, one is Albanian. So they come into the school and the principal tells them to teach him something.

"The American goes up to the board and writes 2+2=4. So the principal says, 'All Americans know how to do is make money.'"

Antonio laughed a little.

"Then the Italian comes in. She starts to write something on the board but she gets hungry and orders some pasta. The principal says 'All Italians know how to do is eat pasta.'"

"Hey!" said Antonio.

"Last, in comes the Albanian. She finds some money the principal left on the desk and hikes up her skirt. The principal gets up and says, he says, 'All Albanians know how to do is . . . .'"

She couldn't finish. Antonio put his arms around her but she pushed him off. He'd known her since she was a girl, since before the Tyrraneans had come. She'd worked long hours as a maid so that she'd never have to degrade herself. In the twenty-fourth century, being Albanian had been the least of her problems. But things had changed.

"That joke is so awful," she sobbed. "They don't know anything about us."

"This isn't happening," he said. They turned the corner onto a larger road. Up ahead he could see some kind of construction site. Cranes and bulldozers moved metal beams around. The noise was deafening.

"They won't be able to hear us over that racket," said Elona. "Listen, I know some people who are forming a group. They're going to give it to the Tyrraneans right where it hurts. I want to join, too."

"But Elona," he said, "they could send us all into sub-space with a couple of bombs. We'll never win."

The brightness in her eyes dulled. She took his hand and started crying again.

"I say we should get out of here. We'll escape," Antonio said, "from the museum city and go someplace like Milan. Life is normal there, I hear. The Tyrraneans and the Italians live together as one people."

"But how will we get past the guard-bots at the gates? They shoot on sight."

"I know some people with connections. We'll get a couple of scrambler suits. That way, we can slip right past them."

Antonio put his index finger into the glass tube and a wave of heat moved across it as the machine scanned his vein structure. An unusually pale Tyrranean named Tippu, whose wide back slumped like the side of a hill, typed commands into a computer on the desk.

"You're all set," said Tippu. "You're cleared for security inside the Uffizi. You understand that you need to be extremely careful around the works?"

"It's always been that way," said Antonio. "Even during the floods, the government protected them. People drowned so that these things could be saved."

"All right," said Tippu. "You're to be stationed in the Caravaggio room. Some of the visitors might try to touch the paintings. Just tell them to back up. And remember to speak only twenty-first century Italian—you're here to keep the place period true."

"What if they don't listen to me?"

"We can't have oily fingers touching the precious works. Keep this neuro-pistol on your belt; it will paralyze the central nervous system of anyone who can't control themselves. Call me if you have to use it."

Tippu had him change into the white shirt and black slacks that were the uniform of the Uffizi guards, then brought him up to the Caravaggio room and left him there. The museum opened shortly and from that moment on the gallery was packed to the windows with Tyrraneans. Antonio considered himself a fan of great painting, but he'd never seen anything quite like the way these people stared into the works, their eyes gaping wide, their lips quivering, their hands clutching at their robes. He watched two young girls in Italian clothes staring for what seemed like hours at Caravaggio's painting of Bacchus.

"See how he's got those fig leaves in his hair?" said one of them.

"I know. It's beautiful."

"It makes me wonder why we keep them in this dirty, ugly, twenty-first century. There are museum cities all over America and Asia from that period, and we have only two in all of Italy."

"It's true," said her friend. While she looked young, her eyes and cheeks sagged dramatically with an exhausted look special to the Tyrraneans. "At first everyone wanted the twenty-first century, because that was what their great-great grandparents remembered. But people are getting bored with the highways and taxicabs, and the immigration conditions are hard to replicate. It won't be long before we have the votes we need. Then we'll feel as human as the man in this painting all the time."

"That would be incredible," said the first girl.

"*Scusi,*" said Antonio, careful to speak Italian. "You're too close to the painting."

The girls nodded blankly and backed up, their eyes still locked on the pleasures promised by the curves of Bacchus's soft white body, his dark eyes twinkling beneath his fig-leaf crown as he curled his fingers around the neck of an elegant silver wineglass.

As he left the building after work, Antonio nearly tripped over an old beggar who sat cross-legged on the ground in front of a small wooden bowl, whimpering and rocking back and forth. Antonio was about to curse him when he noticed who he was.

"Umberto! What are you doing here?"

Umberto looked up at him through the stiff white hair of his eyebrows. His lips pulled back from his teeth in an expression that mixed anguish, rage, and sorrow in equal portions.

"They caught me selling a three-dimensional vidcam," he said. "I lost my kiosk for selling off-period tech. Curator said he had an opening for a beggar so here I am."

"I'm sorry," said Antonio. "It's too bad that you're not at the kiosk anymore, because I could actually pay you now. I still owe you some money from before."

Umberto rocked forward, his face still locked in that furious expression.

"Listen," said Antonio. "Me and Elona would like to go for a walk. A long walk, you understand. We'd like something that would help us blend in."

"Take a long walk up my ass."

"Umberto, I'm serious. You know how to get things. I'll pay you well."

"Hmm, I'm not sure. Come and check with me next week."

"Oh, thank you," he said. "Thank you so much."

He said goodbye to Umberto and turned the corner to visit Giovanni's butcher shop. How different it felt to see a friend and not have to beg from him! How different it felt to have a plan, a future. He walked into the shop and spun on his heels.

"Buongiorno, Giovanni," he said. "I have good news for you. Soon I'll be able to start paying you back. I'll give you a hundred Euro as a first installment! What do you say to that?"

Giovanni's broad face pinched into wrinkles at the corners of his eyes. "I would say congratulations, Tony. But there's something you need to know first."

Cold fear washed over Antonio's glee. "Is it my mother? Another vice?"

"No."

"Well, what then?"

"It's Elona. She was arrested by the police today. It wasn't far from here. I'm not sure of the nature of the crime but she's being held in the-"

Giovanni kept speaking, but Antonio did not hear. He felt as if he'd been punched in the guts by the cold double arms of a security bot. He pulled out a chair, tried to sit in it, fell. Giovanni came and picked him up off the tiled floor.

"Cameras?" Antonio gasped, peering into the corners. "Are there cameras in here?"

"No," said Giovanni, but Antonio didn't believe him. Tears were running down his face. He couldn't bear to be under their gaze. How could they do this to him? How could they take her away, just as he'd been preparing an escape? They'd let him have his joy for an hour or two and then made it disappear, just as surely if they had shot it with a sub-gun.

He dashed outside and headed across the square to the corner where he kept his Vespa. On the way, he passed the tall black vendor who sold masks outside the Uffizi. The man was loading all the unsold masks into a sack of frayed burlap. He turned his smooth face to Antonio and gave him a crisp nod.

"What do you want?" said Antonio.

"You don't look happy," said the vendor, speaking Italian with a strange accent Antonio couldn't place. "You walk like you were carrying your own gravestone on your back."

"That's not far from the truth."

"Why don't you come with me, then? My name is Yusuf. I'd like to show you something."

"Come with you? I'm not coming with anybody!"

But even as he said this, he was taking his first steps behind Yusuf's swirling purple robes. He was glad to follow someone, instead of having to decide for himself where to go. They crossed the Ponte Vecchio and headed into the southern quarter known as the Oltrarno. They wandered through narrow streets where the evening sun threw diagonal shadows across buildings in pastel shades of umber, lavender, and orange. Then Yusuf found a rusty old security door over a garage. He opened the padlock with a key, lifted the gate, and put his sack of masks inside.

"Come in," he said. Antonio obeyed. Yusuf shut the door behind him, then crouched down on the floor. Underneath a piece of moldy plywood was a long tunnel leading down. It must have been part of the old sewer system, thought Antonio. But it was dry and led down towards a flickering light below.

Antonio's feet hit a concrete floor. He looked around and saw tables where people sat, laughing and talking. Some voices spoke in Tyrranean, others in a strange clipped dialect that only after a moment did he recognize as twenty-fourth century Italian. It was the language of his youth, but it had been so long that he understood only half of what they said.

"What is this place?"

"A secret," said Yusuf. "Hundreds of years ago it was used to plot against the royal families. Today it's back to a similar purpose. Tell me your name."

"Antonio Buccini. Why have you brought me here?"

"Don't you know? This is a place for the ones who don't like living in a museum. I thought you looked like one of us."

"That's crazy," said Antonio.

"Are you?"

"I don't know. I can't think straight. My girlfriend, they threw her in jail. I don't know how long for."

"You sound like one of us. You look like one of us. I think you are one of us."

"I don't even know who 'us' is."

"Let me tell you. I used to be a lawyer in Accra, Ghana. Then the Tyrraneans came and turned back the clock on us to the seventeenth-century Ashanti empire. A rival tribesman sold me to a Portuguese trader who brought me here in a galleon. I had to laugh when I found myself not only a thousand miles away, but four hundred years in the future."

"And two hundred years in the past," said Antonio.

Yusuf laughed, a deep sound that echoed in the underground chamber. "From the true date of 2310, yes. We call our group the Sundial Brigade, because anyone who watches the movement of the sun cannot deny the passing of time. Join us."

"I don't want to hurt anyone." Antonio had always been the most peaceful of boys. He'd never played with guns as a child or enjoyed those popular halluci-domes in which his friends played mutant musclemen who beat each other to a pulp.

Yusuf's smooth face gnarled, turned ugly. "We need you, Buccini. It used to be that a people was bound to suffer if there was oil under their land. These days it's the same with ancient ruins. They'll take you back to the fifteenth century, don't you see that? What if they prefer Giotto to Caravaggio? You could find yourself in 1285 with no running water, living on gruel."

"I told you, I'm not the right man for the job."

"Buccini, we need someone inside the Uffizi. We need someone now. We need you."

Antonio hesitated. "Listen," he said. "Lashing out at them is not going to make them act better. Now, I've asked my friend for two suits of scrambler camouflage. I'm going to wait until Elona gets out and then I'm leaving the museum city."

For a long time Yusuf said nothing. The whites of his eyes blazed in his dark, sweaty face. He spat on the ground, his phlegm landing just centimeters from Antonio's shoe.

"All right," he said. "Get out of here."

That night his mother was full of talk.

"I'm a software programmer," she said, slicing a piece of veal into pieces and putting the first one into her mouth. "I specialize in AI automobiles."

"Mother, please."

"They will hear, you say. I don't care. First, they told me what to do. I said no and they made me fat. But still I would not obey. So then they made me drink." She tipped her glass back, drained it, and tossed it at the window. The Tyrranean childrens' mouths opened in fear and they scattered away. The glass bounced harmlessly off the window, then shattered on the floor.

"Still I said no," mother went on. "So they made me smoke. Now they've taken Elona. What else can they do to me?"

"I don't know, mother. I really don't."

"If I'd known that it would be this way, I would have fought them from the beginning. I would have told them to leave us with our swollen seas." She got up and pulled the window open. The cool, evening air tasted of lemons.

"You hear me, Martian pigs?" she screamed. "You're never going to get another minute of pleasure from me, do you hear? Because I'm through. I'm totally, totally through. I'll never act in period again as long as I live."

Antonio pulled her away from the window, shook her by the shoulders. "Jesus Christ, mother. What the hell are you trying to do?"

"I want them to know," she said. Tiny red veins swelled in her drunken eyes.

Antonio heard footsteps behind him and turned. Moddo's round face was drawn into a stubborn glare.

Antonio shrugged and laughed it off. "*Buona sera.* She's drunk, that's all."

Water droplets hit a white-hot skillet and the little red gun appeared in Moddo's hand. "We've done all we could for her," he said. "She has all the worst habits of the period."

"I'm not comming another bit in old-fashioned Italo as long as I flux," said his mother. Antonio heard the twenty-fourth-century Italian and tried to cover her mouth. *"Let the drox lip up to the sky for all I gloam!"*

The red gun buzzed and quivered in Moddo's hand. Antonio jumped back. The air around his mother crackled and frothed with a curious steam filled with points of radiance, like thousands of microscopic fireflies. Then she vanished, along with her clothes, her spectacles, and her shoes.

"I'm terribly sorry," said Moddo. "If it helps you stay in period, you can imagine that she died in a car crash. All right?"

Antonio could hardly speak. Fractured words scanned and tilted in his mind, but they were eclipsed by a great sun of rage and sadness that had nothing to do with language as it rolled across the sky of his mind.

The gun slowly turned until it was pointed at him. His lungs felt as small and narrow as string beans as he apologized to his mother's murderer.

A few days later, he went back to the garage in the Oltrarno. He knocked but no one was there. He sat down in the doorway and waited with his head between his knees. Some Tyrraneans passed and photographed him but he did not care. Hours passed before Yusuf came, dragging his sack of masks behind him.

"I'm glad to see you're here, my friend."

"They killed my mother, Yusuf. I finally saw the sun."

"Hold on a little longer." Yusuf pulled open the padlock and the security door flew up with a rattling howl. "We have work for you to do."

Antonio had arranged with Umberto to pick up the bomb early on Monday morning and he came five minutes before the prescribed time. Umberto was there, sitting cross-legged on the cobblestones of the Ponte Vecchio.

His small wooden bowl contained a few euro and assorted coins.

Umberto got to his feet with a groan. Antonio followed him to his old kiosk and watched as the old man squeezed into a narrow space behind the wooden structure. The stones scraped Antonio's shoulders and hips as he slipped in after the old man.

"Open your bag."

Antonio loosened the straps. Umberto reached into the ragged folds of his clothes and placed a compact metallic object into the bag.

"It has an adhesive back," said Umberto. "Attach it to a wall. Then pull out the long pin. Turn the front of the bomb half a turn clockwise. Put the pin back and run."

"How far do I need to go?"

At that moment, a footstep scraped on a cobblestone and Antonio heard the hum of ventilation suits, so close that he could feel the airstream sweeping across his face. He stood so still he thought his heart might stop.

"Are those people back there?" asked Tyrranean voice.

"They're probably only urinating. A common practice in this period. Come take a look at these painted tiles in the wall."

The men walked away. Antonio would have collapsed if the space had been wide enough to allow it.

"Next time they could have a sub-cam and detect the bomb," Umberto whispered. "Get out of here."

"No," said Antonio. "I need to know who gave this to you."

"Can't tell you."

"I could die today."

"I know that. But this is dangerous information."

That made him want it even more. But Umberto gave him a hard push into the street that ended the conversation.

As Antonio headed to the Uffizi, he concentrated on putting one foot in front of the other. He turned into the little plaza between the two wings of the museum, which was almost completely filled with Tyrraneans, all of them searching for themselves in the gesture of a statue or the shape of a cornice.

His stomach seemed to be burning, or freezing—he couldn't tell which—as he walked past the statues of Giotto, Galileo, Boccaccio, Dante. Poets and kings, scientists and queens. All of them would die—even their memories in the minds of public would die—so that the Tyrraneans could see the Earth for what it really was: a growing, living, fighting, screaming thing, where the shadow on the sundial never stood still, and humanity could never be trapped in amber like a fly.

Antonio finally reached the entrance to the museum. Before he went inside, he took a moment to gaze at the statue of Dante Alghieri. His face was bitter and intelligent, almost alive despite his marble skin.

"I'm sorry, Signor Alighieri," said Antonio. "But this time the inferno has camera flashes instead of fire pits, tourists instead of devils. It's worse than you imagined."

He stepped up to his door, waved his finger in front of the scanner, and slipped inside. He followed the hall to the dressing room and pulled on the black slacks, the white shirt. He took the neuro-pistol from his locker and clipped it onto his belt.

In the Caravaggio room, he took one last look around at the paintings. Staring into the sweet eyes of Bacchus, he cursed the Tyrraneans one last time. Damn them for making our greatest works into the bars of our prison, he thought. Damn them for seeing authenticity only in the past. And damn them for making me do this.

He took the bomb from his bag and peeled the plastic off the back, revealing a sticky gum. Following Umberto's instructions, he pulled the pin, turned the face, and stuck the pin back again. His heart crashing in his ears, he gently stuck the bomb to the wall next to the painting.

"Oh, Signor Carravaggio, I'm so sorry."

Immediately, he heard a hiss from behind him. He whirled and caught sight of a sub-cam in the corner of the room. He'd been seen.

He dashed through the door, then followed the hallway past the other guards, putting one foot in front of another as if nothing had happened. The earliest guests were just arriving. He stepped around them as he descended the stairs, ignoring their questions about where to find this painting or that one.

Halfway down the stairs, he saw Tippu with a sub-gun in his hand. The gun twisted. Antonio grabbed a Tyrranean by the arm and pushed him in front of himself with one hand, his other grasping desperately for the neuro-pistol. A second later, the Tyrranean's falling body was no more. Antonio leveled the pistol at Tippu's sagging form and fired.

People were screaming, and, somewhere, the heavy footsteps of security bots were shaking the ground. Antonio clawed his way through the crowd, pushing Tippu's paralyzed body onto its side and shoving his way out the door. Angry cries sounded behind him as he zigzagged across the plaza. A hand fell on his shoulder and he screamed, ready to fire the neuro-pistol again. His eyes caught on a sheer purple robe, a tall figure. He stopped, totally confused.

"Yusuf?"

Yusuf stood silently with his hands over his head. With a hiss and a flash of tiny fireflies, a glass bulb the size of car appeared in front of them. Yusuf opened a door and stepped in, then pulled Antonio after him. The bulb rose high into the sky, even as Tyrraneans pointed and shouted at them.

"But you're, you're . . ." Antonio grabbed one of Yusuf's hands and saw long scars across his palms where the sub-space keychips had been implanted.

"It's true," said Yusuf. "I'm a Tyrranean. I've never been to Ashanti. Another vendor told me that story and I liked it better than the truth."

Down below, every window in the Uffizi building burst outwards, throwing sparkling slivers of glass high into the air as jets of pink plasma flowed out in pressurized streams. The building shuddered once, twice, as iridescent flames crawled up and down the walls. Sections of the building slumped and melted, stone turning into white hot cream. A moment later, the building shuddered again and exploded upwards in a blast of black dust, pink gas, and white smoke.

Antonio gaped. It was all gone. He didn't know how, but it was gone.

"It's a type of sub-space bomb," explained Yusuf. "It creates a portal to the pressurized inner core of a gas giant planet which exists in sub-space. The portal closes after a minute to keep the destruction focused."

Down below, however, the plasma was still flowing. Human bodies contracted into black skeletons in seconds, then crackled into dust. Streamers of twisting gas rose into the sky. They coiled around the glass globe, but did not damage it.

"I need some answers now," Antonio said. "Who gave that bomb to Umberto? Was it you?"

The smile on Yusuf's smooth face seemed so typically Tyrranean that Antonio could hardly believe he hadn't noticed before. "No. I'm an exile without access to weapons. I've lived like you people for years now, because I spoke out against the museum cities."

"Then who? Who did it?"

"Someone inside, very deep inside. He's a Tyrranean politician who opposes the museum cities but doesn't want to face the consequences of saying so in public. He believes the Tyrraneans won't stop building museum cities until they come to see them as dangerous. So he passed the bomb to the Sundial Brigade."

Antonio watched the toxic clouds roil beneath, liquefying every building in their path. The portal seemed to have shut, but the twisting spirals of gas already covered whole areas of the city. The wind was picking up, blowing them to the east. Antonio strained his eyes, looking for the prison where Elona was being held.

"I'm worried about Elona," he said. "Can't you do anything? She's there, in the prison."

"Then the gas has already got her, Tony. Don't feel bad. She would have wanted this."

"No!"

"Some things are worth dying for."

"Like what?"

"Like your humanity. You know how we need to see that."

"What is that supposed to mean?"

"I may be a dissident and an exile, but I'm still a Tyrranean. My people will remember this day as a nightmare for years, but eventually they'll see it differently. What just happened here is the most human thing I've ever seen. It's beautifully true to period."

Yusuf was looking down at the destruction below with an odd expression, his eyes wide, his lips quivering, his dark fingers rubbing at his robes. He looked just like the tourists in the Uffizi as they studied the paintings there. He put a large hand on Antonio's shoulder and shook his head.

"Maybe this will satisfy us once and for all."

'How I took care of my pals.'

Elizabeth Sourbut

The airlocks open thirty seconds before the drop, and the wind howls in. Loose straps start to flap and anyone who's lagging behind scrambles to seal up his visor. The sergeant heads for his place by the inner door. But Tony doesn't wait. He's always the first one on his feet and today he heads straight for the opening and just keeps walking like the floor goes on forever, and as the fierce gravity takes him and whips him out of view, I can see his legs still walking, just like he has somewhere to go.

"Man," says the new kid Raoul, his voice grating right in my ear over the comm. "That guy ain't afraid of nothing."

"You're wrong." It's Seymour who says it, but it might have been any one of us. We all know, and we nod, agreeing. The kid frowns, not getting it. Then he glances back at Tony's seat and his eyes go wide as he sees what Tony left behind.

Then it's time and the sergeant's counting us out: one, one, one, a tap on the shoulder and you're out, and even sealed up in your armour it's like the wind's eating your face. We fall like rocks for half a klick. Then the 'chutes open with a wrench that'll take out your shoulder if you've done up your harness wrong, and acres of toughened fabric billow out into the poison air. After that we fall like snow, drifting down gentle as you like to fall soft on the target and smother it dead.

Tony missed the target, and he fell like a rock all the way. See, the kid was wrong. Tony ain't afraid to die – that way he's just like the rest of us. But he is afraid to kill. That's why he walked out on us early. That's why he left his 'chute stashed under his seat. So he'd land like a rock too and the only thing he'd kill today would be his own self.

Don't be too hard on him. We've all got something. Some thing that defines us, if you boil us right down so you can say: "Oh, yeah, so-and-so, that's what he's all about."

Tony's all about not killing, which is tough on a marine. Tough on the rest of us too 'cos now we got to concoct a story, and make sure we all stick to it, the kid too. 'Cos if we don't and they find out he killed himself on purpose so he couldn't kill any Sticks, then our Tony won't be coming back at all. Oh, we'll still see his chump walking around barracks, and he'll still answer to his name, but we won't see that gravestone grin no more, and when you look in his eyes there'll be nobody in there looking back out.

No, if we get our story wrong, they'll re-adjust Tony and then he might as well be dead for real, and that walk on air will be the last walk he'll ever take as a thinking human being. And I don't want that to happen. Tony's my pal and that's my thing, the thing I'm all about. I look after my pals.

So now we're all back, some of us with new chumps, a few with the same old mugs as before. And we're all sitting around and bragging about how many Sticks we killed. Raoul says he took out forty-five, but he's a kid so we let him.

Me, I bit it this time, along with most of the guys. The Sticks are getting wise to us. The first few times, they just stood around and looked at us as we marched right into those branch and moss settlements the brass call towns. We thought they was rooted, and they might as well have been. They just stood there while we sprayed them with lead, and down they went. They look all dried up, but don't believe it. When you shoot one, it bursts open and gunk comes out, thick and orange and smelling like nothing on Earth. Which figures. It burns if it gets on your skin, but then so does what passes for air.

Yeah, they was easy meat at first, and we took over their world. The transgalactics set up their mining enclaves, and we thought peace-keeping was gonna be easy. But the brass judged it wrong. Those skinny-looking Sticks ain't never given up, and they've finally figured out how to fight back. So down we're floating, soft as you like, and they're ready for us. They've got these catapult things and they fire phosphorus at us. It hits the 'chutes and up they go like flares and then we're back to rocks again, falling too fast.

I'm supposed to land in the big open circle the Sticks always have in the middle of their towns, but without my 'chute I can't control my descent, and I fall more than a hundred metres short. I'm lucky though. I hit a big moss roof and it breaks my fall so when I land I don't hurt myself much.

So I jump up and grab my gun and I'm about to start firing when I take a good look round. Then I stop. I can't help it. I fell into the middle of this green, mossy room and there's a bunch of them all staring at me, their mouths and eyes open in great round Os, just like a person would be if they was surprised. Some of them are real small, and the big ones have their arms round them, those great long fingers with their joints like cankers spread across the chests of the ones I guess must be kids.

Apart from their grey, flaking skin and the fact they're taller and skinnier than any fancy hooker I ever saw, they look just like regular folks, sitting down to a quiet evening in, as well as I can remember suchlike from before I got recruited. And I can't do it. I never had no problem with killing them before, but then I never saw the little ones before. I never saw them at home, just living. So I lower my gun and give this kind of stupid bow and mumble something they'll never understand, like, "Sorry about your roof," and I stumble out backwards, sweating like a pig.

Outside, things are real bad for our guys. There's bodies scattered all along the street, half the company it looks like, bones broken, suits ruptured, guys flopping like landed fish, trying to breathe and gulping as their throats close up. The domes say there's oxygen in that air just like back home, but what gets us is the fluorine and it don't matter how much oxygen is mixed with it. Once you get a good whiff of that stuff you're gone.

I still gotta help them 'cos they're my pals. So I start running around, dragging the injured under cover, yelling for backup on comms. But I can't kill no Sticks, not today. Maybe not ever again, and that makes me sick 'cos our platoon's already got Tony, and what're we gonna do now there's two of us won't kill?

I figure I've saved several guys, but then I'm surrounded. Eight big, adult Sticks with murder in their eyes and it makes no sense I can't kill them neither, but I can't. And they do that thing, that horrible thing they do. All together, they twist off one of their own hands at the wrist and burning orange gunk sprays all over me and eats through my suit. I smell the stink of that alien air and the next thing I know I'm waking up in a tank and that offensive's over and my chump didn't do much good after all.

So now I'm sitting in the mess hall in my new chump. The domes say they're all the same, force-grown clones of the first me, but they never feel quite right for the first few days. So there I am, pulling my fingers 'cos they feel too short, and cussing long and loud to get the new voice broke in right. One by one the guys turn up, and Tony's last of all. I wanna talk to him but then the sergeant comes in and rest time's over.

"On your feet, chumps!" he roars. "Get out on that ring you wretches." And we all jump up and thunder off to the high-gee exercise ring, trying not to trip over our brand new feet, gawky as teenagers growing into our perfect new bodies.

Wretches they call us and reches we are. That's short for direches, or digitally reconstructed humans if you wanna be a dome about it. And what that means in the real world is you can kill us as often as you like but we always jump back up. An endless supply of disposable bodies, the same set of battle-hardened minds. It costs a lot to train up a modern marine, more than it costs to grow new chumps for us all and pour us back in each time we go down. Just like downloading music, and not much more complicated.

So here we are, pounding round the ring in our brand new chumps, and my left knee don't click no more, and that's a good thing.

I get my chance later when we're all in the commons after chow. I'm polishing boots, and Raoul's putting his gun together, over and over. He still ain't quick as the rest of us, but he's getting there. He's pleased with himself 'cos he came through this time with his face intact but that's no big deal. You win some, you lose some, and it's pure chance which.

Then Tony comes over, grinning his tombstone grin. "Some of the fellas say you didn't do no shooting this time," he says as he sits down. I don't give no answer right away. This is what I wanna talk to him about, but now we're here I don't know what to say.

He looks at me sidelong and says, "When I was a kid, just twelve years old, my dad reckoned it was time to teach me how the world works. He was a big-shot, senior brass. Still is. Did I ever tell you that?"

He didn't, but he doesn't give me time to say so before he carries on.

"It was the Doughnuts back then," he says. "You remember them? All eyes and fingers and that damn great hole through the middle. My dad, he planned a lot of that campaign. Got promoted for it when we'd blown them away. He was real proud of his medal. Kept it on display, and told me all about how he'd planned the destruction of a whole planet-load of big-domed critters. I think he'd died twice by then. Not much by our standards but those deaths meant a whole lot to him. All the brass have died. You know that, right?"

"Everybody dies," I squeeze in, but he's already going on with it.

"Anyway, my dad had been telling me about the brave marines who do all the damage, and I think he felt bad that they'd died so often and he'd only done it twice. I still think it was more about him than me when he took me outside and told me to defend myself."

I look at him then, and he's staring across the room, his eyes unfocused, and I know he's back there, back in a time that seems more real to him than where he is now. And I realise suddenly that he's always been there, that somehow he never left that moment.

"He wanted me to kill him, and I wouldn't," says Tony. I wait for more, but he's stopped, so that must be it. I don't get it.

"He wanted you to kill him?" I repeat. "Why?"

"He'd only died twice, and it wasn't enough, not for a war hero like him, so he figured he'd sort out two things at once. He's a great one for efficiency, my dad. He'd teach me about death, and he'd increase his own chump-count, both at the same time." Tony looks at me then, and his eyes are blank and there's no grin at all. "All the times he killed me afterwards, a new way every week, it was because he wanted to die. He wanted to be a real hero, a proper soldier, but he was brass, and brass don't go to the front lines. They wouldn't let him get into any real danger, so he took it out on me."

"But it was the first time that mattered," I say, and I don't know where I get that from, but I know it's true.

"Of course," he says. "It's only the first time that ever matters."

I laugh at that. I can't help it. "Hell, I don't even remember my first time."

He looks at me funny, just waiting, and I wonder what he wants. Of course it ain't true, what I just said. Hell, everybody remembers their first time.

"There were six of us," I say. "Young, loud, full of spunk. It was before the Doughnuts, before the Ghosts even. We was at peace then, had been since my granddad's lot pacified the Squid. Me and the lads, we'd just finished a big construction job, ore-hauler for the asteroid run, and our thumbs were charged with cash, so we were out for a good time."

As I talk, the memories come clearer till they're like a holo-soap they seem so real. I'm striding along the dark street, my boots slipping on the rain-slicked cobbles. The air's full of the smell of frying seafood from the fast-food joint we've just left. I'm munching battered squid – not the big-domed kind we took the planet from, just the regular ones. They're salty and sour. It's a taste you gotta get used to, but once you got it, it stays with you.

We're laughing and loud, arguing about which club we want to hit next. Then Ghulam squeals and Axel pitches face down right in front of me so I trip over him. That saves my life because the next flying blade slices right over the top of my head. I roll over and peer back the way we came and I see them, five chumps in black, swinging a blade in each hand, looking for the next easy target. The other three lads are still alive, down on the cobbles beside me, cowering behind our dead pals, and I can smell the stink of fear.

I know we can't win, not against these guys, so I tell the others to wait till I move, then run, get the hell out of there. It would have been nice if they'd said, "No way, we're staying with you," but I see the whites of their eyes bobbing up and down as they nod.

So I take a deep breath and stop thinking about it. I leap up, yelling loud as I know how, and charge straight at those murderous chumps. They're so startled I think I might make it as far as the first one, but then there's a flash of steel, a flood of something hot and sticky pours down my chest, and then all the colour's washing out of the world and my legs seem to melt under me.

"My last thought was for my pals," I say, looking up from my hands to see Tony staring at me. "It was a stupid thing to do, but I had to look after my pals."

He nods. "I know. You always do that."

I shrug. "Pals are important. Two of 'em did get out that night. I saved two."

"That's good. You've got a good fixation. I wish there were more like you."

"It ain't a fixation," I grumble. I don't like that word, makes it sound like I'm stuck in one place.

"Yes, it is," he says. "You've said it yourself often enough. We've all got something, some thing that defines us. I don't kill. You help your pals. The first time I died, my dad was trying to make me kill him, and I wouldn't do it. He pushed it too far trying to goad me into cutting his throat and I died begging him not to make me do it. You died looking after your pals. And look at us now. You figure it out."

I can see where he's going, but it don't make no sense. "It's just one death," I say. "What does it matter what it was like? We've all died a hundred different ways."

"No," he says, "we've only died once. All of us, we only die once, even the brass. After that, we're just echoes of our real selves. They record us and store us and pour us back in, but there's something missing, something all their fancy technology don't pick up. We can move, we can eat and shit and kill. But we can't grow, we can't change. All we can do is re-live that first death a thousand different ways."

I shake my head. I don't want to believe him. "No," I say. "There's something makes us who we are, and it's still here." I thump my chest and it hurts. I'm alive, all right.

Tony nods. "I know," he says. "That's the worst thing about it. We're trapped. Even the domes, and the brass too, though I don't think they realise it. But we're all dead, all the same. And unless there's someone out there powerful enough to stop us, we're going to keep right on repeating the same old patterns until we've killed everything else."

I think about what he's saying, and maybe because I've just been telling him about it, I taste that squid again, and it makes me drool. I ain't tasted nothing that good in a long time. Come to think of it, I ain't had that much fun in a long time. We wasn't much, just a bunch of construction workers off on leave, but we sure knew how to live it up. And when I remember that night, it has a kind of glow to it. Nothing that's happened since can match up to the way it felt then – to be young and alive and ready for anything.

Tony's watching me, and he nods like he knows I've got it.

"So what I'm wondering now," he says, "is exactly who you think your pals are these days."

I laugh. "Ain't that obvious?" I look around the commons, at Raoul slapping his gun together and bragging some more, at Seymour and Chen and all the rest of the guys who were happily slaughtering Sticks just a few hours ago, and suddenly Tony's question ain't funny no more.

"They're called St'x'iouk'os," he says, clicking his throat in the middle so it sounds more like he's clearing out phlegm than speaking.

"What are?"

"The people who live on this world. They had a global culture for more than ten thousand years before we showed up. You know what we were doing ten thousand years ago?"

Now it's my turn to look sideways. I'm looking for the dome hidden under his crew-cut. "How do you know stuff like that?"

"Officer training. Told you, my dad's brass, and I was supposed to be too. But they threw me out, so now I'm here, just another chump. Powerless to change anything."

"What's to change?" I say. "The world is what it is."

"Funny," he says, and scratches behind his ear. "I thought you changed today."

Then it's lights-out and we can't say no more. I lie awake in my bunk for a while, staring into the darkness. I can see the faces of those skinny little kid Sticks – St'x'iouk'os – in their moss-lined house, and I feel something real strange in my chest. For the first time ever, I feel like they're my pals too.

We get some quiet time after that. It happens sometimes, the St'x'iouk'os warriors stop raiding the mining enclaves, fall back into their towns and villages and leave us alone for a while. I dunno why. So Tony takes me to see this pal of his, a dome. I ain't never talked to a dome before and I keep staring at his head. I can't help it. It's all swole out at the front above his eyes and there's lumps behind his ears. I wonder if his neck gets tired holding it all up. Just as well they ain't born the regular way 'cos their mothers would never squeeze out more than one.

He grins and ignores my stares. I guess he's used to it. "So," he says, "a chump who wants to know about the St'x'iouk'os. Wonders never cease. Won't it be harder to kill them, if you know they've got thoughts and feelings too?"

"I ain't gonna kill 'em no more," I mutter. "It ain't right."

He raises his eyebrows till they're squashed right up under that dome, and nods at Tony. "I'm amazed," he says, "but you were right. This one's changed."

"No I ain't," I say. I don't wanna change. "It's just – there's more folks need me for a pal than I thought."

"He looks after his pals," says Tony.

"Ah," says the dome, like that explains everything. "OK, in that case let me tell you all I can about your new pals, shall I?"

He sounds like one of them teachers I had in grade school and I scowl and shuffle my feet. I'm taller than him and nigh on twice as broad in the shoulder, but he still makes me feel like a kid again and I hate him for it. But I wanna know about the St'x'iouk'os, so I just flex my hands and crack my neck bones and manage to stop myself killing him.

He lifts an induction net from his desk and points to a chair, so I sit and he fits it into place. It's the first time I've gone under the net in this chump, and the sockets are shiny and new. The jelled plugs slide home one by one with a sharp buzz as each contact bites.

It ain't like a training download. That's short and quick and repeats stuff lots of different ways so we all get it. This one's for domes and it goes on and on till it feels like someone's stirring my brains with a spoon and it's all going so fast I can't see nothing but a blur. My ears are crackling and popping and that ache in my chest from last night gets stronger until it feels like my ribs'll burst open.

Then it's all gone, and I'm kneeling on the floor with my arms wrapped round myself and my face is wet and the dome's ripping out the plugs fast as his delicate fingers can move.

"Is he all right?" says Tony, and then he's kneeling in front of me and peering into my face. "He's crying," he says, like he don't believe it.

I straighten up and scrub my face on my sleeve. "We killed millions of 'em," I say, only it comes out all pops and clicks and something in my throat feels like it sprains.

"Don't try to speak it," says the dome. "Humans can't pronounce the sounds. But you'll be able to understand them now, and they have a tactile version of the language you can use."

"Tactile?"

He taps real quick on the back of my hand. "Sorry about the overload," say his fingers. "I forget you people aren't used to so much information all at once."

I stare at his hand, fingers dark and slender, so different from mine. I could crush that hand as easy as a St'x'iouk'os crushes twigs to get at the soft pulp inside. What's going on? How can fingers talk?

"My head's all stuffed." I reach up, scared I've grown a dome like his, but all I feel is the same old heavy brows and flat forehead of every chump I ever had.

"You'll be all right in a few minutes," he says. "You need to process it and you don't have as much grey matter as me."

I get up and start pacing round the room. The walls are grey and bare and it feels cold. The room needs more green. There's nothing alive in here except us, and that ain't right. "You need some moss in here," I say, and they laugh.

"It's taking," says the dome. "So, do you want to be pals with the St'x'iouk'os?"

I nod, dumb, and my head fills with more pictures. There's dead people everywhere, their limbs broken, orange lifeblood draining into the ground. The sacred rooting grounds have been violated, the priests massacred. And the children… I see fat, pig-like creatures throwing children onto fires like bunches of firewood. Then I blink and see humans, but they're still doing it, they're still murdering the children.

"Why?" I say, but I know why. The strip-mines are everywhere now, ripping into forests and swamps, taking chunks out of mountains. The St'x'iouk'os ain't got many places left to live, but they're still fighting. This is their world, they're rooted deep in it and they won't ever stop trying to protect it.

"They ain't never mined," I say, amazed. "They take chunks of stuff out of rivers if they find it, gold mostly. But they don't mine. And they don't farm neither. They won't cut into the land. And they don't understand how we can be so wicked."

"Neither do I," says the dome softly. "Do you?"

I shake my head and my throat closes up as I remember the dozen or more pacifying missions I've been on since we got here. I've killed more than my share of these gentle people, and I used to laugh about it with the other lads. Stupid, ignorant Sticks just stand there like target practice while we spray them with lead.

But now I know. I know they ain't never killed, not one of them before we got here. They didn't even know it was possible. Their people die, but only of natural causes or accidents. They drink sunlight and suck the pith out of saplings, and sometimes they lick soil to get the salts they need. And the rest of the time they dance and sing and play.

"What can we do?" I say, and my voice cracks, but I don't care.

The dome smiles. "We've been working on that," he says. "We've got a plan, and here's how you can help."

It ain't exactly fair, but I get that I'm less important than a dome. And Tony's got connections that might be useful later on, with his dad being brass and all, so it's gotta be me does it. I don't like it much, but the St'x'iouk'os are my pals, and I always look out for my pals.

"When?" I say.

"Tomorrow," says the dome, and Tony nods.

"It's gotta be soon," he says, and slaps me on the shoulder.

"Tomorrow," I say. "OK."

But tomorrow ain't quite arrived when the general alert sounds and we all tumble out of bed and into our boots before we're half awake. They line us up on the high-gee parade-ground and show us what happened and the guys all roar in fury and it's only me and Tony can understand what we're seeing.

This is why it's been quiet. The warriors were fermenting. They used to be priests, not warriors, and before we arrived it was a sacred ritual. They'd ferment just enough so they could spray the newly adult saplings to start off their first baby-budding. But this time they went on twice as long till they was almost as swole up in the body as a chump, their trunks all fleshy with sperm. Then they sneaked into six of the enclaves, all at once, god knows how. They must have been planning it for a long time. They ran into the mess halls or the dorms, four of them to each enclave, and when they was good and close to a bunch of miners, they burst open like over-ripe fruit and green sperm shot out and sprayed the miners. Like their blood, it burns humans and dozens of men died.

Of course they're all reches, same as us. What the Sticks ain't figured out even after so long is they can't kill us this way. I guess we all look the same to them so they don't get that we come back. Every miner there'll be poured into a new chump by tomorrow and back ripping up the ground a day after that.

But the St'x'iouk'os was dead all right. Two dozen of the oldest and wisest sacrificed for nothing. As the men roar their fury, Tony and I look at each other and nod. I ain't been feeling good about it, but now, seeing them St'x'iouk'os bursting open like that, I feel my heart swelling so big I'm scared I'm gonna pop too, right there on the parade ground, and what good would that do?

But it ain't gonna happen today. Every unit is called up for reprisals and Tony and me's going planetside just like everybody else. The plan's gonna have to wait.

The quickest way back is to stay alive, 'cos they don't always pour us back in right off. It saves on chow if they leave it a couple of days, and we don't want to waste no time. St'x'iouk'os are dying all the time. So today Tony straps on his 'chute just like the rest of us, and though he's first man out like always, he lands safe.

I join him on the outskirts of town. Intel says there's a band of warriors holed up here, and that makes the townsfolk collaborators and legitimate targets, but intel don't know shit. Of course there's warriors here. They're the town priests, they're rooted here, where else would they go? The townsfolk ain't collaborating with nobody, they're taking care of their own, and you look me in the eye and tell me you wouldn't do the same if someone invaded your world.

There ain't nothing we can do except watch as the guys charge in and start shooting. Neither of us can shoot our own men. Tony ain't never killed no-one, and the lads are still my pals. So we watch and wait and hope it won't go on too long.

Then my comms buzz, and I think we've been spotted. But it's Tony's pal the dome, breathless and scared.

"They've discovered me!" he yells. "I'm trying to wipe all records, but I had to warn you. They might – "

The comms cut out then and it goes real quiet inside my head, quieter than I can ever remember. Tony grabs my arm and plugs in a hard commline so I can hear him. He's swearing the air blue.

"What?" I say. "We can do it without him."

"Don't you get it?" he yells, and pounds the side of his helmet. "It's gone. The uplink's gone."

He's right. That's why it's so quiet. The link with the station, the realtime update, it's stopped. We ain't getting no data, and we ain't sending none neither.

"Our templates!" yells Tony. "They've cut us off from our templates!"

I look up, like I can see the station way out in orbit, and I think about what that means. Everything we do now, even this conversation, it'll be lost when we die. Nobody's recording us, there ain't no backup. Next time we wake up in a tank, all of this might as well never have happened. It makes me feel lonely. All those other copies of me up there, they'll never know what it was like to stand here and be all alone. It seems kind of pointless to do anything now.

I start to walk towards town, but Tony tackles me and brings me down before I've gone five paces.

"What the hell are you doing?"

"Getting shot," I say. "I wanna go back to the station."

"Don't you understand?" he hisses. "If they've cut off our uplink they know we're in on it. They'll re-adjust our templates. If you die now, that's it, pal. They ain't never gonna bring you back."

I feel my jaw drop open as I stare at him. I know he's right, and I've seen enough zombies to know what that means. They'll use our chumps as front-line cannon-fodder, two dozen of the same man shoulder to shoulder, and they won't even notice.

"So this is it," I say. "When we die now, we're really dead."

"It's all right for you," says Tony. "You was gonna die today anyway. But what's my dad gonna say? They'll probably strip his commission 'cos of what I'm doing here. Shit." He buries his head in his hands and carries right on swearing. Seems like he never thought this through too good.

I look back at the town. Most of it's burning, and I can see St'x'iouk'os running all over, trying to get away. Some of the lads let them go, but a lot use them for target practice, like I used to. It's a massacre.

"We gotta get back to the station," I say. "I gotta go through with the plan."

"How? You think they'll just let us march back onto the transport like nothing happened? The sergeant will know by now. It'll be shoot on sight."

He's right, of course. "So what do we do?"

"I don't know!" he yells. "Do I look like a dome to you?"

He don't look much like a marine neither. He's shaking so hard his armour's rattling, and I figure it's up to me. But what do I know?

Well, I'm a marine. I know a lot of stuff about surviving, and that's what we gotta do now. Survive. Dead or alive, we can't get back to the station, so we need to find somewhere to hole up. Tony's in a funk, face-down on the ground, so I grab a solid piece of armour, and pick him up.

I can't carry him far. Even with the servos in my armour he's too heavy, but I get him away from the fighting, maybe far enough, before I have to drop him. He curls up into a ball and wraps his arms round his head. I plug in my commline and yell at him, and pound his armour with my fist, but he just lies there.

When I look up, we're surrounded. St'x'iouk'os move real quiet when they want to. There's more than twenty of them, but these ain't warriors. They're young saplings and their kids, and I can tell they're scared.

Very slowly, I move my hand where they can see it, and start tapping on Tony's leg.

"Friends," I tap. "We no hurt you. We help you."

They stare at me, all their eyes going big and round, and I know they ain't never seen a human could do the tapping talk. I know I'm real bad at it, but I'm sure they understand. "We no fight. We protect earth with you. Our soldiers kill us if they find us."

There's a sighing sound, like wind in the trees. It goes all round us and I realise it's them, relaxing. Then three or four of them start clicking and popping all at once, and I can't make it all out, but they say we should go with them. They know somewhere we'll be safe.

Tony looks up then, and when he sees the St'x'iouk'os so close he starts rattling again.

"Quit it," I say. "They wanna help us."

So now here we are in a St'x'iouk'os village, and ain't that the weirdest thing? I figure we got maybe a month before the recycling units in our armour finally quit on us. We can't never take it off or the air'll choke us. I'm already sick of sucking nutrient broth from a nipple, and the water tastes more and more like piss each time it goes round, but I'm still alive, and so's Tony.

There's three priests in this village, and we sit with them every day, trying to figure out what to do. We tell them what we can, but we don't know nothing about the enclaves so it ain't much. When we talk about the chumps, they just stare at us like they don't get it. I try, Tony tries. We tell them every way we know how, but they can't get it. When you're dead you're dead, and your body goes to nourish the earth. Nobody don't never come back.

So we give up on that, but we tell them, "Don't kill the miners. It don't do you no good. They grow up like mushrooms overnight. There'll always be more." And that they do get. But then they want to know, what can they do instead? And we don't have no answer to that.

"I gotta get back on the station," I say to Tony, and he says, "We can't. Alive or dead, there's no way back."

And when I hear that again, that alive or dead, I get the answer. I ain't never had a good idea in my life before, but this one's good. This one's gonna work.

The St'x'iouk'os help us. They got this real smart comm-system where they pound on hollow tree trunks, and they always know what's going on. Anywhere on this continent, if humans come down to "pacify" the folks, everyone knows about it before the next nightfall. They know more about our strategy than the domes have figured out, so maybe those great swollen heads don't make them so smart after all. When we tell the priests what we're planning they agree to provoke reprisals. We gotta get it right, 'cos St'x'iouk'os will die because of this. If we screw up, they die for nothing.

After two weeks, they get us where we need to be. They can see the transports coming in way before we can. They got eyes better than hawks, every one of them, and they're pointing and clicking softly while we're still staring at empty sky.

"I don't wanna do this," says Tony, but at least he's stopped rattling. "I don't wanna see 'em."

I don't neither, but it's the only way. The priests and us, we've fixed it so they gotta send a lot of ground troops into real dangerous terrain. We lie in wait, close but not too close, and watch the men 'chute in. There's dozens of them, and the first wave don't act too smart once they're on the ground.

We tap goodbye to our St'x'iouk'os pals, and they click and pop a quiet thanks. Then we're off down the slope and into the thick of it.

These lads don't react when we show up. They're zombies all right. But I'm still freaked when I see inside the first visor and it's my own face staring back. Reminds me of that time they was short of trained men and ran us all in parallel for a while. I met myself once. Hated the guy. I wasn't the only one felt that way – there was fights in barracks all the time, guys out to prove to themselves that they was the toughest one. It got so bad the brass had to give it up, so now we just come back once at a time.

But after you're re-adjusted it don't matter. The domes leave just enough of the template so it can bond with its chump, and they need that 'cos nobody can run your chumps but you. But they wipe most of the thinking part. This guy don't know me from Adam, he just looks at me and runs on, and goes down sprayed with gore 'cos he didn't see the trap set up right in front of him. That's why they don't re-adjust us all. A good soldier has to be able to think for himself, and even the brass can understand that. They only use zombies when they need numbers.

Looks like the numbers are telling right here, but that's 'cos it's supposed to. The St'x'iouk'os have set things up real good. A few of their warriors will die today, but most of the bodies have been brought in from the funeral grounds after special prayers have been said, and arranged to make it look like our boys did a lot of damage.

Tony and me just have to run about like our zombies and avoid getting sprayed. The St'x'iouk'os reckon they can tell us apart, and it seems they can, 'cos no gore comes anywhere near us. They leave some of the zombies standing too, though I can see they could have taken them all.

Then all at once, the zombies stop dead. The recall must have sounded, but we can't hear it 'cos we got no comms. They turn round and start marching and we join them, walking stiff like they do, letting our faces go slack. I'm so tired after two weeks sleeping in my armour it ain't so hard to blend in, and we march onto the transport right under the sergeant's nose.

So now here I am, lined up with my own zombies in the low-gee of the spindle. That's why I liked my idea so much. It don't just get us back on the station, it gets us into the tanking cylinder. They don't waste chow or bunk space on zombies. Any that make it through, and that ain't many, get stuffed right back in their tanks till the next mission.

The tanking cylinder's bolted onto one end of the spindle so it sticks out past the habitat and exercise rings. No-one gets in here except the domes that grow the chumps, and the zombies coming back from a mission. Guards unlock an armoured door with retina scans and thumbprints and voice recognition, two guys working in tandem either side of the door.

Tony's lot go through first, five of them plus him, and I half see him glance at me. I'm staring at the wall, thinking about porridge 'cos I figure that makes me look like the rest of them. Tony looks too sharp. I'm scared the guards'll spot him, but they're bored and they ain't looking closely. Nobody's ever done this before, so they don't expect it. They just glance up, not even as far as his face, and let him through.

I'm sweating. I shuffle along, staring at the back of the zombie in front of me and wondering if I look that slope-shouldered from behind. It's better than thinking about why I'm here. It's almost over, and I'm terrified. After more years than I can count, and three major campaigns, this is my last mission, the one that just maybe can wipe out the all bad things I done before.

Then we're in and the reinforced door's swinging shut. It's huge in here, fifty metres across and four hundred long and it feels like being outdoors. For a moment I gape at the rows of tanks vanishing into misty distance. Two domes are herding Tony's zombies onto a conveyor strip that'll take them to the holding tanks. They're fast and efficient, but they're bored too, and they sure ain't expecting what happens next.

I turn and slam my fist into the control panel beside the door, smashing it open. Then I rewire it the way our pal the dome showed me, and the whole can goes into lock-down. Nobody's coming in after us now. At the same time, Tony's yelling at the three of him that haven't already disappeared into the distance, and together they start herding the domes away from the action.

My zombies look at me. Their faces are nearly blank, but I know what those expressions feel like from the inside, and I can see they're confused. I'm not sure what they'll do next, but I know it'll be violent. "New orders," I say. "We're smashing the tanks."

They don't move, so I run to the nearest tank, grab an oxygen cylinder and slam it into the transparent wall. Cracks like a spiderweb shoot out from the spot where I hit it. For a moment I think it's not going to break, but then it starts to bulge and then it shatters. A wall of stinking pink slime hits me in the chest and I stagger.

Inside the tank, something moves, and a long brown sausage slithers out, arms and legs flopping like it's got no bones yet. Its face ain't finished and its gaping mouth's got no teeth, but it squeals like a pig being slaughtered as it hits the floor and starts to shrivel. I hit it with the cylinder to make it shut up, and one of my zombies laughs.

"Me," he says. "Me."

I give him the cylinder. "Yeah, pal. You. Go for it."

My zombies set to work, and the shattering tanks and squealing of half-finished chumps is so loud I figure they can hear it in the officers' mess. There's thousands of tanks in here, we'll never smash them all, but that's not the plan. It just gives the zombies something to do.

The domes are yelling threats and Tony's yelling back. Sounds to me like he's starting to panic again, so I move faster. The controls I need are about twenty metres away, right by the emergency airlocks. The dome said he'd sneaked in a trojan horse program. I dunno what that means, but he told me what I need to do and I do it.

Right up to the end, then I hesitate. I know I ain't really killing no-one except myself and Tony by doing this, and we're dead already, but it still feels like murder. I know the templates are stored in a different part of the station, and I know the guys'll still be there, waiting and ready. They just won't have bodies to be poured back into, so next time they go down, that's it for this campaign. It'll be years before the brass can get another tanking cylinder all the way out here, years before they can grow any more chumps for the marines and miners, and maybe the St'x'iouk'os can figure something out by then.

My hand's trembling over the last circuit. All I have to do is stick this wafer back in and the airlocks'll blow right along the cylinder and the decompression'll rip it apart.

There's a viewport in the airlock, and I can see the planet spinning past as the can rotates. I've only seen it from space once before, and that was when we first got here, years ago. It's much greyer now, and there's parts of it where the strip mines are so big I can see them even from up here.

That settles it. The St'x'iouk'os need me more than the lads in my platoon. By now the drumming on the hollow trees will have told everyone what we're doing up here. I've got pals all over the planet. I'm blessed to have so many. I hope the cylinder explodes 'cos then the St'x'iouk'os will see it and they'll know I stood by them.

I press the wafer home and the airlock flies open. A hurricane springs up from nowhere and I'm blown out into the dark and it's colder than I could have believed. It would have been nice to have seen those St'x'iouk'os faces one more time, their eyes and mouths open in great round Os of amazement, but at least I know I done the right thing.

At least I know I looked after my pals.

2020: I AM AN ANARCHIST

Gwyneth Jones

1: The Blue And The White

Kulak knew before he had been in Brighton ten minutes that they were going to kill him. He had travelled by train, to avoid the stop and search roadblocks that would be making motor travel into town hell on earth. He was alone, disguised and maintaining phone-silence. He'd got away with it at Victoria, but in the Brighton concourse his heightened, super-acute senses had told him immediately that he'd been made. The enemy was armed: he saw automatic rifles, openly displayed. The sense of danger thrilled him, as he surged with the heaving crowd of singing, shouting fans, scattering the old ladies, the soft domestic males, the women with kids, who hadn't had the sense to stay at home. Stripped of his car and his mates he was naked, and his reputation meant that there would be no mercy: but that was just the way he liked it. Passing through the forecourt gates he caught the eye of one of the riot-visored police...and stared, deliberately.

My name is Kulak. You know me, but do you know what that means, ignorant pig? It means I'm a hard-bitten, smart, feared, man of the people, immune to your social controls. Take me down if you dare.

They let him through, with barely a glance at his ID.

So that's their game, he thought. No bullets. Plain clothes police assassins moving with menacing slowness through the crowd, using Kulak to guide them to the comrades. But he had many faces, many aliases. He shoved his way across the road, into a pub, and minutes later had emerged from the cubicle in the lav in faultless drag, his 'trainspotter' outfit stuffed into a stylish pink duffle. He paused to check the mirror, while the men at the urinal peeked and leered: he feared no suspicion. Bold tarts are always muscling into the Gents, in crowded situations. Women, he thought. Fuck 'em. They don't deserve the attention they get. If the enemy took him now, and beat him and raped him in some dirty cell, he would feel her pain with a vicarious thrill. But it wouldn't happen. He was invincible. The coppers should have opened fire in the crowded station while they had the chance, but the bastards hadn't dared to do that. Morality is weakness. As he left the pub, two (Concealed Weapon Squad) Brighton policewomen, standing at the bar, glanced at each other and shook their heads. They'd watched the transformation scene in the lav on their wrist screens. There was a CCTV camera in every gents' public toilet cubicle in the town: perfectly legal, and perfectly visible; for the citizens' own protection.

'Some mothers do have 'em,' muttered one.

'It's a shame to take the money,' said the other; and they laughed.

But Kulak saw the Queen's Road, engulfed in Union Jacks, laid out before him like an emblazoned, canopied parade for a conquering hero. In the lav he had transferred his blue and white cross of Scotland lapel pin, from inside the hood of his 'trainspotter' anorak, to his bra-strap. It would have been safer to bear no mark at all of his allegiance, but honour is more than safety. He could feel it there, like a hard, ironic, secret promise. Here we go, here we go, here we go.

The girl was kept spreadeagled on the bed, tied by the wrists and ankles. Popstar posters on the walls, duvet with a pattern of hearts and teddy bears: she'd been raped, and raped, for five days and nights. The guys let her get up to use the toilet, and fed her on biscuits and water. In one bizarre scene Tom, the plumber, had been seen feeding her crackers, while Harry the law-student porked her, one hand behind him to hold his trousers so his jerking bum would not be on show. Harry's modesty, which had become a running joke, made the other guys hysterical; the girl, whose name was 'Boobs', sobbed open-mouthed, spraying poor Tom with masticated Sainsbury's High-Bake.

When the rescue squad broke in she'd been left on her own, crying in the dark. Released, she clung to Maudie, raised her bleared, docile underclass face with a smile –and then frowned in puzzlement, because they'd moved her out of shot (of course, she knew exactly where the cameras were). She was still wearing fragments of her clothes: the blue dress bunched around her middle, torn remnants of her knickers. They made her roughly decent and got her out of there... then Maudie and Trevor took her to the safe house; which wasn't far away. Success of phase one.

2. The Red and the White.

The town centre had been closed to traffic, everyone would have to walk to the Brighton Centre, where a vital match of the greatest sporting tournament of the year would be played out today. The police reported three hundred thousand people pouring through the flag-smothered streets, insanely more than the venue could hold: but the fans didn't care. The tv stats were recordbreaking: topping 15 million British viewers alone, two hours before kick-off. 'Who's got the rest of them?' muttered Bridget to her best mate, Raisa –fellow production assistant on Fantasy And Truth, the brilliantly successful cultural comment show. It was a joke, but Raisa had a literal mind.

'House of Correction,' she answered, seriously. 'They changed their schedule, remember, for the tournament? Really in-your-face of them.'

House of Correction belonged to a rival company, and FAT had been snubbing them, in spite of their ratings. Their chutzpah, in switching from late night to midafternoon –for the benefit of people who 'weren't interested' in the great national sporting event, had been relegated to news snippets and noted as a big mistake. Bridget giggled cynically. She had been shocked when she started working in television, and found out that the notorious gang-bang show was actually real, not faked at all. But she'd got over that.

'What about Battle Royal?'

'Battle Royal' was Middle-England protestors, having pitched fights with the developers' security and the police, over the routing of a new motorway up in the Midlands somewhere (Bridget was unsure of the geography). It was proving to be very good tv. 'Battle Royal is next week, girls.' Colin's richly nuanced, mocking voice made them both jump. 'Let's concentrate on patriotic passion this afternoon, shall we? How about a few more flags in here, eh?' FAT's presenter, handsome, groomed and gleaming, was something of a national icon himself: and he knew it. He left them, shortly to reappear on the monitors, as the run-up started running. FAT was doing an intellectual round table, a stylish choice sort of forced on the show by the fact that the BBC had cornered actual commentary and expert discussion of the game itself.

'What many people don't realise is that this is highly environmentalist,' said a famous female academic. 'EAT IT tells us that it is not what we consume that pollutes, it's what we don't consume. It's not what we use that causes the extremists to protest, it is what we, er... our waste and excess-'

'Environmentalist,' murmured Raisa, 'Protests...'

They were supposed to be tracking peaks, in the focus group polygraph response to buzzwords: but Bridget's mind wandered. For ages and ages, she had been the ditz who still thought that EAT IT! was just an incredibly stupid and gross game-show, something you wouldn't even watch if you were drunk and lonely and stuck with nothing to do on an early Saturday evening. She'd been living in the past, imagining that 'sport' meant things like football, and cricket, and tennis; and maybe strange things like rowing, that only got famous when there was an Olympic Games. Or snooker, that was annoying because they put it on in place of Bridget's favourite interactive fantasy programme. Then suddenly, it had seemed as if she woke up one day to find the ...er, stuff, was everywhere. All over the television, all over the newspapers, all over people's conversations. She wasn't stupid. She understood that it was totally important for people to have something to wave the flag about; and that EAT IT!, had the major, major advantage that the English team was not going to get knocked out in the first round, causing the audience to switch off en masse, and infuriating the advertisers. She understood that in twenty-twenty UK outrageous fun is what everybody is having, and she didn't want to be a prude. But excuse me, isn't the Pooh-Stakes just a tiny bit, disgusting?

In her early days on the show Colin had taken her aside and spoken to her sternly, about remarks of that kind. That had sobered her, briefly, because she loved her job: but she'd gone on giggling whenever she forgot herself, which was often. The whole thing was just so blegggh and silly. Her awakening had come, with a total shock, when she looked at her payslip one month and noticed, good grief, a huge MINUS figure, big as a mortgage, where her pay ought to be. Luckily, (and thank God, before she'd made a complete fool of herself by ringing accounts), she'd remembered a little inside-pages newpaper item, which had said the government was now allowing private companies to buy up student debts, as a tax break…

She could still get teary-eyed and shaky, if she let herself remember that awful moment, or if she let herself think about how the minus figure, which of course got bigger every time she was 'paid', might keep her the bondservant of whoever owned her debt, for her entire life. Being sold into slavery by your government isn't exactly what you expect, when you have three A levels, a bright personality and a fairly good degree in media studies.

But she tried not to think about it, and mostly succeeded.

She had stopped laughing at the Pooh-Stakes, from that day onward. She understood what it was all about, now. Put on your shortest skirt, flirt with the boss, agree with everything he says, or you will be heading down porcelain alley with the brown stuff. And that isn't funny at all.

The rest of the squad disbanded. Only Maudie and Trevor were directly involved in phase two. Maudie, who was a doctor, examined Boobs and found her to be in not too bad shape, considering. They gave her new clothes and money, and told her where she was. They told her she was free to go, but they advised her to lie low here for a few days, before she got in touch with her family or friends.

They had to keep her in the basement, because they understood that she was not very bright, and she wouldn't be able to remember things like not to open curtains. But she was comfortable: bathroom ensuite, tv, nice food. She ate heartily, though she'd been childishly thrilled to discover she'd lost eight pounds!, during her ordeal. And this was the hardest part, because they had to spend time with her, it would have been cruel to leave her alone. But it wouldn't be for long.

They sat and talked, in the safe house kitchen, doing a bit of soul-baring. Maudie was a retired GP, Trevor was an off-duty community constable. Maudie had started off in eco-protest, which she now realised had been just selfish NIMBY. She'd thought nothing of the rest of the mess, until her own patch of lovely countryside was attacked… Trevor believed in the law, in justice, and protecting the gentle people from the bastards of this world, but being a policeman is an authority-kick. He knew he enjoyed that; and that the nice, spruce uniform was a factor-

3. The Green and the Gold and the White

Kulak reached the Brighton Centre an hour before kick-off, still maintaining phone silence. His authority was such that he didn't need to communicate with the shock troops. They would not meet until they had witnessed the victory of Scotland the Brave, which was absolutely certain, because the Welsh were crap at the post-modern beautiful game: and then, going into action like the superbly trained commando agents they were, they would rip the Brighton Centre apart, dealing a crushing blow to the morale of the English team, whose home stadium this was. They knew the price of this action would be high. Kulak and his men would be trapped inside the building, when the police counter attack began. They had no fear, no regrets.

The organising body of EAT IT!, had decided, after what happened last year, to limit the mayhem by moving the crucial matches away from the national teams' supporters: which was how Wales came to be playing Scotland in Brighton. The ploy was having limited success, judging by the hordes of ticketless Welsh and Scottish fans, in full regalia, who could be seen in the huge crowd on the seafront, chanting and rushing the barricades, ignoring police loud-hailer instructions to disperse. But the mood was good-humoured. There were big screens, heavily guarded by armed police, so everyone would get a chance to see the match. Everyone here would feel specially a part of the event that was driving the whole country wild with excitement. Little did the police know that their defences were futile. A cold and brilliant mind, impenetrably disguised by the bold tart persona, Kulak approached the security gates. Already he could feel the razor-sharp satori of the violence to come. It did that to him. When he went into action with the blue and white warriors, everything vanished. He was so focused he didn't know what he was doing. No shame, no guilt, no pain. He placed his duffle on the Xray machine roller, stepped up to the mark and smiled for the camera, with chilling confidence. He sashayed through the metal detector and presented his perfectly forged ticket, with the appropriate photo-ID. (He had many, he was always prepared.) A guy like a brick outhouse in a yellow fluorescent bib picked up the duffle from the roller, peeked inside and smirked. So what, fucker?, thought Kulak, noting that face for later attention... Cross-dressing isn't a crime.

'Ooh, bejasus,' said the EAT IT security officer who had taken Kulak's ticket. 'A special ticket. Bring your bag and come with me, Missis, or is it Sor? We're giving you the deluxe treatment.'

Next thing Kulak knew, he was being strong-armed along behind-the-scenes corridors, determined to keep silent though it cost him his life. No leader is indispensable. The shock troops would go on without him. He was shoved into a bare, grey hangar of a room, with oil stains on the ribbed concrete floor. A half dozen big men, wearing stewards bibs or security uniforms, were waiting there. The men who'd brought Kulak in sat him on a metal-framed canteen chair, jerked his arms round the back of it and got handcuffs on him. Kulak stared defiantly. 'You're not the fuckin' police,' he said. 'You can't touch me.'

They laughed. With one motion, as if they'd choreographed this, they stripped off the bibs and the EAT IT! uniform jackets – revealing teeshirts emblazoned in gold and green and white, and printed with the map of the four counties. Oh, God. A shudder of horror went through him. He had fallen into the hands of the Irish, the most feared of all hard bastards in EAT IT! hooliganism.

One of the former 'stewards' pulled up another chair and sat down opposite Kulak, four-square. 'The fockin' polis fockin' sold you to us, eejit,' said the Irishman. 'An' you'll tell us nothin' becos there's nothin' we don't already know, Kulak alias Jayne Busty, alias Firestarter, alias wee Robbie Thistle, alias a phone book of other fockin' stupid pseudonyms. We know why you're here, you and the other haggis-arsed boyos. Now we're going to tell you our plan.'

Kulak's eyes were drawn, irresistibly, to something that stood on the floor beside the other man's chair. It's white, it's ceramic, it's a china bowl, with a handle, shaped something like a teacup for a giant… The big Irishman smiled.

'We'll have the gentleman down to his smalls, lads.'

What's that beside the teacup? A knife and fork, laid on a white napkin.

The men uncuffed him, and made him strip to the 'bold tart's' push-up bra and lacy thong. They found the concealed weapons: his cosh, his knuckles, the dismantled plastic gun in the false-bottom of the duffle; his make-up bag of ammunition. They said he didn't understand the terrible beauty that had been born, out of this last grotesque flowering of the national pride of the UK, but today he would serve the beautiful game more truly than ever before. He was to lead his troops in a pitch invasion, and destroy Scotland's victory.

Kulak agreed immediately, weak with relief.

They laughed. They told him words meant nothing, he must show his respect in a more solid fashion. Horrified by the urgent pulsing in his bowels, he cowered, as the men loomed over him. When they showed him their heated electric curling iron, fear the betrayer took him by the sphincter muscles. He performed, right there in front of them; and when that was done, they made him take his own excess, and chew, and swallow. In abject tears then, only anxious to please his new masters, he babbled the truth: he warned them that an invasion would not have the effect intended. Scotland the Brave would be given a replay and beat the snivelling Welsh another day.

'Mebbe so,' said the chief of the Irish. 'Except, Lizzie Mountbatten is ours, too, my lad. Your team captain has took our money to thump a punter, namely you: an' after last year, you know what that means.

Disqualification from the tournament.

Kulak was appalled. Lizzie, though a mere tart, was the hardest little bad taste merchant ever to come out of the glens. No one could touch her glory.

'Oh, God, please no!' moaned Kulak. 'No, not Lizzie! She wouldna!'

Boobs sneaked out of the safe house at around two am on the night after they had rescued her. Maudie and Trevor watched her leave, on their own infra-red surveillance. They tracked her progress, as this determined teenager made her way across town to the secret location where the House of Correction was filmed; and crept back into the mock-up suburban house where she had been held prisoner. They had known that she would do this. There was no hope for Boobs. House of Correction 'stars' were chosen through an audition process designed to single out the terminal cases of celebrity culture.

But she was a different playmate now. She was carrying polio and a virulent form of anthrax, engineered by the terrorist cadre using generic biochemical supplies and information downloaded from the internet; and a human form of myxomatosis, stolen from a government lab at Porton Down. They switched on the tv and saw her welcomed back into the game: her escape from the do-gooders would be a huge boost for the ratings. With any luck, no one would suspect a thing until all of Boobs's contacts, the tv people and the eager amateur rapists, basically, started dying... They checked their suicide note over carefully, printed it out and took their own pills. Terrorists who believe their cause is just must die, if they are prepared to deal out death themselves.

'Suffer,' said Trevor,' with hope, or without it.'

'Suffer,' agreed Maudie. 'But someone's got to stop this.'

The policeman and the middle-class lady gave each other a hug, and shook hands. In a few hours, each of them would suffer a massive heart attack. It's a very painful way to go.

4.The Jack

The live audience (composed mainly of English and Irish fans, with a small enclosure of carefully vetted and contained Scots and Welsh) roared as the teams marched out, and took their places at opposing ends, under the glare of the tv lights. Union Jacks flailed madly. The Irish and Northern Irish match officials found fault with the state of the pitch, causing a delay that was discussed with inventive but increasingly strained logorrhoea by the team in the commentators box. EAT IT! etiquette prevented them from remarking on the effect of all the hot lights on the vat of brown solids that played such a vital part in the first half ritual; but this whole thing stinks...was getting hard to avoid.

Nobody up there knew that the real reason for the delay was to give Kulak the opportunity to muster his cohorts, and announce the new battle-plan.

'This is the ideal popular sport,' said the prominent Asian novelist on the round table, back in London in the tv studio. 'A final squeeze of the majestic peristalsis of capitalism, freeing our competitive instincts from the absurd complexity and and needless athleticism of the past. EAT IT! has a profound purity-' They were on a break, but he wasn't taking any chances. Pundits can fall down porcelain alley too: he never bit or even nibbled the hand that feeds.

'Capitalism,' murmured Raisa.

'Mm,' said Colin, looking thoughtful. He leaned back in his comfy chair, and announced quietly, addressing his production assistants off the set, 'Girls, I'm getting feed from Edinburgh. Before we go back to Brighton, can we come up with some soundbites to deal with an English defeat?'

Oooh. This was the first year the tournament had gone fully international, with French, German, Japanese and USA teams participating. The English were supposed to be in an easy group, but rumours had been growing that the national coach was not happy: and the team was not in good shape for the US match, scheduled next week in Scotland... Bridget was surprised to find she genuinely felt her heart sink. England losing, it can't be good, however silly and bleggh... Wow, she thought. Maybe I'm learning to be content with my lot. That's a result! She thought about it, and offered, into her headset mic-

'Err, how about, defeat would be an iron turd, grinding into the faces of the working classes forever?'

'Oh, I like that!' Colin laughed, eyes sparkling. The female academic and the Asian novelist smiled politely. Then the presenter frowned. 'Hm, I'm not sure. Can we say working classes on television?'

'No,' said Raisa, unexpectedly. 'It sounds stupid. Say, all the people.'

'Okay, the people it is-'

The shock troops had agreed to the premature pitch invasion readily. The plan to wait until after the game had always been a little subtle for them. The moment came. Jon MacReady, thirty-something unemployed university graduate from Midlothian, dressed once more in his male clothes, received the Irish signal, and stood looking at the scene below: a little lost, a little hesitant now, at the last. Strange thoughts went through his mind. If the EAT IT captain herself would take a fall for filthy lucre, what price national pride for anyone? What's behind it all?, he wondered. Isn't this flag waving, chanting and brawling over nothing rather meaningless? Am I really so stupid and cruel, in my original nature? Could I change...? But his head cleared, his throat opened in a warrior's roar. The blue and white commandos rose up.

An uncontrollable free for all ensued, in which the contrived stunt with Lizzie proved irrelevant. EAT IT! vetting measures had failed: most of the live audience rushed to join the secret army, and the teams themselves entered furiously into the fray. The Wales-Scotland game ended in anarchy that would leave four contestants (as the players were known, for old time's sake) dead, plus a never-released number of punter casualties...

But for Jon, there came a second moment of epiphany, down in the mêlée. Suddenly he understood everything. He knew that sectarian pride is but a trumpery thing, and that Lizzie's defection was true to the deeper code. Raising a shit-smeared, transfigured face to the bright tv lights, he yelled in ecstasy: 'I LOVE Great Britain!'

Strong Brown God

Kari Sperring

Ordith crouched in the shadow of the drowned man, and counted her crimes. In Citizens' Square below her, people gathered outside the high gates of Pump Station Four. Overhead, the great pipe of Aquifer Eighteen hummed and thrummed. At her back, the rusty access ladder was cold and damp. It lacked perhaps one quarter of the dial until noon: time enough to finish what she had started.

For four days and five nights, it had rained without ceasing. In Six and Thirty Sectors, concrete shacks squatted window-deep in water, disgorging their few contents into the streets. Pots cracked against pylons, blankets festooned the fountain heads like weed. The small-holdings of Fifteen and Twenty Eight Sectors were mulch and swamp, their harvests of brassica and onions gone to feed the eels and the water-snakes. In Sectors Twelve and Twenty One, the petty shops were ankle deep in water. The city throbbed under the labouring of pumps.

The price of root vegetables had risen for the eighth time in that month, and the Water Tax was up by another two marks. The Sluice Masters shook their heads, and spoke of regret and overwork. But their homes and fields, cut higher up the city-scape, stood safe and dry, and their tables were full. Ordith knew that: she had seen it. It was their due, her mother said: the Sluice Masters, after all, took on deadly work to keep the city from drowning. Toxins ran in the mud dark waters of the vast delta, impregnated the iron of the pumps and locks, the tanks and pipes and valves of the city's water system. Under their thick grey uniforms, the skin of the Sluice Masters cracked and bled, their mouths ulcerated, their stomachs grew cancers. Without them, without the lore of purification, the citizens of the city would die, of poison or of drowning.

'Nobody is poisoned by the rain or the floodwater,' said Ordith, stubbornly.

'But they drown,' said her mother. 'And the crops are poisoned. And look what happens to saboteurs.'

Saboteurs were drowned, their bodies turned soft and green by the toxic waters. Above Ordith's head, the drowned man hung in testimony, swinging slowly to and fro with the shaking of the aquifer. It was said that the Sluice Masters looked likewise, under their thick garments.

Peering in through a window at Pump Station Two, Ordith had seen a Sluice Master without his grey garments. His frame had been round and soft, that was true, but his skin was white and smooth, without lesion or blemish. The common citizens were thin and spare, and many showed the ulcers and sores of hunger, as rain or flood poisoned their crops.

In the count of her crimes, that act of spying numbered low. Ordith fingered the spine of the book in her pocket, compact and hard. One crime for each copy hidden in the husks of the rice she threshed. One for each night she crouched outside a hut in Sector Six, a shop in Sector Twelve, a barn in Sector Nineteen, watching for the Water Guard and listening to the printing presses thump and rattle. One for each pamphlet she had slid under doors or tucked into shutters. One for each time she had drunk untreated water fresh from a roof-trap and suffered no ill effects. Rather bigger crimes: each time she had come into the city with her body swathed wide, paper wound tight under her clothes. More still, with each trip she had made up the ladder at her back, bag and pockets filled with copies of the forbidden book.

The Operation of Hydraulic Systems. It was no larger than her palm, clad in thin brown wood, like a child's primer, the copy she clutched in her pocket. Her brother Fareis had brought it home, that evening six years ago, when she was nine and he thirteen. He had had it, he said, from a stranger he met in the paddy fields. He had pored over it by night, reading in the low glow of the kitchen fire, while their mother worked her shift at the cloth mill. It had frightened Ordith. Hydraulic was a lore word, safe only for the Sluice Masters. Her brother would die, poisoned by the print.

He had laughed at her for that. 'Printed words can't kill you.'

He had been wrong. In the square below, the numbers of people grew. Ordith wriggled, felt the ladder bump her shoulders. After today, she would not have to worry if the rust marked her clothes. Six nights ago, the Water Guard had raided a shed in Sector Six, a shop in Sector Twenty One. They had seized three printing presses, eighteen bales of paper and seven living souls, the seventeenth such raid in a little less than a year. Saboteurs, said the Sluice Masters, plotting to open the sluices, break the aquifers, breach the tanks. Look, they said, what had happened last year, after the dykes were mined around Former Sector Twenty Seven.

For the five nights after this latest raid, water had flooded through Sectors Six and Twenty One, Twenty Eight and Thirty. 'We must bear it,' said Ordith's mother. 'We live downslope.'

'Sector Two is no higher,' said Ordith, 'and it's perfectly dry.'

'Don't talk nonsense,' said her mother. 'We have enough trouble.'

But it was no nonsense. The Sluice Masters lived mainly in Sector Two, close to the Main Filtration Centre. 'It's to do with the sluice network,' Fareis would have said. 'The Sluice Masters can channel the water wherever they want.' But Ordith, more circumspect, had said nothing. She was no longer sure she might trust her mother.

The square was crowded, now, men and women pressing up to the Pump Station Gates. Some of them held papers, blotchy with cheap ink and rain. Prices and taxes: Fareis had said that this protest would surely come. And Ordith had been waiting. She could see the Sluice Masters gathering on the other side of their gate, flanked by a handful of Water

Guard. She rose, stretching cramped muscles, and picked up her bag. Her next crime was due. She began to climb the ladder up the aquifer pylon. As she moved, her brother's body jounced and swung. Reaching the top, she threw him a kiss, before crawling out onto the catwalk that crowned the aquifer. In her swamp-coloured clothes, she was scarcely visible. Down in the square, the crowd muttered and shifted. A few men pushed at the gates. A Sluice Master waved his arms and shouted, words washed away in the rain. The Water Guard raised their carbines, muzzles facing the crowd. As Ordith reached the last joint in the aquifer, she halted and laid down her bag. The great pipe hid her from the guardsmen. Against the high upper edge of the joint, she had piled the spoils of her earlier trips, copy upon copy of the little brown book. Below her, the Sluice Masters yelled about their troubles and sacrifices. The crowd grumbled back about prices and food.

'Anyone can run a water system,' Fareis had said, hands resting on the frame of his printing press. 'You just need the instructions. It doesn't take special powers and the system isn't poisonous. It's just rusty.'

Ordith rose to her feet, high over the square, and made a funnel of her hands. As loud as she might, over the crowd, into the rain, she shouted 'We don't need the Sluice Masters. We can run things by ourselves.' One by one, heads craned upwards to stare at her.

Ordith began throwing copies of the book to the crowd..

John Brown's Body (an alternate history)

Lucy Kemnizter

Springfield, Illinois, State Register [Democratic]
(20 October 1859)

The telegraphic dispatches yesterday morning startled the public with an account of one of the most monstrous villainies ever attempted in this country. It was no less than a bold move on the part of a party of abolitionists and negroes to take possession of one of the national arsenals, at Harper's Ferry, with the military stores and the public money there deposited. Under the lead of the most infamous of the Kansas crew of black republican marauders, Ossawatomie Brown, the insurgents, to the number of five or six hundred, attacked and took possession of the whole town of Harper's Ferry, including the government buildings and stores, stopped the mails, imprisoned peaceable citizens, and, in a move both unrepentant and cowardly, left as swiftly as they had arrived, bearing off with them a good portion of the stores and money, and leaving behind them a manifesto declaring their intentions of carrying out many more similar foul deeds.

Early January 1860

"I believe I'll go with the old man."

Four men standing at the edge of a field in the middle of the cold night with a triple deadly choice. They can *go for the north star,* or they *can go with the old man,* or they can go back where they came from. If they decide to go home they may be beaten, maybe mutilated, maybe killed: any of those possibilities becomes more likely the longer they wait to make up their minds and return. If they decide to *go for the north star,* they will be chased with hounds and hounded through the courts, but if they make it to the border they will be free, though forever separated from all of the ones they love.

If they *go with the old man* they'll take weapons in hand and strike against the places that were their homes, secretly, daringly, under the cover of night, taking the lives of those who kept them.

The men are slaves, and they stand here with a choice. The known, with the prize of servitude and abuse: the risk of freedom, with a prize of an ordinary quiet life: the risk of war, with the promise of an end to slavery.

"I believe I'll go with the old man."

Lazarus says these words solemnly, as an oath, as he steps to the side of the conductor who will take him *down the old man's branch line.* Benjamin Shoatt steps to the side of the conductor who will take him north. George Shoatt hesitates, hangs back. Enosh Shoatt looks to the faces of his three brothers — brothers in name, though their mothers are all different, because they carry the name of their master — and studies his three futures in their eyes.

The night is silent as a winter night can be.

The conductors are patient, but their patience has a limit. Enosh knows this. They were frank with them when they met here at the limits of the property where the big old trees stand. The moonlight white on the Spanish moss, casting shadows on the ground. "You have an hour to decide."

Enosh is a young man, with skin as dark as a French plum, eyes wary from a life of capricious demands and punishment. He's strong and he looks it. He's intelligent, and looks it, knows many Bible stories by heart though he cannot read. It's against the law to teach him. Enosh pictures himself behind a plow in Canada, growing white corn to feed a passle of pretty babies. A free wife. A Bible and an almanac and the ability to read them.

He pictures himself with a gun, shooting his master in the face. He winces at the imagined blood and exposed bone.

He pictures himself returning, beaten till the snow-splashed ground is spotted and stained with his blood.

If he goes with the old man, he will most certainly die violently. But he will die a free man, fighting for freedom. His family is all gone, mostly sold but some prematurely dead of overwork or maltreatment. He has nobody to hold him here. There is nobody who will be devastated by his early death.

The stars have moved since they arrived at this spot.

He puts out his hand to give farewell to his brothers.

"I believe I'll go with the old man."

more from the *Springfield, Illinois, State Register*

It was scarcely credible, when the first dispatch was received yesterday, that the object of the ruffians could be other than plunder, but late dispatches, including those we publish this morning, show, conclusively, that the movement was a most extensive one, having for its object the uprising of the negroes throughout the south, a servile war, and its consequences — murder, rapine and robbery....

Brown, though a blood-stained ruffian, is a bold man. As a black republican he practices what his leaders preach. As it is urged by statesmen (save the mark!) of his party that there is an "irrepressible conflict," he wants it in tangible, material, shape. He believes in blows, not words, and the Harper's Ferry villainy is the first in his line of performance.

Late January 1860

Some days later, and some distance from home, Enosh and Lazarus have been split up and conducted through the forests on different paths – not paths, through different trackless forests and up and down desolate hillsides. From time to time they are blindfolded, so that when the time comes that they might be captured and tortured they will have no useful information to reveal.

The way to the old man's branch line is long and convoluted. Enosh and his fellows have traveled long hours every day, more at night than in daylight. Their direction has turned and turned again through the forest. A long time ago they left Virginia behind. Now they're in the disputed territory held by Indians and refugees: people who have no love for the Americans who are surely looking for them. Now and then they visit some of these people, wary on both sides, exchanging gifts and intelligence, concealing more than they reveal. More than once on this difficult trek Enosh wishes he had never seen the conductors. Or had returned with George, though he's sure that George has suffered greatly for having witnessed their departure.

Every night they pray. They pray as they walk: they pray when they stop to rest: and they pray when they get up to walk again. The prayers are long and fervent, eloquent and sincere. They are the most beautiful words Enosh has ever heard.

Always excepting those words he spoke, himself: "I believe I'll go with the old man."

The old man is in the mountains, they say. They say he is in a cave, high up in the crags, that his friends move him from time to time so that even if the American soldiers could get a scrap of information from a captured warrior, they would never find John Brown or his friends: only a cold cave, long since abandoned. "How do we know where to go?" Enosh asks.

"We don't, until we do," is the answer.

And they don't, until they do. The conductors begin to scrutinize the forest for signs. They discuss the placement of stones and twigs, blazes on tree bark: always in that vague, *signifying* way Enosh knows from slave quarters. He accepts that they don't want him to know what they are saying. He is not yet a member of the Provisional Army. Not yet to be trusted.

The way up the mountain is long and cold. The path is unreliable, icy, loose. More than once Enosh is saved from falling by his companions. The sun glares against the rocks and snow. Though his ears burn from the cold, his back sweats.

Without any clear indication that they are doing it, they arrive at the cave. It's much warmer within. They've got a well-formed fire for John

Brown and some other wounded men. It's not as smoky as you might expect. These people know what they're doing.

The meat that Enosh is given is the best he's eaten, and not just because he's underfed from the long trek here. It's a good-sized piece of a shoulder of venison. There's coffee, too, and corn bread.

And after supper, the old man pulls himself painfully to a sitting position, and Enosh gets a chance to talk to him. It's such a holy moment. Enosh wants to express his respect somehow – but they don't allow him to. Here the men are all equals, even John Brown.

He's so frail: he's old, yes, but also, he has never completely recovered from the wounds he received when he carried off that first successful foray at Harpers Ferry. That pivotal moment when the nascent Provisional Army was born against all odds, when the old man gave his one of own sons and nearly his own life for the lives of the slaves. Enosh, thinking about this, looks on the pale old man with his flowing beard and burning eyes, and he is awed, and grateful.

As frail as he is, old Brown is alert and personable. Enosh has never had a conversation like this. Not with a white man. At times the pain becomes too much and Brown has to pause, let his eyes roll back and simply breathe. But he doesn't lose the train of the conversation. To each of the new recruits he has something to say. When his eye falls on Enosh he says, "Your manhood is here, in fighting for your own freedom."

And Enosh feels it.

more from the *Springfield, Illinois, State Register*

The leader chosen was just the man to initiate the work. Bankrupt in fortune and character, an outlaw and an outcast, he was just the man to commence the work which ultra Abolitionism, through its diligent Parkers and Garrisons, hope to reach the millennium of their traitorous designs. Their open-mouthed treason, which culminates in precisely such outrages as that at Harper's Ferry, is but the logical sequence of the teachings of Wm. H. Seward and Abraham Lincoln – the one boldly proclaiming an "irrepressible conflict" between certain states of the Union, because of their local institutions, and the other declaring from stump and hustings, the country round, that the Union cannot continue as the fathers made it – part slave and part free states.

February 1860

Enosh has been learning to read. The woman who is teaching him and four others was also a slave in Virginia, and she learned to read in a cave like this one. Her text is the Bible – Exodus.

He has been learning other things too. The care and use of weapons. Geography, particularly of Virginia. Some history.

For a few days he thinks he is in love with his reading teacher, but she is married. He's respectful, doesn't say a thing, but she knows. She says, "If we live through this, I'll find you a wife in Jubilee."

He smiles, shyly, and reads from Chapter 2, verse 11: "And it came to pass in those days, when Moses was grown, that he went out unto his brethren, and looked on their burdens: and he spied an Egyptian smiting an Hebrew, one of his brethren."

He takes a deep breath, and she nods. "Go on."

"Twelve. And he looked this way and that way, and when he saw there was no man, he slew the Egyptian, and hid him in the sand."

It's exalting, to read these words, to hear them coming in his own voice from the page.

more from the *Springfield, Illinois, State Register*

Who is so blind as not to see the inevitable tendency of black republican teaching? Now we have a bloody, glaring, ghastly fact before us. The "conflict" by blows has commenced. The proofs of an extensive and ramified organization is disclosed, the object of which is to stir the southern slaves to bathe their hands in the blood of the whites of the south. Traitorous scoundrels, with white faces, but black hearts, lead them, and the country is stunned with their deeds of infamy, treason and blood.

Such is the ripening of the black republican harvest. Can an intelligent people doubt that to such ends the maudlin philanthropy, the hypocritical cant, the blatant demagogism, of black republicanism, tends? "By their fruits shall ye know them." Disunion and bloody anarchy.

April 1860: Sumter, South Carolina

This bustling town is named for the architect of the plan to pay Revolutionary War soldiers in human beings instead of money. General Thomas Sumter, the Gamecock, the war hero: the entrepreneur: the statesman. The slaveholder and defender of slavery.

In this county there are numerous people who claim descendancy or some kind of relationship with the man, or with Francis Marion. These people haven't been dead long enough for their relations to forget them, but there's plenty of room for vagaries anyway.

Enosh has come here shuffling, pulling a handcart seemingly laden with agricultural implements. He hasn't forgotten how to act the part. He and eleven others are following the white man named Barclay – Mister Coppoc – who has presented himself as looking for land to settle with these twelve "servants." Two of them are women. They're in town for a few days, getting the lay of the land. Since Master Barclay is looking for land to buy, there's no harm in him sending his servants around with letters of introduction, to look at land and ask questions of the neighbors. They are very well-behaved and intelligent slaves. Nobody has to know that when they sit down for supper, they all sit at the same table and everyone there is a Mister or a Ma'am.

There's a particular place they decide they all like for their purposes, and they begin the final stages of planning for this operation.

"We may not live through this," Mister Shields Green says. Also a former slave, he is a veteran of that first famous raid on Harpers Ferry, where twenty-one men – not the five or six hundred reported in the *Register* – seized the weapons which Enosh and the others brought into town, concealed in hand carts and a wagon. He always says this. He's the one who first said "I believe I'll go with the old man," and established it as the understated slogan for slaves who choose not only to be free but to fight for their freedom. But he always says this other thing, too, "we may not live through this."

As usual, his answer is a chorus of assurances that they'd all rather die doing this than live without confronting the slavers in their homes.

and before I'd be a slave I'd be a free man in my grave

The target is the home of a judge who has served several terms in public office. It's a large home even by plantation gentry standards, and is often the scene of grand parties, where most of the men and women of that class gather in their finest clothes, displaying their most genteel behavior, their most refined wit and most tasteful appreciation. Deals are made here – not on paper, but in the warm matrix of mutuality and friendship.

There's going to be a party at the great house soon: the judge's son has turned twenty-one, and has returned from school in England. The judge is proud of his son, who has trained in medicine. The plan is that he will increase the efficiency and cost-effectiveness of their slaves, as the older son has increased the efficiency and cost-effectiveness of their crops.

They've been working and working on a plan to make their entrance to the property appear innocuous. Mister Coppoc has obtained an invitation to the party and will be bringing a few of his "servants" with him. At the appointed time, some of the others will appear, claiming an emergency that necessitates their speaking to their "master." Mister Coppoc will join them outside. On various pretexts the others will lure the servants out of the house and down to the stream that marks the property line.

And then Enosh and three others will fire the house.

more from the *Springfield, Illinois, State Register*

When men, by specious demagogism, in the name of freedom and liberty, daily labor to weaken the bonds of our glorious governmental fabric, the work of sages and patriots, themselves the holders of black men as slaves, is it to be wondered at that ignorant, unprincipled and reckless camp followers of the party for which these leaders speak, attempt, practically, to illustrate the doctrines which they preach, and in advocacy of which they seek to obtain control of the national government.?

More than half the guests of the party have survived the burning, but the house has not. Several of the servants were willing to go. All but two of these have *gone with the north star:* new freedmen to till the thin, rocky soil of Canada. Now, another group is heading down the old man's branch line.

Enosh isn't with them.

A flaming timber caught him and pinned him beyond the sight and hearing of his comrades. As the masters sorted out what happened they found him, bound him, and took him to the jail. Enosh was relieved not to find any of his fellows there. Only he was caught. He knows what awaits him: torture, trial, and a slow death. He is afraid, but not more afraid than he has been most of his life.

"You're one of Old Brown's," a man says. Enosh knows him to be the young son of the old judge, and a survivor of the fire, come down to the jail to express his anger for the cold-blooded murder of his father and his mother. The judge's son can hardly hold himself upright, his burns are so bad. Enosh's burns and injuries are enough that he cannot even sit, let alone stand. Some of those injuries he received at the hands of his captors.

"You're Old Brown's dupe," the judge's son says again. "You've been corrupted and sent down here to murder us in our sleep."

You were not sleeping, Enosh thinks – he would not speak aloud now if he could – *I saw you out there behind the house, and I know what you were doing. Mister Coppoc stopped you, or the girl would have been in as bad a condition as you.*

"You'll never overthrow our civilization," the judge's son says. "You're nothing but fanatics. You worship a false God and you have no sense of right and wrong. We are stronger than you. We'll find your Old Brown and crush you all." He swings a weakened fist into Enosh's face. He does more damage than he might have, because he connects with bones that are already broken.

Enosh looks at the ceiling, trying to put into his mere glance all the defiance he cannot express in any other way. He feels his mouth fill with blood. He remembers the old man coughing, and the way his followers supported him as he strove to empty his lungs. There were nights the old man lay as still as Enosh lies this day, when life seemed to be packing its bags to leave.

As the judge's son leaves another man arrives with a pan of water and a towel. He washes Enosh's face and body – not tenderly, but not viciously either. Then he leaves. When he returns he's carrying a bowl of broth and spooning it into Enosh's mouth. Enosh doesn't fight it, but he doesn't help either. Some of it goes down the wrong way. The man doesn't apologize. "You know," the man drawls, "They ain't going to find your Old Brown. Not alive. The old man's been dead a long time, that's why we ain't heard anything from him. I'd lay a gold dollar he'd never let you niggers do this without him if he wan't dead. He never could miss an opportunity to wave his saber. You got yourselves some other traitors sending you down here."

Enosh considers the theory. Though he knows that as of a couple of weeks ago, the old man was more alive than Enosh is now, it's quite plausible that he's dead by now.

"They's them that says that old man's the only reason you boys can be got to do such stuff. I believe they're wrong. I believe there ain't a thing will stop you but a full-on extermination effort."

The man grabs Enosh by the face and twists him so he can see his face. "We're going to burn you out, boy, just like a nest of vipers. Which is what you are. And you, boy, we're going to keep you alive. We're going to keep you alive though you wish to God or Satan we don't. Because you're going to heal, and when you heal, you will talk, by God you will talk and you will tell us where to find your filthy comrades. Because that's the only way we're going to let you die."

Enosh stares at him. If in the horrors of the night before – the screaming of the guests in the great house, the smell of charred wood and flesh, his own pain and fear – had driven his certainty from him, this man would remind him:

"We're going to tear you limb from limb. We're going to catch your friends and feed the bucks to the does. We're going to hang the white traitors and grind the blacks. Our institution will survive. Our traditions. Our values."

Your institutions abuse us and you profit from .our abuse, Enosh thinks. Your traditions made my mother a beast of burden and a plaything for a drunken boy. Your values have a stench to them.

"You disgust me," the man says, pushing Enosh back on to the bench where he has been lying since dawn.

Enosh gathers all his strength to croak out a few words. "No. I frighten you," he says, and he's not sure his vocal chords or tongue or lips have moved correctly to form the words, but he can tell the man gets the gist of what he's said, and that he has hit true.

Be the Bomb you Throw

Katherine Sparrow

"Tell me a secret," Theo asked Lilly.

"You sure you want that?" Her body lay pressed along the length of him, belly to belly, and everywhere their skin touched they stuck to each other with sweat.

She rolled away from him and stretched off the single-sized bed in Theo's dorm room. With a dirty towel she wiped herself off, then grabbed her bag. As she unzipped it the odor of unwashed clothes and mold mixed with the smell of distressed latex.

Theo peeled off his condom, tied it off, and held it up to the light streaming through his dorm window. "I made this," he whispered.

"What?"

"Tell me a secret."

"Here," she handed him a book. *The Art of Sabotage* was written with a permanent marker on its spine.

"No," Theo said. "A Lilly secret."

"A book is like a secret. We'll both be able to talk about it once you've finished, and no one will know what we mean, except us." She used her best 'I'm your professor and I know what's right for you' voice.

"I love you," he whispered.

"What?" Annoyance flickered over her face.

"Nothing." Theo wanted to hear that she loved him back, that she had a dream last night where he saved her from some blobby monster, or that, at least, the sex was good. That kind of secret.

Instead, Lilly rubbed herself again with the dirty towel and started dressing. He couldn't take his eyes off her as he watched her misshapen bits disappear. Her tiny penis lay nestled limply amid kinky red pubic hair. The first time he saw it, he wanted to ask her about it, but since that felt rude, he just pretended like it was normal. There was nothing wrong with her vagina, at least. Her sweet spot. Her red-brown girl iris.

Cunt, she insisted on calling it.

Cock, she would add, holding her dick out to him, though Theo wanted none of that part. He ignored it, even when it spurted out wisps of effeminate and insubstantial whiteness. It was nothing compared to his own... cock juice.

Theo wanted to ask more from Lilly, beg her for more, but instead he took the book into his hands.

The cracked leather spine felt fragile, and the edges of the pages were stained with dirt and grease, like all of Lilly's belongings. His school lay between the edge of the city and the foothills of the Sierras, and she lived out in the woods with a pack of crippled dogs. One-eyed Lucy, three-legged Lucifer, Tumor Benjy, mangy Molly, and distemper Lexi.

Lilly wriggled into her tan canvas pants and pulled a faded T-shirt over her small, hard breasts. The shirt read, "Beef: It's what's rotting in your colon!" She tied her brown hair back into a knot and slung her bag across her back.

"When can I see you next?" Theo asked.

She shrugged, then repeated the motion and swung her arms around. Lilly was always turning everything into yoga. She had a theory about yoga and longevity. Lilly had a lot of theories.

"After class? On Wednesday?" Please?

"That's March 31st. Almost April first," she said.

"So?"

"April Fool's Day. My favorite. I'll come, but you have to read the book."

A dog barked outside. Others joined in, until there was a whole pack of them yelping.

"I have a meeting that night, so it'll have to be right after class," she said.

"What kind of meeting?"

Lilly walked to Theo and laid one finger across his mouth. "One secret at a time," she said then left his room, slamming the door behind her.

He pulled the curtains away from his window and watched her call her dogs out from the woods behind his dorm. As she walked across the quad, people kept their distance from her—not just because of the dogs, but because she wasn't the kind of person you should be seen with. Lilly was the kind of girl Theo's parents warned him about when he left for school. The kind of girl he'd insisted over and over didn't exist anymore, or if she did, that he'd stay clear of her. Lilly walked with long yoga-strides. Theo watched until she was gone with a gut-level dread that he'd never see her again. Which was stupid—she had to see him. Lilly was his Wilderness and Technology seminar teacher.

He flopped down on his bed and grabbed her book.

"The Art of Sabotage," by Zachary Gray, the first page said. What's sabotage? he wondered as he noticed there was no RFID tracker embedded in the front cover. He flipped to the back, but there wasn't one there either. Not only was there no identification, he saw as he checked the spine, but there was no place where it had been removed.

Everyone has a right to know what everyone else is reading. It's one of the basic freedoms. Why would Lilly disobey the law? If they catch me with an unmarked book, I'll get questioned, and my name will be in the paper, along with all the other people who read perverted stuff, Theo thought uneasily. Not that anyone was likely to catch him, but still. Lilly just walked around with a book like this in her bag? Some secret all right. What would she give him the next time he asked for something?

Chlamydia?

Still, it was from Lilly. Theo opened the book to the first page. The layout was all messed up, like the layout guy was on pinx and couldn't see straight, he thought, then realized the book was a copy of something handwritten.

The Art of Sabotage

Zachary Gray

> *"The first principle of nonviolent action is that of non-cooperation with everything humiliating."—Mahatma Gandhi.*

This book is dedicated to all the queers, mestizas and passers, for teaching me about the in-between place that still exists, and what we must do to protect it. This is for all of you: one more secret history they don't want you to know.

I am writing this memoir from a prison that every country will insist doesn't exist. If anyone says that it does they are called conspirators, crackpots, or insane. If they persist in saying it, they are put under surveillance.

We are moved around from prison to prison, blindfolded and trussed as we are thrown onto airplanes like luggage, then put into identical facilities. The changing odor of the guard's farts from cabbage, to beans, to beef is the only clue as to what country we're in. Our own food, just like our prison, remains the same gray-protein-slop and pale vegetables.

It's not a bad prison as such places go. Everyone here is a politicalista—taken away from the world for their ability to sway others. It makes for a lively place full of the kind of people I always wanted to know, when I was on the outside. We have organized over time to demand pens and paper. We sit in our cells and scribble out manifestos that would change the world, if only they could escape the confines of these windowless walls. We swap drafts with each other and offer up passionate critiques.

Our prison is not violent, except when food becomes scarce, or the guards become bored. Some days our cell doors open, and we are allowed the freedom to walk around and visit with each other. Other times our doors stay locked for weeks. No one knows why. Part of the power of any prison is the ability to change things without reason or recourse. Our politics and rhetoric, drawn from hundreds of movements across the world, fade as we stay here longer and longer and all that seems real is the coldness of the steel rimmed toilets, the mold on the walls, and the rats who refuse to become pets and remain our eternal enemies.

I write this so you'll know some of who I am. I'm not writing to discuss my confinement, though we have all become a little obsessed with our detention as the years and decades pass us by. These words I write have a different purpose: to educate. I hold the impossible hope that my words will slip out through one of the liminal places—the neither here nor there—and come to exist in the world where action is still possible. I want this, even knowing my story could never exist freely out there.

They were so smart to get you to monitor each other's readings, then slowly take away the books that no one dared touch. They were so smart to get you to want that.

Stories were what made me, back when libraries had whole shelves of untagged books on the subject of dissidence. Stories slipped into my life with an alchemical magic and created me anew. They are our best and brightest liminal space.

Theo wanted to run. He wanted to burn the book and wash his hands a dozen times, but where could he set a fire that wouldn't be picked up on the grid? And wasn't his genomic signature already sweated onto the pages? That couldn't be erased. Neither could the knowledge already slipping into his consciousness.

Theo turned the page.

First off, there is the matter of sabotage. It is an old word, blacklisted and venerable, steeped in the blood of French weavers. The weavers were the poorest of the poor who wore rotting wooden shoes hewn from willow-wood. A peasant's shoe, the sabot, was far different than the soft leather and horse-hoofed heels of the gentry.

The loom owners brought in mechanized looms, and the weavers no longer had work. They threw their sabots into the machines. Sabotage, it was called—an act against property and wealth. A direct action against that which destroys one's ability to exist. Sabotage grew more nuanced over the centuries, and described the pantheon of actions aimed at weakening an enemy through subversion, obstruction, disruption, or destruction.

I am using a precise definition because words change over time. Like decency and the public good. Like sabotage, which has disappeared from our literature altogether: expunged from the world's history so that we will forget the tools our fore-mothers gave us.

Telling you my story, imagined outsider, is an act of sabotage, because I'm hoping, with every drop of ink that bleeds onto this paper, that through subversion I will change you, and you will take action against our common enemy. May this book become a bomb that explodes the mortared walls they have built around your heart.

Waiting for Wednesday, and the moment when he would see Lilly again, Theo read Gray's book every day. He was careful not to fall behind in his studies or be late to class. That would cause a whole cycle of events to happen that he didn't want: they'd install a room eye, a roommate, study partners, and if all else failed, give Theo an "I can eye cam!"—a camera embedded behind his eye that would record all his actions and offer up helpful advice. No, Theo didn't dare allow any of that to happen. He read Gray's book late at night when everything else was done.

It was full of definitions of words that were vaguely familiar, or completely unknown to him—phallocentrism, the imaginary domain, anarchy. The stories Gray told infected his sleep and waking life—often in class Theo would find his mind drifting off and having imagined conversations with Gray. At night he'd dream of prison: of concrete walls and never seeing sunlight. The book affected him like a low-grade fever.

At class on Wednesday, Lilly had singed hair and burn marks on her knuckles. Her eyes ignored Theo as they examined the lumps of underclassmen flesh sitting before her.

"How many of you know what vivisection is?" Her voice was angry and hoarse.

Images of monkeys with syringes in their eyes, cats with intestines spread open, and mice with metal tubes exposing their brains flickered on the screen over her head. Lilly's laser pointer slashed across the creatures' bodies.

"Vivisection is where we must start, in discussing whose body is penetrable, whose not. This is the central problem of humanity's interaction with the world: the way we treat everything that is not us as garbage."

A girl raised her hand. "You mean we should start treating everyone like people?" she asked. The girl had started wearing muddy jeans and tangled hair since starting the class. She smiled expectantly.

Lilly snorted. "Like people? Where would that get us? Two thirds of the world is hungry. Should we treat the world like that? No. We must learn from the natural world. Humans are doomed, unless we learn from all life."

Another boy raised his hand. "Doesn't the natural world eat each other?"

Lilly turned on him. "It does. It gives and takes, it creates a web of interdependence. Only humans take and don't give back," she said. She paced up and down the room like a tiger stalking its next meal.

Theo thought about how he'd been drawn into her class when he walked by the door and saw her standing inside, magnificent. Not pretty. Not sweet. Radiating power. She had approached him after class and asked about his thoughts on the wilds.

Theo told her that man was made to have dominion over the world. He didn't think about it; he just said what he'd always been told. She grinned at him ferociously, took him into the woods, and (as she called it) fucked him. Later, she asked Theo what his name was.

Lilly stopped pacing and glared at the class. "Let's be honest about the human species and domination. We need to become something new. We cannot continue to be our feeble little female/male human selves. Evolution is not moving fast enough. What should we do?"

"Breed?" a boy asked then blushed.

"Don't be stupid," Lilly said.

No one else spoke. Theo looked away from her and wondered who the hell had let Lilly become a teacher. He stared up at the eye embedded in the ceiling, and wondered what the people on the other end of it made of Lilly. Its red light was off—the camera didn't seem to be working.

Later, as the afternoon unfolded around Theo like a graphic movie, he told her, "I read your book."

Theo searched Lilly's eyes for a reflection of himself as his spasms became smaller and weaker inside of her. He'd sprayed his room with PhereMans (TM) before Lilly came over, but they didn't seem to be having the desired effect. She was not swooning from the cat-piss smell of "The power of pure male essence." Her hand reached between them and stroked her penis distractedly.

"Not all of it. I knew you wouldn't," she said. "That's why I gave it to you early."

"Some of it," he agreed. "I've been busy."

Her upper body moved away from him in cobra pose even as her legs stayed wrapped around his hips.

"I know what sabotage is," he whispered.

"Do you know the why yet?"

"The 'Y'?"

"The why we have to break the machine with our peasant parts," she said, lecturing a slow student. She got off the bed, stretched upwards, then bent forward into the downward dog pose.

"Why do I love you?" Theo whispered.

"That's the second time you've said it. Are you sure?" Lilly flexed one foot to the floor, then the other. Her ass wriggled gloriously in the air.

"What?"

"That you love me."

Theo blushed—his already sex-flushed body grew darker. "I think so. I've never felt like this before."

"Obviously. But you have to read all of Gray's book tonight."

"It's just a book, Lilly. None of it's real, not like us." He got dressed, clumsy in his body because she watched him.

"Promise you'll read it?" she insisted.

"Sure, fine."

"It's not just a book, Theo. What if I told you I was Gray's descendent."

"Are you?"

"In an evolutionary way, yeah." She popped up onto her feet and reached her hands over her head. Her belly tightened. Her breasts bobbed up and down as she stretched. "Being in love means being vulnerable: being penetrable. You want to come to my meeting?"

Theo didn't know what he wanted.

"Please? I think they need to meet you."

It was the first time she'd ever wanted something from him. He closed his eyes and let the delicious feeling move through him.

"It's another secret, isn't it?"

"Yes."

Even though her last secret disturbed him, Theo was hungry for more. "I'll go."

Her dogs waited for her outside the glass doors of Theo's dorm. They pressed their noses enthusiastically between Lilly and Theo's legs. She held his hand as they walked across the quad, then through campus toward the city. Something was different between them. It seemed like she actually liked Theo.

"Where'd you grow up?" he asked.

"In a commune, in the country."

"Commune?"

"A collectivized family where not everyone is genetically related to each other," she said.

"How was that?"

"Good. I had a lot of sisters, so it never felt like we got enough attention, but there was a lot of love, too."

"All sisters?"

"Sort of."

All of them, like her? It must be some weird genealogical fluke. "Lots of Lillys," he whispered, liking the idea.

"What?"

"How long have you been teaching?"

"What? Oh, that." She yoga shrugged. "All my life. Never."

He didn't know what to say about that, so they walked on and Lilly looked a million miles away. They took the bike path—filled in concrete over the old train tracks. A man yelled at Lilly to leash up her dogs as he whizzed by on his bike. Mangy Molly, the most able of the pack, chased him for a while before stopping to scratch herself.

The path ended and they walked farther south. Single story houses stood side by side under the blue LED light of streetlamps and faintly glowing red eyes.

They walked on to where there were less houses and no more surveillance. Theo felt uneasy about being somewhere no-one could watch. Lilly led them to the old abandoned Riverside Theatre, sitting all haunted-like up on a hill. Someone had busted open the padlocked door. Lilly slipped inside, and her dogs, one by one, hobbled after her. Theo looked in every direction twice to see if anyone was watching, then followed. It was dark inside except for some randomly placed tea-lights that showed Lilly walking up the rotten-velvet hallway. The air smelled smoky with an undercurrent of mold. He heard talking ahead of them.

"I've brought someone," Lilly called out.

The voices stopped.

"Who?" someone asked.

"I brought *him*," Lilly said.

"Here? Why?"

"I think you all need to meet him."

Theo was flattered that Lilly had talked to them about him. Maybe he meant more to her than he thought.

He ran up the hallway to where it led into the theater and grabbed Lilly's hand. Distemper Lexi nipped at his pant cuff. "Hi, I'm Theo."

Some of the theater seats had been dragged in front of the old movie screen. They were arranged in a circle. A small fire burned in a pit dug into the cement floor in the middle of the chairs. It was the only light in the room. Theo looked at the walls and ceilings, but saw no eyes.

"Hi, Theo," a man called out in a mocking sing-song voice. His womanish face looked Theo over, then he shook his head. "A goddamn child. Jesus, Lilly."

"He's nineteen. Enough moralizing. We don't have time for it. Are we ready?"

The man winked at Theo. He was Indian and wore loose-fitting, sloppy clothes that looked like they came from the bargain shop. He introduced himself as Riffraff. Beside him sat two brown-skinned girls—one asian, one mixed—in black hooded sweatshirts and identical bleached hair. They held hands and were named Spleen and Splotz. Beside them sat a white man in a sharp business suit (Jerry), and next to him an older woman busy knitting a red skull-cap (Mathilda).

"Deer in headlights, babe in the woods," one of the brown-skinned blondes muttered.

"We don't think it's fair," the other one said.

Lilly snorted. "It's more than fair. A plan's a plan, even when you're faced with the consequences."

Theo didn't know what they were talking about, and it made him uneasy. It felt like they all knew something obvious that he should know.

"We all start out ignorant," Lilly added, and looked at Theo pointedly. "There's no other way." She flopped down on one of the chairs.

Theo nudged tumor Benjy aside, who yelped when he poked his lump, and sat beside her.

"What'd you think of the book?" Mathilda asked.

Reading the book felt too secretive to speak about out loud. Had they all read it too? "I keep dreaming about prison," he said.

"Keep reading to the very end," Mathilda said.

Lilly cleared her throat and everyone's torsos shifted to orient toward her. Even though they sat in a circle, she clearly held power in this group. "We need to finalize the sites, and make sure we have clear access to all of them. It's going to be a long night. Jerry?"

He held up a ring of keys and passcards. "Good to go."

"Except Biotech One is out—they updated their security system and there's no time to hack it," Mathilda said. "Symbios will work, though we're still not sure what they're up to."

"We found out they bought some Amish genome in the last month," Spleen/Splotz said. The other one added, "And five hundred Onco mice. Oh, and research ran a demo and had 64% conversion."

"Good," Lilly said. "My people have made the..." she looked at me, then looked at the others knowingly. "They're ready to go."

"Any problems?" Riffraff asked.

Lilly held up her burned hands, then interlocked her fingers and stretched forward. "No."

"What about him?" Mathilda asked.

"Everything's going as planned," Lilly said.

Theo sat there stupidly, feeling their eyes watching him. Why did they think he was any part of this?

"Be careful, Lilly," Riffraff said.

"I never am," she said as though agreeing with him.

"I didn't understand most of that," Theo confided in her on the walk home. Her hand slipped into his.

"I know. Do you have any idea how close this planet is to environmental collapse?"

"Sure, I guess so."

"Ten more years like the last ten, and that's it. You know about manufactured evolution?" It was too dark for Theo to see Lilly's face, but he guessed that she looked angry.

"Sure. Fish into tomatoes, or that corn that took over all of Mexico."

"Human organs into pigs, vaccinations into mosquitoes, frogs into rice," Lilly lectured, her hand squeezing Theo's tight. "Once you've been genetically modified, you can't evolve anymore. We destroy everything, then make it so they can't adapt."

"Well sure," Theo said. "But there's nothing we can do about it."

"Doing nothing isn't neutral. Humans are the ones who need forced evolution."

"What?"

"Sabotage."

Theo breathed in the dangerous, subversive air all around him. Being with Lilly was like stepping into a different land that no one had told him existed.

"Lilly, you'll get in trouble."

"Ten years, Theo," she whispered. "We are neck deep in trouble. Don't you think we should do something?"

"But... think about what happened to Gray."

She stopped walking. The moon emerged from behind some clouds and the light made a halo around her body. Her dogs surrounded her like prostrate disciples.

"I love you," Theo whispered.

"That's the third time you've said it, so it must be true." She took him off the bike path, hopefully out of site of the eyes, and ringed by dogs and moonlight, made love to Theo in a sweet way that was so different from the other times. She was a languid creature, twisting and moaning above and below him like they were both underwater, coming up for breath with great breaching cries.

Only later, after she had kissed him in his doorway and Theo stumbled love-drunk up to his room, did he think about what he'd done, and how they'd both loved it. Taking that small bit of flesh that shouldn't be there, putting it into his mouth, teasing it until it came, then eagerly swallowing the bitter fluid.

"Beautiful, not gross," Theo whispered. He felt confused about Lilly, and about her talk of destroying things. She was joking, right? She was using metaphor. He picked up the book, because he'd promised her he would.

I have grown depressed as I write down these thoughts, and have not written for weeks. It's all so pointless. It's a silly game to keep away my malaise. I know this, but as my protein block arrived vermin-gnawed and under-cooked this evening, I promised I would continue to put my pen to paper and write it all down as though I matter. I promised myself I would finish this, no matter how sisyphean the pursuit. It's that, or give in to the overwhelming despair that leads so many of us to hang ourselves from the rusty plumbing pipes.

Have I spoken yet of my own history? I arrived at university a dull boy, but quickly fell in love with an older dissident who corrupted me in all kinds of delightful ways. He introduced me to a new life wrapped up in the old one. We existed in a wonderfully liminal space, apart yet part of our world.

Liminal? Think of the part of the beach that is half the day underwater, half above. While neither sea creatures nor land-dwellers live there, some life exists there. In hard times, we must exist where others cannot. Reading these words is liminal, if indeed, they are ever read. Liminal is a moment where you no longer exist fully in the confines of their world. When society is bad, as it has been for so long, one can only widen these temporary zones. That is the reason behind sabotage. To create liminal space, however momentary, where everything is possible.

This is what my new friends and I discovered as we read and argued theory. Then we grew discontent with mere theory. So we made bombs. It's easy to make a bomb. The natural world is extremely explosive, almost as though the earth longs for destruction on her behalf.

We targeted corporations that were deforesting the world. We laid our bombs via bike messengers and temp workers in dozens of buildings, then detonated them one by one as weeks and month passed by. No one died: we always alerted the buildings hours in advance.

Our city became obsessed with the question of who would be bombed next. And did you know Cargill was destroying the rainforest? Liminal moments grew.

Then, three bombs went off instead of four, and a building stayed upright. The faulty bomb detonated when the building was full of cops and firefighters.

Twenty-seven people were murdered. Read these words and think of all that lost potential. All those families ruined, because I made a bomb and placed it there. But does any corporation stop and think about what it does?

I keep thinking there must be creation with destruction, but I am not sure how this would be done. It is for others to figure out. What I do know is that you must take action, or all life will disappear on this planet.

Zachary Gray's handwriting ended mid-page, but it wasn't the end of the book. There were pages of bomb recipes, lists of books, and instructions on how to do abortions, lock-picking, hacking electricity, and police surveillance.

Then, as Theo turned to the last page, the handwriting changed to Lilly's writing. In her sprawling script she had written a list of places and addresses: most the major biotech labs in the city. At the bottom of the list she'd penned in thick letters, "All fool's fall—bring down the empire April first."

Theo dropped the book. Then picked it up. Then threw it across the room. They were planning on bombing buildings tomorrow? Yes, that's what that meeting was about, wasn't it? What did Lilly expect him to do?

It all felt too real; too close to him. Concrete prison walls loomed up all around him.

Terrorist. Pervert. Murderer. They would call him, and worse.

No, Theo thought. I can't. I won't be part of this. An almost instinctual need to keep safe—to stay on the right side of society—pulsed through him.

Theo pulled on his coat, grabbed the book, and left his dorm. He sprinted all the way to the nearest police station underneath lamp-eyes that recorded his every motion.

The cops raised their eyebrows and shook their heads. They asked him if this was some kind of fraternity joke, or an art project. They made him sit in an uncomfortable chair in their vomit-hued waiting room. When he didn't leave, someone came out and looked at his book. They ushered him back to a windowless room and heard his story.

They sent in half a dozen different men to ask the same questions. They pumped his stomach to get a DNA match on Lilly then left him alone. He sat there for hours, feeling violated and wondering what they were going to do to him. Theo thought about how he would do anything to stay out of a prison like the one Gray described. He thought about Lilly, and how he was betraying her. Finally, a cop came back into the room.

"Theodore," he said as though they were friends. "It's good you came to us, but what the hell were you thinking?" He leaned back in his chair and studied Theo. "How does a kid like you get involved in something like this?"

"She was my teacher," Theo said defensively, then whispered, "she taught me so much."

"Right. There's no such class offered at your school. We checked."

"But I was enrolled."

"Yeah, yeah, yeah. A bunch of kids were enrolled in it—your terrorists hacked into the university's system. That doesn't mean you weren't in on it. Was it some kind of recruiting scam?"

"No. I don't know."

"You don't know anything. You're just an innocent kid. Except you came to us late enough in the night so that we couldn't check the buildings. Sure, Theo."

"Huh?"

"You knew we wouldn't get your full story until after midnight. It's against policy to send in our bomb squads on the day they're set to explode. But I'm sure you already knew that."

Theo shook his head. "I'm trying to be one of the good guys."

The man slapped his meaty hands on the table. "We didn't get a good DNA match on your man-girl either, but found that weird shit in your stomach. I don't know what's going on with you, kid. It's not illegal, but eating worms?"

"What?"

"Right, you have no idea what I mean. You're damn lucky you come from a good family and have no priors. There's nothing we can stick on you. Yet. Set up an appointment for eye-cam surgery on the way out. We'll GP chip you until then. All for your own safety, of course." He sneered.

After they shoved the GP into his arm, Theo stumbled out of the police station into a sunny day. He stood under the blue sky, glad in every molecule of his body to be free. It took a moment to notice the buzzing of dozens of sirens across the city, and the whoomp-whomp of helicopters overhead.

With a sense of unreality, he walked to the nearest biotech company—Symbios. It was exactly like bomb threats Theo had seen on TV. Lines of police made a perimeter a block out from the building. They wore so much riot gear they looked like robots. Thousands of people stood behind the steel perimeter fences, waiting with a raw and violent hope that something bad was going to happen.

All this because of Lilly, he thought, and didn't know how that made any sense. Theo slipped into the cafe across the street, got a coffee, and went outside again to watch the show.

As more and more people swarmed to the barricades, Theo thought about the line he'd drawn between himself and people like Lilly and Gray. Liminal doesn't exist, he thought. You're either normal, or not. You're either safe, or not.

Theo's stomach rumbled as he sipped the coffee. It made him think of the cop's weird joke. Worms? Why would he say that?

A ground shaking thwump, then another, and another filled the air. The Symbios building shook. Its windows shattered outward. With a metal groan, the whole building shifted to the left and fell to the ground. A grey wall of smoke puffed out from the building and covered everyone. People screamed, then started coughing. Theo breathed in building particulate and a bitter, chemical smoke. He was blinded and bent over hacking.

He heard more explosions farther off. The filthy air began settling to the ground in a pea-soup fog. People moved about like zombies, pushing into each other and moving spastically. Cops yelled through bullhorns for everyone to disperse and go home. Theo did his best to move toward the university. There were too many people everywhere.

More booms sounded from across the city. Theo kept slowly moving toward his school. The air was almost clean by the time he crossed the street to the university, then walked toward his dorm. Theo's breathing was smoke-ragged, and he just wanted to sleep. He wanted to wake up and watch it all on the nightly news like it had happened somewhere else, to someone else. He felt tainted by the police, and by Lilly.

A woman stood to the side of his dorm in a thin-slit suit: typical corporate wear. She stepped toward him. It was Lilly.

A dog howled from the woods behind her. She walked briskly to him in her spiked heels.

"I... I betrayed you, Lilly."

"I know. We hoped you would. Our covenant states we must give humanity a chance. I let you read the book, and let you decide what to do. You told the police. So the buildings were empty, and there was a huge crowd of people around the buildings. If you hadn't done that, we wouldn't have detonated the bombs. You wouldn't have breathed it in."

"No! It's not my fault. I tried to stop it. Are you here... are you here to take me with you?"

Her face softened behind her pointy glasses for a moment, and she patted his head like he was one of her dogs. "No, Theo. I'm here for my book."

"I gave it to the cops."

"Idiot." Lilly stepped toward him and kissed Theo, parting his lips with her tongue and pressing into his mouth. Then she withdrew and turned away from him. Lilly was the wilderness, the dangerous, the liminal. Theo watched her go.

The eye in the quad watched him. His newly embedded GP chip itched. Dogs surrounded Lilly as she disappeared into the woods.

"I don't love you," Theo whispered. His throat burned with ash and lies.

Their manifesto appeared seven days after the April Fool's Day Attacks on ten cities. No one had died, except for a couple of old ladies who had heart attacks. No one had got caught—it was like the terrorists never existed. Except for some conspiracy theorists, people were already starting to forget about the whole thing.

Their manifesto appeared when it was too late to do anything. Theo sat in his dorm waiting for the police to show up and arrest him. He kept waiting for punishment, as he writhed inside his own body, but no one knew that he was the one who'd made it all possible. Maybe, with all the changes going on in the country, no one cared. Nothing at all happened to Theo. Except the obvious.

Execution Morning

Marie Brennan

"Remember to watch the sky," Sarienne told her assembled soldiers, projecting her voice loudly enough to reach the back rows. "And the crowd. And the ground." Her laugh had little mirth in it. "Watch everything. You never know where they might come from."

Several heads nodded. She scanned the ranks of her soldiers, evaluating each expression, noting the ones with a gleam in their eyes. She distrusted that gleam; it was the mark of a zealot, and while zealots performed their duties eagerly, they were also hair-triggered. And that was the last thing she needed tomorrow.

"Let's make this clean," she said at last. "The Empress wants it done right. Dismissed."

The soldiers saluted and departed. Sarienne, left alone, rubbed her face and sighed. *Bedtime soon,* she promised herself. *One last thing to do.*

The prison she went to was cramped and dark, built by the Mittrich, not the Elesie who now ruled their lands. Sarienne nodded to the guard at the front door. He unlocked it for her, announcing into the antechamber, "Captain Chemand to see the prisoners!"

Four checkpoints later, she entered a small room and returned the salutes of the three soldiers inside. One of them leapt to his feet at her nod; she waited as he went to the heavy iron door and spoke through the grate. "Reneur Domérage. Captain Chemand will be entering."

After a moment there came a murmur of acknowledgment. The guard opened the door, and Sarienne stepped inside.

The man seated in the chair did not look up. His attention was fixed on the two women and one man chained to the opposite wall. Sarienne's skin prickled at the tension in the air; was she imagining it, or could she feel the power Domérage was using to keep the prisoners under control? She never ceased to be amazed by the security measures she had been ordered to take. Had her prisoners been anything other than Kagi, they would have been easier to guard.

Had her prisoners been anything other than Kagi, they would not have been shape-changers. And that, after all, was where this began.

"Any difficulty, Reneur?" she asked the seated mage.

He shook his head. "None."

"Very well. I'll be retiring soon; Lieutenant-Captain Alée will continue to check in with you until dawn." She glanced at the prisoners. "May I speak with them briefly?"

He nodded. Reassured that she would not be disrupting his concentration, Sarienne stepped forward and met the eyes of the prisoners. Light blue on one woman, ice-green on the other and the man, unlike the familiar grey of the Elesie and startlingly alien. All three glared at her. Even in the dim light of the prison, their skin glimmered with a faint silver tinge, beautiful and compelling. Looking at them made Sarienne shiver. She'd never been so close to Kagi until these three were arrested.

"Tomorrow at dawn you will be escorted from here," she said to the prisoners. "For your crimes the judges have sentenced you to execution by drawing and quartering." Her mouth opened to continue with the standard next line, about their right to have a priest of Esterre and Aluseme, but she closed it before the words could escape. Esterre and Aluseme abominated shape-changers; the Kagi did not worship them.

"Prepare yourself," Sarienne said instead, the words cold and hard.

The two women looked at the ground, coldly ignoring her, but the man glared directly at her through a fringe of silver-grey hair. The hatred she saw in his pale green eyes froze her bones. The soldiers who had captured him said his otherform was a leopard; she saw it flicker, deep in those eyes.

He would tear my throat out in a heartbeat, if only he could.

He had not blinked. Sarienne tried to keep her gaze on his, but his eyes defeated her. She turned her back on him and left the cell, hoping Domérage hadn't noticed her discomfort. *I've never been hated that strongly by anyone.*

"I'll see you at dawn," she said to the guards, then left the prison.

"Why drawing and quartering, anyway?" she asked Terlieu as he helped her remove her armor. "Of all the ways to execute them, why *that* one?"

"What do you care?" he asked, unbuckling a strap. "They don't have souls anyway. It doesn't matter what we do to them."

"They may not have souls, but they have entrails, which will be removed and burned in front of me. That's not what I'd call a pleasant way to spend the morning."

Terlieu's look was equal parts surprise and amusement. "Are you *squeamish?*"

Sarienne glared at him. "Disemboweling someone in battle is different. You're busy trying to keep his friend from bashing your head in; you have other things to pay attention to. This . . ." She swallowed, but the sick taste in her mouth remained. "I'm just glad we're executing all three at once. At least we'll get it done quickly."

"I wouldn't call it *quick*," he said. "The whole point of drawing and quartering is to make the death slow and painful."

Sarienne would have preferred him not to remind her. She had seen the punishment carried out once, six years ago, in Eles. That time, though, she hadn't been presiding over it. And the bastard had deserved it; he'd tried to assassinate the Empress.

As if he'd heard her, Terlieu spoke again. "Anyway, they deserve it. Can't let people commit treason and get off lightly."

The words came out before she could stop them. "Is it really treason?"

Terlieu actually dropped her chain-mail hauberk onto the floor. He stared at her for a moment before picking it up once more. "They conspired against the Empress. Besides, even though they're Kagi, the Mittern Province is part of Eles now."

Sarienne bit her tongue rather than respond. She'd said too much already. Mittern had been an Elesteir province for only a short time, but since the Conquest everyone who resided there was a subject of the Empress, regardless of race; to conspire against her was treason.

But Sarienne was not convinced the three prisoners lived in Mittern, and didn't simply have the bad luck to be captured there. They claimed they were travelers. Of course, they also claimed they were innocent. Sarienne didn't believe in their innocence, but they might be foreigners. In which case their crime was conspiracy, yes, but not treason – and their deaths should be cleaner.

A servant entered the room and bowed to them both. "Captain, you have a visitor. The Imperial Prince is here."

"What?" Sarienne stared at him. "Which one?"

"Pendrois, Captain."

Pendrois. At least it isn't Ecques; there's a small mercy. "Please, show him in." She snagged her tunic from the back of the chair and did up its high collar. It would not do to receive the Prince half-dressed.

Pendrois was shorter than Sarienne, but his ego filled the whole room. He strode forward and nodded at her bow. "Captain Sarienne Gorin Chemand. My mother sends her greetings."

"I'm honored that she has sent you to us, your Highness. May I introduce my second-in-command? This is Lieutenant-Captain Terlieu Claretes Alée." Terlieu bowed and received another curt nod. "Did you just arrive?"

"Yes." Pendrois eyed Sarienne, then answered the question she couldn't politely ask. "My mother sent me to observe the executions tomorrow."

To observe – not to oversee. Sarienne thanked Esterre and Aluseme that the Empress had sent Pendrois, and not his brother. Rumour said Ecques had strange powers, that he could even spy on the thoughts of others. She didn't need the Empress' son overhearing her doubts about the validity of the evidence against the Kagi.

"The executions are scheduled to begin at dawn," she said, covering up her pause. "Would you like me to postpone them until a later hour?"

"That won't be necessary. Just give me a room, and I'll go right to sleep. I'm looking forward to being there."

The servant stepped forward without being prompted; Sarienne gestured to him. "Guriér here will take care of your accomodations, and I will send someone to wake you before dawn."

Pendrois nodded. "I shall see you tomorrow, then, when we take care of those Kagi criminals."

When the Imperial Prince was gone, Sarienne sagged into a chair and exhaled.

Terlieu grinned at her; he knew her opinion of the Prince. She just hoped he didn't guess the depth of her hidden doubts. Terlieu wasn't rabidly religious, but neither would he question the legitimacy of this execution. "So we'll have an Imperial audience."

"Just what I wanted," she said sourly. "He'll be here to see the chaos."

"You really expect trouble?"

"Don't *you?*" Sarienne sat up and gripped the short strands of her hair. "We're executing three Kagi on grounds many have condemned as flimsier than a balsa-wood fan. And the Kagi hate us. Don't you think they'll take this chance to make trouble?"

Terlieu shrugged. "So what? Our men will handle them. I'm sure Pendrois will appreciate it; did you see the look in his eye when he mentioned the prisoners?"

Sarienne had, all too well. The Imperial Family were all deeply religious, and Pendrois was no exception. To him, killing shape-changers was a divine mission. They were soulless creatures, and lower than human; their deaths were exterminations.

She herself didn't care much one way or another. But she couldn't admit that publicly; an officer of her rank was supposed to at least follow the forms of religion.

Instead she stood and massaged one tight shoulder. "Well, I don't doubt he'll get his chance." And he'd enjoy it, too. Sarienne vowed to watch him tomorrow; he had that light in his eye, the light of a zealot. But she was damned if an Imperial Prince was going to turn the scene into a bloodbath on a whim.

"Everything's in place, Captain. We can begin on your order."

Sarienne pulled herself into the saddle of her gelding and glanced up at the keep's clock-tower, just readable in the predawn light. "Five more minutes. We set out when the bell tolls. And where is that damned Prince?"

"Behind you," a smooth voice said. Sarienne turned, cursing her sharp tone. Pendrois, luckily, seemed more amused than offended. "Nervous, Captain?"

"Just trying to make sure everything is ready, your Highness." Sarienne shrugged her shoulders to settle her armor more comfortably. "I've arranged for you to lead the procession, if that's acceptable to you."

"Do you not wish to do it yourself?"

"I'd prefer to stay with Reneur Domérage, where I can keep an eye on the prisoners."

"As you wish." Pendrois raised one eyebrow, then turned his horse and rode forward, to the head of the column of guards.

Sarienne stared after him for a moment, then cursed and went to take her place next to Domérage.

The mage sat astride his horse, just behind the three prisoners. His face was tight with weariness, but he had repeatedly insisted on remaining with the Kagi until the execution was over; he was a fanatic for control, and didn't trust anyone else to handle it properly. Sarienne had argued, but in the end he'd won out. And perhaps it was for the best; Domérage was good at what he did. It would take more than a crowd to disrupt his concentration.

She looked past him to the prisoners. They stood, hands and feet bound, each tied to a horse in front by a long rope. Sarienne took up a position next to Domérage and realized too late that it put her right behind the green-eyed man. Though he did not turn to look at her, she could feel his stiff-backed rage. But she was damned if she'd move away from him.

The clock tolled. As soon as the last tone faded, she raised her voice for the whole column to hear. "*Move out!*"

From up ahead, she heard a whinny, and saw Pendrois rearing his horse. Then he trotted forward, and the soldiers followed.

With their ankles bound together, the prisoners had no hope of keeping their feet. The horses they were tied to moved forward, and they all fell heavily to the filthy cobblestones, to be dragged through the streets.

Sarienne and Domérage followed at a careful distance, making sure their horses would not trample the prisoners. Soldiers flanked them to either side, keeping the crowd back. No one had the nerve to throw anything at the Kagi, not with the risk of hitting Sarienne or Domérage, but the screams were deafening, the roar of a maddened beast.

The procession wound through the town at a good clip; Pendrois, up front, was making sure the Kagi would be well and truly battered by the time they reached the scaffold. He kept the pace slow enough to give the crowd time to work itself to a fever pitch, though. The Imperial Prince knew how to milk an execution for the maximum entertainment value.

I just want to get this over with. Every moment we take out here is another moment for someone to cause trouble.

But no one attacked them during the procession, and at last they reached the town square, where a large platform had been erected. Sarienne dismounted and climbed the steps to the viewing box raised above it. Pendrois was already there, smiling and egging the crowd on.

Below, soldiers were dragging the Kagi up onto the platform under Domérage's unblinking eye. The women appeared stoically resigned to their fates, but the man continued to kick and fight, despite his bonds and the bruises he had taken. The mob loved every bit of it. Passive victims were not nearly as exciting.

Sarienne cast a worried look around, keeping both hands on the crossbow which had been waiting for her in the box. The prisoners were strapped down onto their blocks, stretched out on their backs, but with their heads over the edges so they could entertain the crowd with their convulsions. Still no sign of trouble, but she couldn't relax yet.

Pendrois picked up the scroll in front of him and offered it to Sarienne. She refused it with a curt nod, and continued to watch the crowd.

The Imperial Prince shrugged and unrolled the parchment. His voice rang out through the square, even over the clamor of the mob.

"The Honorable and Just Magistrates Lady Labrial Alous e'Vamigne Pellard, Lord Unant Cartie Nesau, and Lady Savoine Queliette Peres have convicted you of treasonous plotting against your rightful sovereign, Her Imperial Majesty Evaine Satie il'e'Cersois Rameaux, Empress of Eles. For these crimes you have been condemned to death by drawing and quartering, after which your heads will be displayed in the Temple of Esterre and Aluseme in Eles as a warning to all who would challenge her imperial authority." Pendrois rolled up the scroll and looked down at the bound prisoners. His smile made Sarienne's skin crawl. "At this point I usually make a comment about hoping Esterre and Aluseme have pity on your treasonous souls. But you are Kagi. You threw away your human souls the moment you changed your human bodies for those of animals." His smile widened. "You will die, and be no more."

The mob screamed its delight with one hideous voice.

Then an explosion shattered the air.

The shock wave made Sarienne stagger. As soon as she recovered, her eyes shot to the wall of the town square, which a moment ago had been crawling with eager spectators. Where they had been, there was now a smoking hole surrounded by charred bodies, and a mad rush of people fleeing the spot.

Her head snapped around; she intended to look to the prisoners. But she made it only partway there. A figure in the crowd caught her eye, and then she could not move.

No one in the vicinity of the platform was moving. A spell held them frozen.

Sarienne stared at the woman in the crowd and knew, even before she saw the lips moving in a whisper, that she was looking at the spell's source. The woman looked Mittrich, but that meant nothing, not when dealing with the Kagi. She alone in the crowd didn't look surprised.

In her peripheral vision Sarienne could just barely see a flock of birds streaking through the air toward the platform. A full dozen birds – some of them large raptors, others tiny songbirds, none of them belonging in a flock together. Kagi. The rescue was underway.

And still she couldn't move. Their trick had worked; the explosion had broken Domérage's concentration and had allowed the mage in the crowd to slam a spell down on the area. She would hold them paralyzed while the airborne cavalry came in. The Kagi would rescue their countrymen and escape.

And Sarienne could not blame them.

The three Kagi were scapegoats, nothing more. Forget the accusation; the prisoners were something to feed the mob's blood lust. And she couldn't blame their fellows for wanting to save them from an excruciatingly painful, pointless death.

She had a crossbow in her hands, and it was pointed right at the mage. If Sarienne could just move her finger, she might break the spell holding them all.

She couldn't blame the Kagi for wanting to save three lives.

But then she remembered the hole where the town wall had been, and the townsfolk who had been on it. The screams of the wounded carried clearly through the air. How many Elesteir and Mittrich dead, just to save three Kagi? How many bystanders slaughtered?

That, she could blame them for.

Sarienne's will focused, and her finger convulsed on the trigger.

Her frozen aim was imperfect, but it was good enough. The bolt slammed through the mage's shoulder, and the spell snapped.

Sarienne did not wait. Domérage's sudden chanting receded behind her as she vaulted out of the viewing box; her feet slammed into the platform, and she had just enough time to draw her sword before an owl fell from the sky and turned into a grey-haired man with silver skin and pale violet eyes.

Freed from the spell, her soldiers joined her just in time to hold back the rest of the arrived flock. They formed a ring around the bound prisoners and cut down the transformed Kagi as they tried to reach their kin.

The fight did not take long. The rescuers' plan had depended on the Elesteir forces staying frozen. The Kagi were not prepared for this resistance.

The white-haired young man Sarienne was battling spun and leapt off the platform, into the crowd. Sarienne was about to pursue when she realized the platform was clear of fighting Kagi; the only ones left were dead or tied down to be executed. She stared into the crowd, but the man was long gone; by now he probably looked Mittrich or Elesteir. There was no point in chasing him.

Her eyes went to the shattered wall, now mostly clear of smoke. At its base she could see charred, unmoving bodies. A lot of them.

Some things she could excuse. And some things she couldn't.

Sarienne looked at the three bound prisoners, and made her decision.

The crowd silenced slowly as she walked over to the leftmost of the Kagi, one of the two women. Pendrois, still in the viewing box, swore.

"Captain Chemand, what are you doing?"

She looked up at him, eyes cold. "Passing sentence. I have the right to amend the decision of the magistrates. I am exercising that right." She raised her sword over the woman's exposed neck. "By my authority as a captain in Her Imperial Majesty's Army, I sentence this woman to death by beheading." Her sword flashed down, and the woman's head fell to the ground some feet below. No one moved to touch it.

"Captain, I command you to stop."

"Your imperial mother did not delegate that authority to you, your Highness. You are an observer only. Thus I must continue as I see fit." Another verdict, another cut, another head.

"I will report this to my mother, and she will not be pleased!"

Sarienne shrugged. "I will make my defense to her." She lined up her sword with the last prisoner's neck. It was the green-eyed man. The leopard flickered again, deep in his gaze. She wondered if it was true, that the shape-changers had no human souls, and what happened to them after they died.

"By my authority as a captain in the Her Imperial Majesty's Army," she said for the third and final time, "I sentence this man to death by beheading."

"Such mercy," the man said, his tone and eyes unreadable.

"I'm making it clean," Sarienne replied, her voice pitched for only him to hear. "It's the best I can do."

Then she beheaded him as well.

Here Comes the Flood

Adam Roberts

I.

The President is on the TV, once again explaining why it is better to send terrorists than troops into Karzistan. The common room is half empty, and several people get up to leave when the President came on. Same old same old. Terrorists the *humane option*. Terrorists—*highly trained and expertly prepared—can defuse the situation—with a hundredth of the casualties of*—'What he needs to do,' says Joe, 'you ask me, is sit there and explain to folk that there's even a difference between terrorists and troops.'

'Come on, Joe,' says Rube. 'You're in the army.'

'I *work for* the army.'

'You are a terrorist.'

'I am a professional.'

'A professional terrorist.'

'I'm a computer programmer,' insists Joe. 'I *programme*.'

'Same difference,' says Rube, and he chugs his beer.

II

Don't listen to Rube. What does he know? This is what happened to Rube on a trip into *North Dakota*, of all places.

He took a car and drove down across the border. He was motoring across open territory that was gray and flat as porridge, and at first it seemed to be going OK. He got fifty km into North Dakota before the fear became too much for him, and he had to pull over. He was a-shaking and a-shaking, and his fingers were fat and clumsy on the lever that opened the car door, until finally he tumbled outside. Into the air, and he was trembling, and sweat was coming out of his skin. He stumbled, he nearly fell over, like a clown, like some slapstick version of running, lurching away from the car (why the *car*? what was it about the *car*?) and was a hundred yards from the freeway before he could stop himself. There he was, solitary and defenceless, all the welter and waste of the landscape around him filled with baleful possibility. Who-knows-what lurked in the emptiness of open spaces. He could barely co-ordinate his fingers to push the right buttons on his phone in the right order. There was no question of pulling down a wetware menu. That was where the problem was, for crying out loud.

'Joe? It's Rube, man, man.'

'I hear you Rube,' came Joseph's voice, made squeaky by the tiny speaker of the phone, scary little device. He could hear the terror in his voice straight away. 'Stay calm, though. It's subjective, you remember that? It's all subjective.'

'It's well and good you saying *subjective*, man,' Rube gabbled. 'It's real, it's a real thing, oh God. I can't go on, man. I've pulled over the side of the road. I'm shaking, man. I can barely hold the phone, man.' He's gabbling.

'What was the trigger? Concentrate, man.'

'I don't know, I don't know. The car maybe.'

It was a brand new car. He'd taken it from the pool that very morning. It was so new that shreds of plastic still clung like snakeskin-slough about the leather seats. It still had that new-car smell.

You know that smell.

Joseph's tinny voice was all incredulity. 'The *car*? How can it be the car?'

'I don't *know*!'

'OK, man, stay calm, man. Only I never heard of somebody afraid of their own car.'

'I don't know I don't know!' Rube was looking back at the car, enamelled and bright, already exploding with reflected winter sunlight. Why was the light so bright in winter? He turned, south, west, north. He turned again south. Blankness, and there was light, and nothing.

Joseph's voice was still buzzing in his ears. 'Where are you?'

'On the freeway. There's nothing about. Nothing, nobody, the landscape is flat. There's a bridge up ahead.'

'A bridge?'

'Some big pavement of concrete poured across some river.' He was looking over the flow of the river The river was gray as salt-water. The river was smooth, as if smoothed by a flat-iron, with only the slightest of trembling bulges at the concrete bridge-legs to show its flow. It was a wide river.

'You think it was the *bridge*, maybe?' Joseph was asking. 'Was that the trigger? Or water? How you feel about drowning, say?'

'I don't know,' said Rube, panting and gasping, more than a little.

'Man, your voice gone all cartoony,' Joe said, trying to put a laugh into it; but Rube's was a mood that was not to be lightened. Joe tried again. 'I know it's disorienting. Listen to me, focus on my voice. I'll come and get you. Maybe I could persuade the army guys to fly in, pick you up?'

Rube's voice became a squeal. 'Don't fly!' He was looking up at the sky now, looking into every corner. It was perfectly nude. There was not a single airplane to be seen anywhere. It was a sky that hadn't seen any planes in many months.

'I'll have to drive down, get you,' said Joe. 'I'll have to clear it with Paula. You realise that?' But this only panicked Rube more.

'Don't! Don't! You'll crash it! You'll go in the river! Don't tell Paula, she'll lock us both away, both away. Man, I can't even *drive* I can't even *drive* the car…' But now Rube was staring at the sun, and it was eating his eyesight. To him it was the navel of threat, it was the solar asshole, and it started to gape before his fizzling eyes: it began a process of swelling and opening, a mouth ready to gobble and to gobble, and he was about to be devoured. He was on the very verge of it. The yellow of cadmium. A sea-weed yellow. Phosphor.

'Rube?' Joe was shouting at the other end of the phone. 'Rube?'

But that was the last of it. There was a sound: maybe a gunshot, maybe a dog barking. The connection went.

III

Joe had to decide what to do. He could so easily have gotten in big trouble.

He pulled a ware-link out of the general mess of menus and connected to Paula. Paul-*aah*! the wags in the main processing room call her. That gaspy second syllable: that's male sexual rapaciousness, is what that is. It's a touch upon the object's unattainability. It's how men cope with the secret terror that beautiful women create in them; that crumby solace of tribal mockery and male ballyhoo. Huh! Paula, that's some body on her. Huh!

They are fooling nobody but themselves, the wags in the main processing room. And Joe isn't even one of them. He doesn't even get invited down the common room bar with them. He spends his days surfing the ware and talking to Rube about classic music, and doing his job.

Joe pulled up Paula's face in his head.

'What?' she asked. None too pleased.

'Hi, Paula, it's Joseph. *There's* a problem.'

'What?'

'Rube went south. I've lost him now.'

'Went south how?'

'In a car from pool.'

'A new car?'

'Yes a new car.'

She didn't sound so upset to have lost Rube. But the car was clearly a different matter. 'Those cars cost *money*, Joe,' she said, her brow folding on itself with crossness. 'I can't afford to go *throwing them away*. So, what happened? He *crashed* the car? Is that it? He got the terrors and crashed the car?'

'Parked it, I think. But he's … uh …'

'You'd better go after him. Does up double, take back-up, somebody good with terrors. Don't go alone.'

And this was exactly what Joe is afraid of.

'But maybe I should go by myself, ma'am,' he suggested. 'There's no point in risking a whole team. I'm confident I'll be able to handle the car. I've got the best capacity results of the, uh.' He was going to say *the best capacity results of the whole team for handling the terror*, which was true, but he was scared enough right now for the sentence simply to trail away.

Oh, sure, he was *scared.* Everything hinged on this moment. Paula didn't realise it, of course, but Joe was painfully aware of the two possible futures: and one was of him in military prison, and the other was of him and Rube getting away with it. For now, at any rate.

Paul stared at him. And the decision came down on the right side of the divide.

'You'd better dose up double,' said Paula, in a warning tone of voice. 'And get down there after him right away, OK?'

As if a double dose would make any difference!

'Thank you,' as he decided it was time for some hyper-politeness, 'ma'am. You won't regret this.'

'What was he doing down there anyway?'

The vehement thumping of Joe's heart. 'He was on a data run, ma'am.'

'Just go get him. We'll talk later.'

'Yes ma'am.'

And Lin was fair *scathing* at Rube getting stuck in the terror. 'What's the story here anyway?' she wanted to know, as Joe got ready to go out after his friend. 'Why can't we leave him there? How dare that little shit get himself lost in a terror! What about my day? I've got programmes to write. What about our co-time, on the Korean programme?'

'I know,' said Joe.

'Little shit—I say we just leave him there.'

'Stumbling around,' Joe had said, a little guiltily, since Rube was his friend, after all. 'Running all over the Dakota landscape with his arms in the air.'

'What was he doing down there anyway?'

'He was on a, uh, a data run.'

'Well go pick him up. If you get into difficulties, Joe, you can believe me *I'll* be *furious.*'

'I'll be back this afternoon.'

The thing that Joe particularly remembers about that rescue trip was his coat. He picked his coat off his peg but when he tried it on it was too small. It was Rube's coat. Rube must have picked up Joe's when he went down to the car pool. *Such* an idiot. I mean, it's one thing for Rube to pull on *Joe's* spacious Buzz Ricksons MA-1: but how was Joe supposed to fit his ample torso into this tight little garment? He wasn't even sure what kind of coat it is. There wasn't even a label on it. It was, like, *a generic coat.* He rummaged some more. There was a pile of undone laundry under the spare desk. There was an old sweater, none of the cleanest, but it had to do. And then he had to hurry, padding up the corridor and Joe jabbing his finger at the lift-call: like he's *stabbing* that little button, pow, pow-pow. Kung Fu. It doesn't make the lift come any sooner.

In the car all the way down across the border and into the US Joe was fine. Then the fear bit into him, but he was OK. He found Rube hiding under the bridge, and he controlled his own terror, and he was able to drive on, and recover what Rube had been trying to recover and eventually he got his friend back to the base.

Rube was the object of a great deal of ridicule after that. People were angry that his escapade had disrupted the running of the base for pretty much that whole day, and pretty much the next day too.

By the Thursday of that very week the terror in Dakota dried up; the whole terror just sank and melted away. 'So what was it?'

'It's some militia,' said Joe. 'The Dakota Freedom-men, I heard.'

'Or the Dakota Minutemen, or the Dakota Independents, or the Dakota shitting Confederates,' growled Lin. 'It's always something like that. Who do these guys think they are? Don't they realise they're messing with my work day? How am I going to get all my stuff done?' She seemed to have shifted her rage from Rube onto the Dakota rebel militia. 'Why do the army bother with terror? Answer me that.'

'Uh, why, uh, why do they bother?'

'If I were in command I'd send in real bombers. Never mind terrorising them, I'd kill them. I'd wipe them out. We got plenty of bombers. Fleets of bombers, send in firebombs and wipe the wasteland clean. *Swarms* of bombers, we got.'

That was Lin's considered opinion. There were plenty of Americans who agreed with her. And the President went calmly on, explaining to the camera's eye and through it the whole country, how much much better it was to terrorise—not only more humanitarian, but more effective, more *militarily* effective. And so on.

Joe can see his own face semi-reflected in the glass of the TV screen, superimposed on the face of the President. The face of the enemy, he thinks. He actually thinks that.

IV

'Kill a soldier,' the President is saying, as Rube and Joe are sitting in the common room watching him, 'and you make permanent enemies out of his friends, his family; out of his sons and daughters; you pass the hatred down the generations. But terrorise him, however ...'

'And you got to spend a bling's fortune keeping him all locked up,' somebody says, loudly, at the back of the room. There is scattered laughter.

'Idiot,' says Rube. It's not clear whether Rube means the heckler, or the President.

'The President,' Lin is saying, in a tone of voice that already contains within it her contempt for that high official, lurking in his bunker somewhere in New Hampshire. 'The President ... the *present* president ... the present *incumbent* ...' Away in the corner somebody is singing, softly, slowly:

O the roast beef of old Texas
And O for old Texas' roast beef.

V.

Joe asks if Rube want-ee go to grab-ee snack-ee. A peck of late lunch. Beer has made Joe hungry. You are always hungry. Church bells clanging at three in the afternoon. Not actual bells, synthetic TV bells, sounding brass, gonging cymbals. The president is no longer on the screen. *You're always hungry, man.* Rube is being genial when he says this, but Joe feels it. It stings him, and he doesn't show it. The larger corpus needs a little more by way of sustenance. The more ample frame, there's no need to get personal. 'You coming?' he asks. 'Not me,' says Rube. 'I'm happy here.' On screen snow is falling on empty benches, like dust from tumbling masonry. The church on the screen is sheet-white, violent white, is pure white. It is old-style TV church, white painted wood slats all the way up the tapering bell-tower.

Joe goes off down the corridors by himself.

White is the color of nothing.

The institute café is empty except for Campbell and Goldsworth, sitting together at a table. It's not lunchtime, and it's not suppertime, and only people who work odd hours like Campbell and Goldsworth come in to pull food from the machines at a time like this. Odd people like them, and Joe.

Through the windows is a fine view of the winter Canadian landscape: snowdrift-free for the moment; a bristle of distant fir on the horizon, shaggy as green bear-pelt. A horizon of foam-colored mountains, gray-brown-cream on their flanks, and lifting their Ku Klux Klan hoods of white towards the blue. A very blue sky; winter blue; with only a bundle of gray and white clouds piled over to the west, threatening to roll in over everything. The clouds lie about the sky like piles of wet white towels, ready for the ringer.

Joe gets a pastry from the dispenser and a fruit-mash in a bottle, and goes and sits next to Campbell and Goldsworthy. Goldsmith? He can't remember. And anyway, they barely nod at him; and as he tries to pry the foil top from his fruitmash they carry right on with their conversation. It's a parent conversation, Joe realises quickly. It's a conversation from which he is by nature excluded.

'Those pills you take at school,' Goldsworthy is saying. 'They're not, like, *seeds*.'

'Seeds!' said Campbell, with enormous dismissive emphasis.

'You know the way sometimes people talk ...'

'I hear you,' said Campbell, in a sorrowful voice. The stupidity of the world.

Campbell and Goldsworthy work security. Since the camp was moved north by the military, and real-live soldiers placed on the perimeter, they've had little enough to do. But they're still in work; still wandering the corridors with their flashlights. Going through the motions.

Goldsworthy is getting a little worked up. 'They're *raw material.* I say this to my son. He don't want to swallow the pills, and I say: its *only calcium* and some metals, and a primer. It's not like the wetware is, like, *threaded* into your brain. You know? Wires and stuff—not like that. It's *grown.* Everybody knows that. Your own body grows it. It's practically a natural thing.'

'Your son's at ...?'

'Meadowvale High. Yours?'

'My wife sent both of ours to a private school in Washington.'

'DC?'

'State. It's a Hubbardian school. We get special religious dispensation. We get State help with the fees.'

'They cool with the wetware?'

'You kidding? They're more than usually insistent. *More* than usually insistent. They think it's a *step* on the road to the rapturous singularity, or something.'

'I said to my boy, look: you want to flunk school? You want still to be in school in ten years time? Or you want to graduate *now?* Wetware just means having the internet in your *head,* I tell him. He likes playing around on the screen-computer at home well enough.'

'What he say?'

'Oh, he's all, but *the terror,* Dad. He says, without the wetware Dad I'd be immune to the terror. I got mad with him, I did. Does he really want to be some hicksman, some backwood pig-farmer without 'ware? Eating roadkill? Or he wants a big city job? Don't he want a half a million a year?'

Neither of these men catch Joe's eye. It does not occur to them to include him in the conversation. Joe starts sensing what his teen-therapist used to call *ants,* ants itching inside his brain. Ants in this context means *automatic negative thoughts.* This is what Joe finds himself thinking, bad habit-wise: they dislike me for my weight. For my nerdosity. My technical rank, which technically outranks them. My knowledge of programming. My ethnic heritage. He thinks: I have no place here.

Joe gets up from the table, and carries his fruitmash with him. He doesn't even bother with the rest of his pastry.

VI

Joe goes back to his office and pulls down the news. Things in New York are stable, according to that crumple-faced guy, the news-guy. What's he called? A camera, slightly wobbly, pans across streets empty of people, save for one or two twitchy souls, muffled up and hurried and none of them looking into the eye of the TV. Some of them are running, ungainly. A car has been driven into the central reservation and abandoned, its grill buckled. The camera pans up. No planes in that sky.

Haley. That's the name of the guy.

He flicks through a series of New York State servers and TV stations. Some are blank. Some are showing nothing but re-runs, old episodes of *Bilko* and *Friends* and *Go On Treat Yourself*. The Bilkos have all been colorized.

And here is the datastick from the morning's work.

And here is emptiness.

And here is a mug with some cold coffee in it. Joes prefers cold to the hot, in many ways. On the other hand, as everybody knows, caffeine makes fear more intense, more tart. He angles the mug and the brown-black disk in it shudders and tilts. Black is the color of *everything*.

Paula pops out a ware-menu in his head. She has the priority access of a boss. There's no need for her to knock. 'Joseph, come up to mine,' she says. Her face is too perfect to be beautiful. Joe is sure of that. Beauty needs some flaw to complete itself; just as courage needs some fear. This seems profound to him. He's pleased to have thought of this. 'Yes ma'am,' he says. But even with the dose of anti-terrific he's already taken, he can feel the tingle of fear in his tummy. His tummity-tum. He's out, he's history—this is it. Dishonourably discharged and the rest of his life in a *military prison*. He can *feel* it.

Joseph, come up to mine.

He leaves his workstation, and goes up to hers. He makes his way through the complex, up to the seventh floor, and waits outside Paula's office. When the door finally pings and he steps through he's surprised to see that she's not alone.

'Joe, sit,' says Paula, from behind her desk. 'Joe, sit-down. Meet McPherson. He's a three star.'

And Joe has no idea what's going on. 'A three star?'

'I swear to *God*,' Paula says, sharply, 'you are the dopiest idiot that works for me, Joe. I swear it. A three star *general*.'

'Sit yourself down, there, son,' says General McPherson.

The general is sitting straight up in his chair like a fairground target: stiff spine, wide shoulders, is a military man. Central casting could hardly have provided a better player for Three Star General: scrubbed and pink-faced with white hair combed back over a broad skull, white eyebrows like toothbrush-bristles one on each side of a fat, pear-shaped nose. His eyes are tiny and do not seem to blink. The cloth of his uniform is thick and green, as heavy as felt, and it is folded over and buckled and buttoned and adorned with those little strips of rainbow color that military men wear. He is every inch the general.

It's the terror of the ocean. The terror of night, and all the *sublime* bag-

and-baggage. Sublimity. Who can even answer the question *why are you so afraid?* It's the *so*. It's that modifier. What are you scared of? Death, you say? But death would be a *release* from all this fear, come *on*. Fearlessness and death are the same thing. So: a dose of an anti-terrific only an hour or so earlier and you're still feeling butterflies in your stomach because you're sitting in front of a senior military officer. Something's amiss. It was never more truly said, death is stronger than life, and stronger than hope, and stronger than time. Death is stronger than exhaustion, and stronger than desire. But fear is stronger than death, evidently.

Joe sits down. He is blinking more than he needs to.

'Good afternoon,' he says, and his voice is quavery. This man could be coming to escort him to prison. But why send a three star general for that?

'I know all about where you've been based, son' says the General. He has been served a cup of coffee. Joe can see it, at the General's right elbow, on Paula's desk. 'That's one of my things, to keep my eye on my people. I followed that story of you going down, picking up your friend. The terrors gut him, but they didn't gut you.' Joe actually hears this *got* as *gut*. His mind stumbles on the thought of Rube being eviscerated. The General's coffee is sitting, untested, on the desk beside him. Threads of steam as fine as dental floss float up from it. 'I know all about you, son,' he is saying. 'I'm in *charge* of what you been working on.'

'Of course,' says Joseph. He thinks to add, 'sir.'

'We're sending you on an active service mission, son.'

Joe can't think of anything to say to this. The only thing that even occurs to him to say hey! I was just watching the president on TV talk about sending men into Karzistan, and now I'm discovering that I'm one of the men. The sneering face of Joe's inner Clint Eastwood mouths the words *you going to die*.

'You look kind of stunned there, boy,' said the General.

He is a three star general.

'I'm sorry sir,' says Joe. 'This is, it's a shock, that's all. I have never been on a mission, sir. Not active service, I mean, sir. I've never been behind enemy lines, sir.' *I mean, look at my fat ass.* He has the presence of mind not to say this last bit.

'I'll not be sending you in alone,' says the General, with the thinnest of smiles, a regular anorexic-style smile.

'I'm sorry sir, this is just sinking in. Me sir?'

'You sir,' drawls the three-star.

Joe thinks of saying, can't you see how many extra pounds I be carrying on my unhealthy body? But he doesn't say this. 'I have *been* on missions before,' as if he needs to clarify. 'When I said I hadn't been on any missions, back then, I meant actual missions—physical insertions. But I've been on...'

'I know how many missions you been on.'

Paula is looking off to one side.

'Is that the kind of thing you mean, sir?' Joe asked. 'Because of course, sir, I'll be honoured to hack into ...'

'Won't work. Remote access isn't viable. Systems are too well insulated now. *You* know that, boy. Karzistan, it borders China, Tibet, Khazikstan. They got exactly seven lines going in. That's actual *pipes*—their wireless is very patchy, *vai-airy* patchy. Mountains, I'm told. At first the Karzi government pled poverty for not uplinking satellites to patch over this, but it's pretty apparent now that it was a security measure. So their whole network, hardware and wetware, depends upon a bunch of *material* connections coming in the country. Seven pipes taking in all the data for the citizenry, and all seven are too well shadowed to let you sit in your office—here—and hack their wetware with some terror—like you did—to Timor.'

'The General was telling me how impressed he was by your work on the Timor mission,' Paula puts in.

'Thank you,' says Joe stupidly.

'We got to put you on-site, inside. This is a twenty-man team, and we'll fly you in. Of course, we won't be able to fly you out.'

They won't be able to fly them out because, if Joe does his job properly, any given pilot will be too terrified to operate a plane safely.

'So how do I get out?' asks Joe. His stomach is crawling. Ants under his scalp. Hunger pangs and fear pangs have the same feel, you ever notice that? And now they're roiling and moiling in his great belly.

'We'll shepherd you out on the ground. Your whole team will take roads out. You know why you're the right man for this? Because you went down into Dakota and rescued your pal when there was that ... incident.'

Rube, curse him, damn him. Joe's only friend, too; and now he's set him up for—

'Some people,' says the General, 'well, well, they function *better* under terror than others. Some people go to pieces. Some people barely scrape by. Others get on with what they gotta get on and do.' He smiled again, the thinnest blade of a smile made of too tough a metal to be bent into a curve. 'That's you, son. That's clear.'

Joe blinks. 'I'm—' he says. Then he says, 'General, I'm scared.'

'But of course you're scared!' booms the General. 'That's what I'm *saying*! People who live life on an even keel, from happy morning to happy evening, them people, when *they* get scared it's overwhelming. But people who are scared all the time, like you my son. Like you my boy. People who are always scared, they get used to it. They adapt. Oh, develop ways of functioning under the rubric of fear.'

'Yes sir.' Flying into the middle of mid-Asia. He could get killed. He'd be there *in person*, huddling around some system's node in some shack somewhere, with half a dozen special ops men in their black suits and their alienizing Darth Vader masks and their guns positioned about him. But he could get shot. This is not pulling three day two night sessions in his own station and pressing buttons to send the data parcels off on his behalf through. This is putting his body in the way of possible harm. Ample body.

Joe's face is motionless, but of course there's no art to find the mind's terrified construction in the face.

Where are the entry points into the ware? How are they sustaining it? Joe knows.

'Are you a religious person, son?' the General is asking.

'Religious?' And for a moment Joe has no idea what the question means. 'Religious? You mean, like, praying God?'

'I mean like the *fear* of God. You know what it means to be Godfearing?'

'General,' says Paula. 'Perhaps we should outline for Joe the prep.'

'Your boy has not answered my question,' says the General.

'I don't,' says Joe, flustered. 'I don't know.'

'We think of fear as an emotion,' says the General. 'It's not that.'

'Not an emotion,' says Joe.

'When the war on terror was just bombs, *they* had the upper hand. Do you know why? Because they were *living*, day-to-day, more *afraid* than we were. We were complacent, and comfortable, and we slept easy in our beds. *They* huddled in caves and listened for the scrape of warplanes against the sky and for death to come screaming down on them. They lived all their days like that. They got used to it. That's the natural state.'

'Not an emotion?' Joe repeats. 'I don't see, General, how ...'

'We think of our fear as an emotion but it's not,' says the General. 'It's a *whole* lot *more* primal than *that*. You really think of your terror finding outlets through the usual emotional vents, sonny? Do you really imagine you *weep tears* of terror? That you *laugh* with terror? That you love with *terror?* No, no. The currency of terror is not tears.'

But Joe can imagine, precisely, huddling himself up foetal-like in the corner and crying and crying. This is precisely how his terror presents to him. He shakes his head.

'I'll tell you the mistake you're making,' says the General. 'Those lesser emotions, those alarmeds or anxiouses or worrieds, sure, they can vent themselves in crying, maybe. They might have access to that kind of catharsis. But *terror*—that's something else. That's as far removed from those tears as is imaginable. A child cries mommy mommy because it's indulging itself and feeling sorry for itself; but you take a crying child and *terrify* it and those tears will dry up. That's terror—because terror is not self-indulgent. It's nothing to do with the self. Is the encounter with the other. Everything else is indulgence, but catching a glimpe of the other: that's stark. This is why the terrorist is always some stranger, because that's in the very *nature* of terror.' The General finally picks up his coffee and takes a sip. There is no more steam coming from the surface of his drink. It's cooler now.

He seems to be thinking. Then he speaks again. 'Fear. Maybe fear is an emotion,' as if this metaphysical question of definition is peculiarly interesting to him. 'But terror—terror—terror, that's something else. That's far enough from emotional as to become almost an anti-emotion. It's not feeling, it's the cremation of feeling. We say *in love*. We say *she laughing in sheer delight*. We say *he turned his face away in grief*. But we are never in terror. Terror, on the contrary, that's *in us*.'

There is a silence. Paula had gone very quiet, unusually for her. She seemed to have gone off into some fugue state.

'You an *atheist*, sonny?' the General asks Joe, in a loud voice.

Normally Joseph might have said, 'sure, yeah.' But right now, he's too scared to think. He literally can't think through the implications of that question. 'I don't know,' he says. His heels are bouncing hurried on the floor in front of him. He could not be more uneasy in his chair than he is. Fidgets. He is starting to sweat. Paula is motionless like a statue. Maybe she's afraid too. 'I don't know.'

The General nods at this answer, as if it pleases him. 'There aren't many atheist soldiers,' he says, as if passing the time of day. 'It don't sit well with the uniform. Holy terror, that's the route to the health of the soul. Dr Stourwater here has your mission briefing. She has a datastick with all the material about the Karzi network, and you'll get a week to pull your attack together. I'm putting the entire resources of this base at *your* disposal, sonny.'

'Thank you,' says Joe, with a dry mouth.

'You put your attack in order, and we'll meet again in a week. The team will swing by and high-fly you to our Indian base.' Randomly, Joe thinks of Roy Rogers, and redskin warriors, but even as he thinks that he knows its inappropriate. Consciousness stewed in TV, that's always been his problem. But he—flat—can't go to the middle of mid-Asia and run about with a rifle. He'll get a phosphorbullet in his ample gut. He'll get captured by the people he's been sent to terrorise and they'll torture him in prolonged and agonizing ways. He wishes he never signed the army chit. He could have taken a civilian job.

'Yes sir,' he says.

Paula seems to be trembling very slightly. 'The General has made it very clear that this is highest secrecy, uh, highest security, top secret. The resources of the base are at your disposal, as he says, but you'll come through me. I'll inform people as and when they need to know. The fewer people who know—and so on. You know the drill.'

'This terror will make us strong,' says the General, as if reading a scrap of paper from a fortune cookie. 'This terror is a glorious thing. You know what I call a soldier without fear? A dead man. My soldiers all got the fear; that's what makes them strong. I'll tell you something else. When mankind had a hundred gods, or a million, our terror happened only within bearable limits. But when we humans gave up the many gods for the one God, we opened ourselves to the one absolute terror. You'll be doing good work, soldier. Important work.'

The General is on his feet. Joe stands. Paula stands. They salute, and the General is gone, and all he says as he leaves is 'you have your orders'.

Paula and Joe are alone in Paula's office.

'Joe,' says Paula. 'Sit down again. Just for a moment.' And Joe does.

VII

Paula makes him sign some documents, and password-tag some ware files. That was the official secrets act, the national reimbursement waiver, the acceptance of medical attention in the event of, all the various stuff. Then she gives him the datastick, with the mission parameters on it. 'You'll want to work hard on that I know,' she said. 'But make sure you get some sleep as well. One week from now you'll be in the field.'

Over my dead body, Joe thinks. But what he says is, 'yes ma'am.'

'All I say is you'll need your strength.'

There's a silence between them for the space of one minute.

'Joe,' says Paula. 'I'm sure this was a shock.'

'This was a shock,' he agrees.

'You'll get a medal.' She smiles. This is her idea of a joke. Joe already got a medal, a gold-colored block, for his work on the Timor mission. But then she says: 'I know it's a startling thing. But it's a great honor. It really is.'

'Serving my country,' says Joe. He's not being sarcastic, though you might think he is. It would be closer to the truth to say he is speaking absent-mindedly.

'People have gotten cynical about it I know,' says Paula. 'But it really is a better way of making war.'

'A better way of making war,' Joe repeats, nodding.

'The alternative—and believe me, the Pentagon is planning this as a contingency—would be fleets of bombers, missiles. You can go in, and you'll hijack a population's mind with terror and the country will grind to a halt whilst ninety percent cower in their cellars. But if you don't go the missiles *will* go in and we'd be looking at casualties in the tens of thousands. That's deaths. That's actual deaths, you know.' Joe wonders why she is so insistent on this point. It may be the case that her own imaginative connection with death is so tenuous that she needs to reinforce it with rhetoric of this sort, by way of convincing herself of the potential horror of it. Look, mommy! Corpses! Joe doesn't need that sort of rhetorical trick. 'These people would die, instead of spending half a year quivering in fear.

In a year's time, when they're back up and their country is functioning, and they're all over their episode ...'

'... apart from the odd nightmare ...' Joe puts in absently.

But this displeases Paula. She dislikes being interrupted. 'The flashbacks can be medically controlled,' she says, in a stern voice. 'But they'll be alive, that's the point. That's what you're giving them. You're giving them their lives. You are saving their lives.'

'*Most* of their lives.'

'Phh,' dismissive, 'some crazies run about screaming and maybe shoot a few people. Some folk react that way to being terrified. But the overwhelming majority will cower and hide. And the casualties will be much much lower than they otherwise would be.'

'I know ma'am,' says Joe; and then, conscious of the implication of intimacy inherent in the fact that she's speaking to him at all in this manner, he says 'I know Paula. Thank you.'

'Report to me,' she says, getting to her feet, 'when you've got an initial sense of the data on that stick. We'll plan out your week together.'

Joe gets to his feet, and looks hard at her face. It is such a beautiful face. It is literally, and without exaggeration, frightening that her face is as beautiful as it is; frightening that any face could be so beautiful. It is a sad thought that he won't see it again. The fear is crawling in his stomach. 'I will,' he says.

VIII

Joe goes down to the dispensary and takes a second dose of anti-terrific in as many hours. He tells a lie to the dose-man. He says that Paula has ordered this. The base network confirms his new status. 'Go right ahead,' says the dose-man.

Joe settles in a chair. Some people take their dose on the run, hurrying on, like a sandwich-in-hand as you rush to your next meeting. But Joe likes to sit, to take his time. The whole point, he tells himself, is *calm*. It's all about *calm*.

The dose goes in. He closes his eyes.

The apples of summer are bouncing heavy on the boughs of endless apple orchards, and it's a strong breeze that moves those boughs, waverly, the *vrai* pulses of life itself, Mexican-waving all along the road as Jo floats past. And it's a weighty series of pendula that swing on the branches. And it's green, and pink-green, and bright yellow. Above it all is the sky; it's summer-blue, as azure as a beautiful woman's eyes.

Taxis are jammed in a long line going over the Brooklyn bridge, all yellow bodies and red brake-lights, like the livery of a New England Fall.

There is birdsong. There's a hushing noise, smoke, or perhaps steam rising from fresh coffee.

White light.

The buzzer sounds.

He makes his way through, and waits at the link for the inner door to open.

As he stands he contemplates Paula's words. The terror really is a better way of waging war, of course that's true. True. Better to scare people than kill them. But somebody else can scare them. It's not for him. There's a hissing noise, momentarily, it lasts for less than a second.

The link opens.

'Rube,' says Joe, waking up to his station. 'I got to have a word with you.'

Rube looks up at him. You can see the beer inside Rube's head, in his eyes, his lunchtime drinking. 'I just got settled here,' he complains, pointing at the fire-up visuals on his workstation's screen.

'Now,' says Joe.

Sighing, Rube gets up and follows Joe out of the main processing room. He says something snappish as the two of them wait for the link to open, but the anti-terrific in Joe's bloodstream means that the words float past him.

Outside they hurry along a corridor. They pass Goldsworthy, the security guy, strolling along in the other direction. They wait until he is out of earshot.

'What's going on, Joe?'

'I'm going,' says Joe. 'You hear me? I'm going now.'

It takes no time at all for this to sink into Rube's consciousness. That might be the beer. But he's perky. 'No kidding? You're not kidding. When—tonight?'

'Now. You want to come with me?'

'*Right* now?'

'You want to come with me?'

Rube scratches his face. 'I don't know, Joe. I just don't think … you know what happened in Dakota. I just don't think I'll be able to function. Once you—you know.'

'Man that's just the *breakout*. That's all that is. I'll get you away, and you'll be fine.' A heartbeat. 'I need you, man.'

'Well this is all very brokeback mountain,' says Rube, not displeased. 'Just so as you understand what we're talking about. Once you set it off here in the base I tell you I'm going to be dead weight. You'll have to shepherd me from the building, and away. I'll be a weeping dead-weight.'

'I'll get you away,' says Joe.

'You might have to drag me, literally.'

'Rube, I could put you over my shoulder and walk away and not feel it.'

'Just so as you know. And then what. A life on the run?'

'We got leverage,' says Joe. 'We got the strong position from which to bargain. Everything is networked. Everything is networked.' He says this almost reverently, as a great truth. 'That's the truth of the modern age. It'll take very little to convince the government of that. You and me, we have the programming expertise to take out *city blocks,* that's how accurate we can be. Terrorise *individual buildings,* once we fine-tune our approaches. We'll be able to stop the whole North American continent, or else maybe just the White House bunker. Or maybe the whole of New York. Or maybe just a dozen TV studios. We can squirrel terror into any target because it's all networked.' This is what he'd wanted to tell Paula when she was giving him her girl-guide speech about how terror was morally superior to war. True, he could have said; but—but—but it puts certain people, people *like me,* in unusually powerful positions. One hacker with a virus can disrupt world banking. One governmental terrorist programmer, like him, could put the terror into the whole wetware networked population. And they wanted to send him into the line of fire?

He thinks not.

'Take a dose of anti-terrific,' says Joe.

'I'm not due a dose until tomorrow,' says Rube,

'It don't matter. I've been given priority. I've got authority. Then we'll get our shit together, and set a terror alarm-call. A ten minute countdown and we'll be in a car waiting driving off as the security start howling and wanting their mommies and trying to hide under the tables.'

'Let's do it,' says Rube. 'It was going to be someday soon, so it might as well be now. Let's do it. What pushed your button, man? You're on fire now. What persuaded you that now was the time?'

'Paula called me into her office. There was a three star general waiting for me.'

The blood drains from Rube's face. 'Man, no,' he says. 'Tell me, not that.' He is grasping Joe's shoulder. This is the thing about fear; it can come clattering into a person's mind from nowhere. You can be as blithe as a baby and then, suddenly, you're thinking *they know about Dakota, they've come to arrest us both,* and your mind is racing: *that's why Joe is pushing to go right now—that's why he wants to get away right now—it's not us slipping away into the wide blue yonder, it's us being chased by military police, that's a whole other game.*

'Will you relax?' says Joe. 'It wasn't that. They still think the Dakota incident was the Dakota Minutemen or whoever. It doesn't occur to them—they're still thinking in conventional military terms, you know? We flattened an entire state. To them that *could only* involve five divisions, and blanket bombardment. They can't educate their hearts about the fact that it could be two guys sitting in a room in front of a computer. They still haven't thought through what wetware actually means.'

'That inset point, that machine,' says Rube, for, like, the hundredth time. 'That's got our DNA all over it'. The machine in question is in some equipment shed or other on base. 'They could check its download log, and dust it for our fingerprints, and put two and two together, and ...'

'They'd do that if it were still in situ. But why should they pick it out of all the other junk in one of this base's sheds? And as long as it's on base why does it matter that it's got our DNA on it?' But Joe stops; because they've had this conversation many times before. Because it doesn't matter anymore; they're out of here—in half an hour they'll be on the open road. And most of all because Joe knows that it's not the machine that is exercising Rube's anxiety. That's not why he keeps going on about it. It's a simpler thing, something much more intimately connected to fear. It's shame.

'I'm sorry,' says Rube, in a small voice, shortly. 'I really thought I could pick it up. But I just—flipped out. I was barely fifty klims into Dakota and I could not even drive a car.'

'It's OK,' says Joe. He could add: though it meant that we came within a sliver of being caught right then. We could both be sitting in a National Correctional Facility, right now. That would have been the end. But there's no point in saying that. They got away with it. And they proved to themselves that they could hack the wetware network with a targeted attack.

'The General didn't come to talk to me about Dakota,' he says, in as reassuring a voice as he can manage. 'And he didn't so much as mention your name. He wants me to go into central Asia. You believe that? He's so impressed by my ability to function in a terror zone that he's sending me on a live-fire mission.'

Rube stares at his friend, and then he starts to laugh. 'Oh he don't know you very well,' he says.

'Let's go, man. Now. To my workstation, to set the timer. Then away, into a car and, *here comes the flood*.'

And Rube says, 'Amen to that.'

He's not wrong, is Joe, when he says here comes the flood. Whether he and his friend get away, find a safe-place, whether they manage to blackmail the State administration into striking a deal for their safety and financial security—and whether the State administration honours any such deal—all that is frankly irrelevant to our purposes here. Because the thing is this: what they are about to demonstrate to the world, once everybody is networked up, then one single individual with enough skill to pull the right thread in that network can declare war on the world. The old world, where only somebody in charge of an army could declare war, is about to pass away. The age of the pure terrorist begins. And the good news is that this way of waging war is very much better than the traditional ways. Because you don't kill so many people: *not nearly* so many people. Hey, Joe!

Count Me In.
Kathryn Allen

London's always been like my second home. From the first time my parents brought me to a rally in Trafalgar Square. I know her alleys and side streets, her walkways and tunnels, her buried rivers and even some of her sewer system. But with a hundred routes to choose from, I walked openly across Westminster Bridge because I wanted to stop by Parliament Square.

On a plinth the size of a hearse, plonked down in the middle of the manicured green – as if walking on the grass is a deterrent to anyone wanting to get closer – stands a statue of John Irving and a representative group of Revellers. He's poised to charge forward, his arms raised and hands cuffed. Behind him a half-dozen faceless 'soldiers', artfully posed to reveal belts or waistcoats of explosives, gaze determinedly into martyrdom.

When I was a kid they'd banned peaceful protest within a whole kilometre of this Square, but they couldn't ban the bombers. Now they're glorified in brass and stone, and life goes on.

The layered ironies make it art.

I've never visited the monument before. It's different. Holograms let you stand on the plinth and stare Irving in the eye, but they can't give a sense of scale. And they don't include the middle-aged man sprawled on the grass, shirt open, trying for skin cancer. Or the two thirty-something women sat on a bench, spooning the latest enriched fruit flavour dieters' germ-culture from reusable cartons. Or the toddler screaming 'no' while he's strapped into his seat and then just screaming as 'mummy' walks away, with the automated pushchair following a lot further back than at her heels.

Some people shouldn't be allowed to have kids. John was right about that, too.

He'd have loved his statue. It's those three inches taller that he always wanted to be, for one thing. And without the wedge heeled eco-goth sandals.

I turn a couple of times while I'm walking away, like I'll catch him waving if I steal another look. But eventually I put the past behind me and start up Whitehall. Heading to Trafalgar Square the obvious way.

When I was five or six, and in London for yet another rally, there was trouble with the police. John Irving dived into the swirling crush of demonstrators under attack, carried me away from Nelson's Column, and declared my parents unfit. From then on I lived with him. I imagine I was reported missing and, eventually, assumed to be dead. I've never felt the need to check those details.

There's a small knot of protestors walking a little ahead of me. They must have come out of Westminster tube station, off the Circle Line from

King's Cross. Should have changed onto the Bakerloo or Northern at Embankment and gone to Charing Cross, but visitors don't always check the scale on those tourist maps.

I speed up, join them, ask if I'm headed the right way for the rally and, no matter we can already hear the crowd's responses to a warm-up speaker, a girl called Stella appoints herself my guide and protector.

All seven of them are from Liverpool: Stella, two lads, and two couples. They make excellent camouflage. One of the couples has been down to London before – they're not clear about which and I don't particularly want to know – but it isn't the guy with the baby carrier strapped to his chest or he'd have avoided the long walk up Whitehall. He's breathing hard and sweating before we reach Great Scotland Yard.

Today's rally isn't a cause likely to be overburdened with representatives from London and the Home Counties. Not many locals, but it'll be big. Perfect.

Before the end of the Noughties, John Irving got tired of peaceful protest. It didn't work often enough. Neither did single cause terrorism. That just gave government an excuse to monitor and reduce the effectiveness of any demonstrations and lobby groups which did. John figured that between preventative detention and intrusive control orders the authorities would gradually weed out from the gene pool the few people with a social conscience who weren't voluntarily removing themselves.

A majority of the population were vegetables. They didn't care. They didn't want to care. Homo sapiens' behavioural instincts were rapidly evolving from the social to the solitary. First the extended family had died, and then the nuclear one, and eventually it would be every man for himself. Not anarchy, but a very governable form of dysfunctionalism.

The Revellers were John's way of saving humanity from itself, by forcing homo sapiens to stay a social animal. That, and he wanted to win.

I saw a couple of unmarked police vans tucked down Craig's Court, but none of my newfound friends did, they were too busy taking in the obvious sights to check out side roads. The vans weren't exactly hidden, intended to be visible although they pretended to lurk menacingly. The hope was they'd deter troublemakers, hoaxers, and faint-hearted Reveller copycats.

Society had been too successful in protecting itself. Homo sapiens didn't have any predators except other human beings and, in the Western world, governments continually reduced the level of violent death their populations were exposed to.

Only people didn't fear death less because it was rarer – they feared it more.

Without predators, human beings had no reason to band together, to watch each other's backs because there might be a lion hidden in the long grass, or a leopard up a tree.

And fear of death helped subdue lingering altruistic impulses. Why step in to stop a woman being raped, or an old man being murdered? There'd be no reciprocation as a pay-off for the risk.

'The only thing we have to fear is fear itself,' John told me, the day he worked out what was wrong. Then he designed the eternal revolution.

He created new predators, to instil a genuine and ever-present threat that would touch everybody, irrespective of class or wealth or race or religion or age. Revellers would appear at rallies, at concerts, at supermarkets, at corner shops, in high streets, and suburban schools. And kill indiscriminately.

John theorised that people would learn to live with death. Would fear it less, because it was ever present.

Life would go on. And each of those lives would be more precious.

Trafalgar Square was filling slowly. By the time we reached the end of Whitehall and crossed the road, my friendly Liverpudlians were part of a crowd numbering dozens, moving to join one numbering in the thousands.

The first speaker had given way to music blaring from a sound system rigged for boosting the spoken word. I saw him though, recognised him, and wondered if he'd managed to persuade any of the early arrivals his cause was just. Mike Martin's wife had been killed in one of the first Reveller bombings. Ever since they'd created the monument in Parliament Square, Mike Martin had been campaigning to have it removed. He'd have spent less time in jail if he'd used a kilo of plastique to do the job himself.

Governments fell because they couldn't protect people from the Revellers. For decades they'd been bragging about how many terrorist plots had failed, how many lives had been saved, and demanding greater powers as a reward. John showed everyone how empty the promise of protection was.

A man, or woman, would walk into a crowded concert hall, or cinema, or public meeting, or their workplace, and play the first verse of the Lennon and McCartney song 'Revolution 1' – the version where a man dead for decades sings 'count me in' instead of 'out' – through whatever tinny little speakers the Reveller could conceal about their person while wearing enough explosives to kill and maim anyone within fifty metres. The song was a countdown. A warning. A message. The Reveller would trigger the bomb on the second 'alright'.

The crowd around me started shuffling closer together, new arrivals joining at the outside edges and putting pressure on the centre, forcing a reduction in personal space. I made idle conversation with my group. Chatted briefly to a man dressed as a pigeon. Cooed at the baby. Waited for the organisers to turn off the music. For the crowd to settle. The rally to start.

In part it was the music gave the Revellers their name. And more than a couple were seen to be dancing in the last minutes of their lives, recorded on surviving police video footage.

It didn't take long before crowds would panic the moment they recognised the first lines of the song. There were copycats and hoaxers: John welcomed them. They might not know what cause they were serving, or how, but they served it nonetheless. Garage bands recorded new versions and even pop stars got in on the act, some with supposedly anti-Reveller sentiments. It was all good publicity. Soon no one could escape the song, or forget they were at hazard.

And the Government, admitting defeat, started making noises about negotiating.

Beside me, Stella was asking if I liked children. Confiding that she was pregnant and the baby due in September. She didn't mind if it was a boy or a girl so long as it was healthy and grew up happy. I smiled, and nodded, and offered her my best wishes for the kid.

The music faded, Father Jaimison crossed the platform to the central microphone and tapped it a couple of times. I could see the sound engineer wince.

"Are we here to save the world?" he said quietly. We murmured 'Yes' politely. "I can't hear you. Are we hear to save the world?" He'd raised his voice, and so did we. The third repeat was bellowed.

The secret service and police weren't as keen to surrender to terrorism, they believed in the myths. But governments regularly bargain with terrorists. When they're not, themselves, terrorists.

I turned traitor shortly after the authorities made their opening approaches. My story was simple and true – I was a stolen child, a victim of brainwashing who'd been groomed to commit suicide – and I convinced the security services of my sincerity. They were more than happy to mount a raid, to snatch victory from defeat, if I was willing to play Judas.

And they also paid well.

It was unfortunate that they got John out of the safe house in handcuffs, despite all we'd done to manipulate a summary execution. But John always had a back-up plan, and Simon was military trained as a sniper. I'm not sure if, even now, more than a few of the police officers involved don't believe it was one of their own killed John Irving. I hope it's a comfort to them, and some compensation for blighted careers.

Revolutions die when their leaders are given power. John wanted to make sure ours kept turning and evolved. To do that he had to become a martyr.

There was a fresh wave of violence and hoaxes. The antisocial helping in their own marginalization. The public screamed for action, and the Government apologised to us. They built the monument, they enacted legislation, they reached out to the disenfranchised and the socially excluded, in the hope that they could bind people together and remove any reason or support for violent protest.

Up on the platform, Father Jaimison introduced the first speaker. I missed hearing her name. She was one of those witnesses to injustice ready to tell her story to a crowd of thousands of strangers.

I reached beneath my jacket, fumbled with the connection between my personal music carrier and the speakers Kevin said would deafen me for the rest of my life. We don't hang the bombs around our bodies any more. There are enough smart people supporting us, and funding us, that these days we're equipped to carry far more powerful explosives the way drug mules once smuggled other controlled substances, and trigger them with a wireless remote.

Stella turned as I started the music, her eyes widening. Paul clutched at the baby, and his lips moved in a mantra of desperate entreaties I couldn't hear.

Further back people screamed and tried to run.

Maybe one day they'll turn on us and hit and kick and smother us with their own bodies, so that even if we do trigger the detonation they minimise the damage to others. Perhaps in fifty years, or a hundred. Or maybe that'll never happen, and the Revellers will keep turning the handle on the never-ending revolution. Predators culling the herd, teaching the rest the value of their lives and of every individual. We've the will, and the way.

I wanted the circularity of being here, in Trafalgar Square, at a rally, to commemorate where John and I first met. The Beatles count me down, count me in, and at the press of a button there's fire in my belly.

The last thing I see are faces. Made anonymous by terror, blanched and blank and empty, like the Revellers on the monument. And I see, in that last white-and-red moment, that we're all equally servants and martyrs to his cause.

I smile. For the first time since John Irving died.

The Last Straw

Hal Duncan

Report of Agent Jack Flash

I land on the red tarmac of George Square, roll, and come up on one knee, arms out for balance, with a natty Kung-Fu flourish of greatcoat, as my skybike spins on through a flap frenzy of scattering pigeons, clips the stone pillar of the Cenotaph, and crashes through the front doors of the City Chambers, blowing wood and glass and blackshirt guards out in a fireball glowing green and brilliant blue with all the super-saturated orgone-vapours of a Triumph V2's fully jizzed-up ray-tanks. Bollocks, I think. I really liked that bike. But, fuck, thing is, I had a little itchy trigger-finger issue with the missile I was meant to use just as I passed over Pitt Street Police HQ and left myself without too many options. Sometimes you have to make a sacrifice, I know, but it's still hard. I really liked that bike.

I flick the roach of my Afghan Black away, and stand to scope my circle of not-so-admirers. Fucking pipers.

After twenty feet or so of space cleared in awe of my lithe and limber landing, most of the square is filled with tourists, but I've landed smack-dab in the middle of the Big Show's backstage, so to speak. The inner circle of my own personal mosh-pit is lined by several hundred pipers, drummers and assorted instrumentalists from all corners of the Empire – but all of them white as Widdemore, of course – dolled-up in every colour of kilt and tunic, toppered with busbies, pith helmets and turban-like towers adorned with peacock feathers, ostrich plumes or sundry silliness. It's Albion's soldier sons come home for the Umpteenth Annual International "How Fucking Loud And Annoying Can These Bastard Bagpipes Drone?" Competition, and I can feel my hardcore hackles a-rising. The bagpipes are a weapon of war, baby; Christ, I never understood why the spooks of Guantanamo use Death Metal for torture when sixteen seconds of the 14th Royal Highland Falangists would have me naming every pet pooch in my family history as an Al Quaeda top dog.

So I'm glad I've already got my Curzon-Youngblood Mark I chi-pistol in my hand, because if any of these biscuit-tin kaffer-killers so much as lets a breath out in the direction of a chanter he's getting a discharge of the most dishonourable kind, I tell you. I click the juice on full to let them know that I mean business. No mistaking that salty-ozone scent-and-tingle of orgone energy that fills the air. Sex pistols, honeybuns. Can't beat them.

– Easy, tigers, I say. You know how fast I am. As fast as you can say-

— Jack Flash! shouts the brightest spark among them, and I spin, brighten him a tad more with a chi-blast in his sporran. First prize, beefcake. Ding-a-ling, ding-a-ling. And your next question, for the cuddly toy, is: how the fuck do I get out of this?

No answer. Shit.

I can see over the heads of fleeing tourists that militiamen are pouring in from the side-streets round George Square. The thopters that nearly brought me down over the M8 are now flitting like bats overhead. And it's only the mob of bandsmen that are blocking the blackshirts from a clear shot at Imperial Albion's Public Enemy Number Nothing, Jack Flash, terror of the tartan traitors, scourge of the Scottish fucking Fascists.

The pipers are gearing up for a charge, I can tell, idiot grunts ready to fall for King and Country if it helps bring down a swaggering faggot anarcho-terrorist who's wreaked royal havoc, I'm proud to say, in the Second City of the Empire today. *Today of all days,* I can see them thinking as they twitch, inching forward at the corner of my eye. *This is our day. This is our* big *day.*

This is Empire Day.

They lunge for me, but instead of trying to take them all I backflip, spring-heeled jackboots firing me high over the head of the first to reach me and up onto the shoulders of the one behind. I don't stop there, kangaroo-kicking myself back up but forward this time and into the thick of them, leaping, loping from shoulder to shoulder, piston heels punching me up through the air and them down to the ground behind. I hurdle, somersault and twist this way and that through the gunfire of the militia, headed for the still-smoking rubble of the once-grand entrance to the City Chambers, but with all the directness of a drunken flea.

With the bastard pipers getting mown down by their blackshirt brethren I could play this game all day, but I've got a job to do and the Fox will yap if I don't do it right, so I snatch a glinting gold baton from a bandleader as I crunch him underfoot, give it a twirl just to annoy them all the more as I set my sights on the goal. Problem is, of course, by now the doors are a kill-zone of cross-fire from inside and out. They know where I'm headed, who I'm headed for — a special visitor for a special day, here to award the winning band with shiny silver trophies and shit. But they don't have a fucking clue what Jumpin Jack is capable of. I make a high jump, tuck and roll, come down, coiled like a cat for one surprise spring, hit the ground and —

— hear that imaginary applause as —

I land on the stone balustrade of the balcony, crouched and grinning like a gargoyle at the Foreign Secretary who stands there gawping out at me through the French windows. The Provost is ranting wildly at four

Special Support men about – well, I can't hear his words but I'm guessing that I've pissed on his parade. I raise my Curzon-Youngblood in a mirror image of this other Jack's rising hand, slowly, surely, until we're both pointing at each other, his finger trembling, my gun-barrel accusation steelcast-steady, chi extending in a straight line from my shoulder to the centre of his forehead.

I give him a second to feel the fear.

Let me drop-kick you an update on the dream-state of the nation. We got ID cards and internment, fucking Special Support forces with their lightning bolt insignias. The thought police I'm fighting are in your head, snuggle-bunnies, and it's time you all woke up to that. The conspiracy is society and every one of you is a fucking sleeper agent of your own worst enemy, the status quo. Scary thought? Scary worldview? As Nietzsche said, all great things must first wear masks of terror in order to engrave themselves upon the hearts of men. You know, I always loved Freddy's one-liners; man would've made a great stand-up. God is dead, boom boom. That kills me every time – *and* makes me stronger too, but then I have a hardy constitution. Others are not so lucky.

The Foreign Secretary, the Jack Straw that broke this camel's back, points at me in silence for an exquisitely eternal second, then his mouth is opening, he's mouthing his horror, and the Provost and the SS men are turning... so I blow him a kiss. And then I blow his fucking brains out.

That one's for Puck, motherfucker.

Charge Sheet for the Arrest of Tamuz Masingiri

Strathclyde Militia
CHARGE SHEET

Defendant's Copy

Division: X
Station Charged: Partick Police Station
Date of Arrest: 24 April 2006
Full name: Tamuz Alhazred Masingiri
Born: 1 April 1984 in Tell-el-Kharnain, Palestine
Sex: MALE
Religion: Pagan

CHARGE(S)
You are charged with the following offence(s). You do not have to say any-

thing, but it may harm your defence if you do not mention now something which you later rely on in court. Anything you do say may be given in evidence.

1 F1900405 – refusal to produce ID card on request.

On 24/04/2006, in Kentigern in the Lanarkshire Region of Caledonia refused repeated requests to produce identification card, contrary to Section 28, Clause-22 of the Sedition and Security Act (1984)

Reply: I told him I didn't have it with me. It's in my flat.

Time charged: 16:46
Date charged: 24/04/2006

Report of Agent Guy Fox

The subway station at Calvingrove is busy with commuters and militia at this early hour. The latter in their black shirts and their day-glo yellow flak jackets form a gauntlet of security, standing in pairs up at the turnstiles, at the bottom of the escalator, and at various points along the platform, checking IDs and scrutinising faces. I hand my chipped card over at the bottom of the steps, wait as it's scanned, then take it back with a polite smile and a tip of my bowler, then stroll out onto the platform just in time for the arriving train. This close to the Rookery – that square mile of ghetto fortress at the heart of Kentigern's West End – it's no wonder that security is tight, the Rookery a haven to the dregs and debris of society, the type one really doesn't want travelling too far beyond their own thieves' den. Sadly, these blackshirt goons are mostly trained to look for punks or razor mods, common-or-garden crims up to the more banal forms of "no good". They're really not equipped to deal with a master soulsmith like myself, moving in an identity forged from the skinsuit to the credit history. I've been Thieves Guild from the age of four and those thirty years have stood me well in my life of subterfuge and subversion. Even the smartpaper nerve-gas pack I'm carrying under my arm is indistinguishable from the newssheet folded round it by any but the highest range of scanners. The wonders of this modern era: so many gadgets offer so many ways to hide a bomb.

I get off the underground at St Enoch's, leaving the newssheet and its contents on the seat, no more conspicuous than the half a dozen *Suns* and *Metros* lying scattered around the compartment.

A short detour through City Central Terminus takes me past a post-box where I despatch the latest batch of anthrax-loaded envelopes addressed to various stars of sports or screens who've publicly endorsed the Blair regime. Craven apologists for fascism every one of them, one can only hope they're shallow enough to open their own fan mail. Outside the front entrance of the wireline station, I climb into a black hack and give the driver a destination that's half-way to the Rookery, doubling back on my tracks; it never hurts to throw a little randomness into one's movements.

I text in a quick bomb threat as the taxi heads up Woodlands Road – using recognised keywords so the authorities will know to take it seriously – then ask the cabby to pull over at a garage for a second. I buy a softpack of Gitanes and pay with a forged twenty, tapping out a memorized number on the phone and sizing-up the chap behind me in the queue while I wait for my change: a normal-looking fellow in a business suit and cashmere overcoat; it seems a shame to land this on him but needs must when the devil rides. I hit *send* on the phone and fumble it towards my pocket with a fistful of coins and notes, clumsily bumping into cashmere man as I turn.

– Sorry, I say. All fingers and thumbs today.

He mumbles his own apology and steps past me up to the counter, no idea that the phone now sitting in his pocket is not his own, or that in five minutes time he's going to be standing in a circle of heavily armed militiamen all shouting at him to *get down on the ground NOW*. Poor soul.

Another hack back to City Central Terminus, a quick change of suit in the public toilets (switching the black I'm wearing for the pinstripe in my briefcase, the bowler for a fedora), then an airtrain over to the South Side, a third taxi, and I'm walking up to the reception desk at the main entrance of Southern General Hospital, handing over an Imperial passport in the name of Dr Reinhardt Starn. This is a long-term sleeper self I've been working on for five years now: a German defector, based in the American Dominions, showing up at conferences around the UK, publishing papers in the journals, corresponding with learned colleagues based in Albion, and awfully eager to at last meet, in the flesh, my fellow expert in the field of biological defence, Dr Shipman... who just happens to be giving the Health Secretary, Jack Straw, a tour of his bleeding-edge research facility on this very day that I just happen to be in town.

– I've told him all about your work, he'd said. He'd love to meet you.

– Well, you know, I'd love that too, Harry, I'd said.

I take directions and a clip-on visitor's pass from the receptionist and, chatting casually with my blackshirt escort, stroll along the corridor to the staff lift, swipe my pass through the electronic lock and, inside, hit the button for Sub-Level 5.

– So with these nanites in his system, says Shipman, a serviceman in Iraq, say, will be able to deal with any of the viral agents or neurotoxins we're currently using on the field. No more incidents like the Basra Barracks fiasco. I understand your people are working on something similar, Reinhardt?

I nod. It's true, actually; my people *are* working on nanotech personal defence systems; it's just that my "people" are not actually refugees from the Futurist Reich working for the Pentagon, but rather Arturo Guevara and his team, down in the Republic of Venezuela, trying to come up with something that might help the New International Brigades in their struggle for freedom. It's a pity the Starn identity gets all the glory, really, because Arturo's work is quite brilliant.

The Foreign Secretary stands gazing through glass into a quarantine room where cleansuited doctors are injecting all manner of microscopic horrors into a test subject.

– And when will it be ready? he asks.

Not soon enough for you, I think. Arturo's bitmites, coded to his stolen DNA pattern and transferred with a casual handshake on our meeting, should already be starting to work their wicked ways, replicating through his system, eating Mr Straw from the inside out. In about six hours time he should look like an Ebola X victim, bleeding from every orifice.

Puck wouldn't have approved, I know. He'd much rather have had the bitmites rewire Straw's pleasure centre with an irresistible scatophilia that would have him eating his own shit, time-coded to kick in with maximum compulsion at some public dinner with the Governor Generals of every Dominion and Protectorate in the Empire. That's what Puck would have wanted.

But Puck isn't here.

Interview with Tamuz Masingiri

DCG: Interview commences 17:04. Present in the room are DC Powell and myself; Cameron Mackie, solicitor; and Tamuz... Masingiri. Right then, Tamuz Masingiri. So why wouldn't you show me your ID card? It *is* Masingiri, isn't it? The fingerprints aren't going to tell us that your real name's Mohammed or Moussaoui or something, are they?

TM: No. That's –

DCG: Because you know we can check these things, don't you? You're not in the desert now, Tamuz. This is civilisation, son. We do have computers, you know?

TM: I'm not your son. And, yes, that's my name. I'm not lying to you.

DCG: Alright, alright. No need to get stroppy, son. I just want to know that you're who you say you are. Cause if you're not, you'd be better to tell us now, than have us find out from the records.

TM: This is stupid. Why would I lie about who I am?

DCG: I was just asking the question, Tamuz. This is just routine. Just for the record, can you confirm that you are Tamuz Masingiri.

TM: Yes. I am Tamuz Masingiri. For fuck's sake -

CM: DC Griffin, do you have an actual question?

DCG: All I want to know is why you wouldn't show me your ID card, Tamuz? You haven't answered that yet.

TM: I told you. I didn't have it with me. I just –

DCG: And why didn't you have it with you?

TM: I forgot it.

DCG: You are aware of the law, aren't you? You know you have to carry it? Someone like you, I'd've thought you'd know that.

TM: What do you mean *someone like me?*

DCG: Just answer the question, please. You *do* know you're legally bound to produce your ID card if requested by a police officer? But, you don't think the law applies to you? Is that it?

TM: No.

DCG: You don't carry your card for political reasons –

TM: No.

DCG: – because you object to them?

TM: No.

DCG: You don't think you should have to carry an ID card just because the government says so? That's it, isn't it, Tamuz?

TM: I told you. I just forgot it.

DCG: Where are you from, son? Palestine, right?

TM: What? Look, I've stayed in Scotland since I was four years old. I stay in Glasgow.

DCG: Scotland? Glasgow?

CM: Hold on. I'd like to talk to my client in private for a second, DC Griffin.

DCG: This is *Caledonia,* son. This is *Kentigern.* You've been hanging around with the wrong sort of people if you're calling it *Glasgow?*

TM: Sorry?

DCG: Are you a rook, Tamuz?

TM: What? What are you talking about?

DCG: You were picked up on the edge of the Rookery. Is that where you live, Tamuz?

TM: I stay in the Halls of Residence on Southpark Avenue. What's the Rookery.

DCG: Oh, pull the other one.

CM: DC Griffin, I need to talk to my client in private now. Please, stop the tape.

TM: Just check with the university and they'll tell you. Take me to my room and I can show you the bloody card.

CM: DC Griffin.

DCG: OK, OK. Interview suspended 17:07.

Report of Agent Joey Narcosis

Joey clicks the radiovision camera into the tripod stand, flips out the view screen and swivels the fitting with the lever, angles it down to centre the hostages in the frame. They're all crying. They all know that one of them is going to die.

Jack and the Fox don't have the emotional detachment for killing innocents up close and callous. Sure, Jack takes out the odd passenger-laden wireliner now and then, but its usually in the heat of battle with a horde of thopters on his tail and militiamen trying to blast his skybike from the air. And, sure, Guy has his schemes of strikes on subways and other such public places, sex-bombs blasting orgone energy through City Central Terminus, prime-time commuters losing their senses to their lust in instant orgies that leave them puking and naked, horrified at the De Sadean excesses perpetrated by their unleashed subconscious; but most of his lethal plans are either carried out at a distances or targeted at the top dogs, the knights and bishops of the Empire rather than the unwitting pawns. When it comes down to it both Jack and Fox need to think their victims deserve what they get, even if it's just for their complicity in the system. Joey Narcosis has no such sensitivities. His actions selected in accordance with the calculus of survival, Joey's so deep-chilled that he even files his reports in third person.

– You can kill Straw, he'd said, but they'll just pull another one out of the vat, burn the meme-pattern into his brain, and bingo-bongo, we've got a new Home Secretary just the same as the last one.

They'd been sitting in Club Soda, two weeks after Fast Puck's disappearance, the evening that the word came back to them about a Tamuz Masingiri being picked up on the edge of the Rookery by the blackshirts in a routine streetsweeping operation. The boy should have had more sense as far as Joey is concerned, should have been pristine clean and with his skinsuit airtight to the dotted i's on the paperwork, but then the fascists might have just been looking for an ethnic to fit-up on a drug-bust – easy way to boost the arrest figures for a slow week. Still, Puck knows when to duck and dodge, should have slipped through the sweep like water through a sieve.

Idiot kid got himself lifted though, and now Jack wants action.

— So I'll kill the fucking next one too, Jack had said. And the one after that. We just keep fucking killing the bastard until there's no more of him left.

— It won't bring him back, Guy had said.

— But it'll send a fucking message, a fucking chi-beam text right in the fucking ajna eye.

— Assassination is just a post-it note, mate, Joey had said. They'll look at it for half a second before they bin it. Christ, who gives a fuck about these muppets anymore? There's always another one to replace the last.

— Unless, Guy had said, we take them all out.

Joey looks at the five hostages huddled on the floor, all dressed in their Guantanamo Bling, as they call it on the street — orange jumpsuits and full body-shackles — wrists locked to the steel belt at the waist, ankles cuffed with a few inches of chain for shuffling. The black hoods are off their heads for now; Joey removed them so he could look into their eyes, figure out which one will give the best performance for the camera, the most frightened. It'll go out live over the aether and, routed through Don Coyote's pirate station in the sky, Radio Birdman, the signal should jack every radiovision set in Kentigern. So he wants it to be good, does Joey, in so far as you can say that Joey Narcosis wants anything.

He scans the line of identikit Straws, looking for the most snivelly and snot-nosed. Frankly they're all much of a muchness. Vat-grown, créche-raised, they're not meant to have individuality; their job is just to eat and shit and sleep until the day comes when they're called upon to do their duty for King and Country, Edward and Albion. That blank idiocy should make for more impact in the footage, right enough, the terror on the face heightened by incomprehension. With the speed of growth, the clones don't get to a mental age of more than five in the time it takes their bodies to mature, so Kentigern is going to be watching a retard beg for his life, for his Nursey, for the safety of the Institution. Add to that the fact that the Straws were snatched en route from the créche to the acceleration tanks to slumber through their breakneck adolescence, and what you have is a retarded *child* begging for his life.

It should make for a good show.

One of the Straws has a wet patch at his crotch, Joey notices; the little bastard must have pissed himself. Well, the fascists do like their Nietzsche and their natural selection, so it seems only fitting to play the game by their rules, show them what will-to-power and might-is-right really mean. He grabs the kid by the shoulders and drags him forward and into centre-frame. The image on the viewscreen is clear and, with a zoom out just a smidgeon wider, the black flag with the white Circle-A, nailed to the concrete wall of the basement, should be visible enough. He checks that the balaclava is tucked tight into the collar of his shirt, straightens his tie and flicks a speck of dust off the shoulder of his black suit jacket. He picks up his katana from the top of the cardboard box in the far corner of the room and walks back to the camera, hits record.

– You getting this OK, he says. Sight and sound?

The laptop sitting open on the box beside the tripod gives a beep, and Joey crouches down, clicks to open the window with Coyote's response. *Loud and clear.* He takes his position behind the Straw and waits for the second beep. There's no need to read it; it means *On The Air.*

He sweeps the sword out of its sheath in an elegant arc that curls round and up and to a stop, to a pause, a stillness among the screams and sobs of the Straws, before he slices the blade down through the neck of the mewling cretin child on its knees in front of him, this symbol of servility.

Perfect timing for the Six O'Clock News.

Interview with Tamuz Masingiri

DCG: Interview recommences 18:00. Present in the room are DC Powell, myself, and Tamuz Masingiri. Right, Tamuz. Mr Mackie tells me you've been spinning him a right wee dreamworld. He thinks you're in need of psychiatric help, but myself and DC Powell here, see, we think there's more to you than you're letting on, my lad.

TM: Where's my solicitor?

DCG: It's gone past that now, lad.

TM: What do you mean? What is this? Is this some fucking TV prank show? Did Jack put you up to this? It's a set-up, right?

DCG: Don't try and play games with us, boy. The schizo routine won't wash. We're no daft, son. We've seen it all before. Wee rook gets caught flying home to his nest, thinks – you know – just flap your wings hard enough, act like a mental case, and we'll call in the shrink instead of Special Support. What was it, Tamuz?

TM: Come on, this isn't funny any more.

DCG: Your prints aren't in the database, Tamuz. You know that? So you're either a ferry-rat with no business being in this country or you have some contacts in the identity trade and a dirty past you wanted cleaned. Either way you're in deep shit, boy. Suspicion of sedition. For the record, Mr Masingiri is shaking his head. Come on, Tamuz. What were you up to when we picked you up? Grazing wallets? Casing houses for the Guild? Drug run? Data courier? Nah. You're old enough to have graduated from the kiddywork long ago. You're into something deep, boy. That's what this loony tunes routine is all about, isn't it?

TM: You're the ones who're fucking loonies. This is all –

DCG: Are you a good Muslim, Tamuz? Pray five times a day? Fast for Ramadan?

TM: I'm not a Muslim. What's that got –

DCG: You don't expect us to believe that.

TM: What? Just because I've got darker skin than you I must be a Muslim? Man, this is sick. This isn't fucking funny –

DCG: Sit down.

TM: Let go of me.

DCG: Sit down. I said, sit down!

TM: Ah!

DCG: You sit down when I tell you to, lad. Now. You have two choices: you can ditch the act and tell me who you really are and what you were up to; or I walk down to Special Support right now and tell them I've got a suspected subversive in the interview room. If I were you, I know which option I'd prefer.

TM: This is all wrong. I don't belong here. This isn't –

DCG: Too fucking right you don't belong here, Ali Baba. You belong in the desert with all your suicide bomber chums. Or maybe it's the Rookery you belong. Come on.

TM: *Ah!* Hey, you can't – *fuck!*

DCG: What are you, Tamuz? A political or a religious? What are you mixed up in?

TM: I'm not answering any more questions. This is fucked up. This is fucked. You're crazy. Where's my fucking solicitor? I know my rights.

DCG: You don't have any fucking rights, son. You don't exist. Suspicion of sedition, Tamuz. That's what it is now, and that means you're up shit creek. Now, I'm giving you a chance, son. You can talk to me or you can talk to Special Support. Your call.

TM: This is bullshit. This is fucking bullshit. Let me out of here.

DCG: You're making a big mistake, son.

TM: Let me out of here. I'm – *ah!* Jesus fucking – *uh!*

DCG: Interview terminated 18:03.

TM: Let me go. Let me go. Let me –

Report of Agent Jack Flash

Crouched on the flat gantry on the roof of the wireliner, the thrum of the Cavor-Reich engines all round, I click at my Zippo again and again, trying to spark it into flame to light my hash cheroot. It's just too damn breezy up here, the ray-tanks of the monster machine sweeping up to each side of me forming a perfect wind-tunnel, billowing my greatcoat peachily but thwarting my best efforts at full cool. Bastards. In the Society of the

Spectacle, style is the psychic weapon of choice, and this is like having your voice crack on you at Rourke's Drift with the Zulus bearing down: men of Harlech, hack cough splutter; sorry, mate, frog in the throat. Can we take it from the top?

Unlit joint dangling from my lips, I clunk my way forward along the gantry, muttering dark curses and radiating Bad Vibes, man, as I slap the Semtex packs left and right, flick the detonators on. Twelve charges, six for each side, is overkill, I know — twice what we planned — but if there's no stone for Jack today, well, a boy's gotta get his buzz some way.

At the front of the wireliner, my wings are waiting where I left them, clamped down with magnetic grapnels. Light as paper, stronger than steel, ray-tanks in the harness to counteract my body-weight, the twelve-foot in span synthe pinions lift with the wind beneath them, fighting to take off on their own. The modified waldoes are one of my favourite toys and I slip in under them, latch the harness shut under my arms and around the waist, shove my hands into the gauntlets, like a knight of yore putting on his armour. Up ahead I can see the junction of the wire, already jacked to take the wireliner off course and south-east, towards Ibrox and the football stadium where the torchlight procession should just be arriving. Thirty years ago that stadium's where the Jews and Asians of the South Side, the Catholics of the East End and the academics and bohemians of the West End were all gathered for the Purification; there's no record of how many had their souls stripped down, their bodies stolen to the service of the Empire, but if Straw had been from Kentigern — it's kind of ironic that this is where they would have brought him to die the first time. Now I can see it off in the distance, getting closer fast, a golden glow from the massed ranks on the pitch lighting up the night. I'd swear I can hear the roar of the crowd, the rhythmic chant, the Seig heils, the God Save the King.

As the wireliner lurches left on its new course, aimed directly at the stadium, I flex the wings and release the clamps, lift up into the air. In the gondola bridge below they'll be pulling levers now, spinning wheels, trying to radio the signalman with a frantic *what-the-fuck*, but the inertial dampeners, the wirebrakes, the retro-jets and the radio — all of that shit is already taken care of.

I spiral up to a safe height on an updraft, hold my position in the air like an eagle scoping the treetops for its prey. I figure distance, height and momentum, hold for the perfect moment before I hit the detonation button.

The *Heidelberg* goes boom.

A few hundred tons of metal and fireball heads down in a parabolic curve, hitting the near end of Ibrox Stadium fast and hard, taking out a solid quarter of the terraces and raining a shrapnel meteor storm on another half. Baby, I can definitely hear the crowd roar now. I flick the wings back, aim myself at the far end of the stadium, at the Director's Box where the Culture Secretary, Jack Straw should be standing behind bullet-proof glass, trying to register the carnage below, the flame and the smoke, the rows and columns of blackshirts on the pitch all broken into pretty chaos, the celebrants on what's left of the terraces piling over each other in panic, the landslides of flesh, living and dead. High up on a scrap of terrace, through the billows of smoke, I spot a lone figure with a camcorder held up to his eye, a vulture in Babel

I hope Coyote's picking up my own broadcast. He fucking well should be; my senses are acid-acute right now, so this report, this vision of devastation, should be beaming out white-hot over the astral airwaves, a psychic EMP in the aethernet of Kentigern's dreams. Radiovision, no matter what Joey thinks, is so Twentieth Century. Old news. This is the Kali Yuga, mate; in a war for hearts and minds, the subconscious is the battle ground. You can switch off the news but you can't switch off a nightmare.

I blast through a billow of hot black smoke a-crackle with orgone blue-green sparks and come out with the Director's Box dead ahead, tuck my wings in tight, a human harpoon aimed at the heart of the Great White Empire. There's no glass made by man can stop this bullet, motherfucker.

Shards spray into the room around me as the window shatters. Wings jerked back, nearly ripped off in the impact, I whiplash forward but manage to pull off the landing neat and square, down on my knees in a jitterbug slide that takes me right to the shiny shoes of the last Straw, the Culture Secretary, minister of bread and circuses for the masses. I rise to my feet, hands out of the waldo-gauntlets now, Curzon-Youngblood in the right, a Scorpio .99 in the left, flicking my arms out in a crucifix of armament, firing left and right, to take down the bodyguards at the corners of my vision without once losing eye-contact with Straw. I holster the guns and take the jack-knife from its sheath at my waist.

He knows we got his vatlings. He knows this angel with shredded wings means not just death but extermination. He knows he's not a human being here, just a poison pen letter to the Blunketts and the Blairs and the thousand other motherfucking muppets waiting to take his place. And we're going to make it nice and personal, signed...

Yours truly,

Jack

Death Certificate of Tamuz Masingiri

Certified Copy of An Entry
Pursuant to the Births and Deaths Registration Act 1953
#
DEATHEntry no: 2313

Registration district: Greater Kentigern
Sub-district: Kentigern West
Administrative area: Lanarkshire

1. Date and place of death:
    Twenty-fifth April 2006
    Partick Police Station Kentigern
2. Name and surname:
    Tamuz MASINGIRI
3. Sex:
    Male
4. Maiden surname of woman who has married:
    N/A
5. Date and place of birth:
    First April 1984, Tell-el-Kharnain, Palestine
6. Occupation and usual address:
    Unemployed
    No fixed abode

7(a). Name and surname of informant:
    Nicholas Griffin (D.C.)
(b) Qualification:
    In Loco
(c) Usual address:
    c/o Partick Police Station, Dumbarton Road, Kentigern

8. Cause of death:
    Asphyxiation
    Certified by J. Tyndall M.B.
9. I certify that the particulars given by me above are true to the best of my knowledge and belief
    D.C. Nick Griffin Signature of informant
10. Date of registration:
    Twenty-fifth April 2006
11. Signature of registrar:
    Derek Beackon

Certified to be a true copy of an entry in a registrar in my custody

The Debt of the Innocent

Rachel Swirsky

On October 11, 2035, Jamie Wrede, R.N., was the sole employee staffing the Neonatal Intensive Care Unit at Temperance United in Martinsville's Pine Ridge district. During the course of her career, she'd been asked to kill nine newborns. That morning, she planned to kill four more.

At 6:45 a.m., Jamie woke and began preparing breakfast for her eighteen month old daughter, Claire. At 7:34, she picked up a "crank call" and listened for three minutes until a series of clicks on the other end indicated that The Brotherhood of Man's part in the operation was going smoothly. "I don't have time for this," Jamie said before hanging up, the signal that her end was proceeding likewise.

At 8:10, Jamie rode her bike to work. She carried Claire in a bike trailer attached to her rear wheel for the first quarter mile to the babysitter's. When Jamie went to leave, Claire screamed and stretched toward her. This was a new trick, learned in the past few weeks. Jamie felt helpless before those tiny red palms, those hysterically waving fingers.

"Don't despair, Claire bear," she said. "We're a pair whether I'm here or there. I swear."

Sometimes the rhyme made Claire giggle long enough for Jamie to slip away. That morning, Claire kept screaming. Jamie left anyway, a pair of tears tumbling down her own cheeks. She swiped them away, ."It's for the good of babies everywhere, and that helps Claire too," she muttered to herself, a variation on the refrain she'd mouthed daily since making her decision to help The Brotherhood.

When Jamie got to work, her friend Panda, an L.N. in Obstetrics, called out from the nurse's station. "Here's the paperwork you wanted on the Feliciano mother," she said, handing Jamie a stuffed file folder. "Did you hear they got the girders done on our nuclear plant? Here's hoping there aren't any more delays. I can't wait to get back to squandering electricity on all the computer hours we can stuff into the day."

"Yeah, me too," said Jamie. She squinted at the paperwork. The hospital couldn't afford electric lights in the corridors. Overcast gray filtered through the skylights, casting a dim gloss on the tile. It was barely enough to read by. "Well, thanks," she said, trying to brush past.

Panda held out a hand. "There's going to be a memorial service this afternoon for the recently displaced," she said. "I just got word, figured you might not know either. Damn internal mail system's still designed like it's on e-mail. You had a displaced baby this month, didn't you?"

"Two."

"Ouch." Panda winced. "I remember the second one. Little blonde baby with crazy parents? Looked kinda like Claire?"

Renée Mercer. Born with a premature shock of white-blonde hair. Almost never stopped crying during her short, painful life. "That's right."

"Do you want to take flowers? Rudolpho's working the morning shift at Posies and Petals today, he can get lilies cheap."

"I won't be going."

Panda frowned. "You never miss a memorial for one of yours. Are you feeling okay?"

"I'm fine. I'm just busy. I have to pick up Claire."

"You take it too personally, Jamie. That girl probably would have died anyway."

A dark-haired man pushed between them, an orderly Jamie hadn't yet gotten to know. He tapped Panda on the shoulder. "Excuse me—"

"Can't you see I'm talking to someone?" asked Panda.

Jamie escaped down the hallway.

She checked her watch. 9:17. She had thirteen minutes to get to the Neonatal Intensive Care Unit and prepare before The Brotherhood of Man initiated their part of the plan.

Andrea Cabral, daughter of Meredith and Brian Cabral. 14 days old. Suffers from perinatal asphyxia due to drop in maternal blood pressure.

The first time Meredith realized she was pregnant – deep in her bones realized it – wasn't when she used the swab test three days after, nor a week after that when a gynecologist confirmed implantation. Nor was it on the bus on the way home, jolting over potholes with one hand under the belt of her waif-waist jeans as she watched a blonde her age fuss over a newborn. Meredith tried to picture the newborn in her arms. What would it be like to coo at a little face that recognized you? An infant who knew you so well it forgot where your body ended and its began?

Experts declared this miracle would happen, *was* happening inside her. To Meredith, it felt inconceivable. When the baby was born, she (by week ten, the echo-cam told them to expect a girl) would see through Meredith, in that uncanny way of children and pets. She'd know Meredith was only pretending to be an adult, how she'd missed paying the credit bill last month because she lost it in a pile of fashion catalogs, how only three months ago she'd been considering quitting her job and buying a one-way ticket to the Great Barrier Reef.

By month five, Meredith worried she'd never get over the feeling she was watching the pregnancy happen to someone else. Every time the baby kicked, Meredith jumped, having forgotten there was something inside her that could kick. Sometimes she found herself heading for the bathroom, and realized she'd been subconsciously getting up to take an antacid, trying to soothe the baby away like a bad meal or a touch of stomach flu.

Meredith's family – both father and husband – was well-off, even though these days that meant taking buses and rationing electricity like everyone else. Seeing so much poverty made Meredith grateful that she could afford the six months off work and still squander electricity on a hot shower when she really needed one, even if it meant an outrageous bill. Money made everything so easy. But it couldn't help with this.

The moment Meredith realized she was pregnant finally came in her sixth month. Shopping at the supermarket, she found herself pulling down a box of green dye. *My little girl will like this*, she thought, *My little girl will definitely be the kind of girl who likes green*. She stopped in the middle of the aisle and thought *How do I know that?* In Meredith's belly, the unborn Andrea shifted, like she was dancing or maybe shouting: *Come on, Mom, of course I like green! Buy it already!*

Meredith became aware of a traffic jam behind her cart. She tossed the dye into the basket.

That night, Meredith decided to lavish electricity on an extra load of laundry. She threw the baby clothes she'd been given into the machine and dyed them all the same searing wattage of four-leaf-clover green.

Brian thought his wife was going crazy when she lifted out the retro zebra print pants which had come out looking like some bizarre kind of lizard skin. Meredith collapsed laughing. "Your daughter's one funny lady, Mr. Brian Cabral!" She kissed him on the tip of the nose, but wouldn't let him take her to bed: "Not when our daughter's watching, Mister. You can wait. It'll give you something to look forward to."

The Neonatal Intensive Care Unit was one of the few hospital locations where electric lights shone day and night. Expensive air conditioning and heat maintained a balmy temperature, both for the babies in their incubators and the staff. Other nurses called the NICU cushy. Sure, Jamie thought, if watching babies die – and having to kill them yourself sometimes – was cushy.

The Cabral baby showed steady improvement: response up, skin color normalizing. The Shaw and Stepanian babies demonstrated normal progress. The Feliciano baby was worse: vitals and responsiveness remained low; risk of hydrocephaly remained high.

Jamie felt only an echo of her usual maternal tug when the Feliciano baby stirred, trying to turn its head so it could keep looking at her. It wasn't his fault that he'd taken Renée Mercer's incubator, any more than it was Renée Mercer's fault her parents couldn't afford enough insurance to make sure their baby didn't get displaced. Four expensive, energy-draining incubators were all Temperance United could afford to run. Under ideal circumstances, newborns born into overfull hospitals would be transferred. Circumstances were not ideal.

How was Jamie supposed to accept that the Feliciano baby had more right to live than Renée Mercer? Yet she had accepted it. She'd displaced eight other babies. What did it mean that it took until Renée Mercer, a blonde baby who looked like Claire, for Jamie to shift from guilt to action?

9:26. Jamie went to the door. An orderly she was friendly with, Laird Douglas, stood chatting with a young nurse. He waved. "How's Claire?"

Jamie pulled aside her mask. "She's fine."

Laird turned back to the nurse. Jamie slipped the pressure lock that The Brotherhood had given her out of her pocket, and pushed it onto the latch. It adhered with a whine. Laird looked over. Jamie tugged her sleeve over the lock and smiled. Laird half-smiled in return.

Shit, thought Jamie. Had he seen? She shut the door. A single, long beep indicated the lock's activation.

9:29. The Brotherhood would begin storming hospital records any minute now. When the distraction started, security should be dispatched to that wing of the hospital, leaving Jamie alone to do her part. In case someone got curious, the pressure lock would keep them out, short of something that could cut through the reinforced door.

In the last days of the oil rush, the hospital had been built to survive a siege. Back then, people still believed China would try to usurp American world domination by force. Now the hospital's solid construction would work against its defenders.

9:32. Still no alarm. The Stepanian baby whimpered, one feeble leg kicking out. Jamie didn't go to her.

9:36. 9:38. Should she start early? But then, if someone saw her, security wouldn't be divided. They'd get past the pressure lock sooner, maybe before she finished.

At 9:42, red lights flashed along the ceiling, a silent warning to the staff to stay put. It was standard operating procedure these days in case of violence. Security didn't want panicked civilians underfoot.

Time to start then. Jamie began the process of pulling out the Cabral baby's nasal cannula.

Roshaun Shaw, son of Bea and Tamarr Shaw. 11 days old. Suffers from sepsis with organ dysfunction in the kidneys and liver.

Bea liked being pregnant. Pregnant meant nine months of not having to worry about her damn weight and getting compliments from strangers at the same time. "You glow, honey" – hell yes she did, shouldn't she ought to?

Bea had been pregnant six times and she enjoyed each one more than the last. Her first two pregnancies she did as a surrogate mother to pay for her master's degree.

Bea had no complaints about surrogacy, it was just that motherhood was better. Take the two couples she contracted with – friends from church, good people. She lived with them from months five to nine, enjoying free rent and hand-and-foot wait service. She sat with the parents-to-be through baby showers, nervous excitement, joyful outbursts, and fights about child-rearing. Sometimes she wondered if she ought to charge therapist rates along with surrogacy, but she never wanted to cancel the contracts, as would have been her right at any time.

The kids, Mary and Ruby, called her Auntie. Their parents made up a holiday for her in July to go with Mother's Day and Father's Day. When Mary got drunk on her seventeenth and found herself stranded in Overton, Auntie Bea got called to haul thirty miles out of the city at two a.m. with an extra bus ticket, and to wipe vomit off the seats afterward. That even though Bea had three children of her own by then.

Tamarr hadn't wanted another kid. It was already hard to manage the cost of raising their herd, as Tamarr called the boys, on the salaries of two high school English teachers. But Bea was decided. She hid all the contraception and said she wouldn't have sex with Tamarr if he used protection – and hadn't he listened to Ms. Addison's health class in the room over? No meant no.

Tamarr held out for six and a half weeks. "I'll name this one," he said when he relented. "And I declare there will be no more dead poets in the family."

Bea had been hoping for a DuBois to go with their Neruda, Langston and Keats. She frowned. "What name do you want?"

"Roshaun if it's a boy," he said, "for my grandfather."

She shrugged and agreed. Three happy hours later, Roshaun existed as one full egg and one self-satisfied sperm.

When Roshaun was born, feeble and unable to cry, Bea wished this had happened during one of those pregnancies she did for money, when she was employee not mother. She thought about Mary's red, grey-eyed newborn face, and Ruby's heart-shaped brown one; if only it had been one of them who'd taken faltering breaths, who'd been hauled away by blue-gloved doctors.

"Your name is Roshaun!" Bea shouted after the people who took him. Weak from the birth, she forced herself to sit up, sweat dripping down her face. "Your father named you Roshaun. Do you hear me? You're Roshaun, and you're going to be all right!"

The Brotherhood of Man approached Jamie the day after she killed Renée Mercer.

The woman, who called herself Slate found Jamie on an empty stretch near Washington Street Market where Jamie biked during her breaks. She liked to sit alone there. It was far away from what had become the two main poles of Martinsville: the depressed commercial district downtown, and the frenetic construction site where Martinsville would eventually get one of its very own nuclear power plants so that in ten or twenty years no more Renée Mercers would have to die.

Slate sat on the curb waiting for Jamie to arrive. "I understand you're unhappy with your job."

Slate looked older than Jamie by fifteen or twenty years. She had a broad, stern face, and wore her hair in dozens of tiny braids pinned close to her scalp. Thin white scars snaked across her face and arms, interspersed with patches of dry, red skin. She looked as though she spent a lot of time fighting or doing arduous outdoor work. Still, she seemed trustworthy. She reminded Jamie of her mother, the way Renée Mercer reminded her of Claire.

Jamie came to a stop in the gutter. "How do you know how I feel about my job?"

"A friend of yours told us."

"What friend?"

Slate shrugged. "A friend, that's all. How many times have they asked you to kill now?"

"I don't kill anyone. We disconnect them from the machines. They die a natural death."

"How many?"

"Eight."

"Including yesterday?"

"...Nine."

"And you don't think that's right."

"I don't think babies should die because their parents don't have enough money."

"I'm here representing people who agree with that point of view. Actually – I think most people agree with it. Yet it isn't public policy. People pay taxes, taxes go to the government, the government gives money to hospitals, corporations run hospitals, and corporations say poor people have the right to live as it doesn't impinge on rich people. And the government lets them say that, because the people in the government either get paid by the corporations, or they own the corporations. Know how they get away with it?"

Jamie raised her eyebrows.

"They play tricks with voters using misdirection, like a magician using sleight of hand. They remind people what life was like before rationing: private cars, computers running all day with no one at the keyboards, a lightning fast world economy with us at the helm. Then they talk about how much more people would have to give up – how many buses to power another hospital, how many electric lights to run the catalog for a library." She shook her head. The ends of her braids rattled like snake heads snapping in the sun. "It's a coin in a voluminous sleeve. The private sector saps more energy than all the rationed households in the nation, and they do it on government subsidy."

Slate tapped her boot against the curb, disturbing the deadfall.

"Why does no one notice? Why aren't the scoundrels voted out of office and chased through the streets like dogs? Because the government protects the fragile remnants of the middle class from experiencing the most insidious and insufferable indignities. They maintain a luckless, down-at-heel class the majority can look down on and think – at least that isn't me. And as long as that balance remains, the deplorable policy of killing infants for watts will continue."

Slate sat up straight, slapping her hands on her knees. "We want to throw off the balance."

"How do you plan to do that?" asked Jamie.

Slate spread her hands. "You want to hear?"

Jamie remembered lifting Renée out of the incubator, cradling the infant's head as she turned her over to Dr. Oppenheimer so he could ease her discomfort until she died. Hard to believe the hands in those gloves were hers. Her betraying fingers. Her blood-stained palms.

Eventually, Jamie would learn that Slate had been a history teacher and a missionary during the end of the oil rush, running a school in Burkino Faso with her husband, Titanium. Like all great pro-life movements, the Brotherhood had many Christian supporters. Slate called them God's own radicals. Though the Brotherhood had no traditional leaders, Slate often spoke for them and wrote the essays that became their doctrine.

Jamie learned all that later. During that first meeting, Jamie was just impressed by Slate's calm, easygoing tone as she spoke about politics, as if she were giving a lecture on something as unemotional as repairing a bike or pruning a bush.

"Let me give you a history lesson," Slate said. "You know about Gandhi? His movement wouldn't have worked if there hadn't been a real threat of violence against the British colonialists. Martin Luther King's sit-ins? Backed by Black Panther fists. Nonviolent alternatives don't become appealing unless there's something to be afraid of."

"That's you?"

"It's our job to show teeth so the moderate voters who make up the bulk of our great land – the folk making baa noises and chewing on the grass as they let other people's babies die – will flee to the peacemakers."

Slate lifted the collar of her fleece and raised her chin, looking Jamie in the eye.

"We call ourselves The Brotherhood of Man."

Jamie had heard of them.

"You're terrorists."

Slate shrugged one shoulder. "We're freedom fighters."

"You want me to do to insured babies what I did to Renée Mercer."

Silence.

"What makes you think I'd work with you?"

"You haven't left, have you?"

"I've got a baby of my own. If I do what you want me to, I'll get caught."

"We all have to make sacrifices. At least if you go to jail, your baby won't be dead, just taken care of by somebody else."

Jamie stared at Slate's scars. They formed a pattern like a web across Slate's shoulders, spider-like tendrils cast across her hands. Scarification. Before the rush ended, Jamie had wanted to become an anthropologist, help people in developing countries. Then the power crises started, funding for international charities dried up with no sign of refilling, there was talk of marching on China, and Jamie figured she'd better help her own people.

She leaned her bike against a tree. Two hours later, she rode away.

Darlita Stepanian, daughter of Nadalia Stepanian. 16 days old. Birth defects caused by extreme prematurity (28 weeks) include dangerously low birthweight and Respiratory Distress Syndrome.

When they bought the dairy farm, Brosh Stepanian and his partner, Miguel Espinoza, were banking on a growing market for milk procured by hand. They had no idea. When the switch to nuclear started, politically-conscious, well-off consumers clamored for low-energy, conscience-salving milk. Simultaneously, the competition struggled under new limits and rising costs. Life got lucrative for Brosh and Miguel. It also got busy.

They were mucking out the stables together one night when Brosh stopped shoveling shit and asked, "What do you think about becoming a father?"

"What are you talking about?" shouted Miguel from the loft.

"My sister's pregnant. She doesn't want an abortion. She doesn't want the baby either."

"Nadalia?"

"Yep."

"But she's sixteen!"

Brosh sat on an ergonomically-designed steel-and-plastic milking stool. A cow lowed and blinked at him. "Mom thinks it would be good to keep the kid in the family. Nadalia agrees."

Miguel jumped off the ladder.

"The kid would be legally ours?"

"Signed contract. What do you think?"

"I don't know," said Miguel. "Isn't this fast?"

"Fast as any yes on a pregnancy test."

Miguel kicked some straw. Finally he said, "Yeah. Okay. I think this could be good."

Having agreed to become parents, Brosh and Miguel disagreed on the next course of action. Miguel borrowed an armload of parenting books from the library, then went back for another stack. Brosh took a more direct route – he practiced on the cows.

"See that little guy with the black head?" Brosh would tease. "He's not going to wait until he gets his driver's permit. Little speed demon will be stealing cars and joyriding to Holstein preschool."

Brosh steadfastly refused to read. After two weeks, Miguel got upset. "You have to take this seriously!" said Miguel. He thrust a pile of hardbacks in Brosh's face. "We've got a lot of decisions to make. Corporal punishment? Yes, no, or only gently? Elimination? Diapers or toilet or let it fall where it may? Nutrition? Should we hire a woman on hormones to breastfeed?"

"We'll figure it out."

"But you need to prepare!"

"Not really," said Brosh. "I'm just comfortable with kids."

They bussed into Martinsville once a month to see Nadalia and Mrs. Stepanian. Nadalia spent her time off school relaxing and spending her allotment of electricity on old movies.

"She shouldn't be gaining this much weight," Miguel said. "And I'm not convinced she's getting enough folic acid. I want to put her on a strict diet."

"Nadalia won't do that, she likes taking things as they come," Brosh said. "Don't worry. My family has healthy babies."

But something did go wrong. Miguel was in the main house, cooking lunch for the crew on the gas stove, when the call came: Nadalia was delivering early.

Brosh and Miguel left their foreman in charge and paid the exorbitant fee to fly to Martinsville. They visited Nadalia, but the hospital wouldn't let them into the NICU. "It's too early," they were told by a middle-aged R.N. with short, bristly blonde hair. "I'm sorry," she added, touching Brosh's shoulder. "I have a little one myself. Just have faith."

They went outside and sat on the steps. Miguel held Brosh. "Nadalia's fine. The baby will be too. And if not – we can get a surrogate or adopt. We'll get a baby."

"A baby?" asked Brosh. "A baby?"

Brosh fell silent. For the rest of their visit, he refused to speak. On the bus ride back to his mother's, over their dinner of cold left-overs, all night as the two of them lay restless in Brosh's childhood bed. Eventually, Miguel paid to change his ticket and flew back to the farm.

Jamie disentangled the Cabral baby from the wires and machines – the baby's first taste of freedom – and set her on the metal exam table. She started on the Shaw baby.

9:51. She wondered how far along Slate and Titanium had gotten in their mission to burn the paper copies of the insurance records. The plan was mostly symbolic. Slate knew they couldn't get all the reams before security stopped them. Even what they managed to destroy wouldn't be gone permanently. Recovering and reprinting the data from a remote site computer would be expensive, but it would get done eventually.

But burning the papers served another purpose, as well. "The Brotherhood has taken responsibility for many acts," Slate said. "But we've kept ourselves faceless. Now is the time for us to come forth."

Slate and Titanium would lead the force to destroy the papers. They'd be the ones to get arrested. Them and Jamie. Twin trials. A married couple of missionaries and a young mother.

"During the civil rights movement, many black women refused to give up their seats. The movement picked Rosa Parks, the best one to swing public opinion," Slate explained. "We want to be frightening but familiar. People must understand that times have gotten so bad that ordinary, rational citizens can commit acts they once would have considered evil. Why do you think we study the Holocaust? History is rife with genocides. We are fascinated, terrified, by the idea that people just like us marched innocents into gas chambers. That's the demon that makes the Holocaust more frightening than Armenia or Rwanda or Venezuela."

Slate gave this speech the last time Jamie saw her alone. They sat together in deserted park. The neighborhood's residents had fled when maintaining detached, suburban-style homes became too expensive.

"Do you worry we shouldn't do this to innocents?" Jamie asked. "I mean, babies..."

Slate tightened her hand around the arm of the bench. She could be frightening when she sat so rigid, every muscle taut. "No one is innocent," she said. "From the moment of conception, those babies benefited from their place in the country's hierarchy. They grew in well-fed bellies, drank water free of dangerous chemicals, reposed in the safety of a womb untaxed by the arduous physical labor of field hands or the unrelenting hours of a sweat shop. Other people made that possible. These babies are born perched atop a pinnacle of human grief. Have you any idea how many suffer to support even America's middle class? And even here, where we bemoan our lost status as economic superpower while still enjoying our privileges as China's second fiddle, even here we sacrifice more lives to the altar of these babies. We toss the uninsured out with the bathwater, as soon as they inconvenience us. These babies are not innocent!"

Jamie looked away. To stare into the heart of Slate's arguments was to stare into the sun.

She lifted the Shaw baby. Jaundice from kidney problems yellowed his dark skin. His eyes slid to her face, then lost focus. She set him down and went to work on the Stepanian baby.

Jonathon Feliciano, son of Petra Feliciano (deceased) and Leonard Feliciano. 19 days old. Suffers from low birth weight, prematurity, and complications arising from spina bifida.

Leo believed in Jesus. More than he did in sky. What was sky? Just blue air. Your eyes could be tricking you about sky. Jesus was in your bones. He was the startle when you woke, the moment of trust before you squeezed your brain into sleep. If Jesus wasn't real, nothing was real.

Petra died in childbirth. She bled a lot. But there was no blood in heaven.

Leo stayed at the hospital. His mama brought him clothes. Black sweaters and black sweats with the tags still on, just bought. He forgot to take off the tags. Petra died, but Jonathon was still alive. Call him Jonathon, Leo told the doctors. Jonathon is a good name. Jesus would like the name Jonathon. Mama liked it. Petra didn't at first, but she'd come around in heaven.

Petra always wanted to fly. She watched birds, any bird. She watched geese when they went overhead honking. If they got too loud, she put her fingers in her ears. She watched airplanes too. She'd never been in one. By the time she got enough money, they were only for rich people and emergencies. They flew past so rare now. If she heard an engine, she'd stop in the street, look up like a kid looking for God, stare up at the bellies of the planes, and spin and spin and spin.

Leo's mama tried to trick him into going home by saying she needed him to carry something heavy in her car. Leo figured it out. He didn't go home with her. She sent his sisters to sit with him while she was gone. They came in shifts.

Petra always wanted to play music, but she couldn't. She was tone deaf. She owned a harmonica. She asked Leo to play the harmonica. She smiled when he did. Sometimes she danced. Leo liked it when she danced.

Leo's mama said that now Petra was gone, he was going to move back home, don't argue. Petra could have taken care of a baby, she said, but Leo couldn't do it alone. That's okay, said Leo, Can I still change the diapers? Leo's mama said he could.

Petra said that when she got to heaven she was going to read the Bible all day, and she was going to make Jesus read it with her because she always wanted to know what He really meant. Becky said she shouldn't say that, the Bible meant exactly what it said. Petra said, Don't fret now, Becky. I don't think Jesus will mind a question or two.

The hospital people tried to get Leo to go home. He said okay and left, but then he just went to sit in the parking lot. People didn't drive like they used to when Leo was a kid, so there was lots of free asphalt where he could sit and think. He fell asleep on the asphalt once and a car almost ran into him. There was only one person in it. Leo had trouble believing it at first. Someone had enough money to drive alone? The person honked and Leo went to sit on the curb. A pair of EMTs passed, pushing an empty gurney. One asked, are you okay? The other said, His baby's sick, and the first one asked, What's wrong with it? Leo tried to explain, but he couldn't remember the right words. He tried to get close: Jonathon got born early and his spine fell out.

Petra and Leo went to school together. Leo wasn't supposed to go to public school, but everyone knew his family. They did something funny with his test scores and said, Okay. You can go to school. Leo and Petra knew they'd get married by second grade. All the boys wanted to marry Petra when they got to high school, but Leo was the only one who was always nice to her, not just when he wanted something.

When Leo tried to do sports and he got clumsy, or when he was dumb in class, people made fun. Petra watched and sighed. She said, It's okay, you're better than them. That made Leo feel better. Petra watching and loving him made everything okay. She was going to do that now, up in heaven. And if Jonathon died, Petra would raise him in heaven, and they'd both watch Leo.

Leo's mama found him in the parking lot. Don't do that you'll get dirty, she said. She brought him inside. I made this for you, she said, and gave him a pie. Leo wasn't hungry so he gave it to one of the nurses. That was nice, said his mama, I brought you up nice. She put her hand on his knee. Things will be okay, you know, she said.

I know they will be, said Leo.

His mama looked at him sideways, eyes narrow in her big, fleshy face. You do know it, don't you?

Leo didn't answer. It wasn't really a question.

As Jamie finished loosing the Feliciano baby, she heard someone pounding on the door. Jamie looked up. Loud, metallic thuds reverberated through the room. So they'd found her. Would the pressure lock hold? No time to be paranoid. The damn things had been invented in India to let wealthy women lock themselves in their bedrooms in case gangs broke into their apartments. They were meant to keep out violent criminals armed to the teeth with illegal weapons. Jamie had to have faith they'd keep out a few security guards for a little while longer.

9:55. The evacuation alarm sounded: a pulsating, screechy whine. The babies kicked and shifted.

"I know," murmured Jamie. She set down the Feliciano baby and grabbed a sterile blanket. She placed it under the babies' heads, fluffing it up so that it gave their tender ears some protection. "It'll be quiet soon," she promised.

She sorted through the boxes she'd restocked a few days ago so that no one would have reason to reach to the back of the cabinets. Behind them, she found the hypodermic needle of morphine she'd stashed there.

"Use tools you put there yourself," Slate had told her. "That way no one can mess with them. This may seem silly to you, but remember: Redundancy's the name of the game. Surprise is the enemy of success.

"When you took the other babies out of their incubators, you let nature and time do the dirty work," Slate said. "This time, you'll have to kill them yourself. Do you think you can do it?"

9:57. The slamming subsided, replaced by the shrill of vibrating metal. They were sawing through. Jamie didn't have much time.

Renée Mercer. Teratogenic disorders of the heart due to maternal exposure to Pentathorinol in the ground water. Deceased, 6 days.

"I don't understand," said Shawna Mercer. "You're going to murder my child?"

"No, Mrs. Mercer," said the nurse. "She's been displaced from her incubator. She's resting now, with drugs to reduce the pain. We won't do anything to make her condition worse."

"She's just been displaced?" asked Shawna's husband, Trent. "Just like that?" He pushed past his wife, staring down at the runt chink of a nurse.

Shawna glared at Trent. She appealed to the nurse. "The Doctor, what's his name, Mr. Opera –"

"Oppenheimer."

"Oppenheimer," Shawna repeated. "He said she wouldn't survive without care," said Shawna. "He said that when he was talking to us about how we'd be going into debt."

"We needed the incubator for another child, Mrs. Mercer."

"Renée needs it too!" said Trent.

"I know, Mr. Mercer. Temperence United is very sorry."

The nurse was short and fat and had some stupid parody of an Asian name like Wei Wei or Chongella or something, but she didn't look Asian. She had dark skin and big, squashed features like a black. Would her kid get tossed out like a piece of garbage?

"Look," said Trent, jabbing his hand into the nurse's face. "I'm telling you, put her back in right now."

"Mr. Mercer. Please calm down. I'm trying to work with you."

"Well, I don't want to work with you. You go get your boss."

The nurse waddled off. Shawna felt so tired. There was hope, there wasn't hope. Renée was going to be okay, Renée was being 'displaced.'

"We'll get this settled," said Trent. "No way they're doing this to us."

Shawna looked up at him. Trent had been such a catch. He'd never even looked at her in high school. The day he asked her out, three years after graduation, with her still working behind the counter at the drug store on Hyacinth Street, that was the best day of her life. She was smart. She should have been able work office while he worked manual labor. They should have been able to get by.

The doctor arrived. Short, Jewish, glasses perched on a blunt nose, curly hair flying. Trent barreled toward him. "You tell me what's going on," he insisted.

Shawna ignored them, went straight for the blonde nurse that had followed the doctor in.

"What's going on?" Shawna asked.

The nurse eyed Trent. Shawna realized she was nervous. She rolled her eyes and grabbed for the nurse's hands.

"Tell me," she said.

An unidentifiable expression crossed the nurse's face. Shawna couldn't make head or tails of it. "I'm sorry. You should have known about the possibility of displacement. Didn't you read the waiver?"

"What waiver?" asked Shawna.

"The one you signed when you came in."

"In the load of papers? When I was pushing out the kid?"

"I'm sorry."

"But the doctor said the Pentathorinol, it's all over in our area. It's illegal to dump near water. Some company must have broken the law. Shouldn't we get paid for that?"

The nurse shook her head. "You might be able to, if you sue the corporation. But the hospital doesn't acknowledge claims until they're settled."

"So that's it? My baby's dead?"

"Not yet." The nurse glanced at the doctor, saw him still engaged. "But soon." She glanced again. "She's comfortable. I promise. She's not fussing or crying."

"You've seen her?"

That unreadable expression crossed the nurse's face again. With a shock that zapped her in the bones, Shawna realized what it meant.

"You did it! You killed my baby!"

"Mrs. Mercer..."

"Don't you finish that sentence! Don't you tell me to calm down! God damn you to hell, you did it, you killed my baby!"

Shawna felt red rise into her cheeks. She knew everyone was staring. She didn't care.

"What kind of woman are you? How could you do that to a little baby?"

The nurse looked down, looked away. Good. Let her be shamed. Shawna became aware of Trent standing over her. The last thing she wanted to deal with now was his stupid bulk. What was he going to do? Hit her?

Shawna collapsed into a chair. Her throat felt raw. "You fucking bitch. I hope you rot in hell."

After she killed the babies, Jamie would be arrested. She would be booked with Titanium who'd tell her, in his terse fashion, that Slate had been shot. He wouldn't know Slate's condition, but in fact Slate would die on a Temperance United operating table in seven hours. By then, Jamie and Titanium would be in separate facilities. They'd be told separately.

Jamie would ask for her husband and Claire to be allowed to come visit her. This would be denied. She'd spend her short call on the phone with Claire instead, trying to coax a few sentences, maybe a giggle. Her call would be cut short by a tall officer with cold eyes who would be unnecessarily brutal when escorting Jamie out of the room.

Titanium would stand trial alone, an intimidating, silent figure. Yet he'd fulfill Slate's requirements for familiarity as well, possessing the build of a football player, the pale skin and blue eyes of a corn-fed boy. The cross he wore around his neck would wink gold into the cameras, drawing the viewer's eye into the flash of realization that here was a terrorist who'd spent three years in seminary school, whose tongue and heart were reverent to the words of Jesus.

Jamie wouldn't stand trial. She'd be beaten to death in a prison brawl. A guard would later be tried for standing by and watching her die. The charges would be dismissed.

Afterward, Meredith Cabral developed panic attacks. They cornered her in grocery stores, on buses, at gardening meetings, at church.

When she got pregnant again, they got worse. Stress led to a premature birth, six weeks early. When the obstetrician arrived to give her a pain suppressant, she thought he was trying to inject lethal drugs into her arm. She screamed and tried to flee. Brian and two orderlies pinned her down as the physician sedated her. Afterward, the obstetrician told her that if she ever decided to have another baby, she should schedule a cesarean. Against Brian's wishes, she opted for tubal ligation. Throughout her daughter's childhood, she loomed as a frail but frightening figure, like a shadow: impossible to read, liable to break down at nothing, in and out of mental hospitals the way other girl's mothers were in and out of salons.

Bea Shaw screamed at the hospital staff. She screamed at the policemen. She screamed at her husband. "You didn't try hard enough! You aren't trying hard enough! They aren't trying hard enough!"

But it was Tamarr who went into the garage where they stored his dad's old car on the grounds that getting rid of it was more fuss than keeping it around, confirmed that a few pints of gas lingered in the antique engine, got behind the wheel, and started the ignition without opening the garage door. Bea found him that afternoon, crying over the kitchen table. He hadn't had the strength to finish.

They sat together, Bea with her arms around Tamarr, until the boys came home. "Make dinner," Bea told them, "You can take care of yourselves one night."

Bea took Tamarr into the bedroom and lay with her arms around him. The sun sank, leaving the room grim and dark. The moon rose, casting a ghostly glow on the sheets and curtains.

Bea held Tamarr some more.

Brosh Stepanian sold his partnership to their foreman and moved to New Zealand to raise sheep with his mother and sister. Neighbor boys flocked around Nadalia like flies to honey. She picked one before she was eighteen, and swelled to a happy, wifely pregnant on his parent's farm.

Brosh found a partner to love in action instead of conversation. Their bond grew in the silences of sweat and straining muscles. When they decided to hire a surrogate, they searched for a woman who shared their interests and contracted with a traveling Japenese artist.

Brosh sent a picture of their baby girl to Miguel, along with a short letter. Miguel wrote back: Congratulations. Wasn't it funny how things worked out? Miguel couldn't see himself as a good father. He liked control too much. Maybe a baby would have forced him and Brosh together when they should have been apart.

Brosh tucked the letter into the drawer where he kept official papers about the farm along with his one photograph of Darlita: tiny, blue-skinned, crying. He never wrote Miguel again.

Leo went home. He moved in with his mom and helped with his sisters' babies. Someone else was always around, just in case.

The children grew older. The sisters weren't home much. Leo was. Weird Uncle Leo. Always smiling. Funny how he looked like a boy, when he was so old.

He prayed all the time. So deep it was like sleeping. Once, when Maria Renata was eight, he prayed so hard that he wouldn't wake up. Grandma sent Maria Renata to get a mirror to make sure he was still breathing.

"Why does he pray like that?" Maria Renata asked grandma.

"He's lonely."

"Oh," said Maria Renata. "Maybe I could fix him up with the hunchback lady. She's always nice to him. She gives him plums from her yard."

"Not that kind of lonely," said grandma.

Maria Renata stuck her nose against the window. "She's out there now! I'm going to go tell her about Uncle Leo!"

Maria Renata had her hand on the doorknob when grandma caught her by the wrist. It hurt. Grandma's eyes were dark and flat, like mud drying in the sun.

"Don't do it," grandma said. "Leave the poor man to his peace."

Another baby was tangled up in the whole mess: Claire McFadden, née Claire Wrede. After Jamie was killed, her father changed their name and moved them to another part of the country where he thought Claire could grow up normally.

As an adult, Claire moved back to Martinsville. She found herself moving eerily in her mother's footsteps: she too went into health care to work with infants, though as a pediatric oncologist not an R.N.

Twenty years after it all happened, a woman putting together a documentary showed up at Claire's door. Buzzing followcams hovered behind her in the entryway, careful not to illegally cross the threshold into private property.

"Could I ask you some questions about your mother?" the documentarian asked. Without pausing for an answer, she went on, her tone rehearsed: "In recent months, some rehistorians have been vocal in their claims that it was the Temperance Massacre that turned public opinion eighteen years ago to pave the way for the Energy Redistribution Act. As one of the key figures in the massacre, your mother could be on her way to becoming a hero in some circles. What do you think of that?"

Claire smiled. She said one thing before closing the door.

"My mother was a monster."

10:04. Jamie held the babies for a moment as she slid the needle into their flesh. Each warm, fleet heart beat near hers for a few seconds before she set the infant on the cold exam table.

Andrea died. Roshaun died. Darlita died. Jonathon died.

Jamie watched the life flicker out of their bodies one after the other, then went to turn herself in.

Bophuthatswana

Lavie Tidhar

Late at night, in Melville
We picked out fat honeyed smiles
From a jarful of eyes on the low table
An Indian woman like copper-red coins sitting on the bar
Loose change in Melville, and the cries
of the Rasta Men, selling dried-out love
On the street outside
Where it is warm
Perfumed cars sashaying down
The parade of bars, cows in pasture
And besides Wesley and me
A beautiful, fat black woman
Smokes a cigarette in tender puffs
Her breath steams up
Apartheid Night
When it rained and the colours
All ran together.

We're driving down Rivonia with the Sandton Towers rising on our left illuminated in neon light like metal spikes driven into a crossroads. Wez is driving. I'm sitting in the passenger seat, rolling a spliff under the dashboard.

Wez is on a retro trip. On the old tape-deck Mango Groove's *Another Country* is replaced by Johnny Clegg and Savuka singing *Asimbonanga Mandela*. Wez lifts one hand off the steering-wheel in a closed-fisted salute. 'Mandela!'

I put the rest of the dope back into the *bankie* and seal it, returning it to my coat pocket. I roll the joint quickly, my fingers smoothing the finished cone as if stroking a lover's finger. I put it in my mouth and spark up and it flares against my mirrorshades like a miniature explosion.

'You know what they call people like us in America?' I say.

Wez looks at me sideways. His pupils are large, his dark hair falling over a delicate oval face. 'I don't know, *bru*. Super-heroes?'

'No, asshole,' I say. I take a hit on the spliff and pass it to him. The smoke percolates through my lungs and the definition of light outside grows sharper. Wez is Chinese and lives with him mum down near Bruma Lake. His mum's a born-again Christian. He is the colour of pine and burnt amber. Beside him, I am Ethiopian Mocha, drunk with cream. 'They call us "people of colour".'

Wez takes a toke on the spliff and shakes his head. 'That's fucked up, *bru*.' The car races down past walled suburban prisons decorated in barbed wire and electronic alarms and "Beware The Dog" signs. 'Does that mean white people are called "colourless"?'

'No,' I say. 'I think they're just called people.'

Wez nods deeply at that. We share the joint in silence, listening to the changing music, as the car goes past Rosebank Mall's fake fairytale façade. On the crossroads we stop. A beggar approaches us with a cardboard sign that says, 'Will work for food.' Wez rolls down the window and gives him a one-Rand coin. The beggar takes it but doesn't move off. Wez shrugs and hands him the remains of the joint. The beggar takes a deep hit and rocks his head. Dark matted dreadlocks shake like a Weeping Willow in a storm. 'What's that you're listening to,' he says, 'The Springbok Nude Girls?' He suddenly grins and I realise he is not that much older than us. His English has an Afrikaans accent and his skin, for all its pallor, still retains vestiges of a farmer's tan. 'I was at the concert they gave at the Rand Easter Show in, what was it, ninety-five, ninety-six? Fucking rocked, man.' He seems to think about it. 'It was *lekker*,' he says.

He looks directly at me, now, and his face loses its grin, his eyes are filled with rain-clouds. 'It's all gone, *bru*. You got to stay in the present.' He shakes his head. 'Shit, for a moment I thought it really was the nineties.'

He ambles away, muttering to himself. Wez winds up the window and the light changes and we're off across Jan Smuts.

'Are you sure we're gonna find some there?' I say. 'Melville?'

Wez shrugs. 'That's what the sangoma said.'

The sangoma's our third. Her name's Lufuno. She is calm where we are manic, cool where we are inflamed. Her name means 'love'. Our names mean shit.

So we're driving to Melville. During the day it is a genteel, quiet street, where white people sit in Europeanized coffee-shops and eat slices of cheesecake and drink espresso and try to ignore the black guys who walk up and down the street trying to sell them factory-produced African curios. There are two second-hand bookshops, run by a German and a Jew, respectively, and lots of bars that remain mostly empty until the evening.

During the day, Melville waits, as if Main Street is holding its breath and the hot air is still in anticipation. Until night falls, and a great lungful of air is released, and the stillness shatters like a mirror breaking into a thousand tiny glass knives.

Wez's fingers drum a beat on the steering-wheel. He looks at me and shakes his head and says, 'Never used to see white guys begging on the street. It's freaky.'

'Yeah,' I say. 'And that *okie* was right. Turn that shit off. What is it with you and the fucking nineties anyway?'

I hit the button and replace the tape in the deck with a new one, and a bass line begins pounding out of the speakers. Wez rolls down the window and the wind comes tearing into the car with the smell of recent rain, blowing away the stale *dagga* smoke. Wez sticks his head out of the window and screams, a long incoherent shout into the night until an oncoming car returns his scream with its horn and he withdraws his head from the window and smiles at me, as innocent as a child. 'I was young then,' he says simply.

We drive past Greenside and onto Barry Herzog Avenue. On either side of us the park looks dark and brooding, cloaked in shadows like the billowing robes of a vampire. I say, 'we both were,' then fall quiet as I think about it. It was a weird time. An end, a beginning... Wez and I hooked up working for an Internet company in Randburg. Under Apartheid we were both classified as Coloureds, a lot less than whites, a little more than blacks. Being Chinese, Wez was fucked both ways. He couldn't get a job under Apartheid for not being white, and he couldn't get a job after Apartheid for not being black. With me it was easier. I was a little of this and a little of that, part-Jew and part-black, like something from Eugéne Terre'Blanche's worst nightmares. Now Wez does a little freelance web design from home and I sell advertising space, and in the nights we fight crime. Sort of.

We arrive at last and Wez parks the car. I think about what lies ahead and tense. Wez notices and says, 'chill, *bru*. We'll do it this time.'

I say, 'Let's hit it.'

We get out of the car and Wez takes the front of the tape-deck with him so it can't be stolen. We go to the booth and it opens.

'Ready?'

'Ready.'

We take out two long knives, their edges surrogated, each ending in a point so sharp it could bleed the air. We hide them under our long black coats. We take out a pair of Uzis and make them disappear inside the coats. Wez takes out two pairs of walkie-talkies he picked up at the Bruma flea-market a couple of months back. They're cheap, plasticky things, but they work, and I strap mine to my belt, along with 50-round magazines, a couple of grenades, a knuckle-duster and a Saturday night special. Wez carefully slings a small black bag on his shoulder. I adjust my mirror-shades.

'Then let's do it,' I say, and we walk up Main Street, towards the bars and the noise and the beckoning lights.

I remember the nineties the way I remember Swaziland, as a rocky terrain covered in clouds like a fog. When I was young and romantic I wrote a poem about Swaziland:

Low-lying clouds rest on the Matsapha hills
precariously balanced

in the stillborn morning air
like sleeping elementals.
it is a gentle landscape:
unevenly divided squares of vegetation
tinged by the syrupy-thick fields of sugarcane
and in the distance, a lonely farmhouse,
a water reservoir
are the only testimonies
to this land's man-made nature.
And a few years later I wrote:
These are empty human spaces
a flat and dusty desolation
dotted by mud huts, dusty brick bottle-stores
and the only growth industry of this region:
funeral parlours.

Perception changes suddenly, like an exploding bomb. Like the nineties.

I remember when I arrived in Johannesburg. I lived with my dad in New York, and he let me go back to be with my mother. He was an African-American who'd been to Africa once and didn't like it. She was a large Jewish woman with a nasal voice and an expensive car. I arrived at Jan Smuts airport and the white people stared when she came to get me, the soft white woman and the tall gangly teenager the colour of scattered ash she called her son.

I remember the wide avenues and the flowering Jacaranda trees in a blooming explosion of purple. She bought me Kentucky Fried Chicken and I ate it on the veranda, overlooking the city that hid beyond the wall and the gate.

It was just before the referendum, when white people voted on giving black people the right to vote. The skies were clear, the African sun was hot on my young face, and the wild scent of earth, of renewal, was in everything. All the *Stop* signs had F.W. sprayed on them. Stop F.W. Stop De Klerk.

Eugéne Terre'Blanche was king.

I watched the Boer Nation on TV. Eugéne, big and red-faced, a barrel of beer full of righteous White-Christian indignation. Eugéne and his boys. I watched the bombs flower over Johannesburg in brilliant reds and yellows, fire and blood. Eugéne and his boys valiantly rode to battle with pipe-bombs and guns, and I watched it on television. I felt like I was locked up, bound within the confines of the house, the garden, the walls, the barbed wire. I wrote:

The sun
The scent of Carnations in the yard
fresh-cut grass, a whiskey decanter
and the even, put-put-put sound

of the electric fence

like a memory of freedom.

I wrote bad poetry and read cyberpunk. After a while I didn't care about the problems. I was in love.

I met Xolelwa. In Xhosa, her name means child of peace. I keep her name inside me like broken glass.

I was in love: with the country I hadn't seen since being a boy, and with the girl who was like me, a composite of opposites, who I met at a party my mother gave, who kissed me under a large African moon and let me hold her hand.

On April 27, 1994, she was going back to New York, to study. I went with her to the airport.

But Eugéne and his boys had been busy.

The car-bomb didn't kill her, only blinded her and tore out her arm, scarred her back and her legs and broke her soul. I crouched beside her, looking everywhere, not knowing what to do, how to help her, how to help myself. Her blood was on my hands, on my face, on my World Peace T-shirt.

And I realised something then. That blood is the life, and that blood was what they fed on, the *Afrikaner Weerstandsbeweging*. And that like Ontlametse Bernstein Menyatsoe in the Bophuthatswana coup I too would pull the trigger if only I could. I too would end them.

Do you remember the Bophuthatswana coup? We're going to reenact it.

No more poetry.

Kwaito music spills out onto the pavement. Wez and I march up Main Street. A rastaman glances up at us, begins to offer us dope, changes his mind. This is the new South Africa, the Rainbow Nation, the land of *Nkosi sikelel' iAfrika*. In the bars we pass, white and black kids are dancing together, getting drunk on Castle Lager and Windhoek and Zambezi beer from across the border in Zimbabwe. Upmarket drinks for upmarket kids. The middle classes always win.

Wez checks out the girls: Indian girls and white girls and black girls and Chinese girls and the beautiful cocoa-and-cream girls from Mozambique. I look at him sideways and say, 'You're too old for them,' and Wez grimaces and lights up a Marlboro.

He says, 'Fuck you, *bru*. I'm not old, I'm *experienced*,' and I laugh.

On the left is a cocktail lounge piping out reggae. I see Lufuno, jerk my head at Wez. He follows my gaze and nods, once. She is sitting with a drink by her elbow, keeping company to a pack of Malawian *Life* cigarettes.

Lufuno stands up when she sees us. Her smile is a sun. We approach her and sit down.

'Yo,' Wez says.

I say, 'Peace,' and we touch fists. A big black man comes into the bar then, and as he goes past he nods at Lufuno. I recognise him. His name's Dayo, and he's Nigerian. He runs drugs down in Hillbrow. He disappears into the back room.

Lufuno sure knows some interesting people. Americans might say, 'colourful', but they wouldn't, not to Dayo's face. From what I hear he has no sense of humour. He's killed more people than I had therapy sessions.

'Are they here?' I ask. Lufuno nods. 'Mingling with the dancers and the drinkers they are,' she says. 'The white children of the night.'

She takes a final sip from her glass and rises, pocketing the cigarettes. She has a scar just visible on her right hand, and though I can't see it I know that under the long sleeve the scar extends all the way to her shoulder and continues down her back. 'Shall we do it?'

'Yeah,' Wez says. 'Let's kill the blood suckers.'

We walk out onto the street and start moving slowly up the road, weaving in and out of the bars and clubs in our search.

They were vampires. I realised it that day at the airport, which was once Jan Smuts and is now Jo'burg International. Names change, and sometimes people, too, but the *Afrikaner Weerstandsbeweging*, the Boer Nation, AWB, they never changed. They lived on the blood of others, have done so for hundreds of years, and when their food finally rebelled against them they rode into town shooting. Remember Bophuthatswana?

On March 4, 1994 – just a month before they blew up the airport – the AWB came to Bophuthatswana, the puppet state in the north created by the Apartheid government.

They came riding into Mmabatho, the capital, in a long convoy of *bakkies* and Mercedes cars. They came armed, with guns and grenades, and where they passed they shot out of the windows of their expensive cars, and tossed the grenades, and wounded and maimed and killed. They came to help Lucas Mangope, the black dictator of Bophuthatswana, but even Mangope's own people revolted against them, and the Boer Nation found itself under attack.

Belatedly, they tried to retreat. Three AWB members, Nick Fourie, Alwyn Wolfaardt and Fanie Heyns, driving their Mercedes at the back of a convoy, exchanged fire with black police. They were hit, and their vehicle came to a halt. Wounded, they demanded medical help.

Ontlametse Bernstein Menyatsoe, a policeman, was one of the men shooting at the convoy. He approached the wounded men. A foreign reporter filmed the whole thing on his camera.

He said, 'What are you doing in my country?'

And then he shot them.

It's an unmemorable place
Made memorable
By the twisting of a broken car
On dark asphalt
A wounded-blue metalled body
Lying in the rain
In a dark-blood road, soaked
By an eternity of green.

Menyatsoe, I came to realise, was one of us. He was a vampire killer. He realised the true nature of the men, and had acted upon it.

No one remembers Bophuthatswana. And the vampires still walk, free.

We split up in our search. The room I'm in is dark and crowded, the music a rising beat that shakes the floor. I walk through the dancers. I am bait. I think of Xolelwa, of her large dark eyes looking into mine. She's married now, and living with her lawyer husband in Cape Town. They both worked for the Truth and Reconciliation Commission. Hearing testimonies, granting amnesty. She moved on.

But I am not reconciled.

My walkie-talkie crackles. 'Anything?'

I say, 'No.'

There is a pause, a crackle of static. 'Lufuno says they are not here, but they are coming. Meet in the street?'

I say, 'OK.'

We meet in the street.

'You said they were already here.'

Lufuno shrugs. 'So fucking sue me.'

She looks pissed off. I re-think my reply, then lose it as I see them.

Two *bakkies*, off-white, mud-spattered: farm vehicles. They park at the bottom of Main Street. Loud Afrikaans music spills out of open windows. They come out, white skin browned by the sun, the blood of a dark continent pumping through their veins.

They are big and healthy, and their leader is a big fat bull, a younger Eugéne Terre'Blanche. They walk up Main Street and we three, Lufuno and Wesley and me, stand in their way.

Their leader halts, and the rest follow. They fan around in a semi-circle that confronts us. The leader looks at us, at me, and grins, revealing sharp white teeth.

He says, 'Howzit, bru.'

I nod. My hand is inside my coat.

'Mind if we pass through?'

I nod again. The leader loses his grin. 'You got a problem with us, bru?'

The butt of the gun is comforting against my hand.

One of his coterie spits on the ground. His spit is dark and thick. 'Shit, Hansie, just push him out of the way.'

The leader turns cold eyes on the speaker, who shuffles back into his place in the formation. 'Shut up, Koos.'

'You should *moer* the fucker,' Koos mumbles, defiant.

'I'll moer you in a minute, Koos.'

Silence.

The leader looks at each of us in turn. His smile returns when he sees Lufuno. He grins at her, exposing those long sharp teeth. 'Why are you hanging out with these two *moffies?*' he says. 'You should come with us. We're going to party up here and have a *jol.*'

Lufuno is silent. Her face is a mask etched with the acid of old abuse. The leader looks at Wez. Looks at me. His smile does not reach his eyes. He nods, once, as if reaching a decision.

He says, 'Get the fuck out of my way, *kaffirs.*'

The other one, Koos, grins at this and says, 'Ja, *voetsek*!'

Then everything happens fast and slow.

The Uzi is out of my coat and firing. The spent cartridges make the sound of a winning slot-machine as they hit the pavement. Beside me, Wez and Lufuno are firing with rapt, intense expressions. The leader ducks behind a blue Toyota Corolla and returns fire. He is furious. I lob a grenade at him and watch the car's window explode into a thousand tiny rainbows. Then someone shoots out the streetlights and it's dark.

Everything happens slow and fast. Tracer bullets like fireflies speeding through the night. The leader shouting, 'Charl, Ryk, Piet, get in the *bakkie*!' Koos lying on the ground gurgling blood. The sound of a car engine starting. Headlights cutting through the darkness like the sun through the shaft of a mine. Bullets hitting metal. Someone screaming. The sound of an engine revving, abruptly cutting off.

Wheels screech and die. I release the trigger and my body thrums with music.

On the ground three of the vampires still live. They crawl out of their car and lie with their backs against the punctured metal. They're bleeding. I motion to Wez and Lufuno, and they scan the area. Apart from the three in the car the only survivor is the leader. Lufuno and Wez drag him from behind the blue Toyota. He leaves a snail's wet red trail in his wake. They prop him against the car and step back.

From the black bag over his shoulder Wez takes out the video camera. He points it and gives me the thumbs-up, but already he wears the detached, professional face of the media.

'Help us! Can't you see we need medical attention! Take us to a hospital!'

I look at their faces, dark now with blood, terrified, hurting, and when I raise my head I seem to see Xolelwa standing above them, blind eyes looking directly into mine, one hand holding scales, the other a sword. She looks into my eyes. She shakes her head. *No*. And then she's gone, like a stealing *tokoloshe* in the night.

They bleed other people's blood.

The leader looks up at me. He doesn't beg. I look at his boy's face and think of Eugéne Terre'Blanche. Even Eugéne's reformed now, they say. Writes poetry and preaches on Sundays. Everyone's a born-again in the new South Africa.

'Help us!'

I pull the trigger.

Winning Friends

Van Aaron Hughes

I scan Jake's Tavern and see no familiar faces. I'm the first one here.

I suppose I should have stopped by the office first, but I thought everyone would be here by now. I had this mental image of being greeted with a big cheer as I stepped through the door. I never was any good at making a grand entrance.

⁂

THE MARSHAL: All rise! Oyez! Oyez! Oyez! All persons having business before the Honorable, the Supreme Court of the United States are admonished to draw near and give their attention, for the Court is now sitting. God save the United States and this Honorable Court.

THE CHIEF JUSTICE: Be seated. We will begin this morning with Case Number 23-1527, Johnston versus the State of Colorado. Mr. Benedict?

MR. BENEDICT: Mr. Chief Justice, and may it please the Court...

⁂

I should grab a table for the group, but I don't. Today I'm the hero, not the pathetic lady sitting at a huge table all by herself. I take a stool at the bar.

I look up past the bar, and Johnston scowls back at me. They'll be starting soon. I just hope somebody from the office gets here before then.

A tall blond settles onto the next stool and turns to me. "Come to watch the show?" Not much of an opener, but at least he manages not to puff his chest out the way men in bars usually do. Or at least, the way they used to back when I actually met guys in bars.

I nod, then again when he offers to buy me a drink. I should decline, but when was the last time a nice-looking man bought me a drink?

"I'm Tom Blondie."

I shake his hand, wondering if there's even a remote possibility I heard that right.

"Vicki Musgrave." I watch his face, but there's no trace of recognition. I shouldn't be surprised. Even with all the media coverage, not much of it came my way. I thought I was going to get fifteen minutes of fame, but only a few seconds trickled down to me.

Actually, I should be pleased Blondie doesn't know who I am. It means he sat here for the traditional reason. Sometimes, lots of times, I get to feeling like an old maid. At least I'm not too old to catch the notice of a strange man at a bar.

⁂

JUSTICE MADSEN: You say that so definitively. Isn't the Constitution intended to be flexible? Doesn't our interpretation of its provisions sometimes change to suit the times?

MR. BENEDICT: Yes, Your Honor, but there are some absolutes. Our respect for human life should not diminish to suit the times. As Justice Thomas explained in his concurring opinion in Graham v. Collins, there are–"

JUSTICE YOURSHAW: Justice Thomas' opinion in which case?

MR. BENEDICT: Graham v. Collins, Justice Yourshaw.

JUSTICE YOURSHAW: When was that?

MR. BENEDICT: I don't recall the exact date. It predates the al-Masri decision.

JUSTICE YOURSHAW: Well, exactly. Isn't al-Masri our starting point? The authority you're relying on is old, old, old.

JUSTICE THOMAS: It's not that old.

(Laughter.)

"It's a very unusual name, but it fits," I say, glancing at his hair.

He blinks three times before grinning widely. "B-I-O-N-D-I," he says.

He has a nice smile. And I have no idea what to say next.

How did I get so out of practice at this? It wasn't so long ago that most weekends saw our group hopping between whichever clubs were hot. That was before Lisa got married, had the twins, before Jess and Lana moved away, before It got Bridget. Times change, and not just for us. You can bet those clubs aren't so hot any more.

I look back at the giant screen behind the bar. I'm expecting Johnston to start yelling, spitting out one of his political diatribes, but he just sits passively through the final preparations.

Finally Blondie says, "He's getting what he deserves, huh?"

"You think so?" To my own surprise, I don't much feel like talking about it. Tonight, the talking should finally be done.

Three people from work walk in together and stake out a large table. My party is here, my excuse to Blondie to leave. But I'm not cold enough to cut a guy off like that. I accepted the drink, so I should at least chat long enough to finish it.

JUSTICE MADSEN: You keep talking about the sanctity of human life as if that's some mantra that can actually decide this case for us. I am not persuaded. The sanctity of human life comes in on both sides of the ECP equation, so repeating that phrase just takes us around in circles. What about the women in this case whose futures were stripped from them? What about the people whose lives could be at stake in future cases? I don't see you showing a lot of respect for the sanctity of their lives.

MR. BENEDICT: Your Honor, I don't think –"

THE CHIEF JUSTICE: Mr. Benedict, your time is up.

MR. BENEDICT: With the Court's indulgence, may I respond to that last question?

THE CHIEF JUSTICE: The Court does allow counsel to go beyond the allotted time when there is a question pending.

MR. BENEDICT: Thank you, Mr. Chief Justice.

THE CHIEF JUSTICE: But I don't think that was a question. I think it was a criticism.

JUSTICE MADSEN: Yes, it was.

THE CHIEF JUSTICE: You may sit down, Mr. Benedict.

MR. BENEDICT: Thank you, Your Honor.

"You don't think he deserves it?"

"Sometimes I'm not sure." Did I just say that?

"Come on, you know what he did!"

They're administering the injection. A cocktail of phenothiazine, haloperidol, and a half-dozen other drugs and chemicals I could have rattled off two months ago. Supposed to heighten his sensitivity. It's pretty doubtful that the injection works, but the important thing is that people believe it works.

"Yes, I know what he did." I know exactly what he did. I saw every piece of evidence. I examined his last victim. Not that it was much of an examination. She was reluctant to talk about it. But I got her to point her right index finger at Johnston. That was all we needed.

"Well, it doesn't matter if he deserves it anyway. It's got to be done for deterrence."

"And what is this going to deter?" I ask.

There's an old lawyers' game, where you argue the side of an issue you know is wrong, just to see how persuasive you can be. Or sometimes just to be annoying. I don't know why I am playing that game, but I seem to be winning. Blondie is getting pissed off, raising his voice a little. "You cannot let a monster like this run all over, spreading It around, and not do something about it."

"What if I don't believe the something we do is going to accomplish anything?"

He seems flabbergasted. "Do you really mean that?"

"No."

"Oh," he says, recovering quickly, "Well, you should say what you mean."

MS. MUSGRAVE: This Court's historical interpretation of the Eighth Amendment is perfectly consistent with the practice of ECP.

JUSTICE ALITO: May I say, this term "ECP" is a delightful euphemism. Is there some reason you don't want to spell out what it is we're talking about?

MS. MUSGRAVE: It is no secret what action the State of Colorado intends. I do not believe I am concealing anything by using that acronym.

JUSTICE ALITO: Not concealing, just sanitizing.

People are streaming into Jake's now. There are a lot of Johnston parties going on tonight. Several more people from the office enter, but they don't see me as they pass the bar.

Blondie puts his hand over mine on the counter. I should pull mine away, but when was the last time anyone held my hand?

"So you agree this is the right thing to do?" Blondie asks me.

I figure he's talking about Johnston, not holding hands. "Definitely, yes."

A passionate cheer goes up around us. I look up at the screen. It's started. They're turning up the heat on Johnston. Literally.

"So why the devil's advocate routine?"

"Sorry," I answer. "I was just trying something different."

Johnston squeezes his eyes shut, sweat beading his forehead, his breathing fast and heavy.

"You've been arguing my side of the debate a lot?"

"Just doing my job," I say coyly.

JUSTICE ATWELL: In al-Masri, the point was to get answers. That's not what you're after, is it?

MS. MUSGRAVE: Correct. We're not gathering information. We're sending a message.

JUSTICE ATWELL: Suffering for its own sake.

MS. MUSGRAVE: No, Justice Atwell, for an important purpose. ECP is a necessary tool if the State is going to perform its proper function of protecting its citizenry.

Blondie pauses while that sinks in. "Your job? Of course! Musgrave! You're one of the prosecutors. You argued the appeals." I try not to look too pleased.

He announces me loudly to the folks at the bar, and I receive several rounds of applause and pats on the back. Fifty feet away, half the professional staff of the Colorado Attorney General's office is celebrating the Johnston case, but somehow I find it more gratifying to be toasted by Blondie and the assembled strangers at the bar.

Johnston's skin is quickly turning beet red, the first blisters starting to form.

The buzz around me finally dies down. Blondie is still at my side, still with a grip on my hand. "I saw your name on the web accounts when you argued to the Supreme Court, but I pictured you as someone older. How did you get to argue such a big case?"

"Well, the Attorney General is a great guy." The Attorney General is a spineless weasel. "He thought I was ready, so he decided I should give it a shot." He thought we were going to lose, so he decided I should take the fall.

Johnston is panting and starting to moan. They say the sensation is like being trapped in a burning room, without asphyxiation to look forward to.

"So you're the best possible person to ask. I'm glad they're doing this and all, but I have to admit I don't get how it can be constitutional."

I smile.

JUSTICE RUMBERGER: I'm with you on the concept that this is an unpleasant necessity, but I have to admit I don't see how it can be constitutional. If this isn't cruel and unusual, what is?

MS. MUSGRAVE: There is no absolute test for what is cruel and unusual. It varies with the circumstances of the crime. The standard that this Court announced in Gregg v. Georgia in 1976 is that, quote, punishment must not involve the unnecessary and wanton infliction of pain, unquote. The punishment here is not unnecessary and wanton, any more than the interrogation at issue in United States v. al-Masri. It is a necessary means, the only means, of deterring this conduct.

I never make it those fifty feet to the AG's party. Instead, I wind up at Blondie's apartment.

We show each other our virus certificates. They're green, clean bills of health. There used to be another kind of "green card," but they don't issue those any more.

Blondie's green card is over a month old, so I should leave, but when was the last time I got laid?

He turns on his screen for a moment. Johnston is screaming, the uncontrolled, high-pitched wail of a trapped animal.

I turn off the screen and lead Tom into his own bedroom.

I tell myself that I'm just randy, that it's been too long. But I know that's not why I'm here. Trouble is, I don't know the real reason I came, any more than I can guess why Blondie went into Jake's tonight and sat down next to me.

JUSTICE YOURSHAW: We allowed this method in al-Masri to try to prevent a terrorist attack. That's not what today's case is about.

MS. MUSGRAVE: I respectfully disagree, Your Honor. Mr. Johnston may attack his victims one at a time, rather than thousands at once as we saw with 9/11 and the Halloween Massacre. But his victims end up dead, and he kills them for no reason other than to terrify the public.

JUSTICE FRANKLIN: You can't think of any other possible motive for these crimes?

Tom is rough with me, almost violent, and as he finishes abruptly, I know I've made a mistake.

But afterwards, he becomes more gentle, caressing and kissing me softly. After a while, we make love a second time, this time slowly and tenderly, and being with him starts to feel right.

Now I know why I am here. It's not sex I'm missing. I am so tired of being strong and independent. I want companionship, even for a single night.

I should know that's not what Tom Biondi has for me. Sometimes you can't see what's right in front of you.

JUSTICE ATWELL: I have no problem defining this as murder, whether or not his victims have died yet. But why isn't capital punishment the appropriate response? Wouldn't that be an eye for an eye?

MS. MUSGRAVE: Because ordinary capital punishment is not effective. A defendant who has It is already expecting to die, and soon.

THE CHIEF JUSTICE: You don't trade an eye for an eye with someone who's already blind.

MS. MUSGRAVE: Exactly.

(Laughter.)

I look down at Tom as I'm getting dressed, and he seems close to tears. "I'm sorry," he says.

I don't know what he means, then suddenly I do. Just like Johnston. He said he was sorry too, and he meant it.

Tom is trying to explain, stumbling over his words, but I don't want to hear it. I bolt for the door.

I run blindly down the street, past the rows of restaurants and bars. From each open doorway, Johnston's screams follow me.

JUSTICE FRANKLIN: So the Petitioner has It, with a capital I. He's going to die anyway.

MS. MUSGRAVE: That's correct. That's why ordinary capital punishment is no deterrent.

JUSTICE FRANKLIN: Well, it would deter him from committing any further crimes.

(Laughter.)

JUSTICE FRANKLIN: You're afraid it won't deter others that also have It, and want to share It. So you want to frighten them with the threat of torture.

JUSTICE ATWELL: But give it the gentle name of "enhanced capital punishment."

MS. MUSGRAVE: They are already under a death sentence from the disease. There's no deterrent unless we impose punishment beyond that.

JUSTICE FRANKLIN: Somehow I just don't think human responses are that simple.

MS. MUSGRAVE: But Justice Franklin, that is not a legal issue. That is a policy decision for the State to make.

JUSTICE FRANKLIN: Perhaps. But I fear this decision is not going to win you any friends.

I wander all night. Time was, a girl couldn't do that in the city. But no one stops me to try to molest me. No one stops me to try to help me.

Sometimes I cry. Sometimes I just feel numb.

I should go to the police, send them after Blondie. I don't. I'm tired of doing justice.

I should go to my doctor for immediate treatment. I don't. I don't want to be told I have It. I don't want to be told I'm dying.

I should talk to someone. I want to, but I can't think of anyone I can talk to about this.

I know that I need to talk to someone. I can't go through this alone.

I check in my purse to make sure I still have my green card. This is going to be a long day, but tonight, I'm going back to Jake's.

I'm going to make some new friends.

Freecell

Chaz Brenchley

> A bomb is an act of beauty.
> A body is a flower, yet to open.
> Blossom falls in the beckoning wind.
> *A bomb is an act of beauty:*

We watched it from above, from behind, from a dozen different viewpoints. Witness was important. Besides, who wouldn't want to see?

Shami had chosen the space herself – a high-grade mall, perfect for her who was a terminal low-grade shopper, perfect for us because these places are so busy, so core, and so carefully supervised – and Tux cut us into ParaSec. We were crushed into a storeroom that day, squeezed between cartons of new hardware for the livebars, the four of us and Tux who takes up no space physically, only all the mental space there is. On a normal day, that is, he takes up all the space. Today – well, today there was Shami. The five of us and Shami, so many images of her, and another on every monitor we could unpack. We pulled them from the cartons, powered them up, linked them in; Tux filled them. He filled our eyes with her, she filled that crowded room.

The boys had brought stills, hardcopy captures from all the times they'd had with her: parties and sex sessions, chill sessions, X-ports. And shopping, eating, talking, all the things she simply did when she wasn't doing anything else. Sleeping. I was surprised, how many shots there were of Shami sleeping. Probably I shouldn't be; the boys did like to share, and whatever they shared together they always wanted to share with the world after.

So many caps, bright memories of Shami in her pomp, in her clothes, in her skin. And suited up outside the habitat, Shami at play in her skypinks, drifting off beneath a lightrider or leading a scramble from the dead pitted mouths of the ramjets to the bright windows of the Bridge. That was Shami to the core, Shami at her best, racing and gambling and breaking whatever she could, records and rules and safety codes and more, snapping off the odd antenna as she leaped for a handhold here, dishing the occasional dish there as her boot scrabbled for purchase. Wherever she went, whatever she did, she always left a trail, detritus in her wake. Broken hearts, broken bones, as many broken devices as she could manage. She'd have been brigged for that if they'd ever caught up, wastage is the one true offence Upside, the core of all law; but of course they never did.

After today, after we were gone they'd find this room enshrined to her, the walls bedecked with her still image, and all these screens replaying what she did today. Then they might catch on, but still they'd never catch up. We ride the leading wave; they push us forward, even as they chase.

Shami was everywhere, and she'd never looked more beautiful than she did on the monitors today. We'd fixed her make-up for her with the tattoo-gun, to be sure it didn't smudge.

Blood rose in full thorn: this wasn't her native mall, and she should have been triggering every alarm ParaSec has, simply by being there and looking like she did. Tux was covering that, though, filtering what the system picked up or else blocking its reaction, so that she could have her day her way. All those lenses were turned on her, but there was only us to see: us and the people shopping all around her, clean and corporate, an exercise in contrast.

Her hair was a crimson crest, and that same colour – selfsame, the tattoo-gun had matched it – was dragged down like leakage from her hairline, as if the dye had oozed and stained her skin. As if. Off her brow, it dripped and streaked like tears down her cheeks; but the heart of chaos is certainty, and down the jawline it turned fractal, dominant, a little scary.

The backs of her hands we'd done like traditional henna patterning, but still in that rich crimson, like blood against her nut-butter skin.

Generally she had more skin on show, but face and hands was it today. For the rest, she was in clothes. Remarkable clothes, clothes that told a story. It was a lie, or at least a fiction, but that was legit; she lacked the body to sustain the lie, so she couldn't even pretend to be faking it. She was dressed that way for herself and for us, and for the moment.

What she wore was miners' gear from the Downside bubble colony: rockboots and padded trousers, hippohide jacket hanging down over her knees. The shoulder seams reached halfway to her elbows. If we hadn't rigged straps to hold them rolled back double on themselves, the sleeves would have swallowed her hands and never given them up again. Then no one would have seen the pretty patterns.

She looked tiny, in those clothes. Well, she was tiny, but she looked absurd, a little kid playing dress-up in her daddy's gear. It was all old stuff well used, the real thing, no kitsch fashion copies with designer stitching and live logos; she'd insisted on that. Ripped seams, scuffed toes, patches on the elbows, the smells of dust and sweat and machine-oil spilled in the dark.

She looked tiny and vulnerable and utterly lost, adrift in that high-status mall and dressed in someone else's dirt. People glanced at her in that way that says "Where's security, why hasn't she been lifted yet? She belongs Downside, if she belongs anywhere. Or lurking in the flea-markets, perhaps. With the other fleas. Not here..."

They gave her room, but never room enough. What's to be afraid of, in a badly-dressed girl? They didn't need to shun her; she was beneath their shunning. If she was in their way, they stepped around her. That was all.

Besides, that little-girl-lost look was unutterably sexy. Here, where the clientele was as brightly polished as the floor, her simple presence was like finding a brothel suddenly open in the lobby of a chapel: shocking and compulsive, attractive on a gravitational scale. She drew men towards her, and women too. We could have boosted that with a pheromone spray, but she said no; she knew we wouldn't need to. Shami always knew.

They came close, they peeped or glanced or stared openly; they swerved around her and moved on, and most of them looked back. Some of them, the young ones, lingered; they murmured between themselves, paused by a display, made large and positive gestures to each other, *I'm sure there was something better back that way* and so somehow happened to end up going the same way that Shami was.

She was a comet with a tail, our Shami, dragging the less committed in her unheeding wake. She knew.

Upside there are malls for the likes of us, malls for the likes of them, malls for those who are unlike anything you've ever seen. But never mind the grav settings and never mind the air, never mind the company, the credit or the clientele: they all follow the same configuration, they're all bent around the same arc of orbital wall and they cling to all the old ways of real-time shopping. There are long galleries for the boutiques or stores or market stalls, extended five ways from a central hub; half a dozen access points, then, but one node, one place to meet, to eat — if eating's what you do — and talk, show & tell, compare & contrast, do everything that's shoppy that you don't actually need to do in a shop.

Shami headed for the hub, and so did half the folk who saw her, and why not? They had nothing better to do with their time; in that echelon, even wastage was let by, even something that couldn't be recycled.

Shami had something exact to do with her time, and she'd chosen it as carefully as she had the space. This was mid-shift; to be shopping now was a statement, an expression of wealth. If you were in the mall, you were not, by any definition, working. By any definition, then, you didn't need to work.

By some definitions, that made you waste, in and of yourself. Here, of course, that didn't matter.

This high in society, to be seen was as important as seeing for yourself. They shopped, they paraded, they forgathered; the hub was crowded, even before Shami erupted into it with her entourage.

Her shriek of hair, above her hopelessly inappropriate clothes and the sense she gave of almost slipping out of them at every step; her entranced pursuit, half the glitteryouth of Upside sauntering so casually at her heels, just hoping to see who she was and what she did, what she was doing here; small wonder if heads turned at her arrival, conversations faltered.

Oh, she knew what she was doing. She walked solidly, determinedly to the heart of the hub, where there was just never quite enough seating; she blinked at all those busy tables, all those curious and bewildered faces;

she glanced behind her at her captive, captivated audience; and then she looked at us.

She'd researched this, all of it, so well. She knew just where the lenses were. She found one, no hesitation, no casting about. And lifted her hands to her neck, and one by one set all her fingers just where they ought to be, under the jawline there, on the nodes we'd tattooed in last night.

A moment before the last finger touched home, she smiled at us all and said, "Contact." Tux caught the sound from somewhere and piped it through to us, one last touch of her voice, and half a breath of wasted air, and–

Connectivity is all.

Power was in her fingertips, the implants that we'd set there earlier this morning. The tattoos were conductive, her skin beneath her clothes a minutely detailed circuit-board, a chart of binary instruction. Those instructions followed intricate paths, and learned, and passed the word along; and the word was *finish*, unless it was *begin*.

Every cell in her body below the neck heard that word, and for once in her life she was obedient. She let go, or they did: all the energy inherent in a biomass was released on the instant.

And was contained, briefly, by that so-carefully-chosen clothing; and that was her achievement, to make herself a bomb.

Half the security lenses went dark, a moment after. We lost all our near views; kinder souls might have been grateful. We were jubilant, celebrating, loving our friend and her success and ourselves too for being her friends, but we still wanted to see; there was a chorus of appeals to Tux, to find some closer feed.

The miners in that bubble Downside wear steel mesh inforcements as standard, against the certainty of being slammed around by tremors, flesh into rock. Wrap that around an explosion – a human bomb, a biombe – and every ripped-open link is a flechette. The boots were steel-lined, for a weightier shrapnel. In an open, unprotected space, Shami in her clothes was simply lethal.

The long views that we had just showed us bodies, wreckage, everything overturned that wasn't torn apart. The display cases in the walls were armoured plass, and even those were smashed.

From distance, all we could see of the bodies was how they lay, broken and thrown. We called that urban sprawl. And giggled, and thought ourselves so clever, and longed for close-ups. Light reflected oddly, darkly all around them; we could intuit, we could understand but we wanted to see. Witness was important. We didn't only want to count the dead, it's not a numbers game, we had to clock the damage.

It's not just a numbers game. Numbers of course are important. There may be no glamour in them, but impact, yes, they do have impact. So long as they're big. These days, you really need three figures if you want the news 'cast anywhere beyond the orbital.

We had that, all of that and more. Shami had that. This was her day, and it was a triumph.

There were figures – the other sort of figures, wet ones – moving among the fallen, of course there were. You never do get all your dead together, all at once. Some of these might even survive – though the heavy metals and other tox that clung to the miners' gear would tend to work against that, in the run. Might be the long run, if they were lucky. But if they were lucky, they wouldn't be here, now, in that condition. Barbed.

There was movement on the edges, around the walls of the hub. Movement away, the walking wounded and the truly, amazingly lucky, the untouched; we didn't care about that. They were witnesses, they mattered, but only generically. What we wanted was movement towards, help on its way – and here it came, magnificently just too late.

Tux must have tipped them off, the Corps, just that calculated little time before the blast. He's good like that.

So in they came, helmets and body-armour and weapons at the ready, just in case; and every helmet had a lens, and every lens was uplinked to ParaSec, so Tux could suck on their feed and give it all to us.

The monitors gave us everything they saw and everything they sent, the whole heads-up display. That's what we used to call them, Heads-Up, HU for short when we were kids and always in a hurry, spraying or breaking something and running away. You'd think it would be hard to run Upside, when you can't get off-station and there are lenses everywhere, but there's always some corner to hide in when you're little and squirmy and not scared of the dark. And that was before we had Tux on our side, fouling signals and fudging records, hiding us in a whole new dimension of concealment.

They – the Corps, HU, and the Council too, all our good governance – thought they knew all about us, but they didn't know about Tux. They thought we were over, finished, dead. And so we were, in any way that mattered; but – well, they didn't know about Tux. Nobody did. They may have suspected something, but it was probably a human hand they thought at work, sabotaging and subverting their precious system. They purged it anyway, at regular intervals and on general principles, but for Tux too – unreadable, unknowable Esparantux, coded in a language no one spoke, he said – there was always somewhere to hide.

Their own safety is their prime concern, when the Corps moves in. Heavily Underwritten, Tux says. I wouldn't know about that, but heavy-handed, that's for sure. Best not to be a bystander. These people didn't know that. Survivors and onlookers, the walking wounded and the simply stunned: they lacked the wit to melt away, and so they found themselves staring into the bellmouth of a piezol, hearing the traditional, thoroughly unofficial warning, *all I need to do is close my fist...*

That was old to us, listening in from our cupboard, we'd heard it all our lives. To them it was shocking, and they were shocked already; this was the kicker, to see their rescue & protection come and have it turn on them, find themselves the wrong side of the weapon.

We saw their fear, their bewilderment close-to, through the helmet lenses. Outrage would come later, no doubt. For now there was only one more unexpected terror to endure, an unfamiliar obedience to authority that till now they had thought belonged to them. They fumbled for ID when it was demanded, they backed off at the wave of a piezol, they stood where they were told and stammered answers: no, they didn't know what had happened here; a girl, they thought, perhaps, and an explosion; no, she hadn't seemed to have a partner; no, there had been no threats, no speeches, no warning of any kind; no, this blood that spattered them, they didn't think it was their own...

For some of them, of course, it was their own. Some hadn't realised until they looked down, saw it, suddenly felt the pain.

No matter; they were walking wounded, they could look after themselves or each other. The Corps didn't do concern. Once they were sure of no second biombe, no sniper in the aisles, no ambush, those helmet-heads all turned away from the margins, back towards the heart, what we most wanted to see.

Close-to, there was nothing leisurely, nothing relaxed about those sprawly bodies. Even those that were still relatively whole carried Shami's eruptive message, writ large in how awkwardly they lay, posed by a brutalising hand; writ small all over, where the spray of shattered steel wire had ripped flesh to the bone.

I could never have imagined so much blood. It had nowhere to pool on the marblised flooring, quicksilver-smooth; it just flowed in search of a drain that wasn't there, sucked this way and that by fluctuations in the artificial gravity. It made a dark mirror that underlay every view we looked at.

People still moved, in every view we looked at. That was the Corps' first role, always, to find the living in among the dead. Once found, there was a quick triage, a rapid assessment of their chances; but the Corps is not medically trained, except in a swift despatch. And wastage is still the ultimate crime, and who would waste air – who among the electors would vote to waste air – or other resources on someone who would certainly be an expensive dependent hereafter? Anyone who hasn't got to their feet and at least tried to get out of there before the Heads-Up come, anyone who can't do more than just lift their head up in hope – well, lifting their head only makes it easier, is all.

The mercy-chord is a neat white plastic box that adheres to the temple when it's put there, it clings to the skin until the HU presses a button. Then it unleashes a disharmonic pulse, a chord that simply undoes the human brain, disrupts its sequencing, makes every separate synapse miss fire all at once, and there's an end of it.

We watched this, over and over. People were alive, and then they were not, and we could see it happen. Shami had achieved the same thing, but not been able to watch; we did it for her, as much as for ourselves.

Tux says the chord is inductive, it resonates through the skull and inward, so the operator is entirely safe. We wouldn't have trusted the device ourselves, we agreed that, but the Corps is trained to be without imagination; Highly Unresponsive, Tux says, when he isn't calling them the Hitler Euth.

Then all the monitors changed to the one image, the one man's work, as he turned from his latest execution and took up another role.

Many of the dead were frankly in pieces, where shrapnel had disarticulated them. Someone had to pick up all those pieces, and the Corps was ready to do that, in the interest of gathering evidence. This man maybe didn't know it as he did it, but he'd just found Shami's head.

That had been her one stipulation, that she wanted to leave her head intact. For evidence's sake, for DNA certainty, *I did this*; but also for the art of it, the style, the statement. *See, my body is my weapon, as it always was — but my face is my own, and will outlive me.*

He picked it up, and for a moment she was there in his hands and we could see her, and oh, but she was beautiful.

A body is a flower, yet to open:

The boys went to the game, of course, together. It's good to share.

Tash and I didn't need to lurk in some unseen space to watch this; the game was out there, public, all but compulsory. Every livebar showed it live on every screen. We got to party while we kept an eye on what our friends were up to. We couldn't talk to Tux, of course, directly; but we knew he was watching us as well, we knew he'd be listening in, he'd find some way to get a message to us if he had to.

We were being perhaps a little more careful than before. The Corps, the Council, they had all thought we were dead before. Ourselves, our cause, our struggle, all finished with, over. Most of us were, indeed. And the cause, for sure. We were the remnant: pitiful probably, hopeless certainly, doomed undeniably.

And yet, they had shrugged us off too soon and we had punished them for it, and that was a victory, no doubt; and tonight was another already. Even before we saw the boys inside the stadium, we'd won. ParaSec was everywhere: scanning, searching, questioning. The start of the game had been delayed, because they were so slow to pass the audience through. The Council would be hating that, every aspect of it; if they could hear the conversation in our bar — and they could, for sure, if they asked to — they'd hate it more. Ridicule is the hardest thing to bear, in the face of failure. They'd declared us beaten, and Shami had shown them oh so wrong in that; and now their hard arm had to underline it, a guard on every corner and no leeway, no grace. Every glance an interrogation: *identify yourself, explain yourself, persuade me*. People talked of nothing else. They were scared, twice scared, of us and of the Corps, and so they mocked us both and the Council too. We didn't care; every laugh was a score for us, a loss for the Council, joy.

Tonight we were joyful beyond measure, because the screen commentary was suddenly turned up loud, just as if someone wanted to drown out all those little conversations all through the orbital, and had given orders that it should be so – but even the commentators at the game were talking about security, because they had nothing else just yet to talk about.

They noted ParaSec everywhere, they couldn't not, and the screens followed their words to emphasise all those helmets, gloves, batons, the inherent threat of power and the manifest failure of the Council to keep the people safe. That would have been enough for us, on any other night; tonight there was more, so much more. There was a special section in the stands, they said, finest views and so close to the Council's own box, set aside for victims of the outrage at the mall. Not many of them, of course, the mercy-chords had seen to that; but there were a dozen survivors in seats and another half-dozen on wheeled gurneys, improvised – the commentators told us – in lieu of the normal powerchairs for security reasons, because a powerchair meant a fuel cell, which might so easily be rigged by terrorists. Better to be safe, and have these unfortunates fetched in by the Corps, happy to be seen to do their part in serving the community...

They were probably not happy, to be wheeling cripples through the station under the lenses' eyes. We were delighted, because two of those cripples were our own best boys, Tanner and Maxie.

Tux had faked their credentials, giving them a whole history of regular Upside life before they were so unluckily caught up in the catastrophe at the mall. Between us, Tash and I with Tux advising, we had done things to their legs that were not fake at all. They did need those gurneys now. On the outside, they sported all the scars and dressings of major surgery, just as all their fellow victims did; and they were of an age, and if the Corps did not remember letting quite so many of the badly wounded live, well, their own records proved them wrong, and there was an end of it.

Soon, there would be an end to it. I wasn't sure that either of the boys could wait for the game to start. We'd done what we could with neural blocks, but Tash and I were like the Corps, not medically trained except in ways of killing; there was abiding pain, however much we all pretended. And more than pain, because we couldn't use the tattoo-gun again, anyone with tats was simply taken. We'd needed to be cruder and more clever, and no body was made to endure what we'd done to those poor boys. They were numbed on the one hand and drugged up on the other, and it left them feeling sick and sore all through, they said. They weren't sure quite how long they could bear it. Kick-off would be good, we all agreed, but if not – well, no matter.

They'd waited for the Council, that at least. There were fanfares and announcements, speeches and entrances, iron-haired men and women dressed to rule and acknowledging the crowd. Tanner and Maxie were below and to the side, a little, but really very close. That hadn't been our aim, but it was a gleeful bonus.

There would be a show, parades and music before the game began. It was too much to ask. Tux found a view that focused on our boys, and that was good enough; that was plenty. He cut it suddenly into every screen in the livebar, likely every screen on the station. People yelled in protest, but they went on watching; there was nothing else to look at.

We saw the boys holding hands, gurney to gurney; we saw them haul each other up, lean in.

We saw them kiss.

This was a truecast camera we were watching through, not a hidden speck of short-range security lens. It must have been right across the other side of the stadium, to see all this and not lose a moment of its image.

We saw the kiss, Tash and I, and held hands ourselves beneath the table.

The boys were each other's catalysts – "as we always have been," they'd said, loving it, wanting no other solution – and their saliva was the vector. The bones of their legs were reservoirs, the marrow all sucked out and replaced with tox, two separate cocktails, harmful on their own, explosive in combination. The moulded plass that made a protective shield for the boys' poor wounded bodies, covering them from the waist down – clear plass, to show the Heads-Up that there was nothing but damaged flesh and bone beneath – was made to shatter, to shard like steel.

We saw them go in a flare of light, a great disintegration. We whooped stupidly into that suddenly silent bar; but Tux was ahead of us, as ever, dialling up the volume even as we shrieked. Not much he could do to disguise our leaping up, and we did that too; but then there was so much swearing, shoving, rushing about in such a small space, no one was likely to remember two kids who were a fraction premature in their reaction, who seemed more celebratory than shocked.

Tux fed the Corps' audio channel all through the station, to let everyone know just how panicked they were, how out of control. No one else would have noticed his own voice among so many, though to us it was sharp and clear, cutting through the hubbub in the livebar and telling us to get out of there, where to go, what route to take.

We did what we were told. Perhaps we skipped it where we should have walked, danced instead of running; but that was all tribute to the boys, Tux must have known that, and he could hide it from any authoritative eyes who might come scanning, now or later.

As we went, we heard news all the way, reports from the bewildered

Corps still echoing down every corridor. Half the Council was down, by the sound of it. Headless Uproar, Tash suggested, but just for a moment there, I didn't want to laugh. A year ago, when we were a Movement, that would have been a triumph; it might even have led to real measurable victory, the whole system down and a new dispensation. Now it was only incidental, a distraction even, not the point at all. Who would stop to think about the thing itself, the achieve of it, if all they did was number and name the dead?

Tux sent us to a public baths, empty, out of use according to the panel by the door. It opened at our approach, though, and locked again behind us. Nobody showers, Upside; water is heavy but energy is cheap, and a little steam goes a long way. Tux gave us as much steam as we could bear, till the walls ran with condensation and there were conspicuously wasteful puddles on the floor, another petty blow for freedom.

I wished aloud that the boys had been the other end of the stadium, away from the elite. It would have kept the action pure, I said, save it looking political. When there's nothing left to fight for, I said, it's a shame to have people misunderstand the fight. They'd pass us off as helpless, hopeless: bitter failures who couldn't recognise their own defeat.

Tash said no. She said it didn't matter what they thought, what they said, what they wanted. She came and lay beside me, warm and wet, a skinful of content; she said this was what mattered, this and this, her body and my own. Beauty is what you do, she said, not how you're interpreted. It's an absolute, she said, it has to be. That's what this is all about, she said; if we can't set our people free, then fuck it, let's outshine 'em.

You know all this, she said, you do. And she was right, of course, I did. So I kissed her and nestled close; and was it Tash or was it me who asked Tux to rerun all that coverage on the screens in the bath-house there, so that we had Maxie and Tanner erupting silently, vastly, continually on every wall, giving a reflective glory of gas-giant colours to the billowing steam...?

Blossom falls in the beckoning wind:

We're ambitious, Tash and I. When we go – soon now, soon – we want it to be effulgent; but it needs to be on a human scale too. No warnings, though, no statements, no messages of any kind. We agreed that after Conclave was betrayed, we last half-dozen shabby survivors watching the bulk of us, the best of us displayed in triumph every hour on the hour while commentators endlessly debated our destruction. From then on, what we did had to speak for itself, these brief parting glances, little glimpses of a waking world. Shami has spoken, and the boys, magnificently so; what else is said comes down to us, and what we can achieve together.

It has to be together. We need to help each other, physically and otherwise. Tux will do what he can, of course, but he has limits and he has his own concerns, which he can't or won't share with us. A rebel program, a ghost in the machine: how could we hope to understand him?

I'm fairly sure he understands us very well. Sometimes I think he made us – not in his image, exactly, but surely to his design. History asserts that the Movement came first, but history can be wrong. Or faked, to give us faith in ourselves. Perhaps he lurked, guiding the early pioneers discreetly from the shadows, and only revealed himself later; or – sudden inspiration! – perhaps he only ever revealed himself to us, his last few surviving children. Those who recruited us, they never spoke of him; he came later, after the betrayal, seeking us out in our solitude, in our couples, in our bewilderment. He brought us together and gave us this last and beautiful purpose, to assert the power of what we do, *sui generis*, whole unto itself.

We don't need to declare our cause; why would we? They know who we are and what we stand for, what we used to fight for. They have the lists of our demands; all that is known ground, quarrelled over, unconceded. They have the lists of our dead, just as we do theirs. We at least will not parade our own, to their shame and our own.

What we will do, we will parade ourselves. Here's joy: the Council – what's left of the Council – has so lost touch, lost confidence, lost control, they've gifted us the only victory we want now. They're casting an appeal, to us directly: to Tash, to Tux, to me, though I don't suppose they know our names or number. 'To the last pitiful remnant of the insurgency' is what they say – see, I said we were pitiful – but even that's a capitulation. They want us to stop killing innocents, our brothers and sisters of the Upside; they appeal to our intelligence, to our humanity, to realise that it achieves nothing. We note that they made no such appeal until we'd killed a few of them, and no doubt others – the human, the intelligent – will note it too. No matter. They ask what we can hope to win, and never understand that in their question is our reply. Just the asking cedes the ground to us.

As an afterthought, a gesture, they invite us to surrender.

That's what we'll do, then, Tash and I. Publicly, in one last arena.

We're not naïve, we don't imagine for a moment that we'll get anywhere near the people who matter. ParaSec will interpose the bodies of the Corps as a kind of insulation, Heavily Upgraded. What they don't understand, what they'll never understand, is that we don't care.

No more multideaths, but so what? It never was about the numbers. Everyone – station-wide, system-wide – absolutely everyone will be watching. Tux will make sure of that. We'll march into whatever space has been agreed, we'll gaze around at whatever cordon sanitaire they've dared to risk themselves behind – and we'll smile at each other, and whisper to each other because there is no point in shouting now, and the words we say will trigger each other's little, little packages, and we'll go off *pouf!* under the bright and fascinated gaze of every lens that could squeeze or argue, bully or smuggle its way in.

Just the two of us, together, that's enough. That's a statement of intent.

I don't know what mess they'll be left with, to clear up after. How much damage can two people do? Two more deaths, numerically that shouldn't matter. Politically, they can try to spin it as their victory, the end of the insurgency, security restored; there's not a chance of that. Who would believe them, or us? Lambs to the slaughter, we're going to look like, two scapegoats sent out as cover, nothing more. Tash and I, we could never be convincing. They're looking for masterminds, Machiavellian corruptors; all we have to offer them is us, young and sweet and hopeful.

Maybe the station will rise up in disgust against the overlords, when it sees us give our pretty lives away.

Maybe not. It hasn't yet, so why would it now? We're not that hopeful, truly.

Truly, what I'm guessing, I think Tux will finish what we started. Once that 'cast goes out, once the message spreads, I think he'll wait till things settle down again, until they think we really are defeated, dead, no more – and then he'll blow the station. All of it. I think he can do that. *Fiat lux.*

I'm sure he'll have cameras beyond the orbital, to see it happen and send the images on. Hey, he's Tux; he'll wait till there are people out there playing X-ports, with lenses on their lightriders. They'll see it, they'll record it; and then that photon-wave will send them riding far, far out into the dark, and they should be glad of that because they'll be surfing ahead of the worse radiation, our own manufacture of solar wind, and just maybe someone will come and find them before their air runs out. If not, someone's sure to come and find their bodies, with their records, what they saw.

The Rural Kitchen

H. H. Løyche

2008-05-19

Dear Mr. Pierre Moisan,

thank you for submitting *The Rural Kitchen*. Having discussed your manuscript, we agreed that the concept is splendid and your research seems thorough. Although charming, the slightly old-fashioned style might however prove difficult to sell, and we need to run some market analysis before taking a final decision. You'll hear from us in approx. three months.

Sincerely yours,
M. Capra, editor
Raspberry Books

The strange fact that nobody took responsibility for the 9/11 attack shows that terrorists do not always wish to deliver a message. The reason therefore is found among the many motives for terrorism, ranging from revenge to sheer frustration. The latter can be observed when private problems like poverty, unreasonable case workers, lack of appreciation, sexual incapability, unemployment, bitchy bosses, or nasty neighbours, build up anger and irritation in a person until he or she snaps. It is obviously the case when somebody gets too sensitive to noise, feels provoked by coughs, and shows hatred towards anonymous, albeit easy-to-recognize groups, such as foreigners, bikers, homosexuals, pet-owners, and Electric Light Orchestra. Unable to fight back, the victims are likely to turn to alcohol, argue with everybody, and beat up their wives and kids. In rare cases, they take hostages, go serial killing, or jump in front of trains as a final manifestation of the general rule:

1. The unloved strive for admiration.
2. The unpopular strive for power.
3. The impotent strive for pity.

The question is not if it can happen to ordinary people, but how and when it ends in violence. And if the fact that the perpetrators refrain from political claims prevent them from being called terrorists, then it is also valid to claim that 9/11 was not terrorism sensu stricto, but merely a large scale act of revenge, inspired by the Hollywood movie *Armageddon*. This distinction between terror and terrorism became clear with the example of the lonely teenage twins, who had had enough of being rejected and put down by class mates. Inspired by the *Home Alone* movies, they began building catapults to terrorize fellow citizens with rotten eggs and doggy doos. When the twins were eventually caught, their ingenious traps had not only spoiled dresses, but injured thirteen people and killed the chairwoman of the local horticultural society. But what else could they do but spend their spare time booby trapping Hastings?

2009-04-07

Dear Pierre Moisan,

it is my pleasure to inform you that *The Rural Kitchen* is scheduled for publication in our upcoming Fall edition. Although several recipes (such as soap boiling and treatment of sores) fall well outside the traditional contents of cook books, we nevertheless decided to include almost all. We believe that your historical angle can add a new dimension to our bestselling cook book series. The only exception is the chapter on practical jokes. We hope you will show some understanding about the situation, but we really have no choice, bearing the Hastings twins in mind. We shall contact you a.s.a.p. about the illustrations, propose a contract, etc.

Sincerely yours,
M. Capra, editor
Raspberry Books

Who crashed the stock market? Who caused the explosion at Tjernobyl? Who flooded New Orleans? In cases without a human culprit, the frustration might be directed at an anonymous crowd, not because of any specific misdeed, but precisely because the crowd did little or nothing. For instance, although meteorologists and relief agencies are often issue warnings several months in advance of African droughts, nobody reacts until the pictures of starving babies appear on tv. By the time the help arrives, their brains and organs are so damaged that even if they survive, they will never live a normal life.

In the early afternoon on the 12th of June 2009, an unknown male caucasian was found dead on Venice Beach, Los Angeles. Two days before, he had checked into the nearby Cadillac Motel using a false name and paying in cash. It is likely however, that he was a medical doctor and had been working abroad for the Red Cross. A witness had noticed him shopping for an enormous number of stock cubes. He described him as a quiet and somewhat shy bloke, certainly not someone you would fear. According to another witness, the man had spent the evenings in the lobby, drinking a few beers and staring at his ballpen, as if grappling with a difficult message he had to write. He never, however, wrote a single word. It is believed that the ballpen contained the Anthrax spores which he added to the lukewarm soup in the water bed, just before checking out. Being only a matter of time before someone drained the water bed, it was likewise only a question of time before a thousand litres of Anthrax were released into the alley behind the motel. Any person exposed to the soup would have caught and spread the disease. Unlike the Anthrax powder used in letters, the virus in the water bed was an unimpaired live strain, highly contagious and capable of killing millions of people. The death of the unknown man himself however, prevented the situation from escalating. A mere dozen people died and the sales figures for soup, water beds, and ballpens dropped only for a while. Unfortunately, nobody suspected that before the unidentified man fell victim to his own terror plan, he had prepared water beds in a hundred motels across USA. It is estimated that within the eight months that he toured the States on a zigzag course from New York to Los Angeles, he produced a hundred thousand liters of concentrated Anthrax. Although many theories were presented, the motive which drove him remains obscure. The leaflet found in his wallet might have been a coincidence: a request to support the starving Africans. It is a fact however, that bombs and soldiers are swiftly shipped to install democracy, but soup and medicine always arrive too late.

2010-06-14

Dear Pierre Moisan,

although expressions such as "liquid bird" are not listed under The Publication Act, the references to c...... s... and other meals are highly problematic. Moreover, illustrations never enjoyed protection by the constitution. As in fact, any correction of your manuscript may prove insufficient to ward off The Censor Commission or boycott of our backlist, I am sad to inform you that I dare not publish *The Rural Kitchen*. I like your writing though, and strongly encourage you to submit another manuscript.

Best regards,
Matthew Capra, editor-in-chief
Raspberry Books

PS. In case you contact me again, please avoid using ballpen.

The new age sects recruited many members around the new milennium. The "Uploaders" for instance, which believed in the preservation of bodies for a future, when they could 'upload' to and live forever in computer systems. They spent a lot of time and money building failsafe and self-sufficient cryotoriums in desolate caves and old NATO bunkers, and a good many families went bankrupt long before they ended up frozen in liquid nitrogen. The members of another sect committed collective suicide as they believed every comet or astronomical event was a sign, that flying saucers were coming to raise their spirits to a state of 'higher' consciousness in another world. They claimed that Hopi Indians were able to interpretate the prophecies of crop circles and shaman ritual drawings at Nasca. Accordingly, they had shared their knowledge with the new age gurus, but not with 'lower' spirits, who might be tempted to misuse it. And who knows, maybe they were better and wiser than normal people? At least they were thinking in advance and offered help in time. With the best intention, they set out to rescue 'lower' spirits, bringing as many as possible along when they left the material world.

Yet another sect believed in Gyp, a godlike creature, which secretly thrived in the telepathic subconsciousness of all minds in the universe. Gyp was distributed wherever living bodies were located, and was said to 'manage' the spirits of everyone. It was Gyp who guided Muhammed, Jesus, and Buddha, and Gyp even came in handy as an explanation for reincarnation: memories from dead people temporarily stored in other brains. But in the fall of 2010, Gyp ran into trouble. A dark (for us undetectable) interrupt field drifted trough the galaxy, blocking all telepathic contact on its course. This blocked the return of spirits to Gyp, which normally took place at the moment of death. You may say, Gyp was threatened by a kind of black hole, sucking in spirit and leaving matter unaffected. To prevent the massive harm, Gyp had to evacuate the spirits of a few hundred solar systems, and the sect was convinced that we were obliged to help. That's why they poisoned food in supermarkets, shot people at random in discos and holiday resorts, and set fire to the cryotoriums to thaw the Uploaders. Was it emergency aid or terrorism?

2011-02-23

Mr. Pierre Moisan,

consider this as a warning. Future attempts to contact my client will be met by legal actions and your letters and manuscripts will be forwarded to the military for analysis.

On behalf of Elderberry Printed Matter,
Ethan Barlow, solicitor

Admittedly, some people do seem debased to an animal-like, instinctive existence, eating, breeding and behaving like soulless flesh machines. And others seem to believe in whatever rubbish they hear or read, like the explanations given, when, in the crazy summer of 2011, ordinary people began killing their own families, and were afterwards unable to give reasonably explanations for their behaviour. Or maybe they couldn't express the origin of their dissatisfaction? Even children and old people went on killing sprees in those days, armed with kitchen knives and garden tools. Hummer owners used their vehicles against each other, and competed to run down bicyclists and pedestrians. If this was for sport, I need not mention what happened to games like darts, golf, or cricket. The pubs were crowded with home defence fanatics and survivalists in blood-sprinkled shirts, boasting about the number of people they'd shot and toasting for the best murder stories. The survivors weren't too eager to get to the hospital. Doctors and nurses were less interested in treatments than in imposing additional pain – not to mention designing new, lethal diseases to try out on the patients. Violent riots started spontaneously – attacks on public schools, football stadiums, airports and so on. Airline passengers agreed to take over their aircraft and crash into nuclear power plants. Firemen became serial arsonists and fought their arch-enemy, the police. Oh yes, this was truly the golden age of terrorism. Everybody was enrolled in one or more terror cells. The secret services had a hard time trying to track new groups and networks, and distinguish earnest militias, like the Lodge of Virulent Englishmen and Armed Resistance to Terror, from mere hobbyists, such as ELM (The Ecological Left's Martyrium) and ELO (Electric Light Orchestra). It seemed like only the most stubborn, insensitive people pretended to maintain a normal life. As if Gyp himself had taken action.

In the midst of the havoc, academics discussed a global, paradigmatic change, but could not agree what it was. Psychologists as well as neurologists investigated the phenomena and suggested all sorts of contradictory explanations, ranging from pandemic virus, through mental disorder caused by air pollution, to mass psychosis triggered by movie violence. The Armenian sociologist Achot Rafaelovitj Kazarian pointed out a fascinating parallel: bodies and nations fell apart, as if cancer cells and human beings were thinking the same: "What has the community ever done for me? I'm not gonna struggle, take orders or behave myself any more. I want my part of the fun – and I want it now!" But whatever results the scientists came up with, they were used as bad excuses for destructive behaviour. When military force was finally introduced, it just added to the problem. Nothing seemed to help, not even the massacre of the Hopi Indians.

2011-12-18

Dear Pierre,

regrettably, I am still unable to publish *Rural Delights*. I am ever so sorry, but it is not solely due to the illegal beans, mustard, or spices mentioned. No matter if you rewrite the entire book in accordance with the PA Positive List, it seems futile to try and publish cook books (or any other kind of literature, for the matter). At least within the foreseeable future. Books have low priority when people need food, water, medicines, and shelter.

Faithfully yours,
Matthew

Experienced first-hand by many people, terrorism is neither a new phenomenon nor an activity restricted to brainwashed fundamentalists, eager to sacrifice themselves. Throughout history, people of alternate beliefs have been forced to obey the majority, innocent families have been exploited and made to pay the price for countless wars, and brute repression and torture formed part of everyday life in many regimes. The reactions were not unexpected. While some groups called for armed revolution, however, others sought peaceful means to defend their right to exist. Because of these disagreements and common concerns among terror cells and similar organizations, violent acts were often organized by contradictory alliances. Individual businessmen and criminals, religious sects, secret services, labour organizations, and opposition parties as well as governments made networks, in which some members planned the terror, others gave the order, still others delivered the weapons, a cell executed the plan, and more cells covered it all up. It was not unusual that terrorists tried to steal the credit for an activity in which they had had no part, or on the contrary, tried to blame somebody else. In the case of the latter, it was typically to help a Bill being passed, or to prevent a party from forming government, or to justify an invasion. Thus, it could be difficult to figure out who took the initiative and for what purpose, and it is ridiculous to state that the culmination of Western interference in the Middle East came on Sunday the 23rd of December 2012. There is no doubt that this date marks the most remarkable terror deed ever; a cheap and easy operation, but nevertheless a record in casualties and material damage. It was also made by one of the most mixed groups ever: an Islamic linguist, a former US Marine, a Greek actress, a Hopi Indian, and a French cookery editor. They did not leave any message, and apart from the consequences, it remains a mystery why they hired a helicopter and flew a few barrels of fabric softener into a volcano on the Canary Islands. Beneath Las Palmas existed a system of bowl-shaped, massive rocks filled with porous lava, and the rock prevented the rain water absorbed in the lava from escaping into the ocean. When the soap-like catalyst was poured into the crater, it reduced the surface tension of the lava and allowed it to float as it never had before. Disaster was inevitable. When the volcano erupted, the lava rushed into the ancient lava tunnels and heated up the water to extreme temperatures. The steam pressure caused the largest explosion in the history of mankind, sending twenty kilometers of mountain into the ocean, which gave rise to a wave several hundred meters high. The wave traveled four times around the planet, sweeping away everything in its course. Island realms were wiped out and coast lines battered beyond recognition. The American East coast, which the wave reached eight hours after the eruption, was most vulnerable. Metropolises like Boston, Norfolk, Providence, New York, and Miami vanished completely. Even cities along rivers far inland, such as Baltimore and Washington, were flooded. Only Europe, the Middle East, and Asia were relatively unaffected, except the weather remained unbearable for decades after, leaving almost no crop to harvest.

2018-10-10

Hi Pierre,

what a surprise hearing from you after all these years! Especially since, some time ago I came across *The Rural Kitchen* in my archives. Ezra has tried out some of the recipes and I have found much useful advice on brewing. Now, I simply cannot resist asking for your permission to distribute handwritten copies among the British island camps. It is my conviction that your work can serve to improve life over here, along with the line of survival guides which seems so popular these days.

One of my co-editors survived as well. He'd been hiding in the wilderness somewhere North of the Arctic Circle since that summer of 2011, when everything went haywire. Didn't even know about Las Palmas.

We don't hear much about the provisional government. They declared the majority of old laws void, but never passed any new ones. My impression is that they don't occupy themselves much with legislation or politics. They are still too busy, trying to restore infrastructure, reopen hospitals and schools, and – of course – solve the nuclear reactor problem and whatever mess from days of yore. Ezra and I volunteered for some work too. We spend much time in libraries, saving books from decay and firewood/toilet paper collectors (God! – how I miss real, soft toilet paper). Although the climate is colder and the sky is eerie, life isn't bad and I actually feel that the present world is a better place. I have come to appreciate the quiet hours, wandering to and from libraries. I'm tinkering over a book on terrorism's impact on literature, but might give it up and begin writing poetry. Almost no fiction is produced over here, and I guess it is because we are forced to focus on practical tasks. Sometimes, when passing through downtown Lambeth, I recognize the shapes of bank and office buildings less than a decade old, and just can't figure out what purpose they served. Odd, I was part of it and didn't find anything wrong. In such moments, I wonder whether those terrorists did us a favour. Forgive my frankness, but I do mean that, at some point in life, a lot of us could have joined the Las Palmas group. I think we were too many for this small planet, and the stress made our minds run wild, until it vanished with the drastic decline in population. Everything was owned or occupied, controlled by a company, manipulated by an organisation, or regulated by twisted laws. We were caught in a damned unhealthy situation, where nobody could move a finger without colliding with somebody else's interest. I worked hard to make a living out of my interest, but my time was consumed by the attempts to sabotage or take over my publishing house. In the end, I couldn't recommend a simple pastry recipe without having two or three lawyers checking its origin and copyrights, making corrections, writing declarations, and answering questionnaires from the Censor Committee – and still being sued. You couldn't read anything without dozens of bar codes, approval stamps, logos, notices, and warnings smacked into your face. Why were they so interested in my modest business? How could cook books possibly offend anyone or threaten somebody's power? The pressure was sort of close to critical mass and meltdown of my mind. All respect to the dead, but thank you, dear terrorists, for lifting the burdens from our shoulders. Now we can move into whatever empty house we please, paint it in any colour, and grow potatoes in the neighbours' sofas if we like. We stay in the old Hercules Buildings though, and the potatoes still refuse to grow. And wow, I sleep so well at night.

Hope you are okay too and find comfort in the sweater (knitted by my daughter Sara). We'll try to make it to the continent when the tunnel is drained, hopefully in the upcoming spring. Then maybe we can finally discuss our common passion in a civilized manner...

Till then, yours,
Matthew

The Laughter of Ghosts

Ian Whates

Everybody had forgotten about the Ghurkhas; everybody except Anthony.

Understandable, of course. The British government had wanted them withdrawn and disbanded years ago – too expensive. Besides, what was the point in maintaining a military presence in Brunei these days? Well, there was always the oil, but apart from that?

It was the Sultan who wanted them to remain. He trusted them more than his own troops and for some reason being so closely linked to Britain and Her Majesty's forces still carried a lot of prestige in that part of the world. So he offered to pay for them out of his own pocket.

How could anyone refuse an offer like that?

So there they were. A highly efficient and lethal military force, part of the British army, recruited from one foreign country and paid for by another. Now that is bizarre. Hardly surprising they were over-looked.

Britain had recalled most of her troops in an effort to defend the sovereign Isle, but everything had happened so fast and some units had simply not been able to respond in time. The Americans' first priority had been to mop up such far-flung forces. There had been some heavy fighting but weight of numbers and superior hardware told in the end. There were still rumours of British troops continuing to fight a guerrilla action here and there, but most had quickly capitulated or been taken out.

To all intents and purposes, it was over. Britain had fallen in a little over two weeks. The French were already submitting tenders for a share of the rebuilding work.

Only in Brunei had any sizable force escaped attention. The Americans relied on intelligence provided by the CIA, which proved to be a God-send. The Ghurkhas did not appear on many of the regular military lists – payroll for example – and it seemed that someone at Central Intelligence had skimped on their homework.

Anthony, who had been responsible for liaison with the Ghurkhas during his posting to Brunei, thought of them as soon as news of the invasion broke. He had watched everything closely from afar – no war could be fought in privacy anymore, every move was monitored and reported by the media, every decision discussed and dissected. He used his own position and contacts to fill in the occasional blanks that the media missed.

Nobody had remembered the Ghurkhas in Brunei.

He determined to act independently and made a point of avoiding all official channels, having no idea which might be compromised and no way of knowing whether any of them at all were still valid for that matter.

He slipped out of Singapore just ahead of the world-wide sweep to round up every senior British diplomat and place them under armed guard 'for their own protection.'

His wife and two children, one little more than a babe-in-arms, had already gone to stay with her mother. She was Malayan and they would be as safe with her as anywhere.

Whilst waiting at the airport he caught a glimpse of a newscast by the US President. He was too far away to hear individual words but could make a reasonable guess at the message in any case. Doubtless the propaganda would be delivered with all the conviction and heart-felt sincerity for which the man was famous.

It was odd coming back to Brunei. Like stepping into another world; a tranquil paradise where the upheavals of the outside were no longer relevant, could not possibly be real. The temptation to stay here and simply vanish was seductive and had to be consciously set to one side. He could probably do it, too. He still had many friends here, locals and ex-pats. He could pick up the threads of his past life and disappear, leaving the world to go hang itself.

For how long, though? Only until reality came crashing in – which it would, eventually.

No, there was little point in playing ostrich by ignoring what was going on. Anthony headed straight for the town of Seria, just outside the Bruneian capital, where the 700 or so Ghurkhas were stationed. With him he carried his kukri, the wickedly curved fighting knife which had earned such a fearsome reputation in operations around the globe. His had never seen service. It had been a gift from the officers of the Ghurkha battalion, a sign of friendship and respect – both of which he was fully prepared to call upon if needed.

In the event, they were not. He was escorted directly to a Ghurkha in colonel's uniform. Instant recognition and smiles all round. Prakash, someone he knew well, thank the Lord.

It emerged that the Ghurkhas had been left here in a vacuum for weeks. No orders, no direction and no ideas. Some had deserted, heading back to their native Nepal when it became clear the British cause was lost, but most had stayed on. These were a fiercely loyal and honourable people.

Impotent and frustrated, they watched developments with dismay, not knowing how to respond. They were as pleased to see Anthony as he was to see them and no one chose to dispute his authority. They were also ready to leave at a moment's notice.

Quite why they should be so patriotic to a country not their own was a mystery to anyone who took the trouble to wonder about it. After all, the British had used Ghurkhas as front line troops for decades, throwing them into one hot-spot after another, all the while proud to count them as part of the British army. Until they were either injured or retired.

A former Ghurkha received a pittance, somehow falling outside the normal benefit package available for regular soldiers. Of course, ministers would quote you the reasons for this if pressed. As far as Anthony could recall, they boiled down to two:

1. The British government could not afford the enormous cost involved.

2. The standard of living is completely different in Nepal, so the usual benefits package is neither required nor appropriate.

Whilst granting there was some validity to the second argument, it still smacked of convenient rationalisation to Anthony, who considered their subsequent loyalty a miracle.

The first moment of tension arose at the airport, as they were boarding to leave. A Bruneian official raced up in an open-top jeep with a handful of regular soldiers, demanding they should stop. Two trucks tore up behind them, disgorging more troops.

It was a surreal tableau. On the one side, a hastily gathered squad of visibly nervous soldiers, doubtless wishing they were anywhere else but here. Facing them: a brigade of Ghurkhas, bristling with weapons and itching for a fight.

The ironic part, of course, was that both sides were paid from the same purse.

In the end Anthony and his men were allowed to leave without needing to resort to violence. Frothing at the mouth he may have been, but even the Bruneian official was forced to concede that there was very little he could do to stop them. Just as there was little Anthony could do to stop the Bruneians reporting everything to the Americans. He could only hope they would choose not to – relations between Britain and Brunei had always been pretty good... Mind you, no British official had ever turned up unannounced and walked off with their Ghurkhas before.

That only left the American spy satellites to worry about. Anthony knew full-well how effective they could be. He also knew their limitations. The Yanks could not be watching every inch of the planet's surface every second of the day, and right now there were plenty of other things going on around the world to occupy their attention. He hoped.

Nor did it seem an unreasonable hope when you considered that for all their famed technology and much-vaunted resources, they had failed to notice a whole force of Ghurkhas. God bless the CIA.

Once they were airborne, Anthony had a chance to stop and reflect on what he was doing, to ponder exactly what had prompted him to take such a direct course of action. After all, he was a diplomat, not a soldier. The only battles he had ever taken part in were fought with words and wits. Potent in their own sphere, but hardly credentials for this sort of undertaking.

It had been a news report – the proverbial straw wreaking mischief on the back of an over-stressed camel – a live broadcast direct from London. Even now he could clearly recall the image of General Weiskopf straddling the steps of St. Blair's, eyes invisible behind designer shades, which themselves were shadowed by his pristine camouflage helmet, the unbuckled straps of which fell down each side of his face and bounced disconcertingly as his jowls worked. The General was announcing to the free world that he and his boys were "proud to be instrumental in liberating the oppressed peoples of Great Britain."

He made a great deal out of his having personally witnessed men and women weeping in the streets as American soldiers sauntered past. An unequivocal display of joy and gratitude, or so the General maintained.

Of course, strictly speaking it was only England and Wales that had been 'liberated', but the Americans had even more trouble differentiating between England and Britain-as-a-whole than the English did.

The horrifying images of kilted highland regiments leading the charge against the barricades at the Houses of Parliament, like berserkers of old, were etched indelibly on his memory.

Anthony had always liked the Scots. Why, some of his best friends were Scottish.

He never had grasped the depth of resentment that some Scots nursed towards the English. He knew it was there, but had always thought it little more than good-natured rivalry, given lip-service without actually being adhered to. It was a shock to discover how much more it meant to some.

Conversely, whilst Scotland declared for the Americans, Wales stood firmly by her ties to England within the United Kingdom, suffering some of the heaviest bombing as a consequence. Ireland stayed out of it, but then they had problems of their own, what with the emergence of the New Irish Republican Army.

Despite their name, the NIRA had little in common with the old IRA, but since when had such details ever troubled the opportunist?

Rumours of funding from the States had yet to be substantiated.

Anthony's thoughts ricocheted back to the present. If someone in Brunei did contact the Americans, so be it. He was taking his Ghurkhas to the one place the Americans would never dream of looking. He intended for them to attempt the unthinkable and achieve the impossible. Someone had to strike a blow for Britain. He wondered whether history would remember him as a hero or as a ruthless terrorist. That would all depend on who got to write the history in question, presumably.

When he first set out Anthony had no definite objective in mind beyond reaching the Ghurkhas before someone else remembered them, giving little thought as to what he actually intended to do with them. But during the flight from Singapore a course of action had begun to suggest itself. By the time he landed in Brunei, it had become a fully crystallised agenda.

This whole situation was monstrous; something had to be done. If he remembered his fables correctly, the best way to kill a monster was to strike off its head.

In this instance, that meant killing the President of the United States of America.

Air traffic in and out of the USA had continued to build throughout the new millennium. Of course, with all the uncertainty of war it had tailed off a little recently, but not by much. After all, the war itself was such a long way away.

US air defences were on full alert, but with such a high volume of traffic it was a hopeless task attempting to distinguish the innocent from the potentially threatening. Mistakes were likely to happen. Only two days ago a civil airliner had come down off the coast of Florida, with no survivors. The official line was that it was due to a mechanical problem, but there were persistent rumours that it had been brought down by American air defence systems.

That old familiar phrase 'friendly fire' had been swiftly dusted down for yet another cruise through the tabloid headlines.

Yes, America was vigilant… after a fashion. The problem was, there was something in the American psyche that just couldn't accept the reality of any threat. After all, the war was over, wasn't it? The Brits were beaten. Anyway, who in their right mind was going to invade America?

Okay, so there was Pearl Harbour, but that had been a hit-and-run raid and when you came down to it, that had been Hawaii. Granted, Hawaii was part of the United States, but it was not really America as such, was it?

Then there was 9-11. A lot fresher in the memory, but time remains a great healer and though America would never forget, the passing of decades had soothed the resultant trauma. It still ached like an old, ever-present wound, but it no longer burned with righteous fire.

No one had ever actually invaded the USA.

Until now.

After discussing alternatives with his officers, Anthony decided the best option was to land in Canada, within reach of the US border. The choice was made that much easier by the location of their objective.

The President was spending time at one of his favourite retreats. Not Camp David, but a sprawling manse in Aroostook County, Maine, New England.

They moved mainly at night, infiltrating the border in small units and regrouping once they were on US soil. During the day they would hide out in deep woods. The greatest threat was from tourists and sight-seers, but they were careful and had a lot of country to hide in.

There was only one incident – a family of hikers: mother, father, teenage daughter and younger son. Their dog escaped, which was regrettable but there was no point in fretting about it. The people were dispatched quickly and efficiently, in accordance with Anthony's standing orders. He was no monster, but knew that surprise was everything. They could not afford the slightest risk of discovery. Still, the executions troubled him despite their necessity. He consoled himself with the thought that on a mission like this collateral damage was inevitable...and besides, how many innocents had died in the UK during the last few weeks? Even so, he was relieved that it was another unit that encountered them, glad that he only heard about the killings after the event.

They lived off the land, not easy with such a sizeable group, but if anyone could do it, the Ghurkhas could. Anthony had once spent four days deep in the Bruneian rain forest with a unit of Ghurkhas on a training exercise. They had brought rations, but on the second night out had prepared a meal solely from roots, shoots and leaves gathered from the forest, flavoured with spices from their ration belts.

Remarkably, it was one of the best meals Anthony had ever eaten.

Maine was a long way from Brunei, but the Ghurkhas seemed to have an instinct for ferreting out the edible and nutritious.

The attack was launched two nights after they crossed the border. The President's retreat lay deep in forest and was surrounded by a wooded compound. The US military were there in force but appeared to be pretty relaxed. There were holes in the security all over the place – partly because this was not the easiest of places to secure but mostly because no-one was seriously expecting any trouble.

In their accustomed small units the Ghurkhas drifted through the defensive perimeter like ghosts.

Anthony was with a squad commanded by a Corporal, Pala, whom he had grown to know over the past few days. Pala and his men were assigned to him as bodyguards. Whether they saw this as an honour or a chore, Anthony was never entirely certain.

He did his best, but he was simply not as adept at this sort of thing as his escort. Inevitably, it was his clumsiness that drew the attention of a sentry. Even so, it was not him that the trooper actually discovered but one of the Ghurkhas, who deliberately left himself exposed so that the rest of the party could find cover.

The sentry came toward the crouching Ghurkha, night goggles down and gun levelled. "Hey Sarge, look what we've got here," he called over his shoulder in a loud stage whisper. "A little guy playing at being a soldier." He was still smiling as the Ghurkha disembowelled him. For his part, the sergeant said nothing; principally because he was busy having his throat cut at the time. Neither of the sentries had noticed the second Ghurkha creeping up behind them.

It was the first time Anthony had ever seen the kukri used in anger, the first opportunity he had to fully appreciate quite how it had earned its fearsome reputation.

They moved on, with Ghurkhas going on ahead to clear the way and avoid any more surprises. The further they went, the more concentrated the security presence. Twice Anthony had to step over the motionless forms of US soldiers before the bulky outline of the manse itself loomed out from the darkness and the sheltering trees.

Oddly, it seemed at first that the front door was unguarded. An illusion that lasted only until it was opened by their own men. Several bodies had been heaped unceremoniously inside, some in uniform and some not – the missing sentries; both military and secret service.

He looked away, concentrating on the house around him, which was impressive to say the least. The entrance opened into a vast high-ceilinged hallway, dimly illuminated by occasional pairs of lamps spaced along the walls. An ornate crystal chandelier hung from the ceiling's centre like some grotesque earring. It remained unlit. His eye was inexorably drawn to the sweeping staircase, which split gracefully to meet with landings that bracketed his position to either side. Several doors led off from the hall to right and left, all closed.

From behind him, somewhere in the night, came the sound of automatic gunfire. It was what he had been half-expecting, half-listening for throughout the mission. The real surprise was that they had managed to come this far without being discovered. In a strange way this long-anticipated sound came as a relief now that it was finally heard, whilst making everything that much tauter and more urgent.

There was muffled noise from behind one of the doors, almost certainly a reaction to the gunfire. A Ghurkha instantly slipped across to stand beside the door in question, moving to grab the figure who stepped through as it opened.

A maid: pretty, slender and young. She wore full maid's dress, complete with white bib-apron and small frilled hat, looking bizarrely out of place next to the Ghurkha in his dappled combat uniform, like some extra who had just stepped from the set of a Miss Marple mystery and found herself in the wrong movie.

Even as that thought crossed Anthony's mind, a hand clamped over the girl's mouth and a kukri flashed.

Perhaps it was the tension of the situation or perhaps just a growing familiarity with violence, but he felt less regret about her than he had on being told about the family of hikers. She was probably secret service in any case.

The gunfire sounded nearer. Corporal Pala and his men went back outside to take up defensive positions, guarding the entrance.

Another Ghurkha gestured him over to a particular closed door, holding up one finger emphatically and pointing to indicate that there was a solitary man inside. Anthony risked opening the door a fraction and peered in. It was the President. He was pacing up and down with obvious impatience.

After some furious signalling, the Ghurkhas reluctantly agreed to wait in the hall. He opened the door and stepped inside; alone.

It was a long room. The far end accommodated a dark wood table, encircled by several high-backed chairs. A log fire, embers aglow, graced an impressive stone hearth to his left.

The only things to adorn the walls were an irregular series of paintings. Preserved in oils, the faces of long-dead men gazed down from formal portraits.

The President turned towards him, perhaps alerted by the sound of the door despite his care.

"About god-damn time!" he exclaimed, before resuming his pacing.

Uncertain who he was being mistaken for, Anthony took a moment to assess the man before him. Slight – far shorter than he looked in newscasts – with a furrowed brow and thinning hair peppered with just the right amount of grey to look distinguished. He wore a suit that might once have been expensive, classy, but now just looked lived-in, as if it had been worn continuously for days.

"Sorry to keep you waiting, Mr. President," Anthony temporised.

"You people really have a fucking nerve! Don't you know I've got a country to run?" He reached the end of the room, swivelled and paced back again, gesticulating wildly.

"Now don't get me wrong, the food here's great and it's good to get away once in a while. I know you're busy men yourselves, what with your corporate empires to oversee and everything, but that doesn't give you the right to treat me like this. A month! I've been late for meetings myself in my time. I could have excused a few hours, a day even... but a month?" He stopped and jabbed a finger at Anthony's chest, "I'm not irrelevant yet, you know."

An assertion which seemed debatable, under the circumstances.

A month. That meant that the President had been here since before everything kicked off.

Anthony thought about the newscasts; that wise, reassuring face addressing the American populace and, by extension, the people of the world, explaining in earnest tones why the invasion of Great Britain was such a regrettable necessity.

Fake, all of them. Computer-generated, an actor, or a combination of both? Not that it mattered, he was just fleetingly curious.

All the while, the man whose face had been thus plagiarised – the

President of the United States, believed by many to be the most powerful man on the planet – had been here in this remote wilderness, waiting for a meeting that was never going to take place. The poor schmuck clearly had no idea of the situation, might not even be aware that there had been a war at all.

Anthony was abruptly conscious of the unaccustomed weight at his belt, where a borrowed pistol rested. He had come here determined to cut off the beast's head. Unfortunately all that was available was its figurehead. But he had to go through with it, didn't he? Some sort of blow had to be struck for Britain, for all the right-minded people of the world, and for the Ghurkhas who were even now sacrificing their lives to give him this opportunity.

"Mr. President, I'm sorry."

The instant his finger tightened on the trigger it occurred to Anthony that he might actually be doing the real powers-that-be a favour – creating a martyr out of a puppet who had already served his purpose.

The man's face showed puzzlement, then shock and complete disbelief. Even at the very end, he never understood.

All along the walls the eyes of dead Presidents stared down at him from their dark, heavy-framed portraits, as if in judgement. Anthony allowed the gun to drop to the floor, his arm suddenly too weak to hold it up. He gazed at the sad, crumpled body for a moment, whilst the sounds of gunfire drew suddenly louder, suggesting that the fighting had reached the house itself. It would not be long now.

Somewhere, he felt certain, the ghost of Bin Laden was laughing.

What We Can See Now, Looking in the Glass

Suzette Haden Elgin

That was the week when Lilani's father was caught and arrested
for two crimes.
First: the crime of crafting unauthorized water.
Worst: showing children one of the ways it's done.
How to dig the hole in the sand;
how to put the cup at the bottom of the hole;
how to lay the sheet of plastic over the top;
how to weight its edges down with stones;
how to set on the plastic the one last stone to make the cone
where the water runs down underneath, into the cup.
"At the end of a long sunny day," he told the children,
"there'll be water in the cup." Unauthorized water.
"Understand," he told them. "And remember.
This water is not *crude* water.
This water comes from the sun, and is safe to drink."
"If we don't get caught," the children said, "it's safe to drink."
And Lilani's father nodded, saying: "Don't get caught."

When the water police took Lilani's father away,
my own father was furious.
"Damn the man!" my father said.
"Now where am I going to find another butler?"
Myself, I thought, "Where am I going to find
another Lilani?"

That was the week:
when the cheapest water at any decent restaurant
went to forty dollars a bottle;
when TransDeltamerican Airlines doubled the price
of water served on its transatlantic flights;
when statistics for Earthwide water-related deaths
were made exempt from the Freedom of Information Act;
when Congress made the drinking of crude or unauthorized water
a felony, trying for fewer deaths;
when Standard Water Corporation proudly announced
third quarter profits of thirty billion dollars.

And that was the week when we celebrated, dutifully,
my parents' fiftieth wedding anniversary.
We sat round our diningroom table together that night;
my parents, and we three wary daughters.

There was filet of sole.
There were little tender lettuces, served whole.
There were small potatoes, roasted in olive oil.
There was night-dark chocolate nested in golden foil.
There was a silver platter of sharp cheese.
There was a basket of flatbread crusted with seeds.

And there was fine water – from a very good year –
a separate glass on the table for each one of us.
My father can afford a separate glass
for each one of us.

My mother gave my father a handsome fountain pen,
and a box of slender bottles of waterless ink.
My father gave my mother a golden necklace
strung with a dozen tiny crystal vials,
every vial filled with gleaming water,
pure and precious and forever shut away.

My sisters said nothing at all.
But I'm not like that.

I stood up, and looked straight at my father,
and I said to him:
"And does the card read 'Let them drink champagne'?"

– Suzette Haden Elgin

Note:

Suzette would like to acknowledge her Live Journal readers' help and input during the crafting of this poem.

Torch Song

Una McCormack

> "If you want a picture of the future, imagine—"
> George Orwell, *Nineteen Eighty-Four*

I

We were up on the Kennet bridge – Tyler and Ness and Ryan and me – looking down along what had once been the river, prospecting. Ivy running up the cracks in the stone and the paint peeling off the railings. Late sun hot and heavy on the back of my neck. Air as dull as it is every day. "What about that one, then?" Tyler said, and pointed down the path.

Old man in his thirties, limping towards the foot of the steps. Stopping at the bottom to catch his breath, one hand on the rail, other pulling at his jacket like he had some kind of dignity. Tyler half-panting by now and not from the heat – but Tyler's cracked, plus he should have known better. You get a suit like that when you get back.

I shook my head, slowly, side to side. Ryan hanging on to my every move, blinking away like the shutter on a camera. "Too easy," he said. "He's falling over by himself, doesn't need us. Right?"

I drummed out a beat with my fingers. Military tattoo. "Wrong," I said. "Wait till he comes past. Have a proper look."

By this time he'd made it to the top of the steps. It had been an effort and he hadn't seen us. When he did, it was far too late. I'd turned round by then. Leaning against the railings, brushing flakes of paint off my fingers, watching him pass. Grey hair, grey skin, sign of a cheap life – but the badge had cost him. Gold with two black bars, one for Aleppo, one for the Khabur valley. I lifted my hand and gave him a smile to show him how grateful I was. He got past as quick as he could.

Time to set Ryan straight. I patted him on the chest where the badge would be. "He was in the desert. We touched him, half the borough's old boys on us by tonight." I gathered up some of his shirt in my hand. "You up for that, Ryan? That too easy?"

Ryan more interested in the ground now, or his feet, something other than me. Blinking faster. "No."

"Who then?" Tyler said, missing all this of course, and: "No rush," Ness told him, relaxed as a pussycat and watching me. "You got your eye on someone, Jay?"

I leaned out over the bridge. From here I could look out up the valley, keeping almost the whole city behind me, see the Westway arcing above the borough on its way out of town. Sunlight on the brown and yellow hills, on the dark green lines of the vineyards up in Caversham. It looked nice. Six o'clock chiming, and people heading down the path to the tube station. I picked out the woman in the green jacket, carrying a brown paper bag.

"She'll do."

Tyler rocking back and forwards; Ness coiling up ready to spring. Ryan almost looking tough again. "Okay," I said, "Let's go." And off they went, off the leash. I pulled my tie straight, so I'd look smart for the occasion, and followed on at a gentler pace.

Ness got there first, just as the woman got to the foot of the steps, cutting off escape that way. Ryan circled round behind. Tyler came face to face with her, backing her against the wall. My little unit, so well trained, it could bring a tear to the eye. "Oh," she was saying, "please, I don't have anything on me, I don't have anything..." then Tyler punched her in the stomach and she was down on the ground, retching, hands splayed out on the tar. When Ryan kicked the bag over to Ness she tried to grab it – stupid, but people do stupid things under stress – and he had to stamp down to stop her. His boot landed just short of her face.

I came to a halt on the second step. Ness was picking up the bag. Security camera whirring behind and above us, monitoring the situation. I leaned against the wall and began to put on some lipstick. A crowd gathering nearby – we were blocking the way up onto the bridge. No-one lifting a finger to help. Why should they? Not like we were doing anything wrong. "Well," Ness said, tearing the bag open, untroubled, "what do we have in here?"

In fact, most of it was rubbish. Some pasta, a couple of apples, a bottle of gin. Down at the bottom though were some cigarettes, and Tyler pounced on them. "Disgusting," he said, as he pulled the packet apart. "Filthy."

"Do you know what they cost the health service every year?" Ryan said.

"Waste of taxpayers' money," Tyler agreed.

"Good job we stopped you," Ryan finished. "Before you made yourself sick. You should say thank you." Ness threw me one of the apples and I took a bite.

"Bloody kids," someone said from the crowd. Not a young face among them. There's a word for that. Projection. It doesn't matter. We're not the ones first turned up the heat, and we'll be heroes soon enough. Tyler had finished pulling the cigarettes apart, and he dropped them on the ground. Ryan ground his heel into the shreds, right up against her face again. "You know, I really think you should say thank you."

"Okay," I said, "we're done." I jerked my head and the three of them pulled back and started off down the path. I bent down and put my hands on her elbows and, as I pulled her up I kissed her on the cheek. "Bye," I said, quietly, as she stared at me, and then I backed down the path, biting into the apple. "Thanks for watching, folks," I said to the crowd, and then I turned and ran to catch up with the others. I looked back over my shoulder once. Someone had come forwards at last to help her. She was crying and my lipstick had left a red gash on her cheek. And that was the third time I laid eyes on Susan.

II

The first time she was coming out of the People's Press on the corner of Jackson's Square. One of the things that made me look twice. An ordinary evening. People sitting in chairs outside the bars playing bad chess and drinking bad gin and not talking about anything that mattered much. I was hovering around waiting for Ness because we'd got our hands on some film tickets. While I waited, I was watching the screens on the side of the press building showing something about how family benefit fraud was big business run by the Triads or the Pope or the Hellfire Club or maybe it was all three and maybe I'm bending the facts but you get the idea. Someone's fatcatting with what should be your money and they're probably not white and they're probably not straight and they're definitely not you and did we mention how you could spot them? A woman came down the steps of the Press in a green jacket cut above her hips and I watched her walk across the square until Ness landed and we had to go inside. The film was boy fucks girl and bad but we heckled through it twice because no-one was going to throw us out.

Second time was just lucky. I was at home with the family in the evening for once. If I'd known what was coming on, I wouldn't have stayed, but they slipped the item in between the thing about benefit barons and the one on STDs they'd been running all month. Two scrubbed-up, healthy-looking NCOs sitting on a beach in Honolulu talking about how great life was and what a good job everyone was doing and how proud they were and so were both their mums. I might be exaggerating. Boy and a girl – that was a nice touch. Michael had been quiet all night, but this set him off, and once he started muttering, I could see mum's hands twisting around and I knew what was coming so I left before the fireworks.

I had more than an hour to kill before I had to be over at the barracks, so I went and did what I always do when I'm alone, which is to get on the tube and put as much of London behind me as I can. I only do it when I'm by myself because I don't like people watching me when I'm looking at the hills. Plus Tyler won't travel on the Goring and City line, because it's pink and that's a fag's colour. There'll come a point with Tyler when they'll have to throw away the key. I'd gone two stops past redbrick terraces when someone said my name.

"Jay? Jay Mason?"

I looked over my shoulder and saw a girl holding a baby and smiling at me. I recognized her at once; we'd been at school together. I hadn't seen her in over a year. The baby was tiny and sweet and it looked like there was another on the way.

"Hello Cath," I said, and shifted along the seat so she could join me. "You're looking well." She was about to sit down when she saw what I was wearing. Her face changed completely, of course. "I should have guessed," she said, nodding at the stripes on my shirtsleeves. "All the same, your family, weren't they?"

And off she went, down the carriage, baby and all. People were enjoying the show, and my cheeks were beginning to burn, so I put my head against the window and tried to cool it. Because the law is the law, and you have to be doing something at fifteen, and I didn't want to pick olives in forty degree heat, and I didn't want to be paid to up the birth-rate like Cath, and there wasn't exactly a family firm, so what else was there to do but collect a set of badges? But then that's the problem with young people today. They want discipline. When I looked up again, the woman sitting opposite was watching me, and I was about to take her up on it when I saw she had a green jacket folded across her knees. She had short black hair and grey-green eyes and she smiled, just a bit, like she was sorry about something. I think that was the moment I got the whole idea.

After our introduction by the bridge, I kept pretty close and made sure she saw me. Followed her from the Press to find out where she lived. Went round after her while she was shopping; found out what she ate and where she got those cigarettes. Sat and watched films over her shoulder. Finally she cracked, late one Saturday afternoon, after leading me half way round Tilehurst. I followed her down an alley where I knew she'd be waiting to tackle me. It still took a minute or two before I had her under control, my hands locked firm about her thin wrists.

"Who the fuck are you?" she hissed, and then: "You're that cow from the bridge, aren't you? What the hell is going on—?"

Bloody hell, but she could make a noise. If she kept on like this the world and his three fucking wives would all be out to have a look. "Calm down, will you—?"

"Calm down? You've been following me around for weeks! Whatever you think I've done, I haven't, I've not done anything, I've not done anything for years, just lay off—!" She started struggling against me.

"Shut up!" I shook her arms hard and pushed her back against the brick wall; it was controlled, to stop her, not to hurt her. "I'm not... You don't have to worry—"

"Not worry?" She'd worked out she couldn't get away and had started trembling in my hands. "I can't get rid of you, everywhere I look, everywhere I turn, you're watching—"

"It's nothing... I don't know... I just thought..." We were face to face, looking at each other. Up close the jacket was embroidered and worn around the cuffs. "You look nice in green." Out loud, it sounded even lamer than I'd intended. She was staring at me like I was crazy. I let go of her arms. "Do you want a cup of tea or something?" I said, clumsily.

Everything was dead quiet all of a sudden. Susan put her hand up to her forehead, and, "Jesus Christ," she muttered, which was only the first law we broke that evening.

III

Susan lived on the second floor of a house two minutes from Tilehurst tube. Her room was tiny – just enough space for the bed and a sink and a couple of suitcases piled up and a floor-length dark-wood mirror standing in one corner to make the place seem bigger. She had put some candles out and thrown some bits of dark material around with a busy pattern on. When I knew her a bit better, I worked out it was meant to be bohemian. In fact, it was a dump, but the water came on twice a day, and the bed was big enough and there was nobody between it and the landlord on the ground floor, so I suppose it wasn't all that bad. I sat on the bed under where the ceiling sloped, with one leg pulled up and the other hanging off the side of the bed, and watched her put the kettle on.

"So. A cup of tea, yes?"

"Thanks." I looked round. There was a flatscreen television lying on its back on top of the suitcases, small and old, but it looked okay. "Does that work?"

"What?"

"The telly. Does it work?"

She shrugged. "I suppose so... I hardly ever use it."

I reached over for it and switched it on. She was missing two channels, so I opened up the back and got to work. She came back and put a mug on the suitcases by me and then stood watching as I played with the tuning. After a bit she sat down next to me and began to laugh. "You're crazy—"

I went stiff. "You know what?" I told her, straight. "Don't ever say that to me again."

"All right," she said, softly. "I won't. Why don't you tell me your name?"

"Jay."

"Hi Jay. I'm Susan."

"I know."

"Of course you do," she said. "Why are you here?"

"Because you said you'd make me a cup of tea," I said, and then Channel 7 came on strong. "There," I said, and propped it up at the foot of the bed. "That's better."

"I said I hardly ever watch it—"

"I wasn't planning to watch it—"

"We won't need it."

I turned round to face her, put my hands around her wrists again, but loosely this time. "It was too quiet," I said. "No-one can hear—"

"Really," she said, and it was like there was some private joke, "we won't need it." I let go of her arms and she reached to turn it off. Then she held my chin in her hand and her breath was warm against my cheek. "But I appreciate you mending it."

The kiss had only just started getting good when – and I'm not joking – there was a blast of trumpets underneath the window. I jumped back like we'd been caught in the act. "What the fuck was that?"

"That," Susan said, as a tune made itself clear, "is my landlord's taste in music."

"I didn't think there'd be a bloody brass band... Is it always so loud?"

"Yes," she said, and as she stretched out on the bed alongside me she kicked the telly onto the floor. "I told you we wouldn't need that."

Night when we got up again. I went to have a look out of the window. The valley holds the street-light and a haze hangs round until morning. "Did you know," I said to Susan, leaning on the wall beside me, "that the reason the birds keep singing all night is that they're confused? It doesn't get dark enough and they think it's still day. They're not meant to do that."

"Aren't you full of interesting information?" She had found a cigarette and lit up.

"You shouldn't do that," I told her. "Not even at home."

"Well, as you may have worked out by now, I don't worry all that much about being unpatriotic."

"Still though, it's bad for you. It'll make you sick."

She reached out to touch my cheek with her thumb, gently. "Thanks, Jay," she said, and then turned away to the window. The streets were orange and empty. Lots of dark buildings that did nothing but rot. "I grew up round here," Susan said. "It was so different back then. There were people, for one thing. Shops. So many things to look at, things to touch and smell. You could hear half-a-dozen different languages, just walking along this road. That—" she pointed with her cigarette at a burnt-out shell on the corner opposite, "—that was the Polish Centre. It's a crying shame."

"Yeah... well... there's more room now, I suppose, isn't there?"

She watched me for a moment, smoked. "You know, Jay," she said, "I don't think your friend on the tube can fill all those houses by herself."

I said nothing, but when she tried to put her arm around me, I pulled away. To be honest, I didn't really know what she was getting at. It's never been any different so far as I can remember. I looked out of the window at the ruin. Michael had told me that Dan had once told him he did it on his first month out with his squad, but I didn't pass that piece of information on to Susan. Then the landlord's music came on again, only this time he was singing along, crooning, and as we couldn't help laughing we had to kiss and make up.

And that was what we did all summer. The heat got worse, got cruel.

Her work and my training shut down till September – nothing else to do but be with each other in that tiny room on that big-enough bed. One night we went as far as we could on the tube and sat on a hill and looked up at the cars turning the arc of the Westway silver with the exodus from the City, anyone who could heading for the country for the season, leaving the boroughs sweating behind. The telly worked fine, but Susan was right and the landlord worked better, switching between big band numbers or ballads from the second war, all about lost innocence, lost love. I saw nothing of Ness or Tyler or Ryan. Sometimes we quarrelled and then kissed and made up. Sometimes we'd whisper along to the words of the ballads. Sometimes Susan would get sad and talk about how it had all gone wrong, how she was making tea and filing paper for someone at the Press who was half as smart as she was and liked her to wear high heels or so she said. There was a story there but I didn't ask. Everyone's had a sad life and that wasn't what I was there for.

It was almost September when I finished it. Traffic had started trickling back into the city and a new front had opened in Guam. I knew the words to a bunch of old songs and every inch of Susan's skin. Time was running out, so one evening I explained why I'd met her, and what I'd do if she didn't do exactly what I said. Because there were laws about this kind of thing, and even though I wasn't underage it wasn't far off, and they wouldn't look too kindly on her. It didn't turn out quite how I'd imagined it – she nearly threw me downstairs. To be honest, I hadn't reckoned on her saying no. Not just because I could hit a lot harder, but because I'd listened to her talk all summer and I'd read the books she kept stashed behind the headboard and I thought she already knew politics didn't stop at the bedroom door.

IV

And then the summer was over, and it was back to business, and they were working us harder than ever. When I saw Ness again, she looked fitter, older. She'd kept training through the heat. Ryan at her elbow. "Not seen much of you this summer, Jay."

"Been busy."

"Or slacking. Playtime's over, Jay," she said, patting me on the shoulder. "We're all grown up now." She still sounded the same as ever, but I've known Ness Brophy since we were putting up sandcastles, and she's had her eye on my stripes from the second I put them on, and I should have known full well she'd never give up.

September wore on, and I was out of options. The heat stayed late, and we had to work hard for every inch of ground we covered, every second we drilled, every pointless dreary task they set us. Late one afternoon, I was heading for home after a run where Ness had set the pace for me like she used to and then crippled me in the last half-mile. The sky was black and blue, and the pressure was building – and then I saw a flash of green against red brick, and knew in the same second just how closely Ness was watching me.

"Not here," I muttered as I went past, and, "Come round later," Susan said.

When she let me in, I couldn't believe it was less than a month since I'd last been there. It was like an age had passed. "Sit down," Susan said, and I did what I was told, perching myself on the edge of the bed, staring down at my boots.

"I want to tell you something," she said, "and then I want you to explain."

It turned out that when she'd been a student, there'd been someone, and they'd been in love, and they'd had a great time together putting up posters and going on marches and shouting about laws and then when the heat got turned up under them they'd both been so terrified they'd sold each other out about as quick as you could make the threats. Same old story. She shouldn't beat herself up about it, was my thought; enough people out there ready to do it for you. I mean, we're only human, after all.

So altogether I didn't care, much, but she just went on and on and I had to get up and put the light on, and I was dead tired and my head was killing, and that storm wasn't breaking, and as I watched and listened, something seemed to crack inside me. First of all I was scared, and then pretty quick I was angry with her, that she'd done something to break me. "Shut up," I told her, but she got angry too, said how she couldn't believe I had the nerve to talk to her like that, and I got up from the bed and rather than hit her I kicked that crappy mirror against the wall, and the pieces flew everywhere.

"Look," I said, and I pulled out the piece of paper I'd been creasing around for the past month, and slammed it into her chest. She took it from me, and read through it, and I saw from her face that she'd finally grasped what was going on. My marching orders.

"I see," she said, much quieter now, and then, "Poor Jay," and again, "Poor Jay," and that second time was what broke me. She put her hands around my wrists, and pulled me to her, and then slid her hands up, and we touched palm to palm for a moment – and then she had her arms around me, and I was crying, for a bad choice I'd made too early and what was going to happen next because of it, for big brothers who come back crazy or don't come back at all, for mothers who are scared when they look at you because it was meant to be different with you but somehow it's all gone wrong again and maybe this time even wronger. I kept on crying until I was empty and when I was aware of anything again, it was some stupid song from downstairs, and Susan holding my head against her shoulder, and we were moving together to the music, and, "I'm here," she was saying, "I'll stay, I'm always going to be with you."

That was the second time I'd misread her, I suppose. First time round I hadn't reckoned on her saying no. But I never thought if I just asked that she'd say yes. And, yes, she said. Yes.

V

Once Susan was up for it, it was easy enough. I couldn't get myself inside, that was the problem. Too young; too suspect. But I had everything we needed. They shouldn't leave all that stuff lying around for us to play with. And they really shouldn't show us how to use it.

I watched it happen from up in the hills, sitting in the shade of an olive tree, with a view right down the Oxford Road. Black ranks marching east into the city. Streets lined with people and flags to wave them off. Glory hallelujah; never been so popular in all their sad short lives. We timed it perfectly, me and Susan, because when the whole parade was inside Jackson's Square, the Press building went up like a light, and what the blast didn't get the shards from the screens would have. And I won't say it was beautiful, I won't say it was right, but I will say all's fair in love and war. All the Berkshires, officers and fodder alike, Tyler and Ness and Ryan among them – it took them all. And if you think that's harsh, then let me tell you this – that they were dead already, and it was better to go on a sweet hot September day at home with their heads full of fiction than fucked and frightened and covered in blood and sand. I took them all, and I took me with them – missing in action, the ghost in the machine – and it was a mercy killing.

Early evening now, and down below the valley is full of fire and fear and panic. Street lights are coming on, and soon it'll all be lost to me, smothered under orange haze. The sky up here's dark blue and medalled with stars and I didn't know things could be this clear. Maybe they've been watching us for weeks. Maybe they've got her, maybe they kicked her door down last night and dragged her off and are making her do again what she did before. Or maybe she's on her way right now, coming to meet me waiting for her here with the sky and the shade of the trees. And then? Then we're off; we'll put the city behind us with its old lies and dead ends. Where are we heading? North, I think, and west, out into the country, over the mountains. It doesn't end here. Over the mountains we will be free. Over the mountains we will wear our dancing shoes.

Minutes of the Labour Party Conference, 2016

Charles Stross

PREAMBLE TO THE MINUTES OF THE LABOUR PARTY CONFERENCE, 2016

Greetings from the National Executive.

Before reading any further, please refer to the Security Note and ensure that your receipt and use of this document is in compliance with Party security policies. If you have any doubts at all, burn this document immediately.

SECURITY NOTE

This is an official Labour Party Document. Possession of all such documents is a specific offense under (2)(2)(f) of the Terrorism Act (2006). Amendments passed by the current government using the powers granted in the Legislative and Regulatory Reform Act (2006) have raised the minimum penalty for possession to 10 years imprisonment. In addition, persons suspected of membership of or sympathy for the Labour Party are liable for arrest and sentencing as subversives under the Defence of the Realm Act (2014).

You must destroy this document immediately, for your own safety, if:

* You have any cause to suspect that a neighbour or member of your household may be an informer,

* You have come into possession of this document via a suspect source, or if your copy of this document exhibits signs of having been printed on any type of computer printer or photocopier, or if you received this document in a public place that might be overseen by cameras, or if it may have been transmitted via electronic means.

The Party would be grateful if you can reproduce

and distribute this document to sympathizers and members. Use only a typewriter, embossing print set, mimeograph, or photographic film to distribute this document. Paper should be purchased anonymously and microwaved for at least 30 seconds prior to use to destroy RFID tags. Do not, under any circumstances, enter or copy the text in a computer, word processor, photocopier, scanner, mobile phone, or digital camera. This is for your personal safety.

MINUTES OF THE LABOUR PARTY CONFERENCE, 2016

1. Apologies for absence were made on behalf of the following:

Deputy Leader, Hillary Benn (executed by junta)

Government, Douglas Alexander (executed by junta)

Government, Kate Hoey (detained, Dartmoor concentration camp)

EPLP Leader, Mohammed Sarwar (executed by junta)

Young Labour, Judy Mallaber (detained, Dartmoor concentration camp: show trial announced by junta)

...

2. Motions from the national executive:

1) In the light of the government's use of its powers of extradition under the US/UK Extradition Treaty (2005), and their demonstrated willingness to lie to the rest of the world about their treatment of extradited dissidents, it is no longer safe to maintain a public list of shadow ministers and party officers. With the exception of the offices of Party Spokesperson and designated Party Security Spokesperson, it is moved that:

* Open election of members of the National Executive shall be suspended,
* Publication of the names and identities of members of the National Executive shall be suspended,

* The National Executive will continue to function on a provisional basis making ad-hoc appointments by internal majority vote to replace members as they retire, are forced into exile, or are murdered by the junta;

From now until the end of the State of Emergency and the removal of the current government, at which time an extraordinary Party Conference shall be held to publicly elect a peacetime National Executive.

(Carried unanimously.)

2) In view of the current government's:

* suspension of the Human Rights Act (1998), Race Relations Act (2000), and other Acts,

* abrogation of the Treaty of Europe and secession from the European Union,

* amendment via administrative order of other Acts of Parliament (including the reintroduction of capital punishment),

* effective criminalization of political opposition by proscribing opposition parties as "organisations that promote terrorism" under the terms of the Terrorism Act (2000),

* establishment of concentration camps and deportation facilities for ethnic minorities, political dissidents, lesbian, gay, bisexual and transgendered citizens, and others,

* deployment of riot police and informal militias against peaceful demonstrations and sit-ins, with concomitant loss of life,

* and their effective termination of the democratic processes by which the United Kingdom has historically been governed,

We find, with reluctance, that no avenue of peaceful dissent remains open to us. We are therefore faced with a choice between accepting defeat, and continuing the struggle for freedom and democracy by other means.

We shall not submit to the dictatorship of the current government, and we have no choice but to hit back by all means within our power in defence of our people, our future and our freedom. The government has interpreted the peacefulness of the movement as weakness; our non-violent policies have been taken as a green light for government violence. Refusal to resort to force has been interpreted by the government as an invitation to use armed force against the people without any fear of reprisals.

It is therefore moved that:

* A National Resistance Movement is created. The Movement will seek to achieve liberation without bloodshed or violence if possible. We hope - even at this late moment - that the government will come to its senses and permit a free and fair general election to be held in which parties representing all ideologies will be permitted to stand for election. But we will defend our supporters and the oppressed against military rule, racist tyranny, and totalitarianism, and we will not flinch from using any tool in pursuit of this goal.

* The Movement will work to achieve the political goals of the Labour Party during the state of emergency, and will cooperate willingly with other organizations upon the basis of shared goals.

* The Movement will actively attack the instruments of state terror and coercion, including functionaries of the government who enforce unjust and oppressive laws against the people.

* At the cessation of the struggle, a National Peace and Reconciliation Commission shall be established and an amnesty granted to members of the Movement for actions taken in the pursuit of legitimate orders.

In these actions, we are working in the best interests of all the people of this country - of every ethnicity, gender, and class - whose future happiness and well-being cannot be attained without the overthrow of the Fascist government, the abolition of white supremacy and the winning of liberty, democracy and full national rights and equality for all the people of this country.

(Carried 25/0, 3 abstentions)

3) All Party members who are physically and mentally fit to withstand the rigours of the struggle are encouraged to organize themselves in cells of 3-6 individuals, to establish lines of communication (subject to the Party security policies), and to place themselves at the disposal of the National Resistance Movement. Party members who are unable to serve may still provide aid, shelter, and funds for those who fight in our defence.

(Carried unanimously)

3. Motions from the floor

The party recognizes that that our own legislative program of the late 1990s and early 2000s established the framework for repression which is now being used to ruthlessly suppress dissent. We recognize that our neglect of the machinery of public choice in favour of the pursuit of corporatist collaborations permitted the decay of local and parliamentary democracy that allowed the British National Party to seize power with the support of no more than 22% of the electorate. We are therefore compelled to admit our responsibility. We created this situation; we must therefore repair it.

Never again shall the Labour Party place national security ahead of individual freedoms and human rights in its legislative program. It is therefore moved that the following quotation from Benjamin Franklin be inserted between Clause Three and the current Clause Four of the Party Constitution:

"They that can give up essential liberty to obtain a little temporary safety deserve neither liberty nor safety."

(Carried 16/12)

...

(END)

Recommended Reading

Anderson, Poul, Martin H. Greenberg and Charles G. Waugh. *Terrorists of Tomorrow* (anth. 1985).

Asimov, Isaac. *Robots and Empire* (1985).

Barnes, John. *Kaleidoscope Century* (1995).

Bartol, Vladmir. *Alamut* (1938).

Bear, Elizabeth. *Carnival. (2006).*

Boyce, Chris. *Brainfix* (1980).

Brin, David. *The Uplift War* (1987).

Brunner, John. *The Sheep Look Up* (1972).

Bujold, Lois McMaster. *Mirror Dance (1994).*

Carter, Raphael. *The Fortunate Fall* (1996).

Cherryh, C.J. *Cyteen* (1988).

Cherryh, C.J. *Downbelow Station (1991).*

Dick, Philip K. *The Man Who Japed* (1956).

Dickinson, Peter. *The Green Gene (1973).*

Disch, Thomas. *White Fang Goes Dingo* (1971).

Elgin, Suzette Hayden. *Native Tongue (1984).*

Ellis, T. Mullett. *Zalma* (1895).

Ellison, Harlan. "Repent Harlequin! Said the Tick-tock Man" (chapbook version 1997).

Engdahl, Sylvia. *The Far Side of Evil* (1971).

Engh, M.J. *Arslan* (2001).

Foster, M.A. *The Morphodite (1981).*

Griffith, George. *Angel of the Revolution* (1893)

Grimwood, Jon Courtenay. *RedRobe* (2000)

Grimwood, Jon Courtenay. *Stamping Butterflies* (2004).

Hambly, Barbara. *The Ladies of Mandrigyn (1984)*

Harrison, Harry. *The Stainless Steel Rat Gets Drafted* (1987)

Harrison, Harry. *The Stainless Steel Rat's Revenge* (1970).

Heinlein, Robert A. *Stranger in a Strange Land* (1961).

Heinlein, Robert A. *The Moon is a Harsh Mistress* (1966)

Herbert, Frank. *Dune* (1965)

Huff, Tanya. *Better Part of Valor* (2002).

Kay, Guy Gavriel. *Tigana (1990)*

Kellogg, Marjorie Bradley. *Harmony (1991)*

King, Steven. *The Running Man (1982)*

Levin, Ira. *This Perfect Day* (1985).

Lewis, C.S. *Prince Caspian (1951).*

MacLeod, Ken. *The Sky Road (1999).*

Marks, Laurie J. *Fire Logic (2002).*

Marley, Louise. *The Terrorists of Irustan (1998).*

Martin, George R. R. *A Clash of Kings* (1998)
Martin, George R. R. *The Armageddon Rag* (1983)
McDonald, Ian. *Hearts and Hands and Voices (1992).*
McKee Charnas, Suzy. *The Furies* (1994).
Moorcock, Michael. *The Final Programme* (1968)
Moriarty, Chris. *Spin Control (2006).*
Niven, Larry. *A Gift From Earth* (1968).
Patterson, James. *Black Market* (1976).
Piercy, Marge. *Dance the Eagle to Sleep* (1970).
Piper, H. Beam. *Uller Uprising* (1952).
Robinson, Kim Stanley. *Antarctica* (1997).
Russell, Eric Frank. *Wasp* (1957).
Shepherd, Lucius. *Barnacle Bill the Spacer and Other Stories* (1973).
Spinrad, Norman. *The Men in the Jungle* (1967).
Strugatsky, Arkady and Boris. *Prisoners of Power* (1977).
Traviss, Karen. *City of Pearl* (2004).
Turtledove, Harry. *The Great War: American Front* (1998)
Verne, Jules. *San dessus dessous* (1889).
Verne, Jules. "Baltimore Gun Club" (1870).
Vinge, Vernor,. *The Peace War* (1984).
Walton, Jo. *Ha' Penny* (2007).
Williams, Liz. *Empire of Bones* (2002).
Williams, Walter Jon. *Conventions of War* (2004).
Wolfe, Gene. *Operation Ares (1970).*
Wren, M.K. *The Sword of the Lamb (1981).*
Zelazny, Roger. *Lord of Light* (1967).

There have been a number of films lauding terrorism: *Shockwave Rider, The Matrix, V for Vendetta* and *Brazil.* In the 1970s the comic *2000AD* ran two long running series in which terrorists were the stars, *Diary of a Mutant* and *Nemesis the Warlock.*

Protagonists in television series such as *Blake's 7, Farscape* and *Serenity* are all terrorists. So too are the heroes of *Star Wars* (that's *the government's* Death Star they are destroying, complete with all the innocent workmen who are still aboard as the characters in *Clerks* observe). The crew of *Babylon 5* start out as government but rapidly move to plot against the legitimate authorities.

Then there is *Dr. Who.* While the Doctor may be a nice pacifist, he has brought down governments and given aid and succor to many terrorists (see episodes such as The Sunmakers", "The Mutants", "Colony in Space", "The Happiness Patrol").

Contributors

Kathryn Allen is a citizen of the glorious independent republic of Yorkshire. A cynical optimist, she maintains respect for the traditional values embodied in tea, dourness, and tweedy headgear, but prefers not to attend cricket matches. Kat still hopes to become a fully qualified English eccentric, despite the allure of writing speculative fiction.

Chaz Brenchley has been making a living as a writer since he was eighteen. He is the author of nine thrillers, most recently Shelter, and two major fantasy series: The Books of Outremer, based on the world of the Crusades, and Selling Water by the River, set in an alternate Ottoman Istanbul. A winner of the British Fantasy Award, he has also published three books for children and more than 500 short stories in various genres. His time as Crimewriter-in-Residence at the St Peter's Riverside Sculpture Project in Sunderland resulted in the collection Blood Waters. He is a prizewinning ex-poet, and has been writer in residence at the University of Northumbria, as well as tutoring their MA in Creative Writing. He was Northern Writer of the Year 2000, and lives in Newcastle upon Tyne with a quantum cat and a famous teddy bear.

Marie Brennan is the pen name of Bryn Neuenschwander, an American graduate student in anthropology and folklore. She won the Isaac Asimov Award for Undergraduate Excellence in Science Fiction and Fantasy Writing her senior year of college, and since then has sold short stories to more than a dozen venues including *Talebones*, *Jabberwocky*, *Shadowed Realms*, and *Weird Tales*. Her novels *Doppelganger* and *Warrior and Witch* are out this year from Warner Books.

Hal Duncan was born in 1971 and lives in the West End of Glasgow. A long-standing member of the Glasgow SF Writers Circle, his first novel, *Vellum*, was nominated for the Crawford Award, the British Fantasy Society Award and the World Fantasy Award. A sequel, *Ink*, is due out in 2007 along with a novella set in the same world, *Scorched Earth*. A poetry collection, *Sonnets for Orpheus*, was recently released in a limited edition by Papaveria Press. His short fiction has been published in magazines and anthologies such as Fantasy, Strange Horizons, Electric Velocipede, *Nova Scotia* and *Eidolon*.

Suzette Haden Elgin is a linguist, writer, artist, songwriter, poet, businessperson, housewife, and grandmother of twelve. Her best known books are the *Native Tongue* and *Ozark* science fiction trilogies and her nonfiction *Gentle Art of Verbal Self-Defense* series. Her most recent books are *Peacetalk 101* (a verbal self-defense sf novel) and *The Science Fiction Poetry Handbook*. She has received the Academy of American Poets Award (University of Chicago, 1955); the Eugene Saxton Memorial Trust poetry fellowship, 1957-58 and the Short Poem Rhysling Award (tie), 1988. Her SFWA website is at http://www.sfwa.org/members/elgin; her Live Journal blog is at http://ozarque.livejournal.com/ .

Kira Franz believes everyone should have the power to make a difference in their world without the use of violence. To that end, she became an attorney and a card-carrying member of the American Civil Liberties Union. She has a number of writing projects in process, but the creative venture that consumes most of her time is raising her new daughter Zoe. She graduated from the Clarion West Writers Workshop in 2005. This is her first published story. Unsurprisingly, she voted for the other guy.

Van Aaron Hughes lives in Denver, Colorado with his wife and three children. Like the protagonist of his story "Winning Friends," he is a lawyer and has argued before the United States Supreme Court. He has written articles for legal publications, and his science fiction, fantasy, and horror book reviews appear at FantasticReviews.com. "Winning Friends" is his first professional work of fiction.

Davin Ireland currently resides in the Netherlands. His fiction credits include stories published in a range of print magazines and anthologies, including *Underworlds, The Horror Express, Zahir, Fusing Horizons, Black Petals, Aesthetica, Neo-Opsis, Storyteller Magazine,* and *Albedo One*. His story 'Resting Place' received an Honorable Mention in the *Year's Best Fantasy and Horror* #18, edited by Ellen Datlow, Kelly Link & Gavin J. Grant.

Gwyneth Jones is a writer and critic of science fiction and fantasy, who also writes for teenagers using the name Ann Halam. She's won two World Fantasy awards, the Arthur C. Clarke award, the British Science Fiction short story award, the Dracula Society's Children of the Night award, the P.K. Dick award, and the James Tiptree Jr. award. She lives in Brighton, UK. She served for four years on the Women's Action Network Committee AI UK in the nineties; she's still an active Amnesty International volunteer.

Vylar Kaftan's fiction has appeared in *Strange Horizons, ChiZine,* and *Abyss & Apex*. She lives in northern California and volunteers as a mentor for teenaged writers. Like most wandering monsters, her politics are chaotic neutral. She blogs at http://www.vylarkaftan.net/ .

For money **Lucy Kemnitzer** has been a factory worker, a motel maid, a tapestry reweaver, a fast food worker at the Boardwalk, a cannery worker, a teacher of at-risk adolescents, a child care worker, a University teacher's assistant in writing and in community studies, an educational research assistant. For no money she has been a union organizer, a food-buying cooperative coordinator, a writer, a peace and social justice activist, a member of the Santa Cruz City Council Taskforce on the Homeless and currently, a watershed water-quality monitor for the Monterey Bay National Marine Sanctuary and a deputy official of the County Elections Department. She has raised two children and had a hand in raising others and is working on her sixth novel.

H.H. Løyche was born in Copenhagen, 1964, studied at The Academy of Art, worked and travelled in Africa and the Middle East. Home again, he became editor of *Nye Verdener* (New Worlds) and worked on various magazines. As a genre specialist, he began writing articles and short stories for glossy magazines and daily newspapers, and his debut as a novelist came with *Støj* (Baffling Noise) in 1996. His novel *Mission til Schamajim* (Mission to Schamajim) is officially listed among the three finest Danish science fiction novels ever. He was awarded a two-year writing grant from The National Art Foundation (Statens Kunstfond). Among his recent works are a science fiction story for movie director Tómas Gislason and a fully annoted and illustrated selection of H.C. Andersen's science fiction stories. Løyche used to be a member of The Writers' Association of Denmark (DF), but left in disgust of his colleagues' unwillingness to fight for their rights. Take a look at his writing on http://www.loeyche.com/

Una McCormack is the author of two Star Trek: Deep Space Nine novels – *Cardassia: The Lotus Flower* and *Hollow Men*, both of which address themes of violent and non-violent political resistance. Her essay 'Resist the Host – Blake's 7: A Very British Future' examines the BBC's SF drama in the context of the British anti-utopian tradition and other television treatments of armed resistance (see *British Science Fiction Television*, eds. John R. Cook and Peter Wright, 2006). She has a Ph.D. in sociology from the University of Surrey and, when not writing, she teaches organizational behaviour at the University of Cambridge.

Ken MacLeod was born in Stornoway, Isle of Lewis, Scotland, on August 2, 1954. He is married with two children and lives in West Lothian. He has an Honours and Masters degree in biological subjects and worked for some years in the IT industry. Since 1997 he has been a full-time writer. He is the author of ten novels, from *The Star Fraction* (1995) to *The Execution Channel* (forthcoming, 2007), and many articles and short stories. His novels have received one BSFA award and three Prometheus Awards, and several have been short-listed for the Clarke and Hugo Awards. Ken MacLeod's weblog is The Early Days of a Better Nation: http://kenmacleod.blogspot.com

Andrew McKie was born in Renfrewshire several months before men first walked on the Moon. He attended Hutchesons' [sic] Grammar School and the University in Glasgow, from which he graduated in Philosophy. After a spell as an ESU scholar in America, he worked as a freelance journalist, and has contributed to almost every British national title and publications as varied as *The Big Issue*, *The Oldie* and *The Spectator*. He is an occasional lecturer and broadcaster, and was for a time research fellow at the Social Affairs Unit, an independent think-tank. He has been a leader writer at *The Daily Telegraph* for more than 10 years and was previously its Deputy Comment Editor. He has been Obituaries Editor of the paper since 2000.

Farah Mendlesohn is an editor and critic. She has published work on Diana Wynne Jones, Terry Pratchett, religion and science fiction. Future publications include a book on children's science fiction, and on the rhetorics of fantastic fiction. In 2005 she and Edward James won a Hugo Award for *The Cambridge Companion to Science Fiction*. She identifies as a Quaker anarchist although that may be a tautology.

Adam Roberts is a writer and academic in his forties; he lives with his wife and daughter a little way west of London. He has published to date six SF novels, the first being the terrorism-glorifying *Salt* (Gollancz 2000) and the most recent being the, now that he comes to think of it, terrorism-glorifying *Gradisil* (Gollancz 2006). These two facts notwithstanding, glorification of terrorism has (until now) not been a conscious goal in his writing. He has also published five novel-length parodies, two novellas, a collection of short fiction, and a number of books of academic criticism of SF and Fantasy. He has won no awards or prizes, and has accrued no evidence of esteem from the SF community.

Elizabeth Sourbut has previously published four SF short stories, in one of which she killed off all the males on the planet. She has been on the judging panel for the Arthur C. Clarke Award, occasionally attends conventions, and even more occasionally joins in with the programme. She lives in York in a shared house full of children and cats, none of whom, fortunately, are her responsibility. However, she is sufficiently interested in other people's reproductive habits to be doing a PhD on the subject.

Katherine Sparrow (nee Howenstine) lives in Seattle Washington with twelve friends. She loves shutting down the WTO, reading utopian fiction, and growing huge ugly squashes in the backyard. This is her first full-length published short story.

Kari Sperring is mostly Welsh but lives in England. She has won fantasy/SF short story writing competitions at Intersection, the 1995 World SF convention and at Newcon in 2005. As Kari Maund she has published five books and many articles on Welsh, Irish, English, Danish and French history. She holds to her old-fashioned Welsh mining valley socialist values, despite everything. This is her first fiction publication.

Charles Stross was born in Leeds and now lives in Edinburgh, where he writes full-time. His novels include *Accelerando* (shortlisted for the Hugo award and the Clarke award), *Singularity Sky* (shortlisted for the Hugo), *Iron Sunrise* (shortlisted for the Hugo), *The Atrocity Archives* (which includes the Hugo-winning novella *The Concrete Jungle*), and others. He is a founding member of the Open Rights Group and is a member of Amnesty International and Liberty.

Rachel Swirsky is a fiction MFA student at the Iowa Writers Workshop where she's excited to chip away at the boundaries between science fiction and literary fiction, and also to write the inevitable stories about corn. Rachel graduated from Clarion West in 2005 and her work has appeared in markets including *Subterranean Magazine, Abyss & Apex* and *Fantasy Magazine*. She likes her politics progressive, her fiction thematically rich, and her humor like her chocolate: dark.

Lavie Tidhar grew up on a kibbutz in Israel, lived in Israel and South Africa, travelled widely in Africa and Asia, and has lived in London for a number of years. He is the winner of the 2003 Clarke-Bradbury Prize (awarded by the European Space Agency), was the editor of *Michael Marshall Smith: The Annotated Bibliography* (PS Publishing, 2004) and the anthology *A Dick & Jane Primer for Adults* (The British Fantasy Society, 2007), and is the author of the novella *An Occupation of Angels* (Pendragon Press, 2005). His stories appear in *Sci Fiction, Chizine, Postscripts, Nemonymous, Infinity Plus, Aeon, The Book of Dark Wisdom,* and many others, and in translation in seven languages.

James Trimarco believes that no type of narrative representation can be made illegal without damaging freedom of speech. His research into the souvenir trade at New York's Ground Zero (with Molly Hurley) has appeared in *Critique of Anthropology and Selling 9/11: How a National Tragedy Became a Commodity*. He's also had fiction in Flashquake.org, *Talking Back: Epistolary Fantasies,* and *A Field Guide to Surreal Botany.*

Jo Walton won the John W. Campbell Award for Best New Writer in 2002, after the publication of her first novel *The King's Peace*. This was followed by *The King's Name* and *The Prize in the Game*. *Tooth and Claw* won the World Fantasy Award in 2004. Her latest novel, *Farthing* (Tor, 2006), is an alternate history mystery; sequel *Ha'Penny* will be out next year. She comes from South Wales, lived for years in Lancaster, and now lives in Montreal.

Ian Watson taught in universities in Tanzania, Japan, and Birmingham UK before becoming a full-time writer 3 years after publication in 1973 of his first novel *The Embedding*, which won the Campbell Award in America and, in France, the Prix Apollo.

He has published 30 novels, most recently *Mockymen* (2003), and his 10th story collection, *The Butterflies of Memory*, appeared in Summer 2006 from PS Publishing.

He has screen credit for the screen story of Steven Spielberg's *A.I. Artificial Intelligence*, based on much work with Stanley Kubrick. His web site is www.ianwatson.info.

After having several stories appear in UK magazines in the late 1980s, **Ian Whates** took a sabbatical from writing in order to 'research' SF and fantasy (i.e. to read copious amounts of both). Clearly the research was extensive: he published nothing further for eighteen years. During 2006, Ian sold stories to magazines and webzines including the science journal *Nature*, *Farthing*, *Forgotten Worlds* and *Afterburn SF* – his story reappearing in their 'Best of' edition. He has also edited and published *Time Pieces*, a limited edition, signed anthology featuring new stories from Stephen Baxter, Jon Courtenay Grimwood, Ian Watson, Liz Williams and others.